A SHADOW BEYOND

EMMA-NICOLE LEWIS

COPYRIGHT

DEDICATION

For my wonderful family.

And for Jennie, who shared and ignited my passion for the supernatural during our teens. Never forgotten.
Thank you.

Thank you to the marvellous volunteers in Eyam who work tirelessly at sharing an important and extremely humbling piece of history. Their knowledge and passion for what came to pass in Eyam, from September 1665 until November 1666, is truly inspiring.

FOREWORD

On the 7th September 1665, the village of Eyam witnessed the outbreak of plague. Located in the heart of the Peak District, Eyam is far from where plague was rife at the time, but a bale of cloth that had been sent from London brought the disease into the village, triggering fourteen months of tragedy.

Between September 1665 and November 1666, two hundred and sixty people in the village of Eyam lost their lives. As the disease rampaged without mercy, whole families were wiped out, sometimes in as little as a week.

However, it was not the onslaught of plague that gives Eyam its iconic place in British history, but the sacrifice that the villagers made to prevent it spreading across more of Derbyshire.

Led by the relatively new and young village rector, William Mompesson and the former Puritan clergyman, Thomas Stanley, the villagers agreed to a 'cordon sanitaire'. Nobody was to enter the village and nobody was to leave.

Whilst many would have been forced to remain in Eyam as their livelihood depended on it, or they had nowhere else to go, these were God fearing times. No matter how terrified the people of Eyam may have been, their oath to God to remain in quarantine would have been taken extremely seriously.

The historical events in this novel take place during the fourteen months that plague ravaged Eyam. Whilst the main plot that follows the tragic and chilling secret of the Thornycroft family is entirely a work of fiction, the story of plague and some of the characters affected by the disease within the novel are based on true events.

My emotions ran high when writing 'A Shadow Beyond'. The history of Eyam is extremely humbling and awe inspiring.

Whether you are familiar with the history of Eyam or not, I hope that you will enjoy the book as much as I loved researching and writing it.

PROLOGUE

25th August 1666 – Eyam

It was dark on the staircase leading to the top of the house. Cobwebs stretched across the walls and mouse droppings had collected on the floor. Dust gathered and the light was dim. This was the forbidden part of the house, where shadows waited for nightfall.

With a shiver, Rachel looked at the door. Its frame was impossibly small, insignificant in comparison to the rest of the grandeur of Thornycroft Hall. Yet what lay beyond that door was the making of the house and all that its inhabitants had become. It was the undoing of the Thornycroft reputation, the reason for her misery and the cause of so much unhappiness.

Something creaked and an icy finger traced its way up and down her spine. Only on rare occasion had she ever ventured up to this part of the house. There had never been the cause nor the permission to set foot beyond the door at the top of the creaky old staircase. Nobody had, aside from Goody.

Goody. Goody Brown. Rachel bit hard on her lip. She whispered the name. There was a coppery taste in her mouth, like blood, thick and unpleasant. Secrets were hidden up in those quarters, secrets that only Goody knew of.

Rachel thought of Goody's tangle of confessions and regrets, riding out into the open on sour breath. They had only been half-truths though, memories muddled together. The truth about what roamed the corridors and banged on the walls at night was still locked away. Rachel thought she had seen it, smelled it, sensed it, heard it before, as had all the staff at Thornycroft Hall. Whispers of a demon, mutterings of a restless spirit of a woman gone mad with grief, every shadowy corner and dimly lit room was rife with those kinds of stories.

Rachel didn't want to see what was behind that door, but now there was nothing left. Everyone was gone. Her time was running out and she needed to know before she too fell victim to the gruesome torture that the plague had brought to her village.

Her heart beat wildly beneath the parchment that she clutched to her chest. Another clue, another confession linked to a mystery so terrible that it made her toes curl.

The door waited patiently for her to open it and she wondered, not for the first time, if the thing that haunted Thornycroft Hall knew her every move.

There were noises that emanated from the top part of the house. Strange noises. Unsettling noises. Noises, that no matter how anyone had tried to explain them away, sounded like something far more sinister than Cook's insistence that it was just rodents and the settling sigh of beams. There were rumours about the house too. Frightening tales. Ghost stories for children eager to scare their friends, women keen to gossip and men telling tall tales as they drank in the village taverns after a day in the mines.

Everyone had once whispered about the dark secrets of Thornycroft Hall, but that had been before they had become mere shadows hidden behind the horror that had hit the village when the sickness had swept in, choosing its victims with careless ease. Now nobody cared about stories of ghosts or demons, not when something far more real, far more threatening was stalking them. The rumours, intrigue and mystery that had once been attached to the great Hall on the edge of Eyam were now in the farthest reaches of people's minds as new nightmares unfolded for them. For Rachel though, those stories were still real and she had been left alone, every day reminded of the sinister darkness that resided in Thornycroft Hall.

Rachel felt as though her boots were stuck to the floor as she stood on the periphery of discovery, stories unravelling through her mind.

It had been the top quarters where the first Lady Thornycroft, Lady Rosamund, had taken her confinement before giving birth to her last.

Rachel swallowed hard.

According to the gossips, after giving birth to that last child, Lady Rosamund had remained confined to the top quarters of Thornycroft Hall, never to be churched because her soul had been possessed and madness had destroyed the woman who she had once been. People laid the blame on Lady Rosamund for her madness and they blamed her maid too. They said that there had been too much interference with remedies and potions in order to grant her a babe that survived birth. They said that all the tinctures, possets, oils and charms had been an invitation for the Devil to step over the threshold of the house. That was how Lady Rosamund had changed. Something unnatural had found safe passage into her, burrowed its way into her flesh and bones until it had found her soul. It had taken her mind, rendered her insane until she had been found swinging from the rafters. That had been nigh on two decades earlier.

In Thornycroft Hall, nobody was allowed to speak of Lady Rosamund. Cecily, the new Lady Thornycroft, had forbidden it. She said that her sin tainted the house and to speak of it would only make things worse. It was a sin to speak her name. Like the top of the house, her memory was forbidden. Lady Cecily preferred to pretend that Rosamund had never existed. People did still speak about her though, in secret. Frightened snatches of conversation, her lonely footsteps heard at night or her shadow seen in a window lit only by candlelight.

Rachel turned to face the line of portraits that were hanging, ever watchful, along the walls. Her eyes trained to the gaps where old hooks remained exposed. Those unsightly blocks of brick between each painting had been where Lady Rosamund's face had evidently once hung. Now those paintings were coveted away, gathering dust in a locked room, where the mournful cries of her spirit and the rattling of chains could be heard.

She felt her pulse quicken. Being at the top of the house was one thing, but being there alone, with nobody left to hear her screams was quite another.

She had seen the grave in the gardens. Unmarked, forgotten, hidden. A mother who had taken her own life and a baby with no baptism, the one they had said had been her last born, flesh rotting away from their bones in ground that wasn't consecrated.

Rachel closed her eyes for a moment, trying not to allow herself to drift to those thoughts. There were rumours surrounding the baby's death too, all of them unfounded and hushed away by the Thornycrofts. A lump caught in Rachel's throat. An innocent life had been taken so cruelly. "Babies die," the physician had evidently stated a little too firmly, so that tongues had been set to wagging about what had really happened up there.

Rachel turned back to the door. It was time to uncover the truth, to face what appalling secret Goody Brown had been holding onto.

She paused, taking stock of the horrors that had unfolded behind the walls of the house. There had been many nights that she had heard the mournful echo of cries and listened to the dragging of dead feet across floorboards. Like others, she had come to fear the idea that the demon had never left, that after Lady Rosamund had died, it too wandered the halls with her lost spirit, searching for another poor soul weak enough to let it in.

When the pestilence had come, ravaging families and destroying a once happy and buoyant place, Rachel could not help but wonder if it was the bad history of Thornycroft Hall that had brought it. She shut her eyes for a moment and steadied herself. It did no good to think of those things now. Goody had held on to some dreadful truth, secreted away behind the door at the top of that staircase. To find it, she would have to face the worst of her fears.

As if sensing her terror, mocking it, something shuffled across floorboards above her. Stifling a whimper, she held her breath. Squirrels and other rodents, that was all it was. She couldn't let it put her off finding whatever clues Goody would have left behind. Before she even realised it, the door was only inches in front of her. Rachel took a steadying breath.

In the past year she had seen the worst of grief, smelled death and the foulness of fear as friends and loved ones in the village had succumbed to the pulsing swellings and putrid rot of the pestilence. The thought was a sobering one and one that reminded her that nothing could be more frightening than that. Trying to ignore the waning light, she reached out her hand.

Slowly, she twisted the handle. The screech of metal on metal caused the walls to shiver but the door remained shut. Tiny crevices around the panel resembled tight lips, sealing away secrets. The shuffling stopped abruptly and her skin shrank as she retracted her hand.

Dusk was setting in so that darkness was seeping along the floors and walls, threatening to engulf her. It made her legs prickle with the desire to run but the house and the village had become her prison.

The parchment crunched in her grasp and she felt the curl of its edge against her forefinger. She had to be brave. Above her something creaked. A foot? The cautious tread of the dead, or the demon?

Rachel directed her gaze to the ceiling but the words on the parchment, what she had learned from Goody Brown, fuelled her to go on. Nothing could make her turn back now.

She reached in her pocket for the large bunch of keys. They felt heavy and cold. As the criss-cross of beams creaked and groaned, the house seemed to shudder. Feeling for the largest key, she pushed it towards the lock and glanced at the window at the far end of the corridor. The burning pinkish red of the sky was swiftly being sucked away. Soon it would be vanquished by the pitch black of night.

With a trembling hand she inserted the key. The sound of the prising back of the old bolt was loud against the silence and the door opened. Stale air accosted her nostrils. In front of her was a steep set of steps. She had to go upwards.

Saying a prayer twice over, she began to climb. The house remained silent as it waited for her next move. Rachel felt along the wall with one hand. In the other she held a tallow candle. Its light was weak, almost useless in the cramped space that wound upwards. She put one foot in front of the other, carefully finding the lip of each step and then sliding the sole of her boot across the surface. Slowly up she climbed, feeling her way until her fingers at last fumbled their way to the coolness of the large bolt on a door at the top.

From somewhere behind the wooden panelling, she thought she could hear the sweeping of a skirt against the floorboards.

Her hand clasped the bolt.

Then another noise, almost inaudible at first. Nails or something sharp dragged across wood, followed by a soft click.

Rachel's mind was no longer lucid. Her body was simply going through the motions of moving from one place to the next. The bolt pinged back and a warm trickle of fluid coursed down her inner thigh, but she cared nothing for dignity. Her legs felt weak but she could not stop herself from entering the part of the house that had for so long been forbidden. A voice in her head screamed at her to go no further, that this would be how she would meet her demise, but the secrets already unearthed gave her determination to ignore those pleas. With trepidation she pushed open the door and stepped inside.

Outside, the sun had disappeared completely behind the white peaks and she hurried to use the taper of her own candle to light the ugly candelabra that had been placed in the room. Her eyes wide, she searched for shapes hiding amongst the shadows and silhouettes of furniture, but there was nothing.

The room was a chamber, basic but comfortable. There was a pallet, a chair, an old dresser, a chest and other old bits of furniture. A dreadfully bitter smell mingled with mothballs. Something scuttled across the floor. The click clack of claws against wood took her by surprise and the pink ringed tail of a rat disappeared into a crevice within the wall. Almost falling over an upturned chair, Rachel clutched at her chest before daring to allow the first ripple of relief to embrace her. "Rats and squirrels," she whispered as she walked around the chair and looked behind her.

To the far end of the room was another door. Her confidence growing, she went towards it and didn't hesitate to push it open.

Lit only by the paleness of the rising moon, the contents of the next room had lain untouched and dormant for so many years. Rachel felt something catch inside of her. She was looking at an old nursery. It had been decorated with such love and care. A mother's love had placed woollen blankets in a crib, had a beautiful wardrobe and chest carved out of walnut wood, a rattle made of solid silver. Nothing moved. Nothing touched. A baby's swaddling had been discarded on the floor and more thrown haphazardly over a chair. Rachel imagined a lonely figure sitting in that chair, a woman whose breasts ached and leaked with the grief of unspent milk as she pressed the blanket to her tear soaked face, contemplating how to stop her suffering after her baby had gone. Choking back a sob, Rachel turned away.

Heartbreak filled the atmosphere of the room. It was a tragedy behind closed doors, so insubstantial in comparison to the cruelty and scale of plague but it was there all the same, locked away, waiting to be uncovered, the story shared. There had been nobody to comfort the grieving Lady Rosamund, nobody to listen, and unburden her from her grief. They had trapped her up there, alone. With all that was precious taken from her, she had been left to rot. Why?

Rachel turned her gaze to the rafters, unable to help herself from searching for any sign of where they had found her stiff body swinging. She hoped that it hadn't happened in this room, the nursery.

Whispering a prayer, she pulled the door shut behind her as she returned to the room that had been made into Goody's chamber and went to the dresser at the far end. Opening a drawer, she felt inside, looking for more truths and clues to what had gone before in this God forsaken place. Nothing. She pulled open another, lifting clothes, shaking out blankets and then another, tearing out the useless recipes and remedies for the stillroom. What good had they been before and what good were they now? With a frustrated cry, she shut the final drawer. There was nothing.

She searched under the bed and behind the grate, checked for unsteady floorboards and loose bricks in the wall. Nothing.

Despondent and exhausted, she sank to the bed and held her head in her hands. All these years of fear, the rumours of a vengeful spirit and a demon that stalked the halls of Thornycroft Hall and yet there was nothing – and no clue as to what had really happened all those years ago.

The sound of the rat scuttling behind the walls reminded her that there never had been anything to fear up in the top quarters, just Goody and childish ghost stories, made more real by the sighs and moans of an old house. Surprised by the vast hollowness of deep disappointment, as a heavy stone in her gut, Rachel realised that a part of her had wanted there to be a spirit or a demon, anything to distract from the horrors of real life and the tragedy that had befallen her village. Anything that would mean that she was no longer alone. A small whimper rose up from her chest. There would be no answers or mysteries solved before the pestilence found her. She would be taken in solitude, with nobody to nurse her or whisper prayers for her in her final moments. The spirit of Lady Rosamund would not be waiting to take her hand. There was nobody. She wanted to weep but her despair was too great.

Then she heard it. A faint rattling.

Rachel looked up. In the curtain of darkness she had missed the arced shape that fitted so neatly into the far wall. A door. She moved towards it. A key jutted from the lock, shivering back and forth. It was as though something was moving it so that it jerked and rattled impatiently. The bitter taste of nerves coated her tongue and it felt thick and cumbersome in her mouth as she reached for the brass ring handle and turned it. There was a click. Without encouragement, the door swung inwards, hitting the wall behind it with a noise so deafening that it reminded her of gunfire. The noise reverberated through her head, sending her reeling backwards for a moment.

She frowned, how could a door hitting a wall make such a loud noise? Something wasn't right. She felt it as she stood on the threshold looking down, her head ringing.

A set of stone steps led down into a room dimly lit by only a few glowing sconces. Convincing herself that the sound had been partly conjured by her own imagination, fuelled by fear, she started to make her way down them.

The stink of rot and dirt clung to the air and she coughed as she reached the bottom step. To her right the room stretched on and at the end, she could see something red. Fabric billowed and throbbed like a ghoulish beating heart. A dress. Another. Then another. They must have all once belonged to Lady Thornycroft. The mad one. The dead one.

Movement. Almost imperceptible in the darkness, but something had shifted. It was just a small movement, like the turning of a head.

Alert, Rachel's eyes were peeled as wide as possible, desperate to see, to spot any threat. There was not enough light to be sure of it, but amongst the dresses she could swear that there was a shape. As her vision adjusted, she felt with a sickening certainty that the shape was moving, only slightly, but it was moving all the same.

It started to grow, as if unravelling itself, until there was little room between the low-beamed ceiling and the top of its head.

With a cry of alarm, Rachel threw herself backwards, towards the base of the steps, preparing to scrabble her way upwards, but the door at the top had shut behind her.

She was trapped. There was an unearthly noise as the thing slowly closed the distance between them. There was nowhere left to run.

The thought sliced through her that she had been right to fear what had skulked in the shadows for so long. Something from the wickedness of the past had remained, haunting Thornycroft Hall.

Before she could even find the first step to climb, the shape violently thrust itself forward and Rachel's shrill scream resounded through the desolate darkness of the house.

CHAPTER 1

Present Day – Eyam

K ate Saunders inspected the map once again and frowned. How, she asked herself, had people managed before Sat Nav systems and Google Maps? All of her technology had failed stupendously just as she had entered the Peak District. If it hadn't been for her father's exceptionally organized 'dad' ways, she would be scuppered. The A-Z had been stashed under the front seat of the old Ford and long forgotten about, until now.

According to the markings, Eyam was the next road on the right. She didn't hold out much hope as she had already made an incorrect assumption that had cost her half an hour of time and it was getting dark.

The sign for the village swung into view swifter than she had expected. Taking the corner, she cringed as the tyres protested. This was not how she had intended on announcing her arrival. In fact, she hadn't intended on announcing her arrival at all, at least not to anyone other than her Great Aunt Edie. Stay for a few weeks or a couple of months, just until Edie was back on her feet properly and then Kate could return to moping about back in Surrey, feeling sorry for herself. That was the plan and the fact that her latest contract at a large banc assurance company had just come to end was a happy coincidence.

A summer in the Peak District was quite different to the plans that she and Richard had made. If things had been different, she would have been soaking up the salty air of the Solent as they prepared to take the boat out of its mooring and around the British Isles.

"Cold beers at sunset, snuggled up watching the foamy crests of the waves," he had promised, making it all sound extremely romantic. That was before Chris though, when there had been no jealousy, no differing of opinions and no police.

Pushing it all from her mind, Kate breathed a sigh of relief. At least she had found the village. Pulling over, she checked her mother's handwritten note giving directions to the house.

It had been years since she had visited, almost two decades in fact. The writing was slightly blurred by a ring from the coffee cup she had rested on it earlier that morning, but she thought she could recall some of the route from childhood memories.

Driving through the village, she flitted between memory and the notes that her mother had provided, looking for the turning to the dirt track that led to the house. Pressing her foot sharply to the brake, she swore as another driver hooted their horn.

She was tired and not concentrating on the road as she should. A curtain twitched and Kate felt her face grow hot. As the car rocked and crunched down the track, she could see the silhouette of Thornycroft, the stonework a welcome silvery glint under the light of an almost full moon.

It was larger than she had remembered with a huge expanse of garden that she could see rambling up and down the pathway in what she assumed would be a sort of organised chaos.

Pulling up, her heart sank as she recalled that there wasn't a drive as such. Aunt Edie had always been fond of keeping the garden just as it was with "no traffic". It would take some effort to drag her bags to the front door in the dark. There were no security lights and so she would have to make do with the torch on her phone.

Finding her way down the uneven flagstone pathway in the dark was a task in itself, but the hunt for the spare key that had evidently been left under the plant pot outside the front door was quite another. She sighed heavily as she counted eight plant pots. It could be any of them.

When at last she had found it, she pushed it into the lock, stepped inside, shut the door and listened to the pleasant click that shut her away from the world. Pressing her forehead against the coolness of the wood, she shut her eyes and blinked back the tears that had been threatening to fall at various stages during her journey.

Leaving Surrey behind with its bad memories and Richard was more of a relief than she had expected. She just hoped that he had no idea that she had driven up to Eyam to stay with her Great Aunt Edie. It was pretty much a certainty that he didn't. They hadn't seen each other in weeks and a restraining order had been exercised, but after the way he had been behaving, it wouldn't surprise her if he did look for her. Richard was nothing if not determined.

Trying to forget the past and think of the present, she snapped on the light switch. The hallway wallowed in a dim yellow glow, made even murkier by the old fashioned lampshades. The house hadn't been updated in decades but that added to its charm. Textured wallpaper that wore the tea stained tinge of age offset a well-worn moss green carpet. It was exactly as she had remembered from childhood. She supposed that as the years had worn on, Edie just hadn't had the money, or the inclination to update it. When Great Uncle Joe had passed it had been back in the early nineties and Edie had lived alone ever since. Loyal to a fault, there had been no new romances and no companionships forged that would at least give her some company. Edie had always been stubborn about her morals and beliefs and to her, meeting anyone else would have been as good as adultery. So she had chosen to live alone, each room proudly displaying memories of Great Uncle Joe through framed photos, the odd certificate and various cups and trophies for his fell running. It was admirably romantic in Kate's opinion, a far cry from modern day romance and it was also dreadfully sad. Someone taken too soon, long before the couple could have started to enjoy the twilight years of their relationship.

Guilt pressed on her shoulders as she wandered around downstairs. Edie had always been so generous to Kate, but as she had grown up, the visits to the Peak District had become less frequent. Instead, Edie had visited Kate's family home, once in summer, every Christmas and sometimes at Easter.

Edie's annual summer trip had been postponed until September due to the cruise that Kate's parents had booked and Kate had been too worked up and embroiled in her problems with Richard to entertain the usual timing of her annual visit. With everything that had been going on at the time, it had seemed far more sensible to wait until her parents had returned and things had settled with Richard.

Biting her lip, Kate looked at a photo of Edie, her head tilted back with laughter, a wide brimmed sunhat toppling from her head. The thought hit her hard. If she had been holidaying in Surrey, the accident would never have happened. Still, it would have been appalling if Richard had accosted Edie with his questions, wild accusations and frustrations.

Choking back a sob, Kate looked around the large house and imagined how lonely it was for one person to be rattling around in it. Edie had never had any children, although Kate had never asked why. Edie wasn't exactly a closed book, but there were some subjects that would be deemed as private, even if it was her favourite niece doing the asking.

It had been a shock when they had heard the news earlier that morning. "A fall. Badly sprained ankle and some bruising, possible concussion too, but apart from that she's evidently okay. " Her mother had relayed the report with tears in her eyes. "A neighbour found her." Pulling out a tissue, she had sunk to the nearest seat and hunched over. "It should have been family who were there for her, not a neighbour."

"Do you know when she was found?" Kate had asked, shocked as she had wondered how long poor Great Aunt Edie had been lying in pain for.

With a shrug, her mother had dabbed at her eyes and sniffed. "A few days ago. Goodness knows how it took so long for them to get in contact with family." They both knew of course that Edie would have refused to give any details, not wanting to needlessly worry anyone, but that fact served as no comfort. "It just makes you think that…" Kate's mother had trailed off as she had slumped on the sofa. There had been no need to finish what she had been saying as the thought was an echo of her own.

"That we should be there more." Kate had taken a seat next to her, shoulders weighted sadly. The suggestion of moving to Surrey had been made straight away over the telephone but Edie's response was predictable. Eyam was her home and Eyam was where she intended to stay.

"Maybe it's better that she does return to her house first mum," Kate had said, draping a comforting arm about her tensed shoulders. "I've finished my latest contract and I need a break away somewhere. I can go up to live with Aunt Edie for the rest of the summer and you never know, I might convince her to move down here."

"I can't leave her Kate. It's not right." Worry was etched into every line on her mother's face. "We'll cancel the cruise."

As she had reached for the phone to get in touch with Kate's father, Kate had stopped her. "Cancel the cruise? You'll do no such thing. It's the holiday of a lifetime. You and dad have saved so hard for this for the best part of the last couple of years." They had been looking forward to the three week cruise for so long that it seemed crazy to cancel it all when Kate was able to go and take care of things.

Shrugging her off, her mother had argued before at last giving in to Kate's reassurances that everything would be fine and that Great Aunt Edie wouldn't want everybody fussing around her. "She won't like feeling like she's having her independence stripped away mum and you have to admit, you'll fuss." That had shut her up. Kate's mum had a heart of gold but she was inclined to attacks of the Mother Hen and that could wind Edie up on the best of occasions. Reluctantly she had conceded to Kate's suggestion and the arrangement was made, with Kate slinging most of her wardrobe into two suitcases, and heading off towards the North of England within the day.

Flicking on more lights, Kate inspected the rooms of the old house. She thought it seemed quite surreal that twelve hours earlier she had been eating a bowl of muesli and wondering what to do with her day. Now she was in the heart of the Peak District, readying herself to help rehabilitate her Great Aunt Edie back into her house.

At least she was far away from Richard and all the trouble he had caused. There was of course the added bonus that she would no longer be subject to the nightly interrogation her mother had taken to giving her about the whole situation. It was a situation that Kate had long since decided she would rather forget.

It was too late to visit Edie in the home but visiting hours were from ten thirty in the morning and Kate had promised that she would be there on the dot. There was a faint hum and buzz as the long strip light in the kitchen whirred into life. It had been a long journey and the first thing she needed was a good cup of coffee. Hunting through the wooden cabinets, she found the last of some instant granules and spooned them into a mug as she waited for the kettle to boil. Taking a look at the kitchen, she smiled whimsically. Warm memories of salad buffets accompanied by a joint of gammon, pickles of all kinds and Edie's famous baking surfaced as she saw the large oak table running through the centre. An assorted mismatch of china jars and containers were lined up along the back of the wooden worktop, either side of the old fashioned Aga, and a riot of pots and pans were hanging from a beam above the table.

Smiling to herself Kate hugged her arms across her chest. A few weeks or months in the Peaks, away from friends, away from family, away from the mess that she had left behind and most importantly, far away from *him* was exactly what she needed. This was her safe haven and a place to think about how she was going to pick up the pieces and start again.

Reaching for a packet of gingerbread biscuits that had been placed next to the slightly chipped china hen bread bin, she felt the familiar darkness drift over her. Whenever she thought of him, that darkness returned. It was like a storm cloud over her head, always threatening to burst. What with the threatening behaviour and the restraining order, she had barely had enough time to think.

She hadn't been sorry to see the back of him. In the lead up to it all, she had fallen out of love. He had become a stranger, not the man whom she had fallen for. Even if she had been up to all the things he had accused her of doing, it was no way for a man to behave.

With an urgent whistle, the kettle reached boiling point. Pulling herself back to the present, she poured her coffee and trained her line of thought back to Edie.

It was all very sad. Kate had known that she wouldn't agree to the idea of living with her parents in Surrey. She loved her independence. Great Aunt Edie was a free spirit and she always had been. With her wild mass of peppery curls that floated girlishly down her back, her bright blue eyes and long floaty skirts, Kate had often mused that Edie had become trapped in the sixties.

Taking a seat at the table, she sadly observed the other seven empty chairs and imagined her Great Aunt alone in such a big house. Thornycroft was only one part of what had once been Thornycroft Hall but it was still a large house, especially for one person. With a heavy sigh she stood up and tipped the rest of the coffee away. Tiredness was creeping up on her and she didn't want a full bladder to disturb her sleep.

There were four bedrooms to choose from on the first floor. Putting her head into each one, she settled on the one opposite Edie's room. It was of a pretty disposition, just beyond the bathroom and overlooking the back garden. She remembered the beautiful view of the fields rolling down to nearby villages, like a patchwork quilt of brown, yellow and green.

Edie's room was at the front of the house. Kate thought it was strange that her Great Aunt should choose the bedroom without the magnificent view but then she remembered her saying something about the bedrooms at the back overlooking a graveyard. Of course, the village had been home to the plague tragedy back in the mid 1600s and many families had ended up burying their loved ones in back gardens or outcrops of land. When Kate had been little, Edie had told her stories of Eyam's history over hot chocolate by the fire but she could only remember odds and ends from them now. The stories had both fascinated and scared her and her mother had been very firm about the details that Edie had been allowed to divulge.

Turning her attention back to the room, it was just as she remembered it, full of paisley and chintz. Even in here, Kate could smell the fragrance of Edie's floral perfume. At the bottom of the bed, there was a dresser and either side was a nightstand, each of them decorated with a cotton doily and holding a stained glass lamp. It was all very twee but cosy.

Heaving the larger of her suitcases onto its side ready to unpack, she wearily eyed the daunting task ahead of her as clothes spilled out over the edges. There would be plenty of time to sort her things in the morning but for now, she just needed the essentials. The wardrobes in two of the spare rooms were huge and took up far more space than a fitted wardrobe would, but still, there would be plenty of space for her clothes at least. Just as well, Kate thought as she unzipped the case, she had never been one for packing light.

"Why do you need that many pairs of shoes? When do you think you'll be wearing those heels? We're in the middle of the countryside for crying out loud and you've brought crystal embellished flip-flops with you!" In spite of herself she smiled as she considered what Richard would have had to say about her packing.

She bit down on her lip. Richard was gone to her. No more. There was no going back.

Without warning, a memory crashed into the forefront of her mind. She remembered the look in his eye when she had told him that she was having second thoughts. Then the phone calls had started, the pleading, the stories and the watching. That had been the worst of it, the endless watching. It had been relentless.

Taking a sharp breath, Kate slumped onto the bed, the paisley covers crumpling beneath her. She had to shut it out. The restraining order was firmly in place and she had not heard anything more from him. Even Chris, Richard's best friend and the catalyst for everything, hadn't been in touch for a while.

At the thought of Chris her stomach gave an involuntary flutter. The saying 'no smoke without fire' was true. She couldn't deny that Chris was attractive, charismatic and charming but that had been mere observation, Richard had been the one who had stolen her heart.

Chris had been a flirt. Competitive through and through, there had always been a cheeky glint in his eye when he had laid on the charms, made her laugh, made her blush, made her think about if things had been different… just once.

She pushed the thought aside. They hadn't done anything wrong. She hadn't. It was just one throwaway thought, one moment of madness. Their friendship had been harmless and innocent. Not to Richard though. Over time he had become wound up, coiled tighter and tighter until one day he had snapped and they had argued but the disagreement had never been put to bed. It had been enough to trigger the onslaught of rows to follow, the behaviour and the eventual calamitous destruction of their relationship.

A good friend to them both, Chris had backed off, given them space to sort things out but things had gone too far. A line had been crossed for Richard who had appeared half mad, obsessed with her movements and obsessed with Chris. Of course, it had all been dressed up as the fact that he cared for Kate, worried about her, that it was Chris who was the crazy one and not that Richard was just damned jealous. He had insisted that Chris was after her and that he wouldn't stop until he had her one way or another.

The wild look that had flashed in his eyes haunted her. Richard had become unwashed, unshaven, broken.

It was probably best that Chris hadn't checked in on her since Richard had received the restraining order, for the risk of making things worse. In Kate's opinion, Richard needed some professional help for his mental health. That was his problem now though, not hers.

Glancing towards the unpacked cases, she chastised herself for letting him dominate her thoughts again and headed for the bathroom.

The tap over the sink rattled loudly, emptying a gush of water tinged with a rusty brown colour. Wrinkling her nose, she wondered how long it had been since it had been used. There was a sink in Edie's room but surely she used the main bathroom too?

When at last the water had run clear, she had brushed her teeth and taken the make up off her face, she flipped out the lights and went to draw the curtains in her bedroom.

The movement outside was sudden but the silhouette had been there long enough to prove that it wasn't just a figment of her imagination. A man. Tall. His eyes had gleamed brightly in the moonlight. It had been fleeting, but he had been there.

Sweeping the curtains closed across the windows, Kate pressed her palm against the wall to keep steady and held her breath, not daring to move. Was she going mad?

Her mind racing, she reminded herself that she had locked and bolted the front door but she hadn't checked the others.

Racing downstairs, she checked the back door and the ones leading from the dining room onto the terrace. Everything was sturdy.

Outside, two cats began fighting, their loud screeches causing her to jump. Maybe the man had just been a neighbour walking his dog. It just seemed like a funny time of night to be doing it.

Suddenly Kate regretted the decision to come alone. Returning to the bedroom, she picked up her phone and scrolled down its contact list for Chris. He could check that Richard was still in his home in St Albans. Chris would be happy to help, he wouldn't mind.

Her thumb hovered over his name for a moment before she threw the phone down on the bed. It was ridiculous. Richard would have no idea where she was. Nobody would have told him and she certainly hadn't been followed.

This sort of thing was what her mother had warned her about, the paranoia, making the slightest thing into an unnerving sinister event.

Pushing back the curtain in the bedroom a crack, she peered out again. The track leading to the house was empty. Nobody was out there. Even the fighting cats had found somewhere else to take their dispute.

Taking a deep breath, Kate perched on the edge of the bed. The man was long gone, probably now sitting in front of his television, with a nightcap or a cup of tea.

She couldn't assume that every shadow, bump or noise would be him, seeking his revenge. It was time to forget and to move on.

CHAPTER 2

Present Day – London

Fuming, he slammed his mobile phone face down on the large, overbearing arm of the Chesterfield. So it was true, Kate had gone. Biting his fingernails, he felt a surge of deep-seated anger well up inside. After all he had done for her?

An image of her face flashed through his mind. Her smile, the twinkle of her eyes and the way her hair tumbled over her shoulders. Of course she had cut it short after everything that had happened. Some silly idea that a haircut would give her a fresh start. Well cutting her hair and running away wasn't going to get him out of her life, not after all of the effort he had made. Clenching his fists, he grabbed his car keys.

It was late when he pulled up in the cul-de-sac that her parents lived on. Parking his car a short distance away, he made sure that nobody was watching before pulling back the handle of the car door, hurrying up the driveway and skirting around the back of the house.

The key had been left in exactly the same type of place that she used to leave it for the flat, taped to the underneath of the green wheelie bin. With a smirk, he ripped the tape off and freed the key before pulling on a pair of leather gloves and wiping it of his prints.

Inside there was a click as one of the security lights came on. They had obviously left a few lights on timers to prevent break-ins. With an ironic chuckle, he placed the key on a table in the hall, removed his shoes and began his search.

Finding Kate's room was easy, even if he hadn't known which one it was. Her scent clung to the air inside it and he lifted the pillow from her bed to his nose, closing his eyes as he thought of her and the feel of her lips against his. A longing inside his chest made him ache. He would do anything to be near her again.

Putting the pillow back in its place, he headed to the wardrobe, carefully opening the doors. Nothing but her old purple mac was left.

Frowning, he turned to the drawers and pulled them open one by one before letting out a roar of frustration and throwing the last one onto the bed. She had cleared everything out.

Taking a hold of himself, he picked the discarded drawer up and put it back in its rightful place before moving on to another room.

By midnight he had combed the entire house and found no hint of whereabouts Kate might have disappeared to. Scowling, he went back to the car, his mind whirling with thoughts of where she might be and whom she might be with. The very thought of another man touching her, brushing his lips against hers or holding her close sickened him.

From the very first moment that he had laid eyes on her, he had known that Kate belonged to him. She had been wearing a deep green dress that had set off the colour of her eyes and her fair hair had been grazing the tops of her shoulders. Her smile had lit up the entire room and when she had introduced herself, the chemistry between them had been palpable. It wasn't right that his so-called best friend had ruined all of that. Thinking of the smug look on his 'friend's' face whenever he had seen him with Kate made all the pent up anger explode. He smashed a fist against the steering wheel, inadvertently sounding the horn. A car approaching from the opposite side of the road hooted back and he swore loudly at them.

When he returned home, he took off his clothes, folded them neatly and lay down on his bed. The mattress felt hard, cold and empty. Inside he ached for her. When they had been together he had been truly happy and now she was gone. Without her nearby, sleep was impossible. It was always impossible. With a grunt he rolled onto his side and lay looking at the moon through the gap in the curtains. His mind would always kick into overdrive at night, no matter how exhausted he felt.

Eventually, he got up and put a navy dressing gown on, pushed his hair back from his face and then rubbed at his cheeks. The gentle hum of the fridge in the kitchen was usually comforting, but now, starved of sleep, it had become an irritating buzz. Pulling a bottle of Malbec from the cupboard, he poured himself a large glass and went through the door that led to the study. Drumming his fingers on the desk he thought for a moment before taking a generous swig of his wine.

Kate glared at him from her place on the desk. Almond shaped eyes bore into his soul, mocking him above a half smile. It was a look that he both loved and hated. Picking up the gilded silver frame, he held it in front of his face for a short while before resting it back down in its rightful spot.

"I'll find you sweetheart." He raised his glass towards her image and turned full circle, staring at each and every photograph that looked back at him from the walls. Kate laughing. Kate smiling. Kate glowering.

She had disappeared without a word. She obviously didn't want to be found. Why was she punishing him like this and what was she hiding from him?

There had been no evidence left at her parents' house and she hadn't told anyone where she had gone. It was clear that she had meant to be lost and to stay lost. She had deleted every single social media account that she had ever owned. There was no way of finding her by the usual means. Not to be put off, he thought some more. He would have to find another more innovative way of locating her. It was all a part of the grand plan that was still taking shape in his mind.

Tracing his fingers across a black and white cheekbone until it brushed against her lips, he smiled. "I will find you."

CHAPTER 3

Present Day – Eyam

Birdsong was what woke her the following morning. It made a pleasant change from the usual rush of traffic and car horns beneath the flat that she had given up before her temporary move to her parents' house.

The bedroom was already awash with light from behind the curtains. Reaching for her mobile she checked the time and groaned. It was far too early to be out of bed, but the room clearly caught the first of the sunlight and her mind felt wide awake and alert. Throwing back the duvet, she got up and pulled on her red satin wrap.

Unlike the London flat she had lived in before everything had unravelled with Richard, it was peaceful, still. The silence was almost disconcerting though, reminding her how isolated the house was.

Rubbing her eyes, she went to make a cup of tea before stopping on the landing. Ahead of her, the staircase that led to the top of the house loomed.

At the very top of Thornycroft was a large annexe type of area. Edie had always referred to it as the attic space.

The attic had been a forbidden place in her childhood. Edie had scared her with stories of things that went bump in the night up there. Still, it was no doubt filled with all kinds of relics as Edie was a self-confessed hoarder and it might be interesting to find a bit of family history.

Forgetting about the tea, she pushed aside the old ghost stories from her childhood and headed straight for the door at the top of the staircase. Trying it, she smiled to herself when it opened. When she had been a child it had always been locked. Back then, Edie had insisted it stay that way. "No place for children," she had warned. "Old floorboards, dust and goodness only knows what else is up there."

The staircase wound steeply upwards and even with her bare feet, Kate thought it sounded as though each step was loudly announcing her intentions.

At the top there was another door. The catch turned. Effortlessly it swung open.

As the sun was still low, it was dim in the attic. Kate looked around, observing the contents of the room through the watery light that was leaking in slowly through the windows.

Off to her right there was another door. It had been left ajar, showing off the room beyond it that was filled with old furniture and crates. Turning back to the main room, Kate looked around her. Amidst stacks of boxes, there was an old trunk, a gramophone with a string of pearls randomly draped across it and various other odds and sods. Warped shafts of sunlight created fractured spotlights for the swirling shimmer of dust motes that danced in the spaces in-between.

The attic was a haven of history. She would have to ask Edie if she could go through some of the old photos that must be stored up there. It would certainly be an interesting pastime to retrace her family history and the attic seemed like an excellent starting point.

Picking up an old dusty photo album from the top of a wooden pallet, she blew on it and turned the page. The plastic covering crinkled loudly as she looked at the grainy black and white photos beneath.

Smiling happily into the camera were her Great Aunt Edie and Great Uncle Joe. They must have been in their early twenties and probably not long married. Behind them was the back of Thornycroft. Hens were running around the lawn and a sheep dog was sitting obediently at their feet.

Smiling as faded memories of her childhood returned with some vibrancy, she turned the pages, remembering the many animals they had kept and the allotment that had been her Great Uncle Joe's pride and joy.

Kate's mind meandered through the precious early memories of helping Edie hunt for eggs from the hens and pulling up rhubarb, strawberries and potatoes with her Great Uncle Joe. It would be nice to sift through those early memories of her childhood with Edie.

Standing up, she decided to acknowledge the noisy grumblings from her stomach and find some breakfast.

As she squeezed her way through the boxes towards the staircase, her thigh brushed passed an old bookcase. There was a thud as something wrapped in a piece of cloth fell to the floor.

Reaching for it, Kate noted that the object had been wrapped in a scarlet cloth. A silver cord threaded through a crystal had been wound around the cloth several times over and tied tightly.

Her curiosity piqued, she fiddled with the knot before giving up and questioning her integrity. This was wrapped for a reason and it had nothing to do with her.

Ashamed for prying, she bent to put the object back in its rightful place and opened the door that led to the stairs.

Another thud echoed around the room and she sighed with annoyance as she went to put it back again.

The third thud caused the hairs on her arms and neck to stand on end. Despite having ensured that she had wedged it firmly back into place, it was lying on the floor again. She stared at it with accusation. The crystal shimmered beneath fingers of sunlight that were feeling their way over it, tempting her to reach down and untie the cord.

With a tut, she shook off the strange feeling that had overcome her and checked the shelf, wondering if it was on a slight slope. There was no explanation that she could see.

Keen to leave the stifling feel of the attic, she picked the bundle up and took it downstairs.

Resting it on the kitchen table, she set about looking in the fridge for any potential breakfast. Settling on an egg and toast, she tried to focus on the day ahead.

It broke her heart to think of her Great Aunt Edie cooped up in a hospital, but at least the primary care trust had moved her to a home temporarily. They were keen to keep her under the observation of staff for a day or two more, but had reassured Kate that it was expected that she could be fully discharged by the end of the week.

Tapping off the top of her egg, she sat down and dipped a soldier, ignoring the temptation to take some scissors to the silver cord that was bound around the scarlet cloth.

When she was finished, she washed up and checked the clock. Almost nine. It would take a good half hour to get to the home and that was assuming she didn't get lost again.

Brushing any crumbs from the table, her fingers accidentally caught the silky red cloth wrapped around the bundle. With a clatter, the crystal fell to the table. The silver cord had frayed enough for it to work its way loose. Beneath the silky ripples of material, she could see a brown leather spine.

Gently, she pulled at the cloth so that more of the leather was revealed. There were no grandly embossed letters on the book, or anything to suggest what it might be. It had been placed on top of something else.

Pulling the cloth away entirely, Kate felt the coolness of wood against her skin as a rectangular box was revealed.

Hesitating, she wondered who had taken the trouble to wrap both objects like that. Kate didn't know much about crystals, but she had heard that they were used for cleansing and healing purposes.

Putting the book to one side, she reached for the box before recoiling. Every instinct screamed at her not to open that little box. She had no idea why, but it felt wrong.

Instead, she reached for the book and turned back the cover. An old musty smell spilled off the pages, each one filled with handwriting, some looking like it had been written in haste. Her Great Aunt Edie's writing.

On the first page there was a description of what had once been known as Thornycroft Hall, the words carefully and neatly scrawling out its history: when it had been built, how the family had come to reside in Eyam and how it had stood during the time that the village had been struck by the plague.

Kate read the entry.

William Thornycroft commissioned the build and it became the main family residence in 1614. Ironically, he died nineteen years later when London suffered one of its outbreaks of plague. One assumes that a business trip must have coincided with the time that the infection had been ravaging the city. William was likely infected on the earliest day that he arrived and taken too ill to return home to Eyam.

He and his wife Charlotte had only one surviving son, Edward, the sole heir to Thornycroft, known as Thornycroft Hall back then.

Charlotte never remarried but had brought a handsome dowry to the Thornycroft family and must have had fine tastes in fashion that were perhaps before her time.

It is believed that following the death of William, she began fashioning Thornycroft Hall with a continental aristocratic feel. Some of those features have been retained in parts of what is left of the house today. For example the oak panelling in the dining room has remained. This room was likely to have been used as a parlour room in those times.

Charlotte died shortly after Edward married. His bride was the daughter of an Italian architect who had been a friend of the family and possibly responsible for the work that Charlotte Thornycroft had commissioned.

I suspect that Edward's choice of bride may not have been Lady Charlotte's preferred match for her son, but I have been fortunate enough to lay claim to an unfinished portrait of the woman who had stolen his heart and it is easy to see why a young Edward may have fallen so hard for her. Rosamund.

Kate noticed that the pen had trailed off at that point, as though Edie had been caught in a daydream. When it picked up again, the letters were more rushed and scrawled.

Unfortunately, this marriage provided no surviving children and it would seem that Rosamund died young. Records show that she took her own life.

I find myself drawn to the nearly finished portrait of this beautiful young woman and I can't help but wonder if there is a deep sadness in her eyes. Rosamund.

This time she had underscored the name and the pen had trailed off again, the page seemingly unfinished. Kate's interest was stirred by the portrait Edie had mentioned in the extract. There was certainly nothing around the house that looked anything like an old portrait, so it had to be up in the top section of the house.

The thought of venturing back made her skin crawl. There was something unnaturally still in the atmosphere up there.

Pushing her curiosity about the portrait aside, she looked back down at the book.

Kate knew that Edie volunteered as a historian at the village church and museum, but she hadn't realised that she had taken such a keen interest in the history of Thornycroft, although it certainly made sense.

"Rosamund." She traced her fingers over the name, whispering it, feeling it on her breath before turning to the next page.

Cecily Thornycroft took Rosamund's place. There are no records of her background so I do not think that she was of noble blood.

No portraits of any of the other Thornycrofts appear to have survived. They have been swallowed in time, perhaps sold off by one of the families who owned Thornycroft long before us. Most likely, they were auctioned whilst Thornycroft was still a mansion, before the rest of it had crumbled and been sold as farmland.

It must have been hard for any woman to fill the shoes of Edward Thornycroft's first wife in terms of her beauty, but it seems that Cecily did provide him with a son, Samuel.

It is hard to find out much more about the Thornycroft family. Edward, Cecily and their son Samuel appear to have survived the plague that hit the village in 1665 until 1666.

Living in the village of Eyam, as a young mother when the plague was rife, must have been particularly hard.

The paragraph ended abruptly. There was plenty of room on the page or the one adjacent to it for additional content, but nothing more had been written. Kate noticed that instead, something had been scored into the page overleaf. The bumps of the lettering pressed out the paper beneath her fingertips.

Turning the page, she felt her insides dip as she stared at the barely intelligible writing and she swallowed back the threat of nausea.

A demon lives amongst us.

Slamming the book closed, Kate was shocked. It was for some time that she sat staring at it on the table, as though it was something foul that she didn't want to touch. Then she noticed that some thick inserts had come loose, their corners jutting from the edges. Something had been stuffed into a plastic pocket that was at the back of the book.

Still unable to bring herself to touch it again, Kate leaned closer to inspect a folded piece of card that was protruding. Her curiosity getting the better of her, she reached for it, tugging it from where it had been secured at the back of the book.

Unfolding the card, she frowned as she noted the circle of letters, numbers and the words in the middle of them, 'Yes' and 'No'.

With a sharp intake of breath, she realised that she was holding an Ouija Board. Edie surely couldn't be into all of that? There was nothing to suggest it elsewhere in the house and she had never said anything. Even when they'd had their conversations about ghosts, it had all been run of the mill stuff, hearsay, rumours, legends and village tales for tourists.

Gingerly, she opened the book again, flicking quickly past the page with the scrawl about the demon. The rest of it appeared to have been filled with notes, as though it had served as a diary.

The first entry was from earlier that year, but the writing was of a different slant to Edie's usual neat scrawl. There was something frantic and hurried about it and the pen had been pressed too hard to the paper. Above the entry was a name.

Rachel.

Kate frowned. Who was Rachel?

As her eyes scanned the page, she sucked in her breath. The diary entry mentioned the family whom Edie had logged as living at the house in the seventeenth century – the Thornycrofts.

The air is thick, stifling. A storm threatens to end our long hot summer with tremendous claps of thunder and a torrent of rain.

It is market day but something is unsettling. Today we had a visitor. Sir Edward bustled her away to his study. Nobody ever goes into Sir Edward's study. Lady Cecily went as white as a sheet and had to lie down.

I don't know who this woman is, but she's created some fuss.

In the village, people go about their business and there is talk of the impending storm. There is other talk too. Gabriel Hounds. I am scared, but then again, fear sits thick like congealed curds in my stomach most days at Thornycroft Hall.

There was more but Kate didn't want to read it. It could easily have been the beginnings of a story that her Great Aunt had been writing, except something didn't sit right. The frenzy of ink that had been sprawled across the page, the Ouija Board and the feeling in those words sent the hairs on her arms bristling.

After stuffing the cardboard Ouija Board into the sleeve, she hurriedly rewrapped the diary and the box back with the cloth.

She had never given the supernatural much thought since childhood and it was uncomfortable to imagine Edie doing this sort of thing. For a moment she questioned her state of mind before batting the idea away. Lots of people dabbled with the unknown and it didn't make them a mental health concern.

A bang on the window startled her and she looked up to see a face. With a scream, she pushed her chair back, spilling the rest of her tea. The face crumpled into a look of embarrassment as a woman with cropped grey hair mouthed an apology.

Leaving the upturned mug and the small pool of dregs on the table, Kate hurried to the door, putting the diary and the box into the cabinet that the telephone was perched on.

"I'm so sorry love. I hadn't meant to startle you." The woman started rushing out an apology no sooner than the door had been opened. "I didn't think. Can I help you clear up?"

Taken aback, Kate stared slack jawed, her mind still on what she had read.

"I work at the museum with Edie," the woman explained, shuffling awkwardly and fiddling with the handle of her shopping bag. "Forgive me for just turning up unannounced, but when Angela said she saw a car outside Edie's place, we assumed there would be some news. Is she okay? Is she here?" The woman craned her neck to try and look inside.

"She's still in care at the moment. I've spoken to the home and they say she's fine though." Kate smiled politely and pulled her dressing gown around her a little more, conscious of her state of undress. "Evidently, she's due to be discharged this week. I'm just off to see her this morning actually. Would you like me to pass on a message?"

The woman gave a sigh of relief. "Oh I'm so pleased. Everyone will be delighted to know that. We've all been so worried. She's been missed at the museum and church. She knows her stuff Edie, and the visitors love her." Clicking her tongue, she rolled her eyes. "I'm sorry," she apologised again. "How rude of me. I'm Lindsay."

Kate stuck out her hand and offered her name. "Kate Saunders. I'm Edie's great niece."

Recognition lit up Lindsay's face. "Oh yes, Kate. She talks about you a lot. You live in London." A smile played on her lips. " And I hear you have a lovely gentleman friend who Edie has been desperate to meet in person. Is he here too?"

Hoping that the rest of her face did not betray the smile that she managed to keep firmly in place, Kate shook her head. "No he's not. I'm going to be staying here for a while, just to help Aunt Edie settle back in."

Lindsay hadn't noticed the change. "Oh that's good that she'll have you here for a while. Well I won't keep you any longer. Please do give Edie our best and tell her not to get all worked up about the museum. We're covering her shifts just fine. Oh yes, and we wanted to give her this." Thrusting the shopping bag she was holding at Kate, she added that they had all put some essentials in there to help Edie back on her feet when she got home.

Taking the bag, Kate thanked her before shutting the door and taking a deep breath. The diary had thrown her off guard and she was sure that she must have looked like a nervous wreck to Lindsay. Still, it was wrapped back in its cloth and that was enough for the moment to keep the contents from playing too much on her mind.

Tapping her fingers against the wall, she pondered about what to do with it. Her eyes trained in on the cabinet she had thrown it inside. From upstairs there was a creak and she thought about the words that she had read.

A demon lives amongst us.

The blue ink was scored into her brain just as it had been scored across the paper.

She needed to get out of the house. The atmosphere had become stifling and close. Everything seemed stuffy and hazy and she was beginning to feel the familiar tightness in her chest.

Doctor Lucas had talked her through how to deal with panic attacks but she hadn't been on her own back then. Until now somebody had always been a stone's throw away: her mother, a friend, the neighbours, Chris. There it was again. There *he* was again.

Squeezing her eyes shut, she tried to block his face from her mind, to forget about the unexplored chemistry. How could she think of it? That would just prove Richard's suspicions right and what would that make her? A cheater, a liar or both?

Marching upstairs, she got herself showered and dressed before heading out of the house into the blazing sunny morning.

******

The home was set against a backdrop of rolling hills and limestone rock. Dahlias, peonies, hollyhock and lilies sent a ripple of electrifying colour across the neatly cut lawns. Their beds had been squared off and not a single piece of gravel from the path appeared to have fallen out of place as Kate made her way to the reception. It wasn't at all how she had imagined.

Clutching a carrier bag filled with several packets of chocolate raisins, some magazines and a mandatory bunch of grapes, Kate found herself standing in the mint green reception area feeling nervous and jittery.

"Not been here before?" a kind voice asked her. It was accompanied by a gentle hand against her forearm. "Who are you looking for? Reception is over here. I'm afraid we need your signature and number plate." A woman with a shock of tight brown curls and kind hazel eyes was smiling at her. The smell of disinfectant wafted into the hall.

"My Great Aunt Edie." Taking a pen, she signed into the register that the woman had directed her towards. "Sorry, Edith Bell. I've come to see Edith Bell. I'm her great niece, Kate." Extending her hand, she wondered if the woman noticed how clammy it was when she took it and introduced herself as Magdalena.

There was a momentary awkward pause and Kate felt the urge to fill the silent void with conversation that would explain away the shame that she hadn't been there to find her Great Aunt when she had fallen. "I live in London. Well in Surrey for the time being. I've just moved back into my parents' home. She was due to visit actually. Usually we call. Someone calls for a chat most days. It's hard with the distance." Unable to prevent the explosion of verbal diarrhoea, she cringed inwardly before asking the question that she wasn't really sure she wanted to know the answer to. "Was she alone for long? After the fall?"

Magdalena cupped a hand over Kate's. "Your Great Aunt is recovering fine from the fall Kate. The hospital wouldn't have moved her here otherwise. They need the beds and we had one free."

"Was she alone though? For long?" Frustrated, she twisted on the strap of her bag. Why couldn't she just answer the question?

Gently ushering her to a door, Magdalena advised that a neighbour had found her soon after the fall. She closed the door to the room. It was quiet inside. Not peaceful, just quiet.

Kate looked at the bland pictures on the walls, speculating whether it was the room that people were taken to when told their relatives had passed away. She couldn't think what else it would be used for.

Magdalena stared at her, taking in her profile, as though working out what kind of person she was.

"I'd really like to see her now please," Kate asked, unnerved.

Gesturing for her to sit down, Magdalena cleared her throat. "As I said, your Aunt has been recovering very well from the fall. The hospital discharged her to us first thing yesterday morning." She smoothed down her white trousers and Kate thought she looked somewhat nervous. "Kate, she has been a little confused."

A cold tongue of dread licked its way up the nape of her neck as Magdalena continued. "Edie mentioned something about being pushed when she first arrived in the hospital. She was quite insistent. Naturally, it was investigated."

"Somebody broke in?" Thinking of the man she had seen lurking the previous evening, Kate couldn't keep the startled tone from her voice.

"No. There was no sign of forced entry. The lady who found her was questioned. Then Edie changed her story. She had been adamant at first. Then she claimed to have got confused and blamed it on the shock."

Frowning, Kate gripped the arm of her chair. "You think that somebody pushed her? Well are the police doing anything further? I've just come from Thornycroft and I would have had no idea that it was a suspected crime scene if you hadn't told me, so they're clearly not doing a lot."

Putting a hand up to calm her, Magdalena shook her head. "There is no suspicion that anybody else was involved. The doctor on duty claimed that the nature of her injuries were not consistent with somebody being pushed and it is really quite possible that a patient suffering a mild concussion could have been confused. My concern is that your Aunt doesn't seem overly keen on returning to her home. She seems scared."

Feeling a knot of frustration tighten in her chest, Kate started to get impatient. "You're confusing me."

Her voice softer and well adjusted with years of training, Magdalena was clearly preparing for her final conclusive delivery. "Kate, it isn't unheard of for older patients to make excuses if they are afraid to return to independent living. Perhaps they would rather not admit that they are struggling to cope. It genuinely may be just a symptom of shock with your Aunt, but I understand that you will be living with her for a while and I'm simply presenting you with the facts so that you can look out for anything that you feel would compromise her safety living alone again."

Sighing heavily, Kate sank back into her chair. "Mum wants Aunt Edie to move down to Surrey but she would never agree to it. She loves the Peaks and she loves Thornycroft."

An expression of understanding and empathy on her face, Magdalena nodded. "Well nobody can force her to do anything. Tests have confirmed that she is sound of mind and we certainly can't see anything that would suggest she would struggle to cope when she is fully recovered, but it wouldn't harm to discuss that option with her. It must be hard living alone with family so far away."

Another wave of guilt washed over Kate and Magdalena touched her hand again. "I don't want to upset you. We all have Edie's best interests in mind."

Swallowing back a lump in her throat, Kate smiled gratefully. "It's nice to know that people care. You hear so many negative things about the whole care system that you

forget that, for the most part, it's filled with peop.
Thank you Magdalena. I really appreciate it."

After a short exchange of detail on how best to
Thornycroft with the minor injuries she had sustained, i
another part of the building.

A conservatory full of wicker chairs with mismatching
In the background, a television blared out a talk show but .
all the thoughts that were racing through her mind. Why v   Was it
connected to the diary and the box, or simply the fact that s   and been on
her own? Had her general health deteriorated? Would she look older and frailer?
Would she blame Kate and her parents for not being around more?

Her nails dug into her palms as she followed Magdalena down an arcing pathway
towards a hunched figure in a wheelchair. The muscles in her throat began to bunch as
Magdalena called out her Great Aunt's name and announced her arrival.

The figure remained motionless. Her injured foot was resting on a fold out chair,
the swelling having subsided but still bandaged. Bruising fanned out across and beneath
her toes, which unusually for Aunt Edie, weren't polished. A pale hand gripped the
plastic handle and Kate could see the familiar emerald stone set in a gold band.

Holding her breath, she edged around the wheelchair, her fingers trailing against the
papery white skin. "Aunt Edie?" she asked. Her voice clashed with something that
Magdalena was saying but that Kate couldn't quite register. The smell of roses tickled
her nostrils and a blackbird bounced bravely onto the rim of the birdbath.

"Sssshhhh. Don't startle him." Edie's voice was coarse and grainy. She didn't move
and Kate still couldn't see her face.

Quietly, she crouched next to the wheelchair and watched as the bird sharply
dipped its amber beak in and out of the water. It was nice that she was sitting in this
spot. Edie had always loved the birds. "Today and yesterday at quarter to eleven. You
could set your clock by him," she mused in a whisper. The garden was peaceful as they
both watched, Kate's hand folded across her Great Aunt's.

"Aunt Edie, it's me, Kate." There was no turn of her head, no warm hug, no offer
of a mint from her pocket. Silence clung to the air. It was thick and uncomfortable, cut
through only by the soft call of a thrush from one of the trees shading the path at the
far end of the garden.

Kate changed her position so that Edie's face was in her view. She regarded the
firm set mouth, devoid of the usual fuchsia lipstick. Her skin seemed grey and heavier,
with wrinkles that ran through it like deep dry rivers. This was not the Great Aunt Edie
she knew. "Aunt Edie?" she asked, her voice small, threatening to crack.

"Edie." Magdalena placed a gentle hand on Edie's shoulder. With a shrill squall, the
blackbird took flight.

"Oh what a shame, he's gone. You scared him." Animated once again, years seemed
to drop off her as Edie turned accusingly to Magdalena. "He can stick around for quite

now. I should really get some seed." The kind, warm expression that
and loved returned, radiating her expression.

an efficient sweep of her hand, Magdalena straightened the footstool that
's foot was resting on. "I'm sure he'll be back tomorrow. Seems like he enjoys his
visits. Tea and biscuits?" she suggested, her voice breezy.

Her eyes twinkling, Edie seemed her old self. "Lovely. Although coffee for me,
please. Kate?"

Nodding, Kate waited until they were left alone before she asked how she was
recovering.

"They say I am confused. I expect they've told you everything. The batty old bag
who thinks that she was pushed." Edie's matter of fact tone took Kate by surprise.

Trying to find the right words, she stammered an attempt at a response.

Clicking her tongue, Edie rolled her eyes. "Oh don't be so awkward about it Kate.
I'd expect that from your mother, not you. It's one of the follies of surviving
everything else in life. We start to lose our marbles. They force that many pills down
your throat when really just a wee dram of whisky would be just the medicine." Eyeing
the plastic carrier bag that Kate had let fall to the lawn, she looked hopeful. "A bottle
in there I hope?"

Giving her a sheepish grin, Kate reached for the bag. "Grapes, gossip and generous
helpings of chocolate raisins. The whisky will have to wait until you're home."

Waving a dismissive hand, Edie grimaced, her thin lips peeling back against her
teeth. "I don't think I'm ready to go back home just yet. It'll be a while before I'm
out."

Frowning, Kate studied her expression but it remained firm. It was the perfect cue
for her to pick up the subject of Edie returning home. "They told me end of the week
and you can be discharged. I'll be staying for the summer, so it'll be easier to settle
back." She had it all worked out as she ran through how she could set up a room for
Edie downstairs whilst her ankle healed, give her a bell if she needed anything, cook
her meals and keep the house up to scratch.

With a light tinkle of laughter, Edie shook her head. "Come home? My dear, I took
quite a fall. I shan't be leaving this place. They only moved me from the hospital
because they didn't have enough beds. I still need to be under observation. So I can't
go back to Thornycroft. I'm even thinking of selling the house. I'm hoping it will fund
what the savings can't stretch to. It's awfully expensive in a home like this one you
know dear."

Appalled, Kate kneeled in front of her and reached for her hand. It felt so small and
delicate in hers. "Why would you want to be in a home when you've got family?
Besides, you love Thornycroft."

Edie's bottom lip trembled but she managed to hold back the tears. "I'm getting old
Kate. You're not even half my age so I don't expect you to understand but I don't

think I shall be returning to Thornycroft." The reaction was nothing like Kate had expected and she remembered Magdalena's observation that Edie had seemed afraid.

"That's why I've come though. I've got the whole summer off. I can stay at least until the end of September and help."

Her eyes gleamed with suspicion at Kate. "What about your gentleman friend? Richard? I thought you two had been planning to jet off for the summer on his boat. 'A Pirate Adventure' you called it."

"Well I've decided to come here now and spend the summer with you."

Raising an eyebrow, Edie glared at her before sitting back. "Trouble in paradise?"

That was an optimistically light-hearted way to describe the situation. Forcing a smile, Kate nodded. "Something like that. We're not together anyway." In a bid to hide her face and gloss over the enormity of her own situation she picked up Edie's cardigan that had fallen to the ground and folded it. "So," she said, mustering all the sunshine she could as she spoke, determined not to give too much away. "I am man free and job free this summer. I'm all yours."

When Edie remained tight lipped and stony-faced, Kate hurried over to crouch by her side and take her hand again. "Come on Aunt Edie, it will be brilliant. Just like when I used to come visit as a kid."

Without even a flicker of changing her mind, Edie stubbornly folded her arms across her chest.

"Look, you can't stay here and you need someone at Thornycroft during your recovery," Kate insisted.

Pulling her hand away sharply, Edie's eyes burned wild. "Don't be impudent Kate. I am not ready to go home and you can't make me."

Kate had never heard her speak like that before. An awkward silence spilled into the air all around them, only to be broken by the sound of Magdalena appearing from the conservatory carrying a tray of coffee and biscuits. Worried that she would be in trouble for upsetting her Great Aunt, Kate tried to smooth things. "Of course not. Whatever you say," she said hurriedly but Edie was glowering at her.

"I want to go inside," Edie demanded, her voice haughty and unfamiliar. "Take me inside."

Kate spent the rest of the visit making small talk and avoiding the subject of Thornycroft or the future. When lunch was called she went to drop a kiss on Edie's forehead before unzipping her bag for her keys.

It seemed surreal that she had resigned herself to never returning home and she wondered what the home would ordinarily do in situations when the patient simply refused to leave.

"So are you planning on house sitting for me?" Edie asked just as Kate stood up to leave.

Sighing, Kate tucked a stray lock of hair behind her ear. "I suppose you could call it that."

"Just be careful."

"Of what?" she pressed her to elaborate, but somebody had come into the room to help her to lunch and it was clear by the way that she was firmly pressing her lips together that Edie wouldn't be saying anything more.

CHAPTER 4

Present Day – Eyam

By the time she pulled up outside Thornycroft, Kate felt dazed and exhausted. Her Great Aunt Edie's words were still ringing in her ears.

The house stood, foreboding, its windows like unblinking eyes and its door weather beaten with chipped paint, hiding secrets within.

Shivering, Kate remained in the car. The thought of going inside didn't appeal. She wished that Lindsay would return, fussing after Edie's state of wellbeing and asking how she had got on at the home but the track towards the house was empty. Perhaps she could do something in the garden instead.

An aesthetic display of hydrangea, lilies and geraniums greeted her in the front garden. The lawn was overgrowing and riddled with daisies, buttercups and dandelions, but it wouldn't take much to neaten it up and a sunny afternoon was as good a time as any to start.

Dumping her bag in the house, she decided to tackle the lawns.

In contrast to the well-maintained flowerbeds and shrubs at the front, the back garden was a wild rug of shaggy grass that had paled under a parching sun. The allotment that Edie had apparently been keeping in shape in honour of Great Uncle Joe had become a tangle of bindweed, suffocating the once neat lines of raspberry bushes, and the tiny orange and blue heads of weeds crawled rampantly across the neglected onions.

An aromatic medley of mint, rosemary, marjoram, chervil and thyme was growing unabated, desperate to be cut back and an untamed mass of cornflowers hung their heads sadly, their once blue brilliance burned away by the summer sun.

The branches of two apple trees weighed heavily with the burden of already ripening fruit, desperate to be picked. A pile of it had already fallen, threatening to rot into the earth and grass beneath them.

Surprised at how much Edie had neglected it, Kate made her way to the shed.

Despite her years, Edie was still a very fit lady with a penchant for gardening and the advantage of green fingers. The upkeep of Joe's allotment had always been of the utmost importance to her since he had died. Whenever she had visited Kate and her family, she would always bring containers filled with seasonal fruit, vegetables and herbs.

Earlier that year, during her Easter visit, she had insisted on pruning the hedgerows and pulling up weeds in Kate's parents' garden, scolding them for leaving it all to neglect.

Kate wondered if Edie was just getting too old to keep up all the physical work required for the garden and she supposed that hiring a gardener would be too expensive, too much like admitting defeat. Bringing the allotment back to its former glory could be an interesting project whilst she was staying at Thornycroft, and she concluded, it could put a smile back on Edie's face.

Underneath some tarpaulin were two lawn-mowers, an ancient rusted old thing that she imagined had last seen light of day when her Great Uncle Joe had still been alive, and a much newer bright orange one.

Pulling back the covering, she inspected the controls, noting the turnkey before going into the shed to find a rake.

The sun beat down pleasantly on her exposed shoulders as she began the hefty task of raking what she could into heavy green bin liners before she could even embark on pushing the mower about. The allotment would have to wait until later.

At the bottom of the garden was a wall separating the property from the public lane behind it. In one direction, the lane led back into the village of Eyam and in the other, to the neighbouring village of Stoney Middleton.

A couple of cyclists passed by, stopping to look at something and Kate remembered that the old boundary stone was a little further down the track.

With a shudder, she recalled the plague stories that Edie had shared with her as a child. The stories had been recounted over sardines on toast for tea or with hot chocolate before bedtime. She had told her how the villagers, in a self-imposed quarantine, would leave money doused in vinegar in the holes drilled into the boundary stone, in return for tools or goods that they needed from the neighbouring villages. According to Edie, there were other sites like it around the edges of the village too.

"Of course, when it was all over, the place was like a ghost town. So they say anyway," Edie had told Kate and she had taken her to see the stone. "See that crumbled old building over there," she had said and pointed across some fields that stretched on beyond the garden. "That used to be part of this house. Was sold on two centuries ago, before it became neglected and ruined." She smiled wistfully, "Still, shows you how big Thornycroft used to be at the time of the plague." Then she had turned her attentions back to the boundary stone and traced her fingers over the surface, relishing the thought of touching such a rich piece of history.

Kate had refused to touch the stone when Edie had invited her to do so. The stone had terrified her. She remembered opening the curtains of her bedroom at dusk, watching as twilight shadows danced across it, imagining the forlorn figures that must have wandered up and down that lane, to and from the village with their money and their supplies.

32

Resting the rake against the wall, Kate leaned over and looked down the well-trodden pathway. Somewhere in the distance a horse whinnied and snorted. The couple had cycled on, leaving her in isolation once again.

Then she saw the lonely silhouette of a man sitting on a grassy bank and staring over in her direction. In his arm he held a large book.

Squinting, she tried to make out the expression on his face. He didn't seem to notice her. It was as though he was looking right through her.

Uneasy, Kate thought about just ignoring him and getting back to her business of sorting the garden, but a knot of anger tightened inside her. It was an intimidating thing to do, standing and staring at somebody's house, especially with no acknowledging wave or any other normal gesture that she would have expected from an innocent onlooker.

A little gate that had been built into the wall led to the lane. Its hinges groaned as she swung it open. The man didn't flinch at the noise.

Kate thought of the figure that had frightened her the night before and marched towards him angrily. Had he been scaring her Great Aunt with his loitering? Was that why she hadn't wanted to return home?

As she approached, she expected him to at least glance up or give her a friendly smile, but he did neither of those things.

"Excuse me?" Irritation spiked her tone. "Can I help you with something?"

The man continued staring past her towards the house. In his hand she could see that he held a pencil, its nib scribbling furiously on the page.

Kate persevered, "You appear to be quite interested in the house and I'm wondering if I can assist you in some way?"

Silently, the man continued to scribble before at last giving an irritated sigh and glancing up from his work. She noticed how dark his eyes were and the angular shape of his jaw. He was probably not much older than herself.

Pulling at the sunglasses that were resting on his forehead, he pulled them back over his eyes and attempted a smile. It wasn't very convincing.

Irked by his rudeness, Kate pressed him again. "Were you stood outside here last night? It's a bit off coming and staring relentlessly at someone's house you know."

He opened his mouth to speak, stopped and turned his gaze towards the house again.

Kate was indignant. "The least you could do is answer me. Are you drawing the house? Who gave you permission? An elderly lady lives there. You could scare her. You might not be on the property, but it is extremely intimidating."

Still he didn't even flinch.

Incensed she went to grab the paper.

With a loud snap, he shut the pad and shifted his focus back to her. "Since when was it a crime to sit and draw?" Tucking the sketchpad under his arm, he stood up from the grassy knoll that he had been sitting on. A few blades of loose grass were stuck to his t-shirt and Kate couldn't help but notice the muscles beneath. This man was lean but strong. She should be wiser than to wind him up.

"I don't like the idea of somebody drawing my house and possibly me. Why on earth would you want to be drawing somebody's house anyway? You have to admit that it isn't something most people would do." Finding a tissue, she rubbed some oil from the lawnmower that was dirtying her hands.

The man regarded her in silence for a minute before pushing his sunglasses back up to rest on his forehead. His expression glowered with the evident inconvenience of being disturbed from his work. The whites of his eyes were a brilliant contrast against the rich darkness of his skin and Kate imagined that if he smiled, he could be quite handsome, maybe even jaw-droppingly so, but this stranger was in no mood for smiling.

"The house is beautiful," he said. "This whole village is. I just like capturing beauty in my work. I'm not in the habit of drawing people. In fact," he eyed her up and down. "I was rather engrossed with the house and hadn't even noticed you before you came marching along the lane shouting at me."

A blush rose from her chest to her cheeks. Had he just had the gall to insult her or was he merely pointing out the innocent passion of his work? Either way, the comment took her off guard and she felt stung. "Well I would rather you came and knocked first if you're going to be drawing the house. I like my privacy."

"Of course. I hadn't realised that Edie had a guest. She has no objection."

Her blush deepened. So he had already sought permission from her Great Aunt Edie. Feeling doubly foolish only served to inflame her temper even more. "If you'd bother to knock to say what you were intending on doing, you'd know."

"My mistake." He sounded dismissive, as though her opinion didn't particularly bother him. "Have a good afternoon and do give my regards to Edie."

He was walking away before she could retort, leaving Kate feeling foolish and angry. She had overreacted but since everything that had happened with Richard, she felt exposed and vulnerable. The last thing she needed or wanted was a complete stranger staring into her house and invading her privacy. The man was rude too. He should have just apologised and explained rather than getting all high and mighty about it.

Pivoting sharply, Kate marched back to the house, cross and hot. She would be sure to ask Edie about him and check out his story.

Finishing what she could of the lawn, she threw down the gardening gloves she had found and sighed heavily. The heat was getting to her. She would have to leave the rest until later, when it was cooler.

Ahead of her, the house looked less welcoming once again. It was like a Jekyll and Hyde house. Whilst the front was picturesque and inviting, the back seemed to have an ugly sneer, as though it was watching and waiting for her next move.

"Don't be so bloody stupid," she told herself, forcing her feet to move so that she could refresh herself with a glass of squash.

Inside, the kitchen was pleasantly cool. Picking up her phone, she checked the signal. No sooner than her thumb was hovering over 'mum', the ringtone blurted out a fanfare of noise that echoed through the house.

Chris.

She had not been answering calls from anyone, but she was lonely and it would be nice to hear a familiar voice. Hesitating, she considered answering it. What harm could it do? Chris and Richard might have been close once, but all of that had surely dissipated after everything that had happened?

"Hello?" She hadn't realised how breathless she would sound.

The voice on the other end was warm, a welcome distraction. "Kate? It's me, Chris. You okay?"

Relaxing, she leaned against the bench and explained that she had just got in from doing the gardening.

With a laugh, he made light of all the time he spent at the gym when he could be keeping active the easy way.

"Easy? You've got to be kidding! You should see the size of this thing!" she said and chuckled, her voice tinkling brightly. It was good to hear a voice from home and Chris still managed to make her feel good. He always knew what to say.

There was some static and a pause. "Well maybe I could come and spend a few days with you?"

The suggestion floored her. Kate stumbled for a response. "I'm not in Surrey." She paused, battling with what details to divulge. "I decided to take a short break. For the rest of the summer."

"What alone?" He sounded surprised and slightly miffed.

"Yes alone. I needed to get away."

The sound of his chin brushing against his phone created the effect of static before he responded. "How about I come and join you then? Seems a shame for you to be going through all of this on your own. You should have a friend by your side."

Was she imagining it, or was there a tinge of hope to his voice?

An image of him accosted her; the way he had looked at her on that one day, the harmless flirtation that had threatened to breach carefully drawn boundaries.

"Oh Chris," Kate sighed, feeling the familiar burden of weight return to her shoulders. "I don't think that's a very good idea, not with Richard."

"Richard?" A cool edge clipped his voice. "What's Richard got to do with any of this anymore? Has he been trying to get in touch?"

Biting her lip, Kate understood the frustration that Chris must be feeling. Richard had betrayed him. He had betrayed both of them. Even a friendship spanning back to their university days couldn't be saved she supposed.

"It's just that it's all so fresh Chris. After everything that went on, I don't want to cause any more trouble for either of us."

More static threatened to break the line as she waited for his response, imagining his ice blue glare beneath tousled sandy hair.

Chris had a unique attractive quality to him, not classically so, but there was something about him and he made her laugh. He knew exactly how to put a smile on her face and given that she had lost touch with so many of her friends whilst she had been with Richard, it was nice having him as a confidant. Chris seemed to be her only friend now. It was pathetic really and frightening how much she had become isolated from her social circle.

Chris had been her rock through it all and she could do with a friend being around. The thought of a visit from him was certainly tempting but it was the last thing she needed. Truth be told, it was the last thing either of them needed. She needed to learn to stand on her own two feet again, not feel afraid of her own shadow, or feel that somebody was always watching her, waiting for her to be at her most vulnerable.

"Richard has a restraining order." A softer tone had replaced his frosty one.

With a bitter chuckle, Kate shook her head. "What good is that? It wouldn't stop him if he saw reason. You know that as well as I do Chris."

"Oh well." There was a long drawn out sigh from the other end. "You know where I am if you need me."

Smiling, Kate felt the tension that had started to build in her back and neck begin to ease. "I know. Thanks for checking in. I really do appreciate it."

"You take care Kate." An abrupt click told her that he had hung up.

The call had at least cleared her head of everything Edie had worried her with.

Taking her squash, she wandered back through to the hallway before stopping, her blood feeling like ice racing through her veins.

On the table, next to the telephone was a dark brown box. It looked just like the one she had found in the attic with the diary, but she was certain that she had wrapped it back in the cloth.

Hovering over it, Kate held her breath as she retraced her steps from earlier. She felt sure that she had shut everything in the cabinet together, along with the keys that locked away the top space of the house.

Pressing her fingers to her temple, she felt her head begin to throb. How had the box got there?

"Just be careful." Edie's voice rang in her head.

"Open it." The instruction was clear as the words, not her own, spilled from her mouth. She said it before she even thought it. Opening the box was not something that she wanted to do.

"Open it." Those words again. Her mouth was telling her to do something that her mind was fighting.

There was something about that box, something that sent shivers up and down her spine and set every hair on her body on end, yet a greater part of her felt compelled to look inside.

Reaching out, she allowed her fingers to trace the rough surface.

This box had belonged to somebody called Rachel. It held a deep dark secret.

Pausing, she wondered how on earth that thought had struck her.

"Open it!"

Recoiling, she held her hand against her chest, feeling the rapid pounding of her heart. This time the voice had come from somewhere in the house.

Sunlight illuminated the wood so that the box was almost glowing. Again, her hand was drawn to it.

Slowly, her fingers curled around the lid. There was no catch to lift but the movement still felt like an effort.

Kate licked her lips. Her mouth was dry and her tongue felt thick and uncomfortable. She wanted to shut her eyes but the same type of morbid curiosity that would keep her watching a horror film meant that she kept them open as her fingers found purchase with the lid's lip.

As the wood parted, she looked at the dark crevice that was slowly emerging.

A sense of unspeakable horror began unfolding inside her. Something glimmered from the depths of the box.

Unable to take the suspense any longer, she swiftly pushed the lid all the way back so that the contents inside were ignited by the honeyed glow of the afternoon sun.

"Rachel!" The voice was very crisp and very clear but she couldn't tell where it was coming from. "Rachel!" It echoed through her head, intensifying the throb so that she began to feel dizzy.

"Rachel!"

CHAPTER 5

August 1665 – Eyam

"Rachel!" Cook's shrill voice echoed through the house, ricocheting off the walls. With the thin watery light of dawn creeping through the shutters, Rachel should have been getting ready for market.

Market day meant that she was expected to buy goods that would help with the running of the house and find ways to help the kitchen impress Sir Edward; new potage recipes, succulent meats, inventive new ways of baking pies. It was stamped in to her every day how lucky she was to be given the opportunity to learn all of the markings of keeping a respectable and wealthy household.

Following the death of her father, the Thornycrofts had been exceptionally generous to take her in as a maid with the sort of privileges that might even one day find her a husband with a more than modest income and good reputation. By virtue of their generosity, the expectations that she was to live up to had turned what Rachel used to enjoy into an event that she dreaded.

When her father had been alive, they had grown, reared and sold produce at market day. Now she purchased goods for the wealthy Thornycroft family.

She had it on good authority that following the Wakes festivities a family of great nobility were going to be passing through Eyam. They would be residing at Thornycroft Hall as guests, and so expectations of Rachel were even higher than usual.

Rachel knew of the family, The Belgraves. They were long standing friends of the Thornycrofts. Sir Edward Thornycroft was involved in business with Lord Belgrave, although Rachel had no idea what he did. According to Lady Cecily the Belgrave family were so well connected that they had even been fortunate enough to dine at the King's Court several times following the restoration of the monarchy. Evidently, Lady Belgrave could be as prone to exaggeration as Lady Cecily, but this piece of news had truly put Cecily into a spin.

The night before, Rachel had inwardly scoffed as Cook had given her the instructions of what she was to look for at market. If what Lady Belgrave had written in her letters to Lady Cecily was to be believed, then surely nothing that they could purchase in Eyam, Bakewell or even from the Chatsworth Estate could be of any match to the type of hospitality that she had grown accustomed to.

Lady Belgrave had apparently described in great detail how at Court they feasted on peacocks and swans and custards laced with spices and fruits. Foods so exotic, that an ordinary person would have likely been sick for days with the richness of it all.

Rachel's shoulders slumped and she sighed heavily. She missed her father so much and her heart never failed to ache for him when she was to set off for the village market or to the Bakewell market.

When he had been alive, he had always seen to it that afterwards, they would enjoy a meat pie, the crusts still warm and the pastry melting against the rich juices inside. They had eaten them together whilst talking about their future on the farm and how one day, he would buy them a croft of their own. The familiar feelings of homesickness returned and Rachel opened up the lid of the bogwood box.

"Rachel!" Cook called out again, impatience colouring her tone, but Rachel needed just a little longer.

Gently, the tip of her finger caressed the stone in the middle of the decorative cross. Her mother's cross. Sometimes it looked yellow, sometimes orange and there were always a few darker flecks running through it.

"This stone is amber Rachel but it's a secret. You must not show anyone that you have this," her father had said to her when he had first shown her the cross. Rachel had only been a young girl at the time, but the memory was vivid. He had sat her on his knee, tucked her long dark hair behind her ear and shown her the box with its secret treasures inside. Whenever she took it from its hiding place, his words echoed in her thoughts.

Her father had been dead for almost two years and her mother had sadly passed when Rachel had been just a babe. The jewellery had belonged to her and he had asked her to covet it away. It was a precious memory, the day that he had given her that box with its special cross inside and other keepsakes. When Rachel wanted to remember she would close her eyes, smell the floral tang that came off the handkerchief that the cross was wrapped in, and think of that day when he had handed it to her.

When her father had first lifted the lid of the box, the amber jewels had glowed beautifully in the light cast from the stars and moon outside of the window. "There is great value in this cross Rachel lass," he had said. "Not just its worth, but its memory." A sad and distant look had clouded his expression and for a moment he had been lost in thought before smiling back at her again. "Your mother would have wanted you to have it."

As he had placed the stone in to her palm and her little fist had curled around it, he had kissed her fingers gently.

Her father had worked so hard to give her a good life, but at times she had caught him looking at her with such sadness and guilt, as though the burden that she had no mother weighed heavily upon his shoulders. He had ensured that she had wanted for nothing though. He had even afforded her an education with a governess, most unusual for a family of their station. Rachel had been eager to learn though and had impressed with her enthusiasm and quick mind. He had always given her praise that his money was well spent.

Somehow she had found the time to learn and to help on the farm and her father always saw to it that although hard, the work they undertook was rewarding and enjoyable.

The days of living on the farm with her father seemed so far away, until in private, she opened the box of trinkets. Then it was as if he was there in front of her again. Rachel was sure she could feel his warmth in front of her face.

"Rachel!" Cook's voice was growing louder and closer.

Rachel's shoulders shook with fright as the pitch of it bounced off her bones.

An overbearing shadow appeared in the doorway just as she had snapped the box shut and returned it to its hiding hole.

"What are you doing up here, whiling away precious time doing nought when there is much to be done?" Cook's eyes blazed from a plump face. Her cheeks were flushed and loose bangs of hair tumbled from her cap.

They had just celebrated the Wakes festival, an annual tradition at the end of August, wherein the whole village would celebrate and there would be much merriment. With a sore head still ailing her after the Wakes festivities at the beginning of the week, Cook's temperament was worse than usual. "It won't do," she scolded. "You have to be at market. The Belgraves are arriving the morrow and there's much to be done. Lady Cecily has instructed that she wants the best jams, honey, eggs and meats and I'm run ragged in that kitchen. You know that. Come along now." Reaching for her, she tried to pull her to her feet but Rachel shook her off.

"I am coming along." Rachel stood up just as the tall willowy figure of Lady Cecily Thornycroft appeared from behind Cook in the hallway.

"Being idle again is she? I don't know why she is in our keep. If it were up to me, she would be out on her ear." Her cold gaze rested upon Rachel and she wet her lips thoughtfully. "I shouldn't wonder if her whole linage was filled with lazy good for nothing women. Still, thank God for small mercies that if nothing else, we have time to teach her how to work." Clicking her tongue and rolling her eyes, she shook her head and looked at Rachel as though she was looking upon a lost cause. "Her head stuck in books all that time has profited nobody. I have no idea what her father was thinking to spend all that money on a governess." She laughed cruelly. It was a loud cackle that made Rachel's flesh crawl.

Lady Cecily continued her callous mockery, "A governess for a farmer's child. Fancy that? What good it has been to anyone, I will never know."

Cook didn't respond. She was too flustered with the preparations.

It was no secret that Lady Cecily disliked Rachel. She had been given a place of employment at Thornycroft Hall after her father had passed away, simply because he and Sir Edward had been friends.

Rachel and her father had been tenants of farmland belonging to Sir Edward and the farm had done well. Sir Edward had deemed Rachel to be too young to keep the farm going and so he had brought her into his employment shortly after her father's death. His generosity seemed to inspire Lady Cecily's jealousy and hatred and the fact that Rachel had an education was a particular point of irritation. She went out of her way on bad days to accuse her of being idle or lazy. This was clearly one of those days.

"If you please Lady Cecily, I have been able to read recipes to Cook and transcribe the ingredients required for medicaments to be made up in the stillroom."

Lady Cecily stared at her, speechless for a few moments, her cheeks flaring with colour. Rachel knew better than to answer back, but she couldn't stand her having a dig at her father who had been the dearest and most loving father that a child could wish for.

"Impudence!" Lady Cecily raged. "Did I give you permission to open your mouth and speak? You'll do well to remember who you are addressing girl. I am the Lady of the house and you'll speak when I say so and not before."

It was preposterous that Lady Cecily held herself in such high regard given the fact that when the late Lady Rosamund had been alive, she had been employed as staff at the house. By all accounts, she had only found herself in a position of such good fortune by bedding Sir Edward whilst his wife had suffered at the mercy of an incurable madness. Everybody knew it but nobody ever dared speak of the fact, not even behind closed doors because Lady Cecily had a talent for hearing everything.

Pressing her hands to the bump that stood out prominently from her belly, Lady Cecily glared at her with warning. "Well make haste before I order Cook to tan your behind. I should want everything to be perfect for the Belgraves. I will not stand for Lady Belgrave turning her nose up at our hospitality. She will be telling us all about her time at the King's court once again I am sure. It was only at the favour of her sister and her husband that she enjoyed that privilege, but she does not let it slip by in any of her letters." If it was possible, she was even more grumpy than usual.

With an irked glare, Lady Cecily waved her hand impatiently. "Coming up here to find out what nonsense has been going on has almost put me to the grave. I'll be in confinement after the Belgraves have left and I shall need help from you. You will need to find the best herbs to ensure safe delivery of this child." Rubbing her belly she cooed something about how perfect her baby would be before gliding off.

Gazing out of the window at the long track into the village, Rachel could see the cart waiting to be tethered to one of the shires.

The day was warm and the smell of cattle dung hung thick in the air. Before they were to leave, she had to go and fill the rooms with fresh flowers from the gardens.

Grabbing her basket, she hurried outside to the rear of the house. In comparison to the truly grand manor houses set within acres of estate, like Chatsworth, Thornycroft was miniscule, pitiful even, but Rachel loved its location.

The lawns sprawled out so that they appeared to mingle infinitely with the fields beyond that led down to the neighbouring village of Stoney Middleton. There was a small orchard and a rose garden filled with blooms that blushed fiercely against the green landscape in the summer. The scent was glorious and was all the more wonderful on a warm day.

With the garden in full bloom, she would be able to arrange a beautiful display that she was sure could even sweeten the sourness of Lady Cecily.

Wandering through the colourful rows of flowers, her basket was quickly filled and she moved her focus to the old disused beehives. There were three and not a single bee buzzed in them. She had never seen them in use.

Cook had told Rachel that the bees had once been the first Lady Thornycroft's love, but after her death, Lady Cecily had put a stop to it. The beekeeper had been given his leave and the honey had stopped.

Holding her basket over her wrist, Rachel wandered over to the disused skeps, their little entrance holes covered over. She wondered why on earth they had bothered to keep them and not just burn the things. Then she reminded herself that there could be no second-guessing the intricate workings of Lady Cecily's mind.

Reaching out, she let her fingers trace the bumpy coarse structure and thought how sweet the honey might have tasted. She dared imagine how different Thornycroft Hall might have been under the rule of the first Lady Thornycroft, Lady Rosamund. Her legend was largely a mystery, shrouded in the horror of demons and ghosts.

Rachel had heard of the portraits that were kept behind locked doors. Lady Rosamund had evidently been a great beauty of Italian lineage, with large blue eyes and thick dark hair that curled dramatically over olive skin. Her smile had been captivating. One that reputedly, any man could become lost in.

It was said that before the madness had taken hold, she had been kind and full of life. It was none the wonder that Cecily had one day demanded that all Lady Rosamund's portraits be hidden away.

As Rachel allowed her mind to wander, she caught sight of the darker patch of land beyond the skeps. The ground was not well kept and not well trodden either.

Nobody had ever said where the first Lady Thornycroft's bones lay, but Rachel thought it was entirely possible that they could be there, under the undulating ground, with her child.

Some of the servants said that they had buried her with the child, lest the demon had managed to get hold of the poor little soul too.

Reflecting on the whispered rumours, Rachel thought about how very sad it was. They said that in an effort to rid her of the demon, Lady Rosamund had been tortured. Rachel imagined how very awful it must have been to be at the mercy of all that, whilst her husband was laying in their bed with his new fancy.

Kneeling to touch the patch of land, Rachel pulled a rose stem from the basket and laid it gently across the uneven earth. "For you Lady Rosamund and your babe," she whispered, before hurrying back to the house.

She did not notice the shadowy face that regarded her from one of the windows of Thornycroft Hall. As suddenly as it had appeared, it melted away into the darkness of the house.

Lady Cecily's personal help, Anna, had been instructed to accompany Rachel to market. Inwardly, Rachel scowled at the fact that she was not trusted to carry the task alone. Anna did not look pleased to be on such a lowly duty either and she complained continuously about Lady Cecily's demeanour all the way to the market, fretting about what the worry would do to the unborn child.

The cart bumped over the dry mud track, making Anna yelp now and again before continuing her rampage of whinging.

Looking away, Rachel muttered and nodded in all the right places, but as far as she was concerned, Anna was as much of a worrier as Cecily.

It was a relief when they dismounted and the shire was taken to the troughs. Listening to Anna go on was not an experience that Rachel relished.

It was busy in the village. The frisson of excitement that accompanied market day hung in the air, mingling with laughter and happy voices.

When she had lived with her father, Rachel had always enjoyed mixing with her neighbours in the heart of Eyam.

Her best friend was Alice Hancock. She had known Alice since she was tiny and being several years younger than Rachel, she had grown to view her as a sister.

Elizabeth, Alice's mother, was a woman of a kind disposition, quite the opposite of Lady Cecily.

The Hancocks lived on the Riley farm, near the Talbot family, at the far reaches of the village. Although they had been trading rivals with Rachel and her father, they had become good friends over the years. Even after Rachel had lost him, she had remained firm friends with the Hancock family and in particular, Alice, who had visited her at Thornycroft Hall with braces of eggs or salted meats.

Unlike Thornycroft Hall, the Hancock house was the way a family home should be: filled with the high notes of laughter, the smell of freshly baked bread, pies and the sharp tang of fruit jam in the kitchen.

Since taking her employment with the Thornycrofts, it was rare that Rachel got to visit the Hancock family anymore, so she treasured what time she could garner with them.

"Have you heard what they're saying Rachel?" Alice Hancock's breathless voice took Rachel by surprise, just as Anna had wandered off after barking instructions at her.

With rosy cheeks and a glint in her eye, Alice took her by the arm. Before anyone could stop them, she was leading her away.

She gave Rachel no opportunity to respond to her question before she continued, nervous excitement getting the better of her. "Remember the calf that strayed into Divine Service?"

Rachel was hardly likely to have forgotten the story of the incident. It had been the talk of the village. Rumour had it that some young lads had driven a poor, terrified, young cow into the church during Divine Service at the Wakes vigil. The village dog whippers had needed to remove it.

The whole incident had upset many, including Lady Cecily, who hadn't even been there, but had insisted that the shock of it all had caused her to take ill for the rest of the day. Some folk were even saying that it had not been an unfortunate mishap, but intended as an insult to the new Reverend, William Mompesson. Rachel hoped that was not the case.

Alice pulled her closer so that she could get her point across. "Well, they're saying that the cow incident is a bad omen and that some of the miners have heard the call of Gabriel Hounds sweeping across the moors at dusk."

Letting out a gasp, Rachel put a hand to her mouth. "Gabriel Hounds?" Gabriel Hounds were said to be the lost souls of un-baptised children that would howl across the moors, portending doom.

"Aye, Gabriel Hounds," Alice confirmed, clearly enjoying being the bearer of such worrying news. "And Catherine Talbot told Ma that she'd had white crickets in her kitchen. So what do you think?"

"What's Ma said to you about tittle-tattle Alice?" Alice's younger sister Anne had sidled up. She was carrying a basket filled with cheeses.

"'Tis not tittle-tattle Anne," Alice protested. "'Tis all true."

"How do you know if you weren't there to witness it?" Despite her youth, Anne often proved herself to be sensible and reasoned beyond her years.

"Come on you two, no point arguing over it," Rachel said, laughing at Alice's angry scowl.

Pouting huffily, Alice let go of Rachel and folded her arms across her chest. "I was at service when the young cow trampled through and I've heard it's a portent. Don't you agree?"

Shrugging, Rachel kept her lips pursed. She didn't like talking about portents and omens, not with all the rumours and creaking floorboards at Thornycroft Hall. "I think people have loose tongues and vivid fancies, is all."

Sticking out her bottom lip even further, Alice was visibly upset that nobody was siding with her. "If Lady Muck let you come to Divine Service instead of being holed up in that dark house with Thomas Stanley preaching every Sunday, you would well have seen it for yourself. Then you'd know."

Thomas Stanley was a previous rector, from the puritan faith. It was no secret that the Thornycrofts didn't support William Mompesson as their reverend. Since the restoration of the monarchy, clergymen of the puritan faith had been forced out of their positions. However, like many other families in Eyam, the Thornycrofts still stood firmly by the puritan ways and they refused to attend Divine Service.

Every Sunday, the village's old puritan pastor, Thomas Stanley, would come to give a private sermon in the little chapel at Thornycroft Hall. Rachel didn't agree, but who was she to give her opinion?

If her father had still been alive, he would have seen to it that they supported William Mompesson, rather than dissenting back to the old ways. He would have supported the King.

The Thornycrofts didn't have the same respect and tolerance as her father had though, especially not Lady Cecily. Still, Rachel couldn't help but wonder how they would behave when the Belgraves visited, who were a family clearly all for the King. If they had been to the Royal Court, then they were bound to be loyal to the restoration, and Lady Cecily was so eager to impress, that surely they would all attend Reverend Mompesson's Divine Service?

Alice sniffed haughtily before adding her final justification that the incident at Divine Service, the Gabriel Hounds and the crickets had to be portents of some kind. "Well, I've even heard that the Reverend Mompesson's wife, Catherine, had cause for concern afterwards. 'An omen', she called it."

At the very mention of Catherine Mompesson's name, Rachel stiffened. She held a lot of respect for the Reverend's wife. If *she* thought that there was something in it, that made Rachel feel uneasy.

"What do you think it means?" Rachel asked, but before Alice could answer, they were all ushered away to their various duties at the market.

As it was the week following the Wakes festivities, it was to be a busy one, with relatives of families visiting. The opportunity for families like Alice's was too good to pass up in favour of idle gossip.

Noon brought with it a close air and a balmy sky. In the distance, the perfect sheet of blue was tarnished with heavy cloud that was seeping across it like a growing bruise. It promised a clean rain to cool the land and sweeten the late summer air. "There'll be a storm later I shouldn't wonder," Anna commented as they loaded up the cart with the goods from market.

By the time they had finished packing away, thick clouds were scudding across the sky.

Despite the weather, Anna's mood was much brighter as she clambered back into the cart. Even talk of the various bad portents that folk had witnessed hadn't darkened her disposition. She seemed excited about some news she had heard of fancy new cloths arriving from London for a young tailor who was staying at the Hadfield's home. "I've had it on good authority that the young tailor, George Viccars, staying with the Hadfields is taking a delivery of some fashionable new cloth from London and will be able to make Lady Cecily a new gown, if it pleases her." She gave Rachel a satisfied grin. "New cloth from London. That will delight her no end."

The smug look she was wearing made Rachel want to roll her eyes. Why she had to please Lady Cecily so much all of the time was a wonder to her. None of the staff were that keen on Lady Cecily. It seemed that Anna was the only one who cared for her at all.

"Rachel lass, after we have taken all of this back, you should come back into the village and arrange for Master Viccars to come to Thornycroft Hall this afternoon, so that he might measure Lady Cecily for a fitting."

Alice was standing nearby and the suggestion was not lost on her as she gave Rachel a wink and a nod. They would take the opportunity to meet and catch up, like old times.

Typically, there was nobody about to help when they returned, and Anna left most of the work to Rachel, insisting that it was far beneath her station to unload the cart.

In the kitchen, Cook was hot and cross. Poor Hannah, the scullery maid, had been given an ear boxing by the looks of things and Rachel vowed to make her a cooling balm in the stillroom just as soon she was back from visiting the tailor, George Viccars.

"I hope you aren't planning on being long, there's much to be done here if we're to prepare properly for the Belgrave visit." Cook glanced impatiently at Hannah whose face was pink from the ear boxing. "I need help here, not hindrance."

"I need to visit the tailor to arrange a fitting for Lady Cecily. I shouldn't be long, not with this storm coming," Rachel replied.

Cook picked up a large spoon and dipped it in the bowl that she was cradling. "Aye, well see to it that you're not."

Rachel took no time to wait and risk being called back. Hurrying to find her shawl and the money pouch that Anna had left for her to secure the services of George Viccars, she was in the large hall when a loud banging drummed through the house. The force and the urgency of the noise was enough to almost cause her to scream.

Jumping, she turned to face the heavy doors at the front of the house. The impatient knocking sounded out again and she looked around anxiously.

Rachel had been given clear instructions that it was not her job to answer the doors to the front of the house. "I do not want our guests to see or hear from you, do you understand?" Lady Cecily had instructed when she had first started her position at Thornycroft Hall. "We have a reputation here at Thornycroft Hall and I shan't have the lowliest of staff answering doors to our guests." Rachel wasn't quite sure just what reputation Lady Cecily thought that she was able to maintain, given that everyone knew of her history, but it would have given her no advantage to argue and so she had accepted it.

Bang. Bang. Bang.

It was as though somebody was swinging a large stick against the doors. She was considering whether or not she should try and find Frimley, Sir Edward's Valet, or Anna, when the heavy swish of silk against the rush matting interrupted her deliberation.

Rachel hid herself from sight under the sweep of the staircase and waited for Lady Cecily to pass. She was muttering something about the fact that none of the staff were ever around when they were needed.

Sir Edward joined her from his study, his face puce with the annoyance of being disturbed from some taxing business.

Rachel slipped further into the shadow, hoping Lady Cecily wouldn't catch sight of her. She was already complaining loudly to her husband about how unacceptable it was that her much needed rest should be interrupted by such a commotion.

Sir Edward threw open the doors with an impatient grunt, just as the elderly Frimley shuffled in from wherever it was he had been.

The scowl on Lady Cecily's face made it plain that she was not pleased with his tardiness, but Frimley was old and wise and he seemed nonplussed by her threatening glare.

"What could possibly be the need for-?" Edward Thornycroft's hands dropped to his sides, his line of questioning cut short as his eyes addressed the person standing on the doorstep.

A woman, almost as tall as he was, glared at him from the doorstep. Her gaze was challenging and her lips drawn tight, with no hint of a warm greeting. In her right hand she held a walking cane, the top of it carved into the shape of a fox's head. Judging by her gait, she did not appear to require the cane for any purpose other than banging on doors.

As Sir Edward found it within himself to utter a greeting of sorts, she lifted the cane slightly, as though the fox would respond on her behalf.

At last she spoke and Rachel could not place an accent amidst the flinted caw of her voice. "Edward." The woman's lips twitched as though they threatened to smile, but her eyes remained hard as flint. She did not seem at all intimidated by Sir Edward's displeasure at her evidently unannounced arrival.

"Goody Brown," Frimley announced to nobody in particular, his voice watery. He clearly recognised her and was eyeing her with suspicion.

There was a short silence before Lady Cecily gasped for air and her body tipped backwards. Her arms flailed uselessly for something to hold on to.

Despite his age and the beginnings of a stoop, Frimley caught her and helped her back to her feet. Sir Edward was too distracted to notice.

"You are surprised?" asked the woman. Beads of perspiration had gathered on her top lip and forehead and her ample bosom heaved, giving away that she was nervous, as well as exerted of her energy.

Sir Edward opened his mouth to respond but snapped it shut again. He turned to Frimley, who was grimacing with the effort of holding Lady Cecily upright. "Take her to her chamber and instruct the rest of the staff that they are dismissed of their duties within the main house until dinner." He looked over the woman's shoulder at the black carriage that was rocking with the agitated tug of the horses. "Have the carriage taken around the back of the house. I shall see to it that the horses are fed and watered. They look tired and you must be too."

The woman showed no gratitude. "'Tis a long journey from York, especially for a woman in my position."

He humoured her no more as he escorted her away from the entrance in order to help her around to the back of the house.

Rachel waited until all was silent again before emerging from her hiding place. There would be no need to stop and listen to any of Cook's demands before she left for the village as she was about to be dismissed of her duty anyway. So she hurried through the kitchen and through the servant door to make good her escape.

For the duration of her walk into the village she pondered over who the strange guest could be. Her appearance had startled both Sir Edward and Lady Cecily.

Edward Thornycroft was a man of steady reserve and not one to come easily unseated. Rachel could not remember a time that she had seen him look flustered.

With her unblinking eyes that could have been blue or brown, depending what light or shadow caught them, the woman had been strange looking. Her expression had been stern but may have once been soft. It was hard to place an age on her as her plumpness flattered her complexion, but Rachel mused that she may have once been attractive, striking even. She could not be a wealthy woman because, although her clothes were neat, they were not of fine materials like Lady Cecily's and her hands were worn, not just with time, but from hard work. Rachel questioned what power she possessed over the Thornycrofts.

Her pondering was soon distracted by the buzz and energy that was still thriving in the village from market day.

When Rachel approached, Alice and her mother, Elizabeth, were still packing away the goods that they hadn't managed to sell. Alice's younger sister, Anne, had evidently returned to the farm to help with her younger siblings.

Rachel reached for a huge slab of strawberry cheese in order to help. "Here let me help you. I will be in the village a while now."

With a kind smile, Elizabeth greeted her before nudging Alice. "No need lass. I can finish up here if you two want to go and have some fun."

Alice needed no further prompts. With a gleeful shout, she thanked her mother and went to take Rachel's hand.

Elizabeth nodded her head towards the fretful sky. "Mind you're back before this storm sets in though Alice. It won't be long now."

Alice acknowledged her mother's warning and tugged Rachel away to tell her some new secretive gossip. "Have you seen Master Viccars today? I heard him promising Mistress Mompesson a new dress, fancy like."

Unlike other men in the village, George Viccars was vibrant and fashionable. His style was modern and from London. Rumour had it that he was a fine tailor in the making and he was working for Master Hadfield, who was still away on business.

With a giggle, Rachel joined in with her friend's musings. "Anna told me about his new cloth from London. I should love a dress to be made for me, in scarlet and green, or the purple of the heather that grows thick on the moors."

Laughing playfully, Alice poked fun at her. "Purple? You should be so lucky Queen Rachel. Find yourself a rich man and maybe a purple gown might one day be yours for the wearing, but even Master Viccars could not conjure such a thing for a country girl."

Pouting, Rachel ignored the comment. She hated it when Alice made fun of her, even in jest, especially as she was far older and prided herself on being that much wiser.

It seemed a pity to spend her precious time outside of Thornycroft Hall sulking and so she chose to ignore the comment and instead suggested that they go and sit on the wall near the cattle troughs. Then she asked Alice the question that she knew would make her young friend giddy with delight. "So do you want to come with me to ask Master Viccars if he'll go to Thornycroft Hall for a fitting?"

Gasping, Alice pressed a hand to her mouth. "Really? Lady Cecily is having a fitting?" She giggled wickedly. "But she will be a horror." Standing up, she began to prance around. "Keep your hands to yourself, lest I should have my husband know of your intent. That's too big, too small, too red, too scratchy. Bone idle man!" She twirled around in a display of mock arrogance before folding over with laughter.

"Alice Hancock, that's wicked." Rachel tried to chastise her friend, but the impersonation was far too like Lady Cecily to stop from giggling.

Alice sat down next to her again and they talked for a short while, laughing together and planning their dreams for the future, all of which involved Rachel escaping the stifling walls of Thornycroft Hall to find a better life, perhaps in York, or even London.

Dreaming of her prospects in York reminded her that the strange woman who had turned up at Thornycroft Hall had mentioned York. It was the city that she had travelled from. Rachel considered telling Alice about her, but much as she loved her friend, she was still young and prone to gossip. Sir Edward had appeared so effected by her visit, that Rachel knew that he would not take kindly to any gossip leaked into the village. There was enough gossip that surrounded the Thornycrofts and his first wife.

Thinking better of it, she hopped down from the wall and suggested brightly that they go and knock at the Hadfield's house.

The air was getting closer and it felt as it always did on the edge of a storm. Elizabeth wouldn't be pleased if she was responsible for Alice getting caught in it and falling ill.

Linking arms, they began to embark on their short journey to the cottage, just as a friendly voice wished them both well.

Biting into a sweet red apple, Master George Viccars was walking past, a spring in his step. He winked at them and tossed a ripe apple towards Rachel, who caught it.

Trying not to look too pleased with herself, she felt her cheeks blush the colour of the apple's rosy skin.

"The orchards are sweet with fruit now," he said and gave an amused chuckle as he noted the colour of Rachel's cheeks. His handsome face was a bright and jolly contrast against the swiftly darkening afternoon.

"Thank you," Rachel stammered, giving Alice a sideways-glance. "Word has it that you're making the Reverend's wife, Mistress Mompesson, a dress." The words tripped off her tongue in a rushed and cumbersome fashion. Inwardly, she chastised herself for appearing so foolish.

"Yes. The material should arrive any day now. Fashion from London. She will look very fine with her colouring as it is." He studied her for a moment, curling his index finger beneath his chin. "You would suit a striking bold colour too. You have a face that could flatter it and carry it off well." He gave another wink, this one exclusively for Rachel, and she felt giddy with the pleasure of being singled out.

Rachel's father had always told her that she would one day be a great beauty who would turn heads, and although she knew that it was sinful to ponder too much about such things, she liked to secretly imagine what it would be like to turn a handsome man's head her way. Even though she knew that he was only being polite and generous with his charming words, George Viccars had just breathed a little life into that secret flight of fancy.

"And what colour would you suggest for me?" Alice chipped in childishly. Not to be outdone, she twirled around coquettishly. Rachel felt her blush deepen as she realised how very silly and immature they must appear to him.

"Blue," he answered quickly. "To match your eyes." With that, he took another bite of his apple and turned his attention back to Rachel.

It was as though he appreciated that she was the older of the two and she would understand that he had to humour Alice. The gesture elevated her mood again.

There was an uncomfortable silence that followed. Alice nudged her sharply in the ribs.

"Ouch. Ummm, Master Viccars?" Feeling foolish once again, Rachel was reminded that there was business to attend to. "Lady Cecily should like a fitting for a dress."

"Yes I spoke with her Housekeeper about that. Do you work at Thornycroft Hall too?"

She nodded. "Anna, that's whom you spoke with. She asked if you might do a fitting for Lady Cecily this afternoon. You see, the Belgraves are coming to visit and Lady Belgrave has dined at the Royal Court and-" she jarred as Alice's elbow prodded her again, cutting her off mid-sentence. Silently she thanked her friend for stopping her from prattling on like an old spinster.

His eyes twinkling with amusement, he looked her up and down before smiling. "I have some matters to attend to now but I could come later if it is convenient?"

Rachel hesitated as she thought of how Sir Edward had dismissed them all until dusk. This was different though. This would make Lady Cecily happy. She agreed.

He gave a cheerful nod. "Good day then." He pretended to doff a cap before disappearing into the cottage that he was lodging in with the Hadfields, just beyond the church. When the door had closed, both girls fell into fits of giggles.

The first drops of rain interrupted them and the streets began to empty fast as the day greyed into an oppressive, muggy gloom.

Saying her goodbyes to Alice, Rachel hurried to the rectory and knocked sharply on the door, waiting to be greeted by Catherine Mompesson's familiar warm smile.

When there was no reply, she frowned and looked around nervously. If she were caught dallying on the Mompesson's doorstep, she would be in trouble.

Unlike his predecessor, William Mompesson was young, with a small family and a sweet tempered wife, Catherine. His predecessor had been reinstated as the village Rector after the restoration of the monarchy, but like William, he had not been held in as much favour as Thomas Stanley had been.

Rachel often thought that if parishioners like Lady Cecily and Sir Edward even gave the Mompessons half a chance, they would be swayed from their allegiance with Thomas Stanley and the puritan faith. In Rachel's eyes, the Reverend Mompesson and his wife Catherine were the most generous spirited and wise people she had ever met.

If it had not been for Catherine's warm heartedness and empathy, Rachel doubted whether she would have ever found a way of coping with the grief of losing her father and their life together on the farm. She enjoyed the little precious time she would sometimes spend with Catherine and her sweet children.

"Rachel?" A gentle voice called her name just as she was about to give up knocking on the door. Arms laden with lilies that were as white as her skin, Catherine Mompesson greeted her with wide dark eyes. "Is everything alright?"

"Aye Mistress Mompesson. Just visiting, is all." The rain had begun to fall in fat drops, plastering their clothes to their skin. It was pleasant, warm summer rain, the sort that Rachel enjoyed feeling drip from her lashes and nose.

Hurrying past her, Catherine ushered her inside. "Don't stand out here to catch your death. Come and sit awhile in front of the fire. William is on errands, although 'tis a thankless task these days." Placing the flowers down on the long table in the kitchen, she looked a little jaded.

It wasn't Rachel's place to ask impertinent questions about what might be troubling her. Besides, Rachel thought she knew only too well the reason for her melancholy. With so many villagers being so dismissive of their post in Eyam, it must be hard trying to keep their heads up and continue to do their work in good grace.

When Rachel had attended William Mompesson's first service, lots of the village had joined her, mainly to learn more about what their new parish clergyman was like. It was a great source of gossip and even the Thornycrofts had attended, Lady Cecily with her nose in the air. Rachel cringed as she recalled how Anna had voiced her opinion loudly enough to be overhead.

"Wet behind the ears," Anna had criticised afterwards with a loud disdainful sniff. "He won't last."

"Nay. He won't make the year," somebody else had agreed. Then, as had started to be customary following service, Lady Cecily had taken tea in the blue parlour with some guests and afterwards instigated the rule that nobody from the household, family members or staff, should attend the Reverend Mompesson's Divine Service again.

Every Sunday, after Thomas Stanley's private sermon in Thornycroft Hall, Lady Cecily would invite friends or acquaintants to take tea with her.

Rachel thought that tea in the blue parlour was her way of showing off her wealth, summoning for the best china, along with the locked caddy that contained the precious tea leaves, and making a great show of preparing it herself, so that Rachel and Anna could be dismissed.

Despite the frosty reception that they had received, the Reverend William Mompesson and Catherine were still in Eyam and people did attend service, although not as many as they had no doubt hoped for.

For Rachel, there was no choice in the matter. She had been forbidden. It was only by good fortune that she had been able to acquaint herself with the Mompessons and she was loath to waste any precious opportunity such as this one.

When she had first met Catherine, it had not been many weeks since the Mompessons had taken residence in the parish. The day had been full of the promise of an early summer, with the soft coo of wood pigeons and the gentle buzz of bees dancing from the heads of the bluebells. Rachel's mood had been unable to match the brightness of the day. Alone she had found a fallen tree trunk on the edge of the Cucklet Delf, a beautiful and peaceful bowl shaped meadow within the village.

The Delf had been one of her father's favourite places to walk. Often, she would go there to gather flowers for his grave when she was overcome with the sadness and emptiness of his loss.

As she had sat, a curtain of despair had enshrouded her. At the time, she had wondered whether she could live through another day. The tears that she had shed over the death of her father had been long spent and all that she had left was an arid feeling of hopelessness.

The weight of her woes and her loneliness had all but broken her that day, pressing her shoulders in to a hunch and causing her head to bow low, caught only by her upturned hands.

Then she had felt a shadow shade her from the warmth of the sun. When she had looked up, she had seen the wide concerned eyes of Catherine Mompesson. She had felt the kind squeeze of her hand upon her shoulder and heard the gentle purr of her words as she had taken the time to find out what was troubling her so very much.

Catherine had encouraged her to talk. She had not offered condescending words of advice. Nor had she given her any stern reminders of how lucky she was to have been given shelter and employment by the Thornycrofts. Instead she had listened, nodded and held her hand. Then she had prayed with her and placed a gentle kiss upon her forehead, so that when Rachel had made her way back to Thornycroft Hall, she had felt as though a great weight had been lifted.

After that day, she had met with Catherine whenever the opportunity had arisen, and so she had found a confidante whom she knew would be one for life.

It had been Catherine who had taken the time to find out how the loss of her father had been consuming her head with such sad and dark thoughts; and it had been Catherine who had dried her tears and held her whilst offering words of comfort. She passed no judgement, but always allowed Rachel the time to talk and to heal. Aside from the Hancocks and Catherine, nobody else had thought to do any of those things.

For Rachel to dare even whimper that she missed her father or her life on the farm whilst under the roof of Thornycroft Hall would have been considered a great insult. With barely anything of value left in her father's will, she was expected to consider herself lucky and prove her gratitude by working for her keep.

With Lady Cecily so adamant that nobody within the household should align themselves with the Mompessons, Rachel's trips to see Catherine and William were shrouded in secret. Lady Cecily would not approve of her timewasting or fraternising with this Reverend, with his fashionable frills on his cuffs and different ways of doing things.

Reminding herself of that fact, Rachel vowed to make the visit a swift one as she followed Catherine's direction to take a seat in front of the fire.

The children were ushered away by their nursemaid and Rachel listened to the increasing patter of rain outside as she broke the edge of the sweetbread she had been handed.

"How is Lady Cecily faring in this heat?" Catherine brushed some crumbs into the hearth. It had been a particularly hot few months and any woman carrying a child was to be pitied.

"Her temper is heightened and her patience shortened," Rachel answered honestly before taking a bite of her bread.

"That is to be expected. You shouldn't think too hard of her for it." Instinctively, Catherine stroked the flat of her hands over her own stomach, as though recalling the memory of pregnancy and the hardship that came with it.

Shrugging, Rachel smiled and dabbed at a crumb on the corner of her mouth. "It's not so different to how she usually is, just a little more often."

"When the baby comes she shall have more than enough to do than keep her attention focused upon you." Catherine smiled warmly as she gave her a knowing look. "I remember those early months well with my two."

"How is the Reverend Mompesson?" Keen to change the subject, Rachel gave her a bright smile.

It was Catherine's turn to look wilted. "Busy. He is doing so much but I can not say that it does our cause much good." She gazed off into the fire. "Such a pity."

"You both do a wonderful job here in Eyam. People will see that one day, I am certain."

Her eyes misted. "You are a good girl Rachel Craven. If only everyone shared your opinion." Taking a seat and smoothing her skirt, she looked to the crackling fire. "Still, let us not ruin this afternoon with such small matters. We can only do what we do." Looking Rachel directly in the eye, two spots of pink began to spread over her pale face so that she looked even more beautiful than usual. "And how are you Rachel?" The question was simple but her gaze penetrating, as though searching Rachel's soul for the answers.

Placing the knot of bread on her knee, Rachel averted her gaze as her bottom lip threatened to quiver. She couldn't cry, not again.

Things had been harder lately. It was to be expected around the time of the Wakes festivities, as she and her father had enjoyed the celebrations that had surrounded it.

Biting down on the inside of her cheek and taking a deep breath, she tried to hold herself together. Surely she had cried enough tears in the time that her father had been gone? Yet the wound suddenly seemed so fresh, like a scab that kept being picked. "As Lady Cecily and Anna remind me, life goes on."

The hypnotic yellow flicker of flames in the hearth distracted her and she listened to the comforting crackle of logs as they fell to ashes. "Times can be hard, not having any family and no grave for my mother," she said, thinking about how the unmarked grave of Lady Rosamund Thornycroft was a sad reflection of how her own mother's life had ended, in ground that hadn't been consecrated, her body lost in a collapsed mineshaft.

She had never told Catherine about the fate of her mother. "When I was a baby, my mother was buried alive in their mineshaft. Pa said they never managed to recover her body. He couldn't bring himself to work the mines after that. He became a tenant farmer for Sir Edward Thornycroft," Rachel explained.

"That is the kind of loss that must be hard on the family. You and your father must have suffered terribly."

With a ragged breath, Rachel choked back a sob. "When he was alive, Pa would take me to the moors and we would lay a wreath every year for her." She looked up and caught Catherine's eye. "I cannot bear to think of her in some unknown space underground. Lonely. Lost in a collapsed mineshaft forever." Shivering, she wrapped her arms about herself. "Do you think she could ever find her way to heaven?"

There was no hesitation in Catherine's response as she nodded. "You say that your father always told you of her kindness. I believe that a good soul will always find his or her way into God's arms, no matter what has happened to their flesh and bone Rachel."

Feeling the warmth of Catherine's hand against her knee, Rachel managed to keep her tears at bay. "I wish so much that I could come to the church for service."

Nodding with understanding, Catherine smiled empathetically. "We are all part of God's family, no matter our status or wealth. Really, it matters not where you pray or how you do it because your prayers will not go unheard." Reaching for the poker, she gently manipulated the logs so that their glowing embers caught some more with a pleasantly soothing hiss. They were wise words, comforting words and with them, Rachel felt some solace.

Keeping her gaze fixed on the fire, Rachel thought how terrible it would be to be buried outside of a churchyard. Despite what Catherine said, it wasn't fair that her mother or the first Lady Rosamund should have such horrible final resting places. Even though Lady Rosamund had taken her own life, the circumstances surrounding it were dreadfully sad.

"Do you think that Lady Rosamund Thornycroft is in heaven?" she asked.

Uncomfortable, Catherine looked away. Everybody knew the story surrounding her untimely death, even newcomers to the parish. "To take one's life is a dreadful sin Rachel." She pursed her lips as though considering which words to choose next, but Rachel was too quick for her.

"Do you think that…." She took pause in her sentence and then a deep breath. The creaks and shadows in Thornycroft Hall had always frightened her but after seeing the spot that she felt certain was Lady Rosamund's grave, and then the strange woman who had turned up at the house that afternoon, she felt especially on edge. She licked her lips. "Do you think that the dead can return?"

Taken aback, Catherine stood abruptly and looked to the window. "That weather is getting worse. I should have William escort you home when he returns."

Rachel didn't want to go home. She didn't want the conversation to end. There was something inside her that was nagging to know, especially after what Alice had said about the Gabriel Hounds, their lost souls wreaking havoc across the moors.

"They say that there is a demon at Thornycroft Hall." She hadn't meant to say it so flippantly, but the words had simply tumbled from her.

A heavy clatter shook the room as the poker that Catherine had been holding rolled across the floor. Catherine stared at her, eyes wide, before attempting to save the rush matting from the glowing orange poker tip.

"I have heard about the Gabriel Hounds and I worry," Rachel continued, wringing her hands together nervously. "People have heard things. Seen things. And at Thornycroft Hall, some say that they have even felt things touch them in the dead of night."

With a gasp, Catherine fell into the chair behind her. "You should not utter such things Rachel, and you should take care to ignore the gossip of loose and ignorant tongues."

Bowing her head in shame, Rachel stared at her hands. "I am sorry Mistress Mompesson, but I am frightened. They say that Lady Rosamund was touched by the Devil, a demon and that she-"

"Yes I have heard all about that and the tittle-tattle that surrounds her fate, but it does no good to dwell upon these things or speak of them. The past is the past. What's been done cannot be undone." She was cross, her tone terse.

Rachel could not help herself. A feeling of dread had been building in the pit of her stomach as though something awful was going to happen. She was unable to shake it. "Do you believe in omens though Mistress Mompesson? Do you believe in…. signs?"

Rising from her seat, Catherine appeared taller and the shadows in the room darkened her face. "This storm is not showing any hint of forgiveness. The children will be restless when the thunder comes." The sound of the front door closing made her shoulders jerk and then a distinct look of relief crossed her face. "That must be William. He will see you home Rachel. You should hurry. I wouldn't want either of you caught out in this weather for long."

As she ushered Rachel out into the porch, she called out to William and insisted that Rachel borrow one of her cloaks.

Fastening the clasp, Rachel noticed that Catherine's hands were trembling slightly. "Keep your faith lass," she whispered, pulling her close for a hug. "You have a good soul and a strong heart."

From somewhere in the distance, the impetuous rumble of thunder crashed above the darkening landscape. "Thank you," Rachel whispered and hurried into the rain with William.

They took the walk through the village at a pace that almost had them running. There was not much point in talking as neither could hear above the smacking of rain against the muddying ground beneath their feet.

Knowing that Rachel would be in trouble if she were caught with the Mompessons, William left her at the gates to Thornycroft Hall and Rachel looked into its face of stone.

The place looked foreboding as the first fork of lightning ripped through the malevolent sky. It was closely followed by a crash of thunder. The storm was much closer and would take some time to pass overhead.

Running to the servants' door around the side of the building, she thought that, above the rain and the clattering of thunder, she could hear cries. Thinking back to the rumour of Gabriel Hounds and the many ghost stories attached to Thornycroft Hall, her heart jerked in her chest.

How had Alice Hancock described the Gabriel Hounds? A thousand lost souls ripping through the White Peaks portending doom, their mouths torn open in permanent screams. Too frightened to remain alone outside for a moment longer, she threw open the door and stumbled blindly into the kitchen.

Nobody appeared to be around. Sir Edward had only dismissed the staff until dusk and so surely Cook would have returned to begin cooking dinner?

The kitchen seemed cold and unfamiliar with nobody fussing about it, no pots bubbling and no glowing fire. It was as though the dark veil that was swiftly falling over Eyam had seeped its way into the house, climbing the walls and suffocating the furniture with its shadowy silence.

Another cry, long, drawn out and pained, crashed through the house. It was coming from upstairs.

Lifting her skirts, Rachel took the steps two at a time. At the end of the corridor, a light was flickering and there was another long groan. The air smelled sour and she hurried towards the light. It was coming from Lady Cecily's chamber, the one that she would soon be using for her confinement.

"Lady Cecily?" Rachel called, but her voice was drowned by another scream.

Pushing open the door, she didn't dare give herself the time to imagine what might be behind it.

Sprawled on her bed, a swathe of watery red staining the blanket and her skirts, Lady Cecily was panting and crying. Her hair tumbled wildly about her face, bits of it sticking to her skin, damp from sweat. Eyes red rimmed with fear, she looked at Rachel. "Help me, 'tis too soon," she whimpered.

"Where's Anna?" Rachel's voice shook. She had no idea what to do.

Lady Cecily was too traumatised to answer coherently. Terror had swallowed her features so that she looked more akin to a frightened animal, wild, irrational and clawing at anything that she could reach for. Her fingers found purchase with Rachel's wrist and she gave her a pleading look. "The baby Rachel. Hasten for help." Her mouth contorted as her body went into spasm and another scream sliced through the room just as a shaft of brilliant white light lit everything up. It was followed by another crash of thunder that pounded across the countryside. "It's coming! I can feel it!" Her frenzied scream tore through the atmosphere.

"Where is Sir Edward? Where is Frimley?" Rachel asked, her own fear making her sound wild.

"Business." Her words were ragged and breathless. "Caught in the storm I shouldn't wonder." Grimacing, she pushed her head back and let out a long pained growl. "Nobody's here. Not after-" She stopped abruptly and looked away, her breath heaving painfully in her chest.

Rachel stared helplessly for a moment. "Should I run for a doctor?"

Another scream ripped through the air as Lady Cecily bunched the sheets between her fingers in agony. "God's teeth lass, just stop asking questions and do something!"

"Aye, of course," she stammered, considering running back into the village to find someone, anyone. It wasn't really a feasible plan though.

With the veins in her neck and either side of her head pulsing so that they looked fit to burst, Lady Cecily screamed again. "Look! Just look down there. See what is happening."

With shaking hands, Rachel pulled up the heavy soaked skirts and looked as best she could but the light was too poor.

Running to the kitchen, she fumbled for more candles and found a blanket. If the babe were to come, it would need to be wrapped. Her hands shook and her heart hammered as she tried to find everything that she needed. Rachel had no idea what to do, but she could not leave Lady Cecily to look for help, it would put both her life and the life of her babe in danger.

She returned to find Lady Cecily gripping the sheets in pain and panic, her breathing wilder and her expression straining with the agony. "Help me," she begged pitifully and Rachel saw the fear in her eyes. The fate of Lady Rosamund's babies hung in the air between them. Lady Cecily was terrified that the same would happen to her child.

Rachel froze, her head swimming with thoughts on what she should to do first. Her legs felt weak as she realised that it was highly likely both Lady Cecily and her baby would die without anybody else there to help.

"Help me, Rachel. You must help." Her voice was growing weaker as her body started to give into the pain.

Another crash of thunder shook the house, swiftly followed by the sharp crack of lightning. From the corner of her eye, Rachel thought she saw a figure hovering in the doorway, watching them.

She looked towards Lady Cecily, but she was too far-gone with the pain to notice.

When the second flash came, Rachel turned fully to face the entrance to the room and stifled a scream. A pale face was inches in front of her, eyes boring into her own.

"Get those candles lit lass. I'll need the light for this." It was the woman who had arrived at the house earlier. Goody Brown, that had been the name that Frimley had given, announcing her arrival. She spoke with authoritative confidence but her expression was grim, as though her thoughts on the likelihood of survival for mother and baby echoed Rachel's.

Without hesitation, Rachel lit the candles and carefully placed them in their holders around the room. As she did so, she heard the sound of Lady Cecily's skirts being ripped, so that the view was clear.

Rachel turned and her stomach twisted at the sight of it. Something was showing amongst the blood and muck. A head. Glistening. "Push Lady Cecily. I see a head," she shouted, not knowing what else to do.

Goody silenced her by raising a bloodied hand.

Lady Cecily was crying and reaching out to grip whatever she could, but it wasn't working. Surely it was dangerous for the baby to stay in that position for too long?

Goody shifted position and Rachel couldn't see what it was that she was doing, but it made Lady Cecily cry out again. Was she trying to do her harm rather than help? Should she run and get help? The storm outside was relentless and Rachel knew it would take her far too long to run through it to find anyone. She felt paralysed with fear and indecision. As awful as Lady Cecily was, she did not wish any harm upon her.

Over the lashing of the rain against the house, Goody began shouting something at her. It took Rachel a moment to understand what it was that she was saying. Her thoughts were too scrambled. Nothing was coherent. Then she was being pulled around to the side of Lady Cecily's bed. Blood and muck were hot and sticky against her skin where Goody had gripped her wrist. "Now you can tell her to push lass," Goody said, the confidence in her voice reassuring.

Rachel raised her voice to a pitch to fight the noise of the storm. "Harder Lady Cecily. Push harder."

With a wretched cry she shook her head, tears and sweat mingling in a salty sodden mess on her face. "Nay. I can't. I can't."

Rachel flashed a look over at Goody who gave her a hard look, as though disappointed in how futile Rachel's efforts were. This was life or death. The consequences of her actions, or inactions, were sinking in, chasing away her earlier panic. She knew that she had to get Lady Cecily to push, stir her out of her weakened state.

Determination took hold of her and she leaned over, pressing her hands either side of Lady Cecily's face so that she was forced to look at her. "This is the first heir to Thornycroft Hall! Do your duty to him!" she screamed, mustering as much venom into her voice as she could. "Even I, a pitiful serving girl could do better than you."

Another shaft of blinding light filled the room and Rachel saw that Lady Cecily's lips were pulled back so that her teeth were bared and her skin was taut. As her expression changed from one of despair to determined, she cried out. A long drawn out howl echoed through the house.

From her position between Lady Cecily's legs, Goody looked up and nodded. "Nearly there lass," she said calmly.

Rachel put her mouth to Lady Cecily's ear. "One more push," she said as Lady Cecily insisted that there was nothing left in her, that it was impossible.

"Think of your babe," Rachel implored her. "Think of the Thornycroft heir. Take a breath and push."

Before she could say anything more, Lady Cecily grunted loudly. "Again," Rachel commanded and with a final howl from her, the baby slipped out.

Stunned, Rachel stared as Goody scooped the baby into her arms, but her expression was dismal. There was no noise.

She held the baby out, as though she suddenly did not want to touch it. For a terrible moment, Rachel thought that Goody was about to drop it to the floor. "Take him," she said sternly.

Him. A baby boy.

Rachel wasted no time, reached out, allowed Goody to place the little bundle into her arms. She looked at the fleshy, bloody pulp that surrounded his tiny body and her world stopped.

Something was wrong. There was still no cry.

All that she could hear was the ragged breath spilling from Lady Cecily's mouth, billowing acrid and sickly in the air.

"'Tis the curse of this place," Goody said. There was no emotion in her voice. "Gone like the rest of them." Evidently her work was done, as she left the room, not bothering to even glance at Lady Cecily who was beyond any sense to notice.

Rachel looked down at the baby. *Cry, cry, cry,* she willed as lightning engulfed the room so that the tiny little form was illuminated, his skin slippery and lips turning blue.

Overhead, thunder rumbled on, its threat still present despite the distance that had gathered. She listened to it continue its destructive rampage and imagined it taking the poor soul of the child with it.

"Gabriel Hounds," Alice had said. "They portend doom."

Had this been what they had come for, to take another innocent life at Thornycroft Hall?

Cry. She pleaded silently and turned the baby, rubbing his back. Tears began to roll uselessly down her cheeks. Still, there was no sound.

Goody had disappeared, not wanting anything more to do with it, leaving Rachel to pick up the pieces.

Downstairs a door slammed and she could hear heavy boots, first on the flagstones and then on the stairs.

Rachel couldn't let this happen, couldn't let an innocent life die in her arms. She poked her finger between the tiny rosebud lips and hooked out a sickening lump of mucus. Ignoring the rising nausea in her belly, she attempted to wrap his little body in the blankets that she had brought upstairs, her heart banging hard.

Then she saw it. The mouth opened and there was a gasp. She saw his little tongue and gums as he scrunched his eyes, balled his tiny fists and let a tremendous wail out.

Through tears, she began laughing.

Sir Edward appeared in the doorway, standing with his mouth agape. Behind him, Frimley arrived breathless, along with Sarah Woodman, a mid-wife from the little hamlet of Bretton on the edge of the village.

Rachel looked up at them. "'Tis a boy," she announced, beaming as the child continued to wail. Gently, she handed the baby to the firm, efficient hands of the mid-wife so that she could sort the cord.

With a look of grave concern on his face, Sir Edward dashed forward as though he struggled to believe the healthy cries that he could hear or the tiny flailing limbs that he could see.

Of course, he had been in this position before with his previous wife. That must be why Goody had referred to a curse being upon the place.

Rachel wondered if the demon that folk said had taken Lady Rosamund's sanity had already been inside her when the babies had been growing. Two had been born blue, another had never made it full term and the last one had lived only a short while, its death shortly before Lady Rosamund's.

This babe was surely quite different though? There was nothing weak about this boy whose cries could doubtless be heard from as far as Stoney Middleton.

She watched Sir Edward peer at him and catch his breath. The hardness in his face melted for a moment as he looked at Rachel. "You delivered him?"

"It was I who delivered him." Lady Cecily moaned from the bed, giving Rachel no chance to answer. "Please, when can I hold my boy?"

"Samuel." Sir Edward took a corner of the blanket that swaddled his child and folded it back. "His name is Samuel." He made a noise that could be mistaken for nothing other than one of joy. "He has your eyes Cecily."

"Aye and your hair Sir," the mid-wife agreed before handing him to Lady Cecily who was propped up with her breast ready to nourish her son.

With a coo, Lady Cecily took hold of him, putting him to her breast and swatting at the mid-wife as she attempted to help. "My boy," she purred with satisfaction. "My son." Beaming with pride, her thumb stroked at the dark swathe of feathery hair on his head. "He has a fine head of hair, the colour of his father's but 'tis thick like mine."

Glancing at Rachel, she pursed her lips and for a moment, she thought that she might offer her some note of thanks. "God has seen it fit to bless us with a strong and healthy lad," Lady Cecily said proudly.

Victorious, she turned her head back to her husband. "I must have pleased Him my darling." The remark was intended as pointed, the meaning jagged and cruel.

As Rachel cleaned her hands using the bowl of water and rags that had been brought upstairs, she wondered if Sir Edward was aware of just how jealous his new wife was of the last.

Glowering, she held Lady Cecily's gaze as she thought of the unmarked grave she was so sure that she had found in the gardens. It seemed dreadfully inappropriate for her to be making such remarks about a dead woman who had been heartbroken by all those children whom she had lost.

There was no comment from Sir Edward, who appeared too taken by the sight of the child, his heir and son, to be listening.

Lady Cecily's eyes had shifted to another focal point as she cooed and purred about what a gift she had provided for the Thornycroft name. There was no mention of Goody Brown and Rachel thought better of it than to say anything more.

Beyond the doorway, in a shadowy nook of the corridor, a cloaked figure hovered. At first she thought it was Goody, but the figure was slighter and shorter. A distant flash of lightning momentarily revealed the glassy gaze of the onlooker and Rachel started. Another flash and the nook was empty again.

Hurrying from the room, Rachel carried a tallow candle, the flame threatening to extinguish with every draught of air.

Footsteps. Above. A shutting door.

Adrenalin fuelling her nerve, Rachel hurried up the stairs until she came to the top of the house and she lifted her hand from the balustrade to feel the spongy layer of dust.

Nobody ventured to the very top of the house, to the hidden quarters. Not even Anna or Frimley. It was forbidden. It was the place where the first Lady Thornycroft had died and the place where the demon that was said to have invaded her body roamed.

Taking a step forward, she lifted the candle to shed what scant light she could.

There weren't many doors, just one behind her, one across the way and the little door that was supposed to lead to the top quarters; the place where the original nursery was situated and where Rosamund Thornycroft had chosen for her confinement before and after birth.

Before she could think sensibly about her actions, she reached out and turned the handle of the door. As she knew it would be, it was locked.

Turning to the door behind her, she tried it. Locked.

She looked towards the final door across the landing and treaded quietly towards it. Even as she reached for the handle she expected that it too would be locked. All the rooms at the top of the house were always locked. That was one of the rules. Nobody goes up and nobody has the keys.

Turning the handle, she heard the whir of brass scraping against brass and then a surprising click as a shaft of moonlight appeared in the now open crack.

Shocked, Rachel let go and watched as the hinges quietly groaned and the door swung open to reveal a room devoid of furniture but filled with white sheets. They were draped over things that were propped at the edges of the room so that they resembled the snowy slopes of the highest peaks in winter.

Crossing the threshold, Rachel tried to quell a cough as the musty smell of age and disuse accosted her throat and chest.

Beyond the window of the room, the storm still made known its rampage, now at a more muted level as it rolled further south. Even the rain had begun to ease.

Without the noise of the weather disguising her footsteps, Rachel would have to remove her boots. She undid the laces and gently laid them to one side before tiptoeing across to the sconces on the nearest wall.

Using her candle to create light, she then placed it carefully on the floor in the middle of the room and reached for the edge of the nearest sheet. Another puff of dust left her stifling both a cough and a sneeze and she waited to regain her composure before getting closer to take a look at what was underneath it.

A large rectangular frame was propped against the wall, another next to it, then another and another. There was a whole line of these frames, their gilded edges demonstrating an element of grandeur. They were the outer edges of something important.

"Portraits," Rachel whispered to herself as she carefully pulled one towards her and repositioned it until she could see the detail of the fine brush strokes.

Large eyes framed by dark circles that the artist had made no attempt to disguise, stared back at her from the subject in the painting. Rouge lips were pursed into a sad looking pout, the richness of their colour exacerbating the pallid complexion of the cheeks. It was a young face, a beautiful face, but one that had been ravished with misery so that the beauty could only glimpse out from behind a mask of sadness.

Resting the painting against the wall, she turned another. This one showed off the curves of a heavily pregnant woman. She wore the same sad pout but there was a flush of natural colour in her cheeks and her long hair was swept elegantly into soft curls that had been pinned to tumble dramatically behind her shoulders.

Caught up in the beauty of the artist's subject, Rachel turned another painting to see a much younger or perhaps just a much happier image of the same woman. Her legs were swung elegantly over the side of a beautiful grey mare and a faithful hound was sitting obediently below her. There was no smile, but a look of confident determination, as though she would swing her legs either side of the horse's flanks and kick it into a wild gallop. There was a wild look to her and a hint of childlike disobedience in her eyes that was fascinating rather than tiresome or petulant. It made her all the more beautiful and Rachel could not peel her eyes away for the want of finding more intrigue in her every contour.

"Lady Rosamund." Her voice was soft but the name chimed loud in the room, its prominence and significance seeming to breathe life into the beautiful faces staring back at her, the faces that Lady Cecily had demanded remain hidden and covered for so long.

A soft thud and the sound of a heavy sob caused her to drop the sheet back over the paintings without turning them back around. She looked towards the door into the blackness of the corridor, but it was as though the sound had come from somewhere within the room.

Looking around, her eyes strained in the dimness as Rachel tried to locate it, but all was quiet again.

From downstairs she heard the cry of a baby and the voice of the mid wife with Lady Cecily. The voices were dulled, muffled by the layers of the house between them, but loud enough to cause alarm. If anyone were to find her, she would be dismissed immediately with no pay and no forwarding employment or home.

Cursing herself for not shutting the door behind her, she quickly snuffed the candles in the sconces and crouched, waiting for everything to quieten again downstairs. She could not risk creeping past Lady Cecily's room and being noticed.

There was another sob and then a rattling noise. Without sufficient light, Rachel could do nothing to locate it.

Shuffling towards the far corner, she curled her knees to her chest and held her breath, waiting.

The sobbing stopped as abruptly as it had started and there was a short silence.

Then came the scratching. Slowly at first but then faster and faster like iron nails scraping against brick. It was unnatural and impossible. There was nobody else in the room. Aside from the covered paintings, it was too bare of any furniture to be hiding anyone, yet the scratching continued and Rachel realised that it was coming from inside the wall.

Pressing her palms against it, she listened as the noise became more persistent. Angry. Then all of a sudden it stopped.

Her mind racing, Rachel tried to think of what might be behind the wall. There were no other rooms to think of. Only the one opposite and of course, the door that led to a staircase that wound up to a higher level of the house. There was nothing behind the wall that she was crouched next to. The scratching was impossible.

Rumours of the restless spirit of the late Lady Rosamund Thornycroft raced through her head and she thought of the cloaked figure in the corridor, there one minute and gone the next.

Rachel wished that she had left well enough alone and simply retired to her little room with her little bed for the night. Now she was left with two dreadful decisions. Remain trapped in the darkness with whatever was behind the wall, or make a dash for it and risk being caught.

Another bout of vicious scratching brought her to a swift decision. Dashing from the room, she carefully closed the door and nimbly ran down the staircase until she was safely behind the door of her modest room.

Even as she lay beneath her sheets in bed, her heart would not quieten and the persistent scratching penetrated her skull, reminding her that something else lived in the house with them, that the corridors and rooms of Thornycroft Hall would never be completely still.

When at last she fell asleep, it was a fitful one and when she awoke, it was with a dreadful start, for she had realised that in all of her haste to leave, she had left her boots behind the closed door of one of Thornycroft Hall's forbidden rooms.

CHAPTER 6

Present Day – Eyam

A persistent, loud thudding stirred her and Kate opened her eyes. The air in front of her was hazy. A fine trail of light, flooded with dust motes, seemed to be snaking in the open space in front of the doorway. She blinked and it began to retreat, like a trail of smoke disintegrating into nothing.

Had she fallen asleep? She didn't think so as she had still been sitting bolt upright when she had come around. She had certainly been daydreaming though. What it had been about, she couldn't quite remember.

The noise persisted, its unwelcome intrusion banging at her eardrums. Kate groaned, seeing the box in front of her, its lid open.

Confused, she shook her head. The banging, she realised, was coming from the front door.

Snapping the lid of the box shut, she pushed it aside and hurried to answer, hoping that she didn't look as dazed as she felt.

"You must be Kate." A well-manicured hand was thrown in front of her and a waft of expensive perfume that mingled with the leathery smell of horse stables tickled her nostrils.

A woman with ash blonde hair styled into a loose French braid was standing on the threshold. "Francesca. Francesca Warren." She was dressed in mud splashed jodhpurs and a t-shirt. Kate's gaze roved up and down her attire. It didn't go unnoticed. "Forgive the mess. I usually come every day for coffee with Edie after I've taken Jack out." Self consciously, she scraped a bright red nail across some dried mud on her knee. "I must look an absolute fright caked in mud and smelling of the stables. You however, look even more stunning than any of the pictures your Aunt keeps."

Embarrassed, Kate opened her mouth to explain that she had only looked because it wasn't every day that she saw somebody dressed in such traditional equine attire.

Before she could even reply however, Francesca piped up again. "Have you seen her yet? Family only they said." With a look of distaste she snorted. "Well I'm as good as but still they wouldn't accept it, never mind that it was me who called the ambulance." Biting on her bottom lip for a moment, she glanced sadly downwards. "Poor dear Edie."

"You found her?" It was the first thing Kate was given the opportunity to say and it came out rushed, almost accusing.

Francesca's head snapped upright. "Yes I did but I checked her vital signs straight away. One of the benefits of being a retired airhostess is the level of health and safety training they rammed down one's throat. I called the ambulance straight away."

Reaching out to touch her arm, Kate smiled gratefully. "Thank you. If it hadn't been for you, my Great Aunt Edie might not have recovered so swiftly."

Something Magdalena had told her replayed through her mind. "I heard the police were investigating the possibility that she had been pushed."

A shadow crossed Francesca's face before she dismissed it with a wave of her hand. "I think Edie had been somewhat confused. The shock I suppose." Concerned, she leaned closer. "I thought she had retracted that statement?" If she hadn't appeared such a lovely, genuine woman on first impression, Kate may have been suspicious, but she seemed a nice grounded person.

"So they say." She opened the door further to invite her in. It wouldn't harm to find out a bit more about her relationship with her Great Aunt. "Why don't you come in?"

Without hesitation, Francesca took off her boots and stepped over the threshold.

As Kate ushered her into the kitchen and filled two glasses with water, cucumber slices and some fresh mint from the herb pots in the garden, she told her about the visit to the home, stopping short at her Great Aunt's reluctance to return to Thornycroft.

Francesca, it turned out, had made firm friends with Edie a year earlier when she and her husband had moved to Eyam.

Unlike Edie's ancient house, Francesca's home was a new development. Being a property developer, her husband had managed to snap up an excellent deal on a sizeable plot of land and they had used the help of a local architect to build their 'dream home' overlooking a great beauty spot.

"It's on the road winding up towards Mompesson's well. Do you know it?" Francesca asked, but Kate only had a vague memory of the landmark, let alone the route leading to it. "Great hill for a run," she added before patting her buttocks. "Keeps these tighter than they were at twenty five."

Kate laughed at that statement. Francesca was easy to warm to. She was open, kind and spirited, that much was obvious. It was easy to understand why somebody as vivacious as her Aunt Edie would find friendship with her.

As they talked, Kate learned that Francesca had retired when she had moved to Eyam from St Albans with her husband Graham. The idea had been to find a quieter pace of life and enjoy the heart of the peaks, but Graham was away far more than he had originally intended. So Francesca had busied herself with finding friends and hobbies to fill her time. Edie had been one of the first people whom she had met and they had clicked instantly.

Like Edie, Francesca had never had children. "Three marriages, six cats, two dogs, a tank of piranhas and a horse but no children." She poked a stray mint leaf back into her glass. "You?"

"None of the above. The last relationship didn't end too well and I'm giving men and their complicated minds a break for a while." Kate bit back from saying anything more. The truth was that she was almost embarrassed by the way things had turned out with Richard. She felt like a fool. She had almost believed him when he'd said the things he had about Chris and then he had shown her his true colours; flying off the handle in public, stalking her and threatening Chris.

With a chuckle, Francesca raised her eyebrows. "You sound just like a man. Isn't it us women who are usually accused of having the complicated minds?"

"Not in this case." Uncomfortable, she shifted in her seat and looked out of the window into the garden. "I'd rather just forget all about it though." Turning back to Francesca, she attempted an airy smile. "That's why I thought it would be perfect to stay here and help Aunt Edie recover. Not that she's planning on any of that." The truth started to tumble out before she could stop it.

"Oh?" Francesca's eyebrows knitted into a frown and her eyes dropped.

Sighing heavily, Kate pushed back her chair and went to fetch the jug that she had filled, before explaining the scene at the home.

"Preposterous!" Incensed, Francesca bit into a piece of cucumber that she had fished from her glass. "She adores you and she adores this house. Why on earth would she refuse to come home?"

Kate picked at a stray bit of wax that had settled into a knot in the wood of the table. "She wants to sell up."

From the look on her face, the words may as well have delivered a punch to Francesca's stomach. "Sell the place? But she loves it here in Eyam. She used to say that it was our duty to keep the history alive. She's a volunteer you know, at the church and museum. That's how I met her. She would often take shifts there, speaking to tourists about the plague era. When I first moved here with my husband Graham, we decided to visit the museum and she was working there. She's extremely knowledgeable and well loved in the village." Shaking her head, Francesca drained her glass and let it fall back to the coaster with a heavy clunk.

Taking a breath, Kate went on to ask Francesca the question that had been playing on her mind since seeing Edie and hesitated. She barely knew the woman, but at the same time, she supposed that Francesca probably had a better insight into her Great Aunt Edie's mind than her. Allowing her shoulders to drop in defeat, she asked, "Do you think something happened that scared Aunt Edie?"

The words were there, large, intrusive. They were like crackling static hanging over them amongst the hectic assortment of pots and pans.

Silence pervaded the atmosphere to an uncomfortable extent before Francesca's frown returned. "What makes you think that she's afraid?"

With a shrug, Kate looked down at the candle wax she had been scratching off the table. It had become a creamy coloured crumbling pile around the wooden knot. "She's convinced that she can't come back here because of her injuries but they aren't even that bad; a sprained ankle, granted it's evidently a very nasty sprain, but apart from that, bruising and a mild concussion. There was something else though and it really concerned me. Aunt Edie seemed scared of Thornycroft."

Francesca's hazel eyes darkened. Her mouth twitched as though she was going to say something, then, as though thinking better of it, she shook her head. "Scared? What did she say exactly?"

There was something about Francesca's reaction that set Kate ill at ease. "I was hoping you could help me with that one, seeing as you used to see her every day."

"Sorry. I don't think I can." Pushing her glass aside, she looked intensely at her. "Do you think I could come next time you visit? I know they said only family, but maybe we could say that I'm your older sister. Maybe I could talk some sense into her. It doesn't seem right that she wouldn't want to return to Thornycroft. She loves it so very much."

Kate didn't need persuading. It would be good to have some company and she needed strength in numbers to help convince Edie that the best thing for her was to return home.

"Listen, I've had a wonderful idea." Francesca switched her tone so that it was bright and airy. "We're having a dinner party tonight. It's a tagine so there's plenty to go around and Graham is a wonderful cook. Why don't you come over and we can get to know each other better. There'll be a couple of people from the village there." She must have noticed Kate's discomfort at the suggestion as she quickly added that it wouldn't just be couples. "I promise you won't feel like a gooseberry."

Against her better judgement, Kate agreed, wondering how on earth she had been talked into it. A low profile, quiet visit had been all that she had wanted and already she was gate-crashing a social arrangement with complete strangers.

Pursing her lips, she leaned against the bench. Surely one dinner party could do no harm? Besides, it would be good to get to know Francesca a little better. With some other guests from the village attending, she thought that it may even help her to find out what was scaring Edie so much.

After Kate had waved Francesca off, she shut the door and turned around. Her heart took a nosedive. She had almost forgotten about the box and the way she had zoned out after opening. Its edge was peeping out from behind the telephone, as though it were waiting for her.

Grabbing a tea towel from the kitchen, she wrapped the box twice over. The diary was still wrapped in the silk cloth underneath it. Picking it up she wondered how much Francesca knew about the box and diary. She had looked concerned when Kate had relayed how reluctant Edie had been to return home. Edie may have told her something. Then again, Francesca's reaction could have just been her worrying for a dear friend.

Kate found a cabinet to tuck the box and diary into, hiding them away, before slamming the door shut.

CHAPTER 7

Present Day – London

The fog in his head was still there when he pulled up outside Kate's old flat. Between his thumb and forefinger, he flipped the silver key back and forth.

There had been no word from Kate and given how she had behaved, running away from him, shunning him, he hadn't expected to hear from her. Still, he wasn't prepared to wait around for her to see sense and come back to him, tail between legs. Good things, he reminded himself, did not always come to those who waited, people had to make them happen.

Cars were parked either side of the road. Two of them had tickets brandished to the windscreens, waiting to be ripped open to share their unhappy news with the owners.

A shiny black four by four had taken Kate's usual parking spot. It gleamed in the sunshine, the gloss to its paintwork giving away the idea of a smart, well-groomed owner. Good looking maybe, a hefty wallet definitely.

Narrowing his eyes, he pushed aside the fleeting thought that she could have met somebody else.

Arm in arm, a couple pushed open the double doors that led to the building where Kate should have been living. They walked out laughing and melted into one another along the road. As their fingers entwined, the woman rested her head on her lover's shoulder and then he loosened his grip, only to drape an arm around her and pull her in close. It was the picture of what should have been.

Angrily he smacked the steering wheel before opening the car door. London was hot, too hot. A circle of damp pressed the pale blue shirt to the small of his back and he grimaced as the heat of the sun pounded at his face. At least in the car he had the benefit of air conditioning.

Crossing the road, he kept his focus on the building. The four-digit code was still burned into his mind. Punching it in, he waited for the familiar buzz that complemented the green light.

With a glance over his shoulder, he checked that he wasn't being watched before disappearing inside and taking the stairs two at a time.

The flat had been stripped bare. Clearly there had been no new takers. His footsteps sounded hollow and lonely against the naked floorboards. Nothing was left to remind him of their memories except for an empty shell.

She was gone. They were gone. A raw wound inside of him gaped open and part of him wanted to sob with frustrated sadness. There was no hint of what once was and what might have been in that flat.

Smoothing his thumb across the curve of the mantel above an alcove that had once been a fireplace, he swallowed back the lump and inhaled deeply, steadying himself.

He had to think. There had to be a way of finding her.

A voice from the hallway stopped outside of the front door. Another two joined it and then he heard the scraping of a key against the lock.

Panicked, he looked around. Nothing was left to hide behind and there were no nooks or crannies to hide in. Slipping his shoes off, he picked them up and bolted down the narrow corridor towards the bedrooms.

The spare room had a cupboard with a built in chest. She had kept her past in there, old boyfriends, Christmas cards, love letters from before mobile phones and Facebook. It spanned across the length of the wardrobe and was fairly deep.

"That'll be perfect for my shoe collection," a female joked when footsteps entered the bedroom and the voices became less muffled.

"Great for storage of blankets and the such like." He assumed that it was the agent who had responded. A crack of light spilled through as the lid was lifted a fraction.

"They said that the last tenants left in a bit of rush." The male viewer sounded irritated and suspicious. "The agency told us that they hadn't made a good job of the cleaning and that there would be a delay before we could view, so we had to wait until we were back from holiday to make the viewing time work."

The letting agent cleared his throat nervously and the lid of the chest was abruptly dropped before he stammered his response. "Well yes, but I assure you that everything is ship shape now, as you can see."

"Did something happen that we should know about?" The woman's light-hearted tinkling tone had been replaced by a suspicion that matched her partner's.

There was a pause and the doors to the wardrobe were gently closed. "Listen, I'm new this week. There's absolutely nothing wrong with the flat. The last tenant moved back to her family home. A change in personal circumstances, that's all. Nothing untoward. She gave the agency a great review and told my colleague that when she's back from her trip up North, she'll be back in touch."

From inside the chest, a slow smile spread across his face. So she was residing up North for a while. That revelation made things a whole lot easier.

"It's a lovely place and this room has a great view." The agent continued his pitch as the footsteps retreated towards the window at one end. "The gardens are communal of course, but they're well kept and you wouldn't know you were in London. In autumn, the shrubs down that path are ablaze with reds and orange. It was planted with a lot of thought. A study desk would be great at this window." There was a tapping sound, fingers drumming against glass. "And of course, the whole place is double glazed so you won't get the traffic noise from out front."

As the voices became muffled again, he waited for the click of the front door closing before he pushed the weight of the lid up.

Dusting himself off, he took his phone out of his pocket and thought for a moment before reselecting her parents' address in Google Maps once again. There had to have been a clue that he had missed there, something that told him where up North she was hiding.

He had to get back in front of her, he had to find his Kate again and make her see that she had made a huge mistake.

CHAPTER 8

Present Day – Eyam

Pressing her lips together so that they were evenly coated, Francesca wrinkled her nose. She looked tired and the richness of the lipstick only seemed to emphasise the shadows that had started to circle her eyes.

Reading the label on the bottom, she groaned and tossed it back into her make up case. Scarlett Rose. Even the name was too young for her.

Scrutinising every line and crevice on her face, she decided that she would have to reassess her colour palette soon. Aging was such an unkind process.

As if to rub salt into the wound, a framed picture of her twenty five year old self laughed back at her. That photo had been taken at the end of her first week as an airhostess doing long haul flights. A puff of blonde, wavy hair flirted with the flawless tanned skin of her shoulders and her eyes twinkled with the carefree spirit of a girl who had thought that the world was her oyster.

Glumly she picked up the frame and then looked at her reflection again. In her opinion, getting older was harder for women. Once upon a time she had tutted and complained at the unwanted attention of men: a lingering stare here, an inappropriate comment there, a flirtatious exchange or a wolf whistle. What she had once taken for granted and even scorned, she now craved from time to time. She was certainly still attractive, but no longer the person who would turn a room of heads.

Chastising herself for allowing her thoughts to become so shallow, she thought of Edie. If she had even uttered one word of her aging insecurities, Edie would have called her a vanity case. "Why can't women these days just grow old gracefully?" she would have asked, before raising a cheeky eyebrow. "Or disgracefully."

Fleetingly, Francesca smiled as she thought of Edie's spirited personality. Then her face dropped.

Since leaving Thornycroft, Francesca's mood had been melancholy. Learning that her dear friend Edie had been so scared, that she was planning on selling up and staying in some home, had been the worst news she had heard in such a long time.

Edie had been her rock when she and Graham had moved to Eyam. Graham was working so hard with the business that he hadn't been around as much as either of them had planned and so Edie had become a close friend.

Her interest in the history of Eyam had been infectious. Francesca had even been reading up so that she could get involved in voluntary work at the church and the local museum. She had agreed to help Edie with her investigation to find out more about the family who had been resident at Thornycroft at the time of the plague, but information had been scant.

As Francesca ran her brush through her hair, she recalled how obsessed Edie had become in recent months. Their coffee mornings had gone from light-hearted chat to profound discussions about the age of Thornycroft and the family who had lived there during the plague, when the house had been much bigger and grander.

What had started as research had soon turned into an obsession. Edie had insisted that the house was hiding some dark secret, but Francesca had no idea where these far-fetched ideas had come from.

Rachel.

The name echoed through her mind, uninvited and terrifying. They had been together the first time that name had been revealed. Then there had been the one who had refused to be identified, but it had been there, with them, in that room, in that house.

Francesca shuddered.

Prior to the accident, she had noticed Edie's change in mood and it had seemed to coincide with her falling deeper into her mission to uncover the truth about the Thornycrofts. It was as though it had consumed her personality, peeling away the kind relaxed Edie, so that only an impatient and frustrated one was left. Now it all made sense.

Consumed with guilt for not noticing sooner, Francesca felt a heavy burden on her shoulders. She shouldn't have entertained the endless searching and investigating.

Kate had asked her if she had seen any signs and she had said no. A terrible feeling of accountability washed over her as she put the hairbrush down and slipped a cocktail ring on to her middle finger. She had as good as encouraged it.

Over a bottle of wine one night, her and Edie had participated in an Ouija Board. It had only been meant as a little fun. Graham had been in Edinburgh for the week and it had been a different way to pass the time. "An adventure," she had called it when Edie had produced the homemade board.

Neither of them had really believed it when the glass had started sliding across the board, both accusing the other of moving it. Then they had gently raised their hands so that only the tips of their fingers had hovered over the base. In fascination they had watched as each of their questions had been answered.

Each evening they had returned to the board, their hearts pounding with anticipation of what would come next.

It had become like an illicit love affair. Even when Graham had returned home, she had made up an excuse to go and use the board with Edie. The board had made her lie to her own husband.

Then it had gone too far. Edie had used it alone, without her. Something had happened, but she had refused to say what. Abject fear had replaced the avid curiosity, and for a while, Edie had seemed a shell of the woman she had once been. Francesca had warned her to leave it, but Edie was a wilful woman. Whatever it was that she had continued doing, had all but ruined her for weeks. Then overnight she had appeared fine again. It was as if she had forgotten about it all and swept the whole investigation under the carpet.

Francesca hadn't pressed her on the subject and they had returned to their regular coffee mornings of light-hearted chat. Then Edie had fallen.

For the most part, Francesca had told Kate the truth about the fateful day that she had found Edie after the fall. She had, however, lied about one thing.

When she had found Edie, broken and alone on the floor at the bottom of the stairs, she hadn't been unconscious. The memory of her bright blue eyes staring upwards, of her mouth pulled into a contorted grimace, still churned Francesca's stomach. It was as though she had been looking at something or someone who had terrified the very wits out of her. Then there had been the atmosphere in the house: ice cold, yet close, almost suffocating. The air had felt full of friction. As Francesca had finished her call to the emergency services and had checked all of Edie's vital signs, she had felt as though she was being watched. Glancing up, she had seen a shadow. It was only fleeting, but something had been there. A dark shape had been hovering. Within seconds it had disappeared.

With a shudder, Francesca stepped into her cream jumpsuit and removed the huge rollers from her hair so that it cascaded into gentle ash blonde waves about her shoulders. Their guests would be arriving any minute and she still had to assemble the canapés with Graham.

Pushing the horrible memories to the back of her mind, she headed downstairs into the kitchen where Graham was uncorking a bottle of Pinot Noir.

As they always did, his eyes lit up with appreciation when he saw her and she allowed herself to bask in the love that he projected onto her before looking away, lost in the loneliness of her predicament.

Graham was a good man and a fabulous listener, but even he wouldn't understand or believe what she had seen at Thornycroft that day, or how much it had affected her.

Pulling open the fridge, she found that the salmon and prawn canapés had already been expertly assembled, so it was just a case of putting the samosas in the oven and chopping the vegetable crudités to arrange around the hummus pot.

Lost in thought, she jumped when the intercom went. With a look of concern, Graham asked if she was feeling okay. Hiding her distraction was next to impossible. She had never been very good at disguising her emotions. "I'm just tired," she said as she picked up a paper towel to wipe her hands. Then she whisked the plate of crudités off to the orangery before hurrying to let her guests in.

******

The Warrens lived in an extremely modern, gated house, along an incredibly steep, windy road that overlooked the village. It was tucked away behind the sprawling green foliage of poplar trees.

74

Pressing the intercom, Kate felt a rush of nerves as she waited for the crackle to fade and a voice to answer. For the third time in the last hour, she asked herself why she had agreed to attend a dinner party full of strangers.

After Francesca's slightly breathless voice sang out over the speaker, the gates opened slowly and the gravel driveway crunched beneath the wheels of Kate's car. She had made the decision to drive rather than get into unwanted drunken conversation with strangers. Now, as she noted Francesca's slender, glamorous frame in the doorway, she felt underdressed, awkward and in need of a drink just to take the edge off. Her host had omitted to tell her just how glamorous the dinner party was going to be.

In a tropical coloured maxi dress, Kate felt that she looked more suited to cheap cocktails on a beach, rather than this sophisticated affair.

"You look stunning. Sensational colours Kate. I love a woman who knows how to make colour pop," Francesca cooed, reaching in to give her a hug and a welcoming peck on the cheek.

Bashful, Kate handed her the bottle of wine she had brought, only to feel even more embarrassed when she was lavished with champagne and canapés.

The other guests had already arrived. A couple, that looked to be in their early thirties, were laughing at some shared joke. They were standing with a man who had his back turned, so that Kate was unable to see his face.

Her stomach lunged. There was no sign of a significant other accompanying the man and she did not want the evening to become on par with a blind date.

She was still hovering awkwardly in the doorway when Francesca returned, announcing that three of the guests had unfortunately cancelled, but that her husband, Graham, would be through any minute.

Engrossed in conversation, nobody else had noticed Kate and each moment was growing increasingly awkward. The man excused himself, leaving the couple playfully bickering over something, before Francesca interrupted to make the introductions.

Miriam and Frankie White were the epitome of the old cliché, 'opposites attract'. Whilst she looked like she had stepped out of a seventies festival, with her Boho dress and wild array of bright copper curls, cleverly arranged to sprawl stylishly from a turquoise head scarf, he was neatly turned out in crisply ironed charcoal trousers and a smart grey polo neck. Frankie was the sales director for a textiles manufacturer and Miriam owned a florist in Sheffield.

Sipping her champagne, Kate asked as many questions as she could in a bid to steer the conversation away from her own situation. She didn't much fancy the discomfort of skirting around her current position in life all night.

"Nick!" Francesca's voice boomed as she left Kate's side to glide towards her other guest. "Nick, meet Kate. Kate, Nick."

Pivoting to face the direction that Francesca had headed off towards, Kate felt her smile freeze as the man approached. The closer he got, the more familiar his dark features and lean but muscular build became. Like her, he was wearing a laboured, polite smile that didn't quite reach his eyes. It was he who spoke first.

"No need to introduce us. We've already had the great pleasure of meeting, isn't that so, Kate?" The dimples she had noticed earlier reappeared. To the outside observer he no doubt seemed friendly enough, but she knew that he was being facetious.

Gritting her teeth, she nodded. She wasn't about to let him get away with it. "Yes that's right. I'm afraid we had a bit of an altercation. I hope that's not going to make things too awkward tonight."

Taken aback by her straight talking, Nick's face dropped. He clearly hadn't been expecting that response.

With a loud chortle, Francesca raised her glass. "A woman who doesn't mince her words. You can tell she's Edie's great niece, can't you Nick?" Gulping back some of her drink, she then chinked her glass with Kate's. "I like you a lot already."

Nick fell into a huffy silence, selecting some canapés before being saved by Graham, who had at last joined them, a red and white tea towel slung over one shoulder and his face pink from the heat in the kitchen.

They managed to steer the conversation away from the altercation that Kate had mentioned, and nobody was too intrusive when it came to her history. As the evening wore on, she began to relax a little more. It had been too easy to take the edge off by accepting a little too much wine though and her journey home was only going to be achievable by foot or taxi.

When Graham cleared the plates and Francesca went to fetch the dessert, Frankie and Miriam had picked up a conversation between themselves that involved a disagreement over whether Frankie had consumed too much alcohol to drive. It ended with the both of them going outside so that Miriam could have her vape. "Giving up has been hell on earth," she added apologetically as they left the dining room.

"Don't I know it, she's like a bear with a sore head when she has a craving," Frankie added, giving her a playful squeeze.

Left alone together, there was a short, uncomfortable silence between Kate and Nick before he cleared his throat. "So how is your Aunt doing?"

"Great Aunt." Folding the edge of her napkin, she corrected him.

With a sigh, he started again. "Great Aunt then. How is she doing?"

Leaning forward, Kate caught his gaze and held it hard. "Scared of returning to Thornycroft."

"Scared?" He looked genuinely concerned.

Scrutinising him for any suspicious reactions, she nodded. "That's right, although I would say that 'scared' is far too mild a way to put it. I'd be inclined to say that something, or someone, has terrified her."

Nick's face crumpled into a scowl when the penny dropped. "Are you trying to hint at something?"

Feeling a rush of angry heat travel up the back of her neck, Kate threw the napkin she had been playing with to one side. "Well I didn't feel altogether comfortable with you loitering around out the back of the house with that sketch pad, and I'm not an elderly woman living on my own."

With a blazing expression, he was defiant. "I happen to be on very good terms with Edie. She's been very supportive of my art."

"So, if you know Aunt Edie so very well, how come she's never mentioned you?"

Her line of fire had been supposed to trip him up. Instead, the frown on his face relaxed as he brought his elbows to the table and rested his chin on his hands thoughtfully. "Tell me Kate, how often do you see your Great Aunt?" The question touched a nerve.

Francesca interrupted the frosty moment, carrying a two-tiered cake stand. "Can't say that they're homemade I'm afraid, but they make such good cakes and desserts in the village cafés that I couldn't decide which one to go for. Take your pick." As she set it down on the table, Graham emerged from behind her, carrying a small stack of black and red bowls.

"Or take a bit of both," he said. "That's my plan. Pecan and walnut tart on the bottom, black forest gateau on top." He set the bowls with precision ordering: red for females and black for males.

Miriam and Frankie had returned from the garden having made the decision to leave the car behind and catch a taxi. Nobody sensed the awkward atmosphere between Nick and Kate. Or at least, they were too polite to mention it.

As they settled with dessert, Francesca diverted the conversation to the forthcoming well dressing event, marking the start of Wakes Week in Eyam. She began sharing her plans for a wonderful party afterwards. "I thought it would be a great way to get to know more of our neighbours better. I feel a bit stuck on the edge of everything here. In fact, Nick and Edie are the only people from the village who we know really well, isn't that right darling?" Her hand rested on Graham's arm and he nodded as he pushed a forkful of tart into his mouth.

"So an after party seems like a good plan. If Edie is better, we can make it a sort of 'pleased to have you back' party too."

Rolling his eyes, Graham joked about never getting a moment's peace in his own house.

Despite the rumble of laughter from around the table, Kate still felt that the tension between her and Nick was an obvious stain on the night. Awkwardly, she dragged herself through coffee before thanking her hosts for a lovely evening, calling a taxi and leaving the rest of them to enjoy after dinner drinks.

Thornycroft was thick with silence in comparison to the Warren household. In a way, it was a welcome relief. She hadn't wanted to spend a moment longer in the company of Nick Delamere.

Kicking her shoes off, she threw on the lights. All she wanted to do was to climb into bed, hit the pillow and fall asleep.

Upstairs, she plumped the paisley pillows on her bed before trying to read for a while, but her concentration was lost. At night, thoughts of how strange and sudden Richard's turn in personality had been, often drifted through her mind. Reading was a good way to combat those thoughts. After turning several pages though, Kate realised that she hadn't taken in any of the words.

Memories of a night out with Richard played on repeat through her brain.

"Chris, again?" he had asked from across the restaurant table. His tone had been incredulous, his voice a little too loud. The fork he had been holding had clattered to the plate, causing their fellow diners to turn and stare.

Kate had been taken by surprise, had felt her skin shade to crimson as the people on the table next to them had watched and waited for her retort.

"What's got into you?" she had hissed over a half eaten bowl of seafood linguine.

Richard had simply taken a heavy gulp of wine and slammed his glass onto the table before chuckling derisively. "I should be asking the same of you Kate. How could you be so naive?" he had asked, picking up his wine glass again and draining it. "How could you be so bloody disrespectful?"

A sick feeling had begun to whirl around inside of her as the scene in the restaurant had unfolded. Richard's voice had increased in volume and most of the restaurant had tuned in for some dinner entertainment.

"Richard, you know that Chris has had a tough time lately and he's your friend. Mine too. I thought you'd be pleased that your best friend and girlfriend actually get along. What's your problem?" The defiance in her tone had not matched the panic building inside her. Every instinct had started ringing the warning bells. This wasn't normal behaviour. To have this reaction because of a simple lunch out with a mutual friend was ridiculous, paranoid even.

"My problem Kate?" He had taken great care in ensuring that her name had rolled off his tongue in a way that made it sound toxic, "My problem is that this isn't just a one off occasion, is it?"

A long silence had dragged out as she had tried to think of all the other occasions that he might have been referring to. There really hadn't been that many though and certainly nothing of much note. Even this one had been irrelevant.

She had bumped into Chris on her way out of the office the day before. He had seemed morose and despite a pressing deadline, she had agreed to go for a quick lunch. That's what friends were for in her opinion, being there for somebody at a time of need. Why Richard would have a problem with that had been beyond her. Nevertheless, his rant had continued after he had summoned the bill and they had walked in a shamed silence out of the restaurant to the taxi rank.

"I don't want you to see him alone again," he had admitted at last, his voice flat and his expression almost dead looking as he had stared ahead, not even turning to address her to her face.

Kate had felt anger at the unjustness of the situation. "That is preposterous. How dare you place those demands on me? You don't own me Richard." Immediately she had regretted those words. They hadn't come out as she had intended.

For a moment, his angry expression had transformed into one of panic, but then his face was stony again. Tapping on the scratched up, mucky piece of plastic that separated the driver from the passengers, he had advised the driver of Kate's address. She had been supposed to stay at his.

"You utter bastard," she had exclaimed before slamming the door and running out into the rain soaked street, mud and water splashing up her bare legs and ruining her coral heels.

The taxi had charged off the minute that she had entered the block of flats. He hadn't seen her in any further than that. That was when she had known that a corner had been turned. Her Richard, her gentleman with good grace, generosity and manners had shown her an ugly side.

That night she had cried herself to sleep with tears that had been a salty cocktail of anger, disappointment and melancholy.

Turning over on to her side angrily, Kate tried to push the memory away. That had only been the tip of the iceberg. She should have got out of the relationship far earlier.

Chris was always going to be faithful to his best friend, but he had as good as admitted that Richard was dangerous. "Don't let him intimidate you, Kate," he had said over coffee, rubbing her arm to show her some comfort when she'd had enough after another disagreement with Richard.

At the time, she hadn't quite agreed with Chris, not understood how a usually unassuming man like Richard could be 'intimidating'. Then the first of the flower bouquets had arrived.

When she had turned the envelope over in her hands, she had seen the love heart and the inscription.

Never doubt. Never Forget.

That had been their phrase. He had coined it after their first lovers' tiff, when they had held each other close, saying how sorry they both were, in between rushed, urgent kisses. It had been their phrase; a phrase written in birthday cards, Valentines cards and whispered as sweet nothings. Words that had previously been meant in a loving way had seemed like a threat when Kate had ripped open the envelope.

With a frustrated groan, she punched the pillow. Why couldn't she just forget him? Even with a good couple of hundred miles between them, he still managed to intrude on her life. She probably wouldn't have been so irritated with Nick Delamere if it hadn't been for what Richard had put her through.

Pressing her face into the duvet, she groaned and punched the pillow again. How could she have let a stupid male get to her so much? His jealousy and insane behaviour had destroyed a part of her soul.

Outside, an owl hooted and she closed her eyes, taking a deep breath. She reminded herself that she was far away from him now and that she was safe. There was a restraining order and so she had nothing to be worried about.

As her breathing mellowed and sleep began to embrace her, the owl hooted again.

In the garden beneath her window, a silver mist spiralled about the wrought iron furniture and crept over the wall into the lane, until it twisted and writhed over the boundary stone.

There was nobody out there to see the shadow that was thrown across the pale green lawn, elongated by a nearly full moon. If there had been, they would have seen that it had been cast from a figure, motionless and isolated in the lonely looking window at the top of the house.

CHAPTER 9

Present Day – Eyam

K ate was waiting on the Warren's driveway as Francesca emerged from the house looking spectacularly glamorous.

"Well I for one am pleased that we didn't go mad last night," Francesca said as she pulled open the door to Kate's car. After settling into the passenger seat, she pulled a bottle of perfume from her oversized shoulder bag and squirted it on her neck and wrists. "I would not have liked to have a raging hangover when visiting Edie."

Kate agreed, grateful for the clear head as they pulled off the driveway to begin the journey to Buxton.

Flipping down the visor, Francesca started to apply some pink lipstick. "Frankie was another story entirely, however. I thought those two would never leave. Had to pretty much boot the pair of them out at gone midnight and he still insisted on another shot of Drambuie for the road. That pair can certainly drink." Pushing the mirror back up, she fluffed up her hair and straightened the teal silk scarf that she had draped around her neck. "I feel like I've been dragged through a hedge backwards this morning."

Smiling to herself, Kate could only describe her first impressions of Francesca as disorganized glamour. Everything appeared to be a rush, as though she was chaotically running from one part of the day to the next. She was already reeling off a number of 'disasters' that she'd had to contend with that morning. It should have been exhausting even listening to her, but Kate enjoyed it. There were no hidden agendas with Francesca. Everything about her seemed to be at face value. She was clearly a good friend to Edie and Kate was pleased of the company on the way to the home.

By the time they pulled up in the car park, a light summer scented shower had begun to bounce from the flagstones. It made the place appear dismal and inside Edie's room, the hypnotic patter of rain against glass added to the mood.

Papery skin hung beneath her eyes and she looked frailer. When she saw Francesca, she scowled before looking away.

Silence filled the room so that it became stifling and when at last Edie spoke, it was Kate whom she addressed. "As you're staying at Thornycroft dear, it would be a real help to me if you could call the Estate Agents and arrange a valuation."

Unable to bear it, Francesca rushed to Edie's side. "Please Edie, this is ludicrous. Why would you want to sell up? You have Kate, Nick, Graham and me and what about all of your other friends, everyone from the village?"

"Haven't you noticed? I'm injured. That's what happens to people when they get too old to live alone." Her response was bitter and so uncharacteristic. "I won't be returning to Thornycroft."

Kate went to argue but Francesca beat her to it. "You had a fall Edie. It happens to lots of people. An accident. I fall off Jack lots when I'm riding but I wouldn't dream of giving up. Why give up on life when you have so much left in you? And selfishly speaking, I miss you dreadfully. I'd do anything to get you back."

There was a pause. Something flickered in Edie's eyes. For a moment, Kate thought she might cry, but she took hold of herself and her gaze returned to a hard, stony glare.

"Don't you think that you've done enough?" Scorn dripped from Edie's words. The comment was left hanging in the room like an awkward guest.

Kate shifted uncomfortably and Francesca stepped back, biting her lip.

"So I take it that you didn't listen to a word that I said yesterday Kate?" Edie stroked the edge of the desk with her index finger as she waited for an answer. "Another sorry symptom of getting old. Nobody ever listens."

There was nothing she could do other than shrug apologetically. "I thought maybe you might change your mind."

"Or you could get help to change my mind." Edie glowered and dashed a look in Francesca's direction. Then her expression softened and her shoulders slumped. "Look, it's very kind of you both to be so keen to help, but my mind is made up. I don't want to return to Thornycroft. As I told you yesterday, these places are expensive. The house needs to be sold."

When it became clear that neither of them were about to change her mind, they sat making small talk for the remainder of the time.

A heavy sadness weighed on Kate's shoulders as Edie eyed her cautiously, looking beyond her as though desperate for somebody to come and tell them it was time to leave. Even Francesca had become lost for words.

Neither of them were used to Edie's mood. She was usually such a happy, carefree and spirited lady, but through the awkward silences, her eyes glazed over and her bottom lip trembled. The whole visit was a disaster from start to finish and not at all the pleasant turn of events that Kate had planned.

It was still raining when they left. Their moods dampened, Francesca suggested that they have lunch together to try and cheer up. "We can buy something from one of the eateries in the village and take it back to the house for some privacy."

"To think that I thought I might be getting some peace and quiet in the countryside," Kate joked as they pulled up in front of the café. It was swarming with people. "I can't believe how busy it is." She took a plastic menu from the top of the counter.

"Not a chance here. It's a popular place, Eyam. You should see it on a sunny weekend." Francesca was fiddling with her bag as she spoke. "You can't move for hikers, cyclists, families, tourists, kids, the lot."

They selected some homemade quiche before driving back to the Warren's house. By the time they were inside the bright kitchen there was a promising break in the cloud.

Suggesting they sit under the gazebo, Francesca handed Kate some plates and cutlery to carry outside whilst she went to get a bottle of wine. "We shouldn't really, but after this morning, I think I need a glass," she admitted, gesturing towards the rattan seating area outside that overlooked a large sprawling garden. "Preference?"

Kate shook her head and waited by the door to the garden.

The pleasant clink of glasses and the sound of a fridge opening accompanied Francesca muttering as she took her time selecting a bottle. "How about this rosé?" She pulled a bottle out of the fridge and nudged the door shut with her hip. "It has a wonderful floral note and a hint of strawberry. I'm not usually a rosé fan. This one is really rather lovely though. Just don't tell Graham as he's a health freak and swears that I drink too much, although he's probably right."

Laughing, Kate felt some weight lift from her shoulders. "Perfect."

Setting the cutlery down on the table outside, she sat down in a chair and leaned back decadently as Francesca brought over the glasses and the wine.

The sun had started to burn through the cloud so that it was becoming more of a melting haze. Inhaling deeply, she let her head tilt back slightly before admiring the view.

The garden was beautifully landscaped. In the oversized pond there was a fountain, the trickle of water spouting from it creating a hypnotic air of tranquillity. With a heartily refreshing glug, the wine was poured into two glasses whilst Kate cut the quiche and spooned out the salad.

"Edie is acting very out of character and I don't think it has anything to do with her injury." After the awkward car journey, Francesca finally said what they were both thinking.

Taking a sip of wine, Kate allowed the tart tang to rest on her tongue and palate for a moment. "I'm glad you said that. What was her behaviour like before the accident?"

Shaking her head, Francesca cut into her quiche. "Fine, nothing untoward." Putting a piece into her mouth, she chewed thoughtfully, and then with a heavy sigh, she rested her knife and fork against her plate. "If I'm being honest, Edie was a little spooked."

Kate's mind flashed back to Nick sketching the house. "Had someone upset her?" The familiar fist of anger balled up inside her.

Francesca's gaze was fixed on something in the distance and she looked uncomfortable. "Not someone. Something."

An involuntary shudder ran up Kate's legs, over her back and shoulders, right up to the hairs on her neck and scalp. The diary and box burned brightly in her mind, their colours, smell and texture so vivid that they could have been on the table in front of them.

Francesca continued her explanation. "She thought that Thornycroft might be haunted." Seeing the horrified look on Kate's face, she corrected herself. "Don't let that get you worried though. Most people have a ghost tale or two to tell here. I mean, who wouldn't? The place is a rich tapestry of history and the stories linked to the plague and the terrible anguish that people suffered are bound to have supernatural connotations." In an attempt to lighten the mood, her eyes twinkled shrewdly. "It's what helps draw the tourists."

Kate wasn't convinced. "Did something happen?"

Loading her fork with more quiche and salad, Francesca shrugged nonchalantly. "People see ghosts, or think that they do. It happens a lot around here." Her tone was light, but Kate felt certain that she was withholding information.

Resting her knife and fork on her plate, she had lost her appetite. "What did Aunt Edie think that she saw?"

A shadow of irritation crossed Francesca's face. It was a subject that she was obviously uncomfortable with.

"Please Francesca," she pressed. "It's important that I understand."

Defeated, Francesca picked up her wine glass, took a sip and sank back in her chair. "Edie was interested in the history of Thornycroft. We both were, but then she started seeing and hearing things."

"What do you know about the diary, the one that seems to log some connections with the spirit world?" She didn't mention the box of artefacts. That had clearly been very old and potentially very valuable. No matter how lovely Francesca Warren seemed, Kate reminded herself that she barely knew the woman and she shouldn't lay too much trust in her.

Panicked, Francesca banged the glass of wine down. "I thought Edie had thrown that out?"

"Evidently not. I found it when I was in the attic. It was wrapped in some cloth and bound with a crystal type charm."

"Yes. I gave her the crystal for protection. I told her to get rid of the diary. What was she thinking?" Standing up, she hurried towards the house. "Wait there."

Confused, frustrated and feeling more spooked by the minute, Kate took a steadying breath. Francesca and Edie knew more than either of them were letting on. The story seemed ridiculous though. Talking to spirits and obsessing over them was something that she had flirted with as a bored teenager. As an adult, she had barely given any of those things a second thought. Trying to calm her thoughts, she looked out across the well-manicured lawns.

Behind her, the crystal chimes danced in a gentle breeze, their pendants swinging together in melodious harmony. There was an incredibly peaceful ambience at Francesca's house. It was a bright contrast to the atmosphere at Thornycroft.

The crystals chimed again as Francesca reappeared holding a large Oriental print box. Carefully, she set it on the table and lifted the lid. There were lots of compartments holding an array of colourful crystals, each one catching prettily in the light. "As you've probably gathered, I do like my crystals and whether you believe in it all or not, I'd like you to take this one." Pulling out a stone that was structured with a lattice of violet shards, she handed it to Kate. "It's an amethyst, a protection stone."

The stone was cool and rough in her palm. It felt strangely comforting to just hold against her skin. "Protection from what exactly?"

Snapping the box shut, Francesca went to pour each of them another glass of wine. "Maybe nothing at all, but we shouldn't have interfered with the unknown the way that we did." Glancing sideways, she gave Kate a sheepish look. "You're right in assuming that the diary is a log of supernatural connections. Edie kept it when we tried the Ouija Board." She paused to sip from her glass and Kate noticed that her hand was shaking. "It really was only supposed to be a bit of fun at first. A way to support our investigation into the house's history but neither of us expected anything that began to happen."

With an encouraging nod, Kate willed her to continue.

"The first time the glass moved, we both assumed that it was the other one doing it, but it started moving so fast and so frantically that our fingers couldn't keep up. It was fascinating and terrifying all at once. We were quite excited about it after the first time, so we started doing it in the evenings - until it all got a little out of hand." Grimacing, she recounted how they had made contact with several spirits. "Rachel was the strongest at first. Then someone or something that called itself Rosamund appeared. The house became suffocating after that. I didn't want to do the board anymore, but Edie insisted. I didn't think that she would go ahead and do it alone. I gave her a cleansed crystal and some silk to wrap the diary inside and told her she should bury it, or burn it. Clearly she did neither."

Gesturing to the half eaten food, she asked Kate if she had finished. Apologising, Kate explained that she was just a little jaded.

When Francesca had boxed up the leftovers and convinced her to keep the rest for her dinner, they had taken a seat in the lounge. Everything was a pristine white and not a single cushion out of place. Kate almost didn't know where to sit. Settling on the end of the sofa, she plumped the cushion behind her and carefully picked up the cup of coffee that Francesca had poured.

"Do you believe that something sinister exists in that house?" Kate held the saucer closely to the cup, worried that she would spill it any moment.

Her hazel eyes serious, Francesca went to say something before thinking better of it. Eventually she answered. "I don't know. I suppose I've given you that crystal which means that I'm not keen on taking any chances. What I do know is that everything was fine until we started dabbling with that damn Ouija Board." She dropped her head into her hands. "It's all my fault. I should have warned her of the dangers as soon as I clapped eyes on the thing. Instead I went along with it wholeheartedly. I even brought the wine the following night and the next and the next. It just went on." She took a moment to look up, mascara streaking her face. "The more we did, the more addictive it became and then–" She stopped and hid her face behind her hands. "We should never have started it."

Handing her a tissue, Kate put an arm about her shoulders. "It's not your fault. You weren't to know. I'll get rid of that diary though. I'm having a bonfire later to burn some of the garden waste. I'll toss it in."

"Promise?" Dabbing at her eyes and blowing her nose, Francesca was a fraction of the confident, carefree woman she had been earlier that morning.

The diary was clearly destructive. It had still had the Ouija Board folded up inside it and Kate fully intended on disposing of that too. She would burn it all.

Before she got up to leave, she felt compelled to ask the question that had been on her mind all day. "How do you know Nick Delamere exactly?"

Her face still puffy and red from crying, Francesca blew her nose again. "The devilishly handsome but oh so broody Nick? I wondered when you might ask about him. You two didn't hit it off too well did you?"

"Why? What did he say?" Feeling prickly, Kate's tone was defensive.

Smiling empathetically, Francesca balled the tissue into the palm of her hand before resting it on the side of her saucer. "Nothing. Nick doesn't say much at all. He's a real genius though. Graham met him through the business and he helped us with this place. Nick's an exceptionally talented architect. Very quiet though. Edie and I are probably his only friends. He's an enigma really. But a real dish, don't you think?"

Flicking a hand through her hair and tossing her head nonchalantly, Kate wrinkled her nose. "I only noticed how rude he was. Rude and miserable."

Raising an eyebrow, the smile came back to Francesca's face, instantly taking ten years off her. "I can see how you would draw that conclusion with Nick. He does himself no favours." She chuckled, "He can be a bit gruff at times but take it from me Kate, his bark is worse than his bite."

"Well I'm afraid I probably rubbed him up the wrong way as I wasn't keen on the idea of somebody drawing the house and possibly me or Aunt Edie. I could have been running around the garden naked for goodness sake."

With a roar of laughter, Francesca stood up to fetch the coffee pot for a top up. "I don't think Nick's quite into life painting. Landscape is more his bag."

Wincing at the heat of the fresh coffee against her top lip, Kate placed the cup back on the saucer. "I really was cross. I just felt so violated on Aunt Edie's part. I don't think he took too kindly to my reaction."

With a dismissive snort, Francesca dunked one of the macaroon biscuits she had put on the side of the coffee saucers. "Oh I'm sure he'll get over it." Pausing, she frowned. "I'm surprised he's still painting."

"I think it was a sketch rather than a painting. Why's that?"

Before Francesca could answer, the doorbell rang and they were interrupted by a rather large delivery.

"Oh damn, I forgot that Graham had said this would be coming. It's his new desk. Just as well we were in." The distraction was enough to throw their conversation off course and Kate left her directing the deliverymen to where the desk needed to be taken and signing paperwork.

She had almost forgotten about the unfinished gardening until she returned to the house and noted the green garden waste sacks that had been emptied. At least there would be room for the weeds that were growing defiantly across the patio at the back of the house. She hadn't even started on that part of the garden and it was probably a good idea to get rid of the old rotting wooden deckchairs and fallen trellis that had been tossed to one side. It was possible that they hadn't even been used since her Great Uncle Joe had been alive.

Her back was aching and her arms sore by the time she threw the last of the burnable waste and junk onto the bonfire she planned to light later. Wine with lunch had made physical activity all the more arduous and when she stopped to sit down, she felt herself in danger of nodding off. To wake herself up a bit, she decided to eat her unfinished lunch and take a brisk walk.

The late afternoon was melting into a glorious evening, with the sky a canvas of gold and blue as she ascended the old farm track that led towards Riley Farm at one end of the village. A small group of hikers passed her with polite acknowledgement. Their bright clothing seemed so out of place and at odds with the softer pastels of the nature they were surrounded by.

When the jazzy murmur of their conversation had disappeared into the village, Kate became starkly aware of how alone she was. It was peaceful and beautiful, a million miles away from the heartache and drama she had been in the thick of back home with Richard. Here in the Peaks, she found it easier to free herself of Richard and his obsession, but she couldn't help missing the companionship and familiarity of having somebody to share the simple things with.

Spontaneously, her mind switched to Chris and his offer to come and stay. It was still tempting but she had spent too much time with him already. Too much time spent with Chris had been the reason for her world falling apart.

After things had kicked off with Richard, he had been there offering an understanding ear, an empathetic shoulder to cry on and…

A twinge of guilt pricked at her, she didn't want to finish that line of thought and so she distracted herself by looking at the view ahead.

As the path wound a little to the left, she slowed, listening to the call of jackdaws that were hidden in the trees either side. Then she saw the sign that pointed out Riley Farm. Ahead of it, the track plateaued slightly.

Stopping, she turned full circle, surveying her landscape. She was truly alone. Everything up this part of the village seemed eerily still.

From childhood memory, she knew that a circle of graves lay up ahead, known as The Riley Graves. Their poignant place in history was marked out by one of the many plaques placed around the village.

As she began to embark on the rest of the path that fit snugly between the patchwork of green, gold and brown fields either side, an unexpected feeling of familiarity rushed over her. It was so strong and so sudden that she stumbled, grabbing on to the grey stones of the wall to one side of her.

Behind her a twig snapped and a panicked thrash of wings echoed through the trees. Whirling around, she felt like she was no longer alone. "Hello?" she called, feeling instantly stupid and vulnerable.

The silence that clung to the air around her was unsettling. It was a peaceful place but now it felt as though the tranquillity had been disturbed. There was another snap and two squirrels bounded from the dense foliage, one chasing the other.

Breathing a sigh of relief, Kate closed her eyes. She was too jumpy. It was ridiculous. She had to get a hold of herself.

Feeling silly, she turned back to the track leading to the graves. It was a beautiful spot and a piece of history that she should take the time to view and respect whilst she was staying in Eyam.

After climbing over a stile into the field that was home to the Riley Graves, she navigated the gently undulating ground, becoming aware of the silence that she was once again engulfed in. The air was thick with it. That was a part of the beauty of the countryside she supposed. The thought didn't offer much respite from the feeling of unease that was creeping up on her.

The grass was soft under her feet, patches of it scuffed away by the tread of visitors so that it revealed the dry, hard soil beneath. Further ahead, she could see the lonely circle of graves. Seven of them. How had the story gone again? She couldn't quite remember. Some poor woman had been forced to bury her family there during the plague.

As Kate got closer to the site, she recalled snippets of the story that her Great Aunt Edie had recounted when she had been younger and she tried to imagine the horror of dragging each body, still not cold and rigid from the onset of death, to their graves.

"Alice." The name came out of her mouth as a choked sob. It meant nothing to her, yet she felt a terrible deep despair clutch at her insides. In her mind she could vividly picture a teenager with yellow curls and happy grey eyes.

"Alice." This time the voice was a whisper on the wind, a sound that rolled about the empty fields. Her heart beginning to race, Kate looked around, but just as she thought, she was alone. The voice had been unmistakable though – a girl's.

The circle of graves lay just in front of her, surrounded by a small wall.

"Alice."

Without looking, she knew that the name belonged within that circle of graves. In fact, she knew all of the names and could picture each of the children, playing, laughing and holding on to their mother, Elizabeth.

"Elizabeth." Shocked, she pressed her hand to her mouth to stop herself from saying more as the name echoed in her ears, uttered from somebody else's lips.

With a gasp, Kate responded to the uninvited and alien thought that struck her. It was not a thought that should have belonged to her. She knew nobody by the name of Elizabeth. There was nobody by the name of Alice in her life either, but as she stood there looking at the silent circle of graves, cracked and crumbling with age, a vivid memory struck her in full colour.

CHAPTER 10

Early September 1665 - Eyam

"Pa said that you'd be wanting the fattest goose." Alice Hancock was standing in front of Rachel, rosy cheeked and breathless. She had pulled a small cart of goods from the farm to Thornycroft Hall. Her dusty boots poked out from beneath the dirtied hem of her dress. It was early in the day to be so hot and fatigued, but from many years of helping her father on their farm, Rachel knew only too well that this was normal for a child like Alice.

She ushered her to leave the cart at the servant's door so that it could be unloaded.

Morning had broken with the earthy smell of ripe harvests and turned over soil on a warm breeze. It was the time of year that usually gave Rachel a feeling of excitement for the plump purple of blackberries in hedgerows, the sharp tang of Cook's cider and the chaotic scatter of scarlet and gold leaves laying on the ground like a royal carpet. There was too much weighing on her mind to enjoy it though.

The house was a whirl of fuss as everyone prepared for the imminent arrival of the Belgrave family. Chores were still to be done, Lady Cecily was audibly fretting and there was merry hell to pay for the fact that George Viccars had not re-emerged to do the dress fitting.

Nobody could have predicted that any woman would want to go through the trial of being measured for and fitted with a new dress so soon after giving birth, but with her vanity and obsession to outdo all others, Lady Cecily defied the mould of anything remotely normal.

There had been no mention of Goody Brown, the mysterious visitor who had helped Lady Cecily give birth. Rachel had not seen her again since that night.

Goody Brown would know that Samuel had survived, that he had defied the curse she had mentioned. Rachel thought it was strange that the help Goody had provided to deliver the child was not acknowledged by anyone. She had simply disappeared after the birth, as though she had never existed at all.

At her insistence, there was to be no period of lying-in for Lady Cecily and although little more than a week had passed, she had already made plans to be churched, summoning for Thomas Stanley, who would also perform the baptism for Samuel in the small chapel that belonged to Thornycroft Hall.

Rachel wondered if the baptism of the boy could even be considered authentic given that the puritan ways were now outlawed and the old puritan ministers were supposed to reside at least five miles outside of their former place of service. Her heart ached for Samuel who had no choice in the matter.

He was proving himself to be a strong baby though, with a cry that could wake the whole household if the wet nurse did not latch him to her breast fast enough.

Rachel had already heard Lady Cecily berating the poor woman, accusing her of neglecting Thornycroft's only son and heir. Already it was clear that she thought of the child as something on a biblical scale and it was no surprise given how long it had taken for her to conceive.

By all accounts, Lady Cecily was an old first time mother, late in her thirties. None of this seemed to give her any cause for concern though and the quest for her dress was giving her a new lease of life since the birthing bed.

Like Rachel, the other staff questioned how on earth she could be measured with any kind of dignity. Her belly was still swollen and Cook had implied with great distaste that there would still be blood for days to come, possibly even weeks. Nevertheless, Lady Cecily had made it clear that she was to be competing with the ladies at Court and so only George Viccars, with his London delivery of cloth, would do. Besides, the dress would be worn at the farewell dinner, which could be at least another week or two away. If nothing else, Lady Cecily's optimism for her swift recovery had to be admired.

Of course, Anna had passed on to Rachel the dreadful earful that she had received for the very fact that George Viccars had not shown, and now Rachel was expected to go back into the village and chase him up. His prompt presence was the desired outcome of her errand, but she was still missing her boots since leaving them in the forbidden room of portraits and her feet were already becoming unbearably sore from wearing her tired old ones. She had tried the door every day since she had left them up there, but to no avail.

"I have never known such fussing and fretting," Rachel whispered to her friend as she helped her offload the cart of goods.

Cook emerged from a cloud of flour. "Aye lass." She nodded towards the cart that Alice had brought and referred to the aforementioned goose. "We'll be wanting the best bird you have. Mind that you just tell yer father to make it swift." Her bosom was heaving with the effort of all the kneading she had been doing and she wiped her floury hands on her apron before inspecting a slab of strawberry cheese. "I've pies and tarts and breads and meats to prepare. I don't have the time to be waiting upon more fowl to pluck."

Smiling sweetly, Alice seemed oblivious to Cook's harsh tone. "Mother said that for a little extra, she will pluck the bird. She also told me to pass it on that she could prepare a jam with the season's apples. It would go well with the cheese and meat. We have an abundance this year."

"No need for any jam lass. The goose will do just fine and never mind the plucking. I don't trust any hands other than these." Cook wriggled her fingers. "Just see to it that it's brought swift." She disappeared back in to the cloud of flour, grumbling something about timings.

Taking Alice by the elbow, Rachel grabbed two baskets and ushered her out to the hens to collect a brace of eggs. It wasn't until they were far enough away from the house and any eavesdroppers that at last she told her friend of her news.

"I heard her Alice. Here in the house. I heard your ghost." Speaking in a hushed whisper, she turned her head this way and that, making sure that nobody was nearby.

"Lady Thornycroft? The first Lady Thornycroft?" Alice was unable to dampen her excited squeal.

"Sssshhhh, we are not to speak her name anywhere."

Oblivious to the importance of stealth when addressing the matter of the first Lady Thornycroft, Alice did not lower her voice. "Where? Where was it? Are you sure?"

Rachel hushed her again and relayed the whole story of Samuel's birth and the forbidden room, before lifting her skirts to show Alice her bare feet. She had removed the old pair of boots that she had resorted to wearing due to the rubbing and blistering that they had caused. "I have no boots. Well, none other than a dreadfully old pair that are long worn through. I left my good boots up there. The door is always locked."

Wide eyed, Alice chewed thoughtfully on her bottom lip. "Who do you think unlocked it?"

"What matter is it who unlocked it? If anyone is to venture in there again, they will see my boots and Lady Cecily will be furious. I'll be out on my ear."

With a breathless giggle, Alice grabbed Rachel's arm. "Oh Rachel, you could come and live with us on the farm. Ma and Pa would love to have you. We all would. Say you will, won't you?"

Smiling sadly at Alice's dreamy expression, Rachel shook her head. "Dear sweet Alice, how I would love to, but there is little enough room for all of you, let alone another mouth to feed." Poking through the straw, she found an egg. "No I shall just have to wait for my moment. Lady Cecily has the key I am sure. When I have been changing the flowers or cleaning, I have seen a bunch of keys that she keeps on a large brass ring. They are often in a dish by her bed. She will be so busy with the baby and the Belgraves now that there is bound to be a time that I can take it, just for a few moments, so that I can go back up there."

Alice didn't look convinced but soon forgot about the dilemma that Rachel faced as they returned to the house, Rachel sharing more details about her experience in the room filled with the portraits of Lady Rosamund Thornycroft.

When they were back at the entrance to the kitchen, Rachel gave Alice a swift hug and pressed a finger to her lips, hushing her when she wished her luck for finding the boots.

It did not take long for Rachel's window of opportunity to arrive. After Lady Cecily had taken breakfast, she complained that the trials of getting everything in place for their visitors had overwhelmed her with fatigue, and so insisted that she needed to lie down.

It was Rachel's duty to bring her a tincture from the stillroom, ready for when she would awaken again.

She waited until the wet nurse was busy with Samuel and listened for the purr of Lady Cecily's snoring, before stealing into her chamber.

The keys were where they always were, placed in the decorative dish on the side of the bed. Holding her breath, she swooped for them.

Lady Cecily stirred in her slumber, but Rachel was careful not to make a sound and then she was out of the room, swiftly taking the stairs that wound upwards to the top of the house.

Even on such a glorious morning, it was shadowy up there. Remembering the dreadful noises that had emanated from the walls, Rachel hesitated at the top of the landing.

Light bled in through the windows, unwelcome and strange in a place where darkness festered. Fractured rays of sunlight made it look like things were moving, shadow people flitting from one corner to another, their hooded eyes ever watchful.

Around the curve of the bannister, the door to the room filled with Lady Rosamund's portraits waited. Downstairs there was a distant clatter and a shout as somebody dropped something in the kitchen.

The atmosphere clamoured at her throat, constricting itself around her so that she struggled to catch her breath. It was a different world to the lively one that she knew downstairs.

This part of the house was one of those places where fear bred boldly, even in the height of daylight. She wanted to turn and run, but she had to rescue her boots. It was more than her job's worth not to.

Hurrying, she tried the first key in the lock. It would not turn, so she tried the second and third and then there was a noise. The press of a floorboard.

Fourth key poised ready to try, she hesitated.

On the back of her neck the hairs twitched and prickled. Slowly she let her hand fall from the lock and she swallowed hard as she pivoted on the ball of her foot.

If it was even possible, the corridor was darker. The sun had been hidden by a patchwork of cloud and all around her everything had dimmed.

Turning to try the key again, something caught her eye. It was in the far corner of the corridor. A shape. A figure all in black that melted back into the wall so that it merged with the stone of the building.

Holding her breath, Rachel squinted. Her imagination was running away with her, scaring her when she needed to be focusing on finding the right key.

Anxiety made her fingers cumbersome and slippery and she dropped the keys. Against the silence of the top quarters, the noise was deafening. Rachel took a step back, slapping her palm over her mouth, afraid that she had alerted somebody downstairs of where she was and what she was doing. She waited for the sound of concerned voices, for the hurrying of footsteps to find out who had ventured into the forbidden section of the house.

There was nothing. People were too distracted by the work that was required to welcome the Belgraves. Swiftly, Rachel swiped for the bunch of keys and straightened.

A pair of eyes watched her. Neither blue nor brown, they stared, their gaze unfaltering. Now that the sun had cast its sparse rays through the shuttered windows once again, it was unmistakable. Somebody was definitely watching her.

The eyes stared from beneath the hood of a black cloak. A woman. As though deprived of natural light, her face was deathly white.

Rachel took a step backwards. The woman took a step forwards, edging closer, until the grim line of a sad mouth could be seen and wisps of peppery brown hair were visible from the sides of the hood.

Rachel gasped, recognising her as Goody Brown, the woman who had visited unannounced on market day and who had helped ensure the birth of little Samuel.

Had she been at Thornycroft Hall all this time, her presence a secret of some sort? Did the Thornycrofts even realise that she was here, skulking around in the forbidden area of the house?

"Lady Cecily will be looking for those I shouldn't wonder," Goody said as she inched closer, holding out her hand, palm flat, fingers outstretched. Rachel realised that she was waiting for her to hand over the keys.

"I can't imagine that Cecily would be best pleased to know who has taken them." Goody's gaze bore into her uncomfortably, as though she was probing to read her inner most secrets. Rachel noticed that she had a hard, wise face. It was the kind of face that looked as though it had seen a lot and for a moment, she considered whether the woman was even real, or just a figment of her tired and frightened mind.

"Come now Rachel. Hand them over." She grinned a toothy smile that Rachel refused to return. How did she know her name? Had she heard Lady Cecily say it during her labour, or had she been watching her, listening to conversations these past weeks?

There was something dreadfully disconcerting about this woman dressed all in black. It was as though she had been in the house forever, as though she had always been a part of it, was meant to be a part of it. She curled and unfurled her fingers, beckoning for the keys to pass from Rachel's hand to her own and eventually, Rachel obliged. As she did so, their hands touched, warm skin glancing against cold skin, rough skin.

Retracting her hand shakily, Rachel held it against her chest waiting for the woman's next move.

"Get gone now," Goody hissed, bringing her face so close that Rachel could smell the sourness of her breath. "This is no place for you." Her eyes surveyed the shadowy corridor, as though looking for something that might be hiding. "'Tis no place for anyone."

She did not need to be told twice. Rushing past her, Rachel raced down the staircase, turning back only when she reached the bottom.

The figure had drifted back into the shadows and the keys were gone. Her chance to retrieve her boots had been lost and now it was likely that her treachery would be revealed.

Hurrying down the next set of stairs until she was back on the ground floor of the house, she ran in to the stillroom and shut the door behind her, closing her eyes as she replayed the image of the secret locked room. So absorbed she had been and so startled by the noises that she had heard, that she hadn't put the portraits back into position under the sheets. Whoever ventured into that room next would know that she had been looking and admiring the beautiful smooth curves and lines of Lady Rosamund Thornycroft's spectacular face. There could be no greater deceit for Lady Cecily to learn of and the punishment would be severe.

As she busied herself with making the tincture for Lady Cecily, Rachel tried to push her vexations far from her mind.

Moving aside the bowl of scented water that she had prepared earlier, she plucked some ginger root from a jar and began crushing it with yarrow flower and chamomile. Despite her obvious distaste for Rachel, whom she considered a burden of charity that had been laid upon her doorstep, Lady Cecily had a clear preference for her work in the stillroom, and it was a place that Rachel didn't mind being with its rich and sometimes foul smells from the herbs, roots, leaves and flowers.

A soft click interrupted her task. She looked up, expecting to see Hannah, coming in from the kitchen, yielding another bunch of herbs to be hung to dry for the winter months. Instead, Goody Brown, the strange woman from the top quarters, was standing in the doorway, her cloak still wrapped about her shoulders as though there was a chill in the air. The way Frimley had said her name rang through her head. Her name had dripped from his tongue like poison.

Dangling from the curl of her forefinger were Rachel's boots. Stern of face, she approached the table, holding the boots high by their laces. "You'll be needing these no doubt," she said, her voice gruff and with no hint of kindness.

Mutely, Rachel took the boots and attempted a smile of gratitude.

Goody stared at her with eyes like flint. "What you did up there is forbidden," she scolded. "It does no good to disturb what is gone. It does no soul any good and no good can come of it. You won't venture there again."

"I was curious," Rachel blurted out in the feeble bid for an explanation.

Goody leaned forward, threatening, her voice a low growl. "Folk should let sleeping bones rest. Respect what has gone before, what has been done, never to be undone."

Shame burned on Rachel's cheeks and she looked to the table, desperate to avoid the accusing gaze of the woman in front of her. "You won't tell Lady Cecily?" The question escaped her lips before she could stop it. There was a pause.

Goody had already started to make her way out of the room. "I won't tell Cecily." Her voice was softer but her back was turned so that her face was no longer in view. "I know how you saved the child, Samuel, and I have no desire to see an intelligent, resourceful young girl turned out with nowhere to go."

Then she was gone.

******

There was a dreadful fuss when the Belgraves at last arrived. Anna was run ragged after being called upon every moment to help fulfil the high demands of Lady Belgrave and her daughter, Bernadette.

For the most part of the Belgrave family's visit, Lord Belgrave and Sir Edward had spent most of it hidden away in the study to discuss a matter of business.

Then there was a scene wherein Lady Cecily took to parading baby Samuel around the blue parlour, proudly showing him off to a collection of coos and proclamations of how beautiful the boy was. The poor child was passed around like a trophy for a good part of the afternoon and not once did he whimper or fuss.

Lady Belgrave had not disappointed the expectations that had been created of her. She was just as demanding and stuck up as the other staff had warned. She had even scolded Anna twice in front of Lady Cecily, who hadn't batted an eyelid. Despite Lady Cecily's own sour nature, Rachel had never heard her speak to Anna in that sort of way before and was surprised that she had tolerated it. However, it seemed that the presence of the Belgraves was treated as some kind of gift bestowed upon them.

It had been a relief when she had been given leave to return to the village to press George Viccars for the measurements that would lead to a dress of fine silk for the Belgraves' leaving feast in the coming weeks.

Mary Hadfield answered the door with a tired face and a look of great annoyance at the fact that she had been disturbed.

"Sorry to trouble you, but I'm here to speak with Master Viccars," Rachel began, but her voice was blotted out by the distressed cries of a child in the background.

Mary didn't flinch at the noise, unlike Lady Cecily would have done. Rachel supposed that having several children hardened her to any distress. "He was supposed to come and measure Lady Cecily," she explained.

"Master Viccars is not well." Mary looked back over her shoulder as there was a shout from one of her older children and the youngest started crying again. "I'll be sure to pass on your message when he is better."

"Do you think it will be soon? Only, Lady Cecily is quite insistent."

"He's laid up in bed. A fever." Her response was clipped and Rachel wasn't surprised, it had been insensitive of her to press, but Lady Cecily would be furious if no dress was to emerge. Mary bid her a good day and shut the door to address the chaos behind her.

Upon her return to Thornycroft Hall, a tray was thrust into her hands and she was instructed to take it to the dining room where the Thornycrofts were entertaining their guests.

Lord Belgrave was speaking in a loud and authoritative voice, giving his opinion on some political matter. Lady Belgrave was nodding with a serene smile, ever proud of her husband's viewpoint.

Sir Edward took a deep gulp of his wine, waiting for the opportune moment to respond. Rachel could tell that he did not agree and that he wasn't going to let the bombastic mannerism of his ego-inflated guest stop him from challenging.

Next to him, Lady Cecily was watching cautiously, glancing nervously at Lady Belgrave and then back at her husband.

Rachel mused how sad it was that a woman of high status should feel so worried about what others thought of her. She knew that if she had the fortune and respect of a noble status, she would enjoy getting involved in conversation and she would not hold back, not like Lady Cecily did.

Carefully, she served the soup bowls and observed the Belgrave children, who were only a little older than her.

Benjamin and Bernadette were both strikingly beautiful with golden hair, peachy skin and eyes of a vivid blue green, like the waters that she had heard existed on tropical shores, where spices were harvested ready to be shipped back to England. Neither of them spoke much, but there was a quiet arrogance about them, in a way that was unnerving.

Rachel noticed how Benjamin in particular appeared to silently appraise every person at the table. His conversation was polite enough, but there was something about his stance and his smile that suggested he was quietly amused at the expense of others.

By the time the meal was finished and Sir Edward had retired to his study with Lord Belgrave, the discussion had been diverted to something of a lighter nature and it was Lady Belgrave's turn to loudly state her opinions.

"Of course Benjamin now leads every hunt," she gushed just as Rachel returned to the room to clear the plates.

Rachel noted how Benjamin looked away, disinterested as Lady Cecily joined in with her acquaintance, impressed by the high praise. "He will make the finest husband in all of England." Lady Belgrave continued her enthusiastic babble about the endless credentials of her son without even a modicum of modesty.

Bernadette's expression had twisted into a mask of envy. Benjamin was clearly the golden child, the favoured one and the one whom Lady Belgrave would back to the end.

The conversation continued with Benjamin in the spotlight. Bernadette's expression hardened and then fell as she took great care in rubbing at an imaginary spot on her dress.

A small wave of pity glanced over Rachel as she subtly observed them.

"Oh you should watch him ride Cecily. It makes my heart swell with pride every time. He joined the royal hunt when we had the good fortune to be at court you know. Even the King commented on his ability and the ladies at court were quite taken by him. Of course, we are selecting his wife very carefully." She turned to look approvingly at her son. "He has the pick of all of England's finest blooms. You can see why of course."

Rachel did her level best not to screw her face up in disgust. Never had she heard anybody unashamedly boast quite so much. It even put Lady Cecily to shame.

Benjamin looked decidedly bored, as though he was well used to the endless stream of adoration. At twenty one he had endured many years of it and Rachel wondered how ruined he must be for it. Instead of basking in her complements and high praise, he turned away, his upper lip curling upwards when Lady Cecily started remarking on how handsome he was. That was a fact that could not be denied, Benjamin had grown into his looks very well and Lady Belgrave clearly fawned over him. It was quite a spectacle and Benjamin needed no tongue to speak of all his richly deserved achievements and of the greatness and grandeur that awaited a young man of his station.

Mutely, he acknowledged the nods of approval and the prompted remarks of how wonderful he was. It wasn't that he was stupid, or that he had nothing to say, but his demeanour held an arrogant air, as though he was of such superior standing, that he need not dignify anybody with a response.

Rachel mused what it must be like to be so adored and to have such expectations placed upon one's shoulders.

When the subject turned back to Lady Cecily's churching and Samuel's baptism, Rachel noted how cleverly she glossed it all over, quick to return the focus back to the Belgraves.

Inwardly she smiled. It would be an utter travesty for the Belgraves to find out that the Thornycrofts did not support the restoration of the Church of England. They adjourned to the blue parlour, Anna sending for nightcaps.

Later, as she cleaned and polished the wood of the table and began to work on the gleam of the candlestick holders, Rachel considered the fact that somebody as fortunate as Benjamin Belgrave, with all of his riches and a destiny carved out in gold, was perhaps more unfortunate than even the poorest of folk. If somebody like Benjamin Belgrave was to fail in any of the endeavours set out for him, he would have a long way to fall from grace.

As she rubbed and shone the last of the candlestick holders, she decided that she would not swap any of her meagre existence for the expectations of somebody with the riches and privilege of Benjamin Belgrave.

In contrast to Benjamin, his sister Bernadette was spoiled and huffy. Bernadette was only a little older than Rachel, a few months from what she had learned. She would have felt sorry for her if the girl had not proved herself to be such a confounding misery.

At every opportunity she would bark some aggressive demand at one of the servants. Rachel could not even imagine the type of employer she would one day make, far worse than Lady Cecily.

She wondered if Bernadette's behaviour was the consequence of being so forgotten by Lady Belgrave's affections. Rachel couldn't help but imagine that, if baby Samuel had a younger sister, her fate would be much the same.

When everyone had eventually retired for the evening, Anna appeared in the kitchen door, her expression dull and fatigued. She reached for some of Cook's cider and poured herself a deep cup. "That woman is exhausting," she exclaimed, slumping into a chair. "I swear I will surely scream if I have to hear of how perfect and wonderful that dreadful son of hers is one more time."

"Do you think they will stay beyond next week?" Rachel asked.

Anna's mouth curled in disgust. "Last time they stayed only a week. This time there is talk of longer." She turned her gaze back to Cook. "Mark my words, I shall turn as mad as the first Lady Thornycroft had been if they stay any longer this time around." At that there was a dreadful thudding from higher up in the house. They all stopped talking and Anna took a sharp breath as a distant moan sounded before fading to nothing.

"You should know better than speak ill of the dead Anna Forest, especially when they could be listening." Cook's voice was an angry whisper, full of reproach and Anna looked particularly peeved at being put in her place by the kitchen staff.

Pursing her lips, she shifted in her chair and drank deeply from her cup before setting it down again. "Superstitious nonsense, just like the nonsense I heard Margaret Blackwell spouting in the village about portents and Gabriel Hounds. I have no time for it."

"Aye and Lady Cecily has no time for mention of the other one's name neither." Cook drained the rest of her drink before looking to the ceiling nervously. "You know the rules and nobody wants to stir up old bones."

Anna had paled significantly. She pushed her cup away before glancing impatiently at Rachel. "What are you staring at? Haven't you got a bed to hurry to?"

Rachel wondered if Anna had also heard the strange noises a few nights earlier.

"Well?" Anna pressed, urging her to leave her and Cook to talk.

She was on her way upstairs when Frimley sidestepped in front of her, blocking her way. "Ah there you are. Sir Edward has requested your presence in his study."

"But the Belgraves…." she began, confused by the peculiar request. "I need to put out the candles in the corridors. Lady Belgrave likes the darkness."

Frimley's pale eyes regarded her impatiently from beneath a bush of grey eyebrows. "Am I to inform him that you have declined his request?"

"No," she said abruptly, worried that he would cause great offence on her part. "No of course not."

Turning to the side, he held out his arm and gestured towards the carved oak doors of the study. "This way then." With a grand swoop, Frimley threw open the doors to allow her into the room. He did not follow and when Sir Edward nodded his head, he pulled the doors shut again, allowing them privacy.

Rachel swallowed hard but her mouth had gone dry. They must have found out about her boots. Goody Brown must have told them of her trespassing after all.

She hovered by the closed doors, her knees beginning to tremble.

Sir Edward had bowed his head to some paperwork, quill in hand. Behind him the log fire crackled, scenting the room with apple wood. A pile of books were stacked on his desk, next to them a decanter of wine and two cups. Lord Belgrave must have been going over some business with him. The seriousness of Rachel's crime had clearly interrupted them.

Candlelight danced across the room from the freestanding candelabras either side of the desk.

With a final flourish of his quill, he set it back into his inkwell before waving his hand for her to move closer, but he did not look up.

Feeling very small and insignificant, Rachel took a nervous step towards the desk, waiting for further instruction of where she should stand and what she was expected to do. None came.

Instead, Sir Edward raised his head and looked her up and down before decanting himself some wine. He gulped it back and poured himself another. Then he filled the second cup and pushed it across the desk. "Please take a seat Rachel."

Rachel understood the instruction, but her legs refused to obey and she stayed stock still, staring at him incredulously. Never had she been offered the opportunity to share a drink with her employer, let alone a cup of wine, and in his study no less. Something didn't seem right. "Well lass? Close your mouth and come sit. It is not such a vulgar request is it?"

At last, she found a way of making her legs move, one foot in front of the other, mutely shuffling forwards. Why would Sir Edward want to take a drink with her? The very idea of it was absurd.

Meekly, she reached for the cup and brought it to her lips. The liquid was spicy and sweet, far better than anything she had ever been given in the kitchen. With a cough, she set the cup back down on the desk and attempted to straighten her composure.

Sir Edward had moved across the room and was lifting the lid of a box. She could hear him fumbling for something and then he was moving across to a cabinet and unlocking it.

When at last he was finished, there were a series of thuds and clicks as he shut everything back up. Then he stood watching her, his gaze penetrating.

Uncomfortable, Rachel took another sip of her wine and stifled another coughing fit.

"Your heart is a good one Rachel." At last Sir Edward broke the silence. "It has not been forgotten or dismissed how you delivered Samuel."

"I was not responsible for his delivery, Sir Edward, it was-"

He held up a hand to silence her. "It does not matter what anyone else says, you are responsible for the fact that my son lives and breathes today. If it was not for you, events could have taken a very different turn." He took another mouthful of his drink. "We have all been too accustomed to sadness and grief in these matters. You refused to let that happen again. I know what you did."

Rachel was astounded. She had brought the baby around before anyone had entered the room. Only Goody Brown had known that he had been born blue. Lady Cecily had been too out of it to know any different. Goody must have told him, but why? That would only show her up for thinking that the child was as good as dead. He did not mention Goody's name.

Uncomfortable, he shifted his steely gaze to the floor. "My wife must not hear of this. She is, I am afraid, a rather jealous woman at times, but her heart is in the right place."

Rachel almost choked on her wine. In her opinion it was highly questionable whether Lady Cecily even had a heart.

He did not notice her reaction. "It was a noble act on your part. I can't imagine that my wife made it easy."

"'Twas nothing any of us wouldn't have done." Her reply was rushed and she wished he would just hurry up. This was not a situation that she was at ease with, but his gaze lingered and there was a strange smile on his face as his eyes glinted in the wavering glow of the candles. He looked pleased, proud and there was something else, admiration.

She wondered if those were tears in Sir Edward's eyes as he thought back to the babies that he had lost and she wondered what fear there was in his heart for his only son and heir. "Samuel is a strong and healthy boy." Her comment was inappropriate. She silently berated herself for her foolishness. After everything that had happened to the babes that Lady Rosamund had birthed, she could be cursing Samuel just by uttering the words.

Taking another drink, Sir Edward crossed the room, the heels of his boots echoing. "Aye, he is a healthy boy and I thank your swift hands for that." Bringing his hand to her face, he cupped it around her cheek and dropped his voice to a whisper. "I thank you for that, Rachel."

He tilted her head upwards so that she was forced to look into his eyes. She noticed that the glint in them had not been from the light, but from un-shed tears.

Unable to find the correct way to respond, the situation was making her tremble. It was not clear what Sir Edward wanted from her. The gesture was intimate and if Lady Cecily was to catch him, she would be livid, but Rachel did not feel that he was of any threat to her, even though they were alone in his study.

Managing a weak smile, she nodded and then she felt something pressed in to the palm of her hand.

"Take this," he said. "It is the least I owe you. We are in your debt Rachel." With a ragged breath, he choked back a break in his voice. "It belonged to Rosamund, my first wife. It holds much value, so hide it well. It is for you to do with as is your own desire."

Rachel gulped and closed her fingers tightly about the object in her palm. It felt like a chain, looped through a large stone and she thought back to the portraits. The woman who gazed out from those canvases had been pressing delicate fingers against a beautiful pendant.

Stunned into silence, Rachel merely nodded.

Sir Edward withdrew his hand and went back to hunching over his quill and parchment on his desk. "That will be all." The official tone had returned and it was as though the moment had never happened.

Dumbfounded, Rachel hesitated, waiting for him to say something else but he simply dipped his quill and took it back to the letters that he had been writing.

Balling her fist around the precious pendant, she pivoted and hurried to leave the room, her cup of wine not even half finished.

"Keep it safe Rachel. Nobody must find that, especially not my wife." As he spoke, she turned back to look at him. He had not bothered to raise his head.

The sound of the quill scratching against the surface of the parchment was all that was left hanging in the air between them.

******

In the following days, Lady Cecily embarked on her habitual parade of Samuel and the usual fuss had been made on cue.

It was a bright morning and Rachel was polishing with beeswax and lavender. Her mind was focused on the floorboard that she had carefully lifted to hide the pendant with her other secret possessions.

Every so often she would look up to see Sir Edward watching her with a shadow on his face before he finally told Lady Cecily that the lad had had enough of his audience.

As usual, she dumped the poor baby on to his wet nurse, as though he was a fine doll easily disposed of, and returned to her room.

The guests slowly dispersed to take a walk in the garden and let breakfast go down, leaving Rachel to finish her chores and clear up after them.

Her stomach was growling noisily but with all the work that was expected of them whilst the Belgraves were visiting, they were breaking their fast far later than usual.

Cook had promised that they could have some of the bread with a little butter and some of the blackberry jam that she had made when they were done. Even she seemed to be breaking a little under the demands of both Lady Cecily and Lady Belgrave.

The other guest, the mysterious Goody Brown, was nowhere to be seen and nobody spoke of her.

Rachel wandered through to the kitchen. Hannah, the scullery maid was breaking a freshly baked loaf and placing it into a bowl. Next to her, Cook was busy spreading a layer of creamy butter onto each piece before dolloping on some of the dark fruity jam that had been left over from the grand breakfast.

Still, nobody knew quite how long the Belgraves were supposed to be staying. There was some hope that they may be planning to leave by the end of the week, but they were famed for overstaying their welcome, so Rachel was not hopeful.

Taking the final bite of her breakfast, she was about to thank Cook when they were surprised by the most awful commotion.

Somebody was shouting. There were more shouts, followed by running footsteps.

Hurrying into the hallway, Rachel was greeted by Sir Edward shouting at her to fetch blankets as he instructed Johnny, the stable hand, to ride to the next village to fetch for the family physician.

For a moment, Johnny stood idle and Rachel thought he looked so pale that he might collapse in front of her. Then she noticed that his arms and hands were covered in blood. Sir Edward bellowed at him to move which seemed to spur some life in to him.

There was no time to ask anyone what was happening and so Rachel simply did as she was told. She had no idea how many blankets would be needed and so she picked up a small bundle.

Somebody shouted something about the stable yard and so, having had no further instruction from anyone in authority, she decided that it was best she hurry out there.

From somewhere nearby there was another scream and then an onslaught of hysterics. Rachel recognised the cries as belonging to Lady Belgrave, who was ushered into the house by Anna and her own maid.

The sound of thundering hooves carried across the courtyard. Johnny had Sir Edward's stallion in full gallop before he had even left the property, so that stones and dust were sent flying in his wake.

Hurrying through the courtyard and towards the stables, she soon saw the men trying to reign in one of the horses. It was Lady Cecily's chestnut mare and she was foaming at the mouth, her black mane streaming behind her as she circled the stables, rearing her legs and whinnying as she hunted for an exit. Rachel could see the whites of her eyes and she thought of the madness that had been the death of Lady Rosamund. There was no doubting that the poor creature was suffering with it.

Then she thought of the stories of the demon that was supposedly still hiding in the depths of Thornycroft Hall and of the noises she had heard coming from the top of the house. Alice's warning of the Gabriel Hounds struck her again. Had this been the terrible thing that they had been portending?

More shouts snapped her back to the moment and then the air was silenced with one terrible bang and then another.

Globules of saliva tinged with scarlet were sent flying in long sticky streaks as the mare thrashed about, before another deafening crack sent her to her knees.

The air was rife with the smell of gunshot and the dreadful scene was momentarily blurred by disturbed dust from where the poor creature hit the ground. As it cleared, Rachel could see that the mare had stilled, her body lying amidst the dust and straw. A pool of crimson began to flow from the ribbons of ebony hair, mingling with the muck and gathering in the cracks of the ground.

Lord Belgrave remained poised, hunting rifle in hand, the shot sparks giving way to a billow of charcoal smoke.

Without time to think, she hurried towards Sir Edward, who was inspecting something in the stable entrance.

Another stable worker was kneeling, his sleeves soaked in red. When he saw Rachel, he grabbed the blankets from her and put them over a shape on the floor, but not before she saw the bloody pulping mess of Master Benjamin Belgrave's once beautiful face.

Bone showed white through fleshy pink and red and his clothes were soaked in blood. One eye had disappeared amongst a mound of raised, broken flesh and his mouth was a messy slash of blood.

"Get her out of here," somebody shouted.

Rough hands pushed her back towards the house and she found herself running past the lifeless mare. The mare's eyes were wide open and staring, flies already beginning to buzz around her head. Flecks of saliva caked her open mouth and Rachel could see where the first shot had glanced across her flank but had failed to penetrate. There was no sign of the second, but the third had embedded neatly between her eyes. Although she tried not to look as she ran past, it was impossible not to.

Back in the house, she raced to her room and reached for the pot under her bed retching and gagging, the bitter taste of vomit in her mouth.

The handsome Belgrave lad, not much older than herself, was quite possibly dead on the straw in the stables and Lady Cecily's mare had been shot dead too. Rachel thought of the madness that she had seen in the whites of the horse's eyes and a cold shiver made her teeth chatter.

When she let herself out of the servant door, she ran around the perimeter of the house and into the gardens, until she found herself by the neat lines of rosebushes.

She turned to look at the great building that had become her home for almost two years, wondering how on earth such a dreadful event could unfold.

Lady Cecily's mare had always been such a gentle beast with a good temperament, so it was quite perplexing that she had taken to such a frenzied state. Something must have set her off, but what?

A shadow passed over one of the upper windows of the house and Rachel speculated whether whatever was haunting Thornycroft Hall could have found its way into the stables and scared the horses?

Feeling as though she was being watched, Rachel wrapped her arms about her body and noted that she was still shaking from the shock. Feeling exposed and vulnerable to hidden eyes that were stalking her from behind the mullioned windows, she hurried back to the house, thoughts of what could have happened churning through her head.

She managed to avoid any orders on her way back in. Everyone was too busy rushing around the stables or standing outside speculating whilst they waited for the physician to arrive. There were whispers that Benjamin wouldn't make it to nightfall, his injuries were so bad.

As she tiptoed back into her little chamber, Rachel wondered again about whether it had been the spirit of Lady Rosamund responsible for the accident. She had heard that animals were supposed to be sensitive to such things.

Her thoughts were interrupted by a bump and the unmistakable sound of creaking floorboards from upstairs.

Creeping from her room, she looked towards the top part of the house. There was another creak. It sounded like a footstep.

Aside from Lady Cecily and Samuel, who were somehow still sleeping in spite of all of the commotion, there was nobody else in the house at all. Hannah and Cook were nowhere to be seen and all of the men were tending to the dreadful business with Master Benjamin.

Stealthily, she worked her way upwards and then tiptoed towards the door that led to the top quarters. She pressed her ear to it, straining to listen.

Gasping, she thought she heard a whispering. It was coming from behind the door, a whisper so soft that it could just be the wind rattling through the shutters.

Holding her breath, Rachel pressed her ear to the door. The whispering stopped. It could have just been the wind, she reasoned with herself, but she recalled how still the air had been outdoors.

Another bang resounded throughout the upper part of the house and a long drawn out guttural laugh followed. The sound was unmistakable. It wasn't the kind of laughter that most folk expressed in merriment, but the sort of laugh that was twisted, mocking and threatening.

Stepping away from the door, she felt her limbs begin to shake. Something was in there and it knew that she was there.

The laughter stopped abruptly just as she noticed the keys that had been left in the lock.

Despite a warning voice in her head, Rachel found her hand reaching for the coolness of the brass and she turned the key. The lock jarred because the door was already open.

She went to turn the handle, but it was already moving painfully slowly. Something from behind was turning it.

Jumping backwards, she ran to the foot of the stairs and watched the door creak slowly open.

"Up to no good again, creeping about like a thief? Spying?" The silhouette of a woman took up most of the doorway. It was the secret, hidden visitor, Goody Brown. Her face was paler than usual and her forehead damp.

"I hadn't realised anybody was in there." Rachel couldn't hide the fear in her voice as the gargled, cruel laughter from moments earlier continued to resound against her skull. She wasn't sure which was the more awful thought, the fact that it could have been coming from the strange woman in front of her, or the fact that it could have been the restless spirit of Lady Rosamund.

Pushing the door shut behind her, Goody locked it and slipped the keys into her pocket. "And so you found yourself a good excuse for snooping then, eh lass?"

"I wasn't snooping. I heard a noise and I thought that…" She paused before diverting the conversation. "There's been a terrible accident, didn't you hear?"

Rounding on her, Goody brought her face inches from Rachel's. "I saw it all from the window." There was no hint of emotion in her voice and no glimmer of horror in her eyes. "Tragic business. That lad may need more than a physician. The rector perhaps?" There was coldness to her demeanour, as though the loss of life, human or beast, could not touch her.

"I saw his face, Master Benjamin's. It was dreadful. So much blood." Rachel felt her hands trembling at the memory. Still the woman didn't flinch.

Her tone was deadpan. "Bad things happen here. Always have." She turned to unlock the door behind her again and without exchanging another word, slipped away.

The family physician arrived swiftly and he was quick to dish out his demands. There were jobs required in the stillroom far beyond Rachel's capabilities, but she had no choice other than to make her way there and try her best.

"Rachel." Sir Edward pulled her aside. Starbursts of lines had become more prominent about his eyes. "You'll need help." He ushered her around a corner, his voice low. "We have a visitor. Experienced in the stillroom, well beyond your years. Better than many physicians, in my opinion. We have not made her presence known." He sniffed the air as though something foul was in it. "She's a character who some would not take too kindly to being here, under our roof. She is our guest for the time being nonetheless and she is a master of the stillroom. Goody Brown is her name. You must fetch her at once."

"Aye, Sir Edward. I'll make haste. Where should I look to find her?"

A hint of a smile played on his lips, but there was no humour in it. "I believe you already know the answer to that, as to the best of my knowledge you have already made Goody's acquaintance."

Colour flushed warmth into her cheeks. So he did know. "I'll go now. I shall do all that I can."

His grip tightened on her arm. "We do not know if the boy will survive. Once you have fetched Goody and shown her to the stillroom with the utmost discretion, see to it that the Reverend Mompesson can come. I'd ask for Stanley but our friends have different views to us." Looking out of a large arcing window into the courtyard below, he began to grind his teeth together. "God's teeth we owe them that much. It was Cecily's horse. Spooked to madness like that. I can only think that…." As he trailed off, his eyes misted over before he caught himself and turned back to look her in the eye. "Bring Mompesson."

Solemnly, Rachel nodded and went to find Goody before making her way into the village.

When she arrived at the rectory, the Reverend Mompesson was still out, but upon hearing the news of Benjamin Belgrave, Catherine insisted that he wouldn't be long and that Rachel should wait for his return.

A basket of apples had been placed in the kitchen, their skin rosy and scent sweet. The rich colours and fragrance of autumn was upon them and Rachel ached to go to the orchard at Thornycroft and fill her own basket with plump fruit. A mulled apple cider would be a sweet warm drink for poor Master Benjamin if he survived his accident and some rosehip and apple jelly would make a pleasing accompaniment to the meats and cheeses that they had been serving. She vowed quietly to herself that if he were saved, she would help Cook make the best meals and treats for him. Nobody should be made to suffer the way that Benjamin Belgrave was suffering.

In spite of the horrible events of the morning, Rachel closed her eyes for a moment and inhaled deeply, savouring the scent of autumn's sweet breath as it drifted in through the open window. It laced the air of the rectory, joined by the earthy tincture of wood smoke. She hoped that this autumn would not be tarnished with the untimely death of the Belgrave lad.

Catherine led her to the garden and Rachel took a seat, waiting as Catherine disappeared back inside to make up a tincture for Benjamin and another to help Lady Cecily in the early stages of motherhood.

When Catherine returned to pick some more herbs, Rachel got up to help her and they talked whilst they worked. In the village there had been more rumours of Gabriel Hounds.

Gathering what was needed, Rachel followed her back into the kitchen.

"Gossip and superstition." Catherine pressed at her herbs. "Don't go repeating such things mind. I don't want the children to hear."

Handing her some thyme, Rachel watched as she expertly manipulated the oil from within. Just as she was about to say something else, there was a frantic pounding against the door of the rectory. A voice, trill with panic, accompanied the banging.

With a quickened step, Catherine hurried to answer, Rachel close behind.

The round face of Mary Hadfield appeared, her youngest son clinging to her skirts and the other sobbing uncontrollably. Her own cheeks were flushed, her face wet and her nose swollen from crying. With trembling hands, Mary reached out to Catherine. "Please Mistress Mompesson. 'Tis George. He's gone."

"Master Viccars?"

Her face crumpling, Mary nodded.

"Gone?" Frowning, Catherine wiped her hands on her apron.

"He was fine only a few days ago." She reached for Catherine's arm, pulling on it as though jogging her memory would help change what had come to pass. "You saw him with your own eyes Mistress Mompesson, carrying the fine patterns of cloth back to the house. Busy he was, working on some beautiful clothes, your dress included and some material to be kept aside for Lady Cecily." Roughly, she wiped her cheek with a shaking hand as fresh tears coursed down her cheeks. "I did what I could but the fever would not break." She began to recount the horror that they had endured over such a short period of time. The angry boils, the worsening fever and the rotten stink. By the time she was finished, Mary's eldest had burst into a fresh wave of hysterics.

A voice from behind them queried the commotion that was taking place. His dark hair tumbling about his shoulders and brown eyes filled with concern, William Mompesson appeared, a book of psalms in his hand.

Mary all but fell upon him. "Oh Reverend Mompesson, please come. You must come at once, 'tis George."

Taking the crying child from Mary, Catherine nodded for Rachel to usher the other into the house whilst William accompanied Mary back to her cottage, where George Viccars was evidently laying lifeless in his bed.

Together, they sat in silence, none of them daring to speak for fear of upsetting the children further.

Outside, birds sang and dogs barked as though it were any other normal day and one of their neighbours hadn't fallen foul of an ailment that had taken his life, whilst Benjamin Belgrave lay broken and dying in a guest room at Thornycroft Hall.

When William returned, all colour had drained from him. Wordlessly, he went to his study.

An uncomfortable silence followed, only to be shattered by the heavy thud of a door closing.

Catherine assured Rachel that she would ask the Reverend to attend Thornycroft that very day, but that she must be left alone with him first.

Agreeing to take the children back to Mary, Rachel hurried out.

Mary Hadfield was calmer and less blotchy in the face when she answered the door. It was a shocked calm, as though she was filled with disbelief and merely in the midst of a terrible dream that she would soon wake from. For a moment, she deliberated over whether she should offer to take the children, but there would be no place for them at Thornycroft Hall and she had to get back there quickly.

With a sombre note of thanks, Mary took the children back in her arms and they sat down on the doorstep, waiting for the body of George Viccars to be taken away.

******

It was late in the day when the Reverend Mompesson arrived at Thornycroft Hall. The physician was still with Master Benjamin and Lady Belgrave had apparently taken a terrible turn. The outlook was bleak.

Lady Cecily was up and about with Samuel, tears still streaking her face from the knowledge that her favoured mare was dead. It hadn't occurred to her to cry for poor Benjamin. Glowering at Rachel, she watched as the Reverend was shown to where Benjamin was fighting for his life.

Word of George Viccars had not reached Thornycroft Hall. Under the present circumstances, Rachel thought that there was little point in telling anybody. The death of a travelling tailor would be of no importance to the Thornycroft household, not compared with the portending doom for the Belgrave family.

It was some time before the Reverend emerged. Despite Lady Cecily's frostiness, he was the epitome of politeness and kindness. His pleasant demeanour made Rachel smile.

Love thy enemy, she thought, feeling even more aligned to the Mompessons and the good that they had brought to the parish.

Goody had disappeared upstairs again, slipped away unnoticed, her work having already been used by the physician to help clean Benjamin's wounds, soothe the pain and prevent them turning putrid.

The rest had been left behind for a servant or family members to administer, morning, noon and night. Nobody thought to question where the salves, poultice or tinctures had come from.

Late afternoon, as the serving staff sat around a stew of potatoes and onions with dumplings, Rachel couldn't find her appetite as she recounted the tragedy that had befallen the Hadfield's home with the death of George Viccars.

As she spoke, she imagined the hideous boils that Mary had described as fat and bloated on his neck and arms. Then she thought of George Viccars as he had been after the Wakes festivities, on market day, with eyes as bright as stars and his thick curtain of hair that had been kissed a bonny shade brighter by the summer sun. It seemed strange to think that she had only spoken with him such a short time before.

Rachel had not known George Viccars well at all, but he had always greeted her with a brightness that would lift her spirits, even on a rain soaked day. It was hard to imagine that handsome smile snuffed out like a candle never to be relit.

"Sounds like plague," Johnny the stable lad commented and Cook swiped for him.

"Don't go saying that in front of Lady Cecily or we shall never hear the end of it and poor Rachel here will be punished for fetching the Reverend Mompesson after he had seen to the Viccars man."

Hannah was aghast on behalf of Rachel. "But Sir Edward instructed her to do so."

"Aye, that may be so, but we all know what Lady Cecily's opinion will be on the matter, so let's not discuss it any further." Cook put an end to the discussion, and Rachel decided to take a walk through the orchard to clear her head.

All the thought of death had reminded her of her parents and tears blurred her vision as she rounded on the smart line of trees that ran just beyond the rose garden.

Dashing the back of her hand across her cheek, she stopped and turned to the lonely patch of land where Lady Rosamund and her baby lay.

The flower she had placed on the grave was still under the stone, its petals curling and tinged with brown as it too awaited its demise. How sad, she thought, that people had to die and leave their loved ones behind. At least George Viccars would have a proper burial. Not like Lady Rosamund, or indeed, her own mother. The very thought squeezed her insides until she felt that she could no longer breathe.

What if her mother was not waiting to meet her in heaven? What if God had not accepted her soul either? What if she was amongst those lost souls of the Gabriel Hounds?

Rachel imagined the Gabriel Hounds the way that Alice had described them to be, fractured images of spirits with elongated mouths stretched into eternal screams as they ripped across the lonely countryside, howling with the insanity of an unfulfilled death.

Kneeling at the barely visible mound that she was certain marked Lady Rosamund's grave, she wept and pressed her palms against the grass.

With no way of knowing where her own mother's bones were, this was a place that she could lose herself in grief.

Whispering her mother's name over and over, she prayed for her soul. Then she cried for Lady Rosamund and then for poor Benjamin Belgrave, who would likely soon be joining them. Then at last she cried for George Viccars and for the loss that his family would feel when word reached them. The sexton would no doubt be lowering his rigid cold body into its grave before his kin even knew.

When at last her tears were spent, the sun had long fallen behind the horizon. Its vermillion glow lit the sky behind a patchwork of cloud as she turned back to face Thornycroft Hall.

Something caught her eye at the very top of the house. A shadow moved across one of the windows, disappearing from view before she could decipher who or what it might be.

A cold shaft of fear ebbed its way through her body. Had Goody been watching her, or something else? The laughter she had heard earlier echoed in her head and the rumours of the demon that had penetrated Lady Rosamund's poor lost soul circled around, taunting her.

It had been in Goody's quarters that they had tried to cast the demon out. The Reverend at the time had known a holy man who had experience of such things. Rumour had it that he had fled from York Minster after the city was taken under siege during the war, that he had been a priest with a darker side, a side that knew about things such as exorcism. Evidently, Sir Edward had paid a handsome sum to rid his wife of the thing that ailed her.

Some of the older staff held on to those stories, telling the newer employees about the strange wisp of a man, with eyes as black as coal and a brown case filled with instruments and phials, some filled and some waiting to be filled. They told of the howls that had bounced from every wall of the house for three days and nights before, at last, he had taken her away with her maid. "Unearthly" was how they had described those howls.

Some said that it had been the demon fighting the holy man, whilst others said that it had been Lady Rosamund, tortured to the brink of death. The imagined screams pierced Rachel's skull as she thought of those tales.

Rachel pressed her hands to her ears in an attempt to shut out the screams, but they were locked inside her head, along with the malicious laughter that she had heard earlier that day.

Running from the grave, she fled to the house, praying that the tormenting noise would cease. Instead, it got louder until she realised that the screaming was in fact coming from the house.

Throwing open the door to the kitchen, she called out for Hannah and abruptly the screaming stopped.

The house was still. Upstairs there was a gentle thud, a door shutting and then the sound of Samuel's cry.

Footsteps hurried across floorboards as either Lady Cecily or the wet nurse hurried to be near him.

Rachel ran up the stairs and stopped short as she saw Lady Cecily in her nightgown, pressing the babe close to her.

"'Twas just a shadow my lamb." She put her lips to his soft tuft of hair. "'Tis gone now. 'Tis gone now." Whispering a prayer, she paced the corridor, her breathing ragged and fear prominently fixed upon her face. She didn't notice Rachel when at last, the baby calmer, she padded softly back into her chamber.

111

CHAPTER 11

Mid-November 1665 - Eyam

Whilst the pained howls of Benjamin Belgrave shuddered through Thornycroft Hall, in the village, it had become unusually quiet.

Johnny had been right in his prediction. As the fertile colours of summer quickened to rich scarlet and gold and the first of the autumnal winds began to strip the trees of their foliage, others had succumbed to the same fate as George Viccars.

Fevers broke into putrid filled lumps and boils that could not be bled of their poisons quick enough. The dead were swiftly wrapped in sheets and buried, and rumours of plague had become fact.

Every week, news of more death or illness was reaching Thornycroft Hall. Eyam was no longer a place where guests would want to outstay their welcome. So aside from Benjamin, who was making a slow but good recovery from his dreadful injuries, the Belgraves had long gone.

The streets of the village were a sad reflection of what they had once been as nobody dared leave their homes unless it was absolutely necessary.

Some of the richer families had moved to alternative residences across the country, or those without land ties had started fleeing to the caves that were carved in to the surrounding landscape. Numbers had been dwindling, not only by people willingly leaving, but by death too.

It was with a sombre silence that the people of Eyam prayed at Divine Service when the Reverend Mompesson asked that they take a moment to remember those who had passed.

Mary Hadfield's youngest son had shortly followed George Viccars to his grave and then her boy Edward had been lost to it too.

News had spread that the Thorpes, Syddalls and Hawksworths had all been struck and by the end of October people feared the worst.

Lady Cecily had forbidden all remaining staff to leave Thornycroft Hall without her permission and had instructed that any who did would not be welcome back. They lived on the edge of the village and as such, were to remain isolated.

"A Kingdom of purity," she said as she insisted that more scented water was to be thrown on the floors. Smells were to be pure. People were to be clean. Nobody was to breathe the same air as her and Samuel. She was becoming a woman possessed. For fear of contamination, Lady Cecily would not even entertain the idea of asking their favoured pastor, Thomas Stanley, to visit the house.

Rachel missed her friends from the village and the Mompessons. She missed the comforting voice of the Reverend Mompesson and she missed catching any time with Catherine Mompesson, who always stopped to enquire how she was feeling and to offer some time to kneel and pray for the souls of her parents and for her own strength and courage. The truth was that she felt lost without the Mompessons or the Hancocks in her daily life, but her employers wouldn't hear of it. They wouldn't let any of them leave the house except for when necessary.

Many of the staff had disagreed with the decision, believing that it would anger God to attend no service at all. Lady Cecily didn't care. Nothing was more important to her than protecting the heir to Thornycroft Hall, her baby boy Samuel.

When the cool winds of autumn took on the edge of the bitter bite of winter, Rachel was too distracted with taking care of the Belgrave boy, Master Benjamin, to notice any of the stranger goings on within the walls of Thornycroft Hall.

Goody Brown continued to mingle with the spiders and the shadows, unseen but always heard. Her strange noises and grunts or bangs, rattles and scratches had become commonplace. She was, Rachel was certain, a mad woman. There was something wild about her, with eyes that looked to have witnessed a thousand horrors beyond what the imagination could muster.

On the occasions that her path did cross with Rachel's, it was always in the stillroom.

Despite her polite and courteous manner, there was a shiftiness to her that could not be placed. She could never look Rachel firmly in the eye and her conversation was often left unfinished, her sentences lingering, as though to continue would risk the unfolding of something dreadful. It set Rachel on edge.

There had been times when she had considered asking Cook about Goody, but her attempts to learn more were either thwarted by fear or distraction.

Looking after Master Benjamin had become her top priority, her duty and nobody else's. Her skills in the stillroom were commended, although, in Rachel's opinion, the spoiled and once handsome young man had simply been very lucky following the accident. Horrific though it had been, his injuries were healing at a steady pace and his recovery was quite remarkable. However, he was silent and withdrawn.

At first she had dreaded tending to him. Every time she had entered his chamber, she had felt his glare upon her and she knew that there were clever, profound thoughts secreted away inside of him. Even though, he had never treated any of the staff with the sort of disdain that his sister Bernadette had during their family's stay, it had been as though he hadn't even noticed them.

In recent weeks though, Rachel had felt the heat from his gaze on her back. There was no vanity in this knowledge that he was paying an interest. She knew her place as a servant of the house and she worried that, in his boredom, she was becoming the object of cruel amusement.

Between his long stretches of silence, he would gruffly ask her to fulfil different duties, some completely unnecessary, and that would prolong her time in his chamber, rather than allowing her to get on with the other chores required of her.

One evening, when she was laying the coal pans in his bed, he demanded that she sit with him.

The request took her quite by surprise, but she knew better than to protest, and so she had sat down, obediently waiting for him to ask her an impossible question, or to mock her in some way.

It was a strange scene. They had sat together in silence, like an old married couple, two companions listening to the crackle of the hearth and the odd hoot of an owl from outside.

After that, the request for her to sit with him had become frequent, and one evening, unable to abide the awkward silence any longer, she found her tongue. "Do you think you shall ever ride a horse again?" Shocking even herself with the impertinence of such a question, she prepared for the onslaught. If the Thornycrofts were to find out she had not kept to her place and had offended their guest, the consequences would be dire. She swallowed, the dryness in the back of her mouth making her want to gag as she chastised herself for such a careless mistake.

For a terrible moment, he did not answer and she was sure that she was going to be punished for her display of disrespect.

He was sitting with his chair turned at a slight angle from her, so that she could not see his face. The silence drew out between them, thickening and making her want to cry out.

With a grunt, he shifted position. Then he took a deep breath. "It is an interesting question and one that nobody else has thought to put to me." He said nothing more for a while and Rachel wondered if she should get up and leave, but he did not seem cross and she wanted to hear his answer.

"I don't think that I should want to go near a horse again, if I were you," she prompted, once more wondering how she could be so stupid as to lose her self-control and voice her less than humble opinion.

There was a low rumbling sound and she realised that he was laughing. "But you are not me, are you?"

Bowing her head, she looked to the floor, regretting her boldness. She had made him angry, she was sure. "I am not and I can not imagine how terrible that day must have been for you," she said, her voice withered.

"But you can imagine can't you?" He picked up his walking stick and tapped it against the floor. "You can imagine what it is like to be me, otherwise you would not have so eloquently voiced your observation."

The stick that he was holding continued to tap out a monotonous beat, its noise pounding at her ears. With a final tap, he expertly flicked it upwards and caught it on his lap. "You are quite astute. Tell me, how old are you? Sixteen, seventeen?"

Even though she couldn't see his face, she could tell that he was smiling with amusement. "I am eighteen, almost nineteen."

"Just a few years younger than me." His shoulders dipped and his tone fell with it. "Sometimes I feel like an old man."

Rachel didn't know how to respond. At that moment, Benjamin Belgrave looked like an old man: hunched in his chair, with his head turned away from her and his stick across his knees.

"If you please Master Belgrave, I must not linger. Lady Cecily will not take kindly to me overstaying my welcome here."

"Pah! Lady Cecily is as much of a dour faced snob as my own mother." He looked her up and down before waving his hand in a dismissive gesture. "Still, you are quite right, you should go. It would not do to be seen fraternising."

As she lifted her weight from the seat, she considered whether he meant that he was fraternising with a servant, or that she was fraternising with him. She wondered if he would turn to bid her good night, but once again, he had fallen into his usual silence.

Reaching for the door handle, she made to leave before turning to look at his bowed head and hunched form. "If I was to imagine myself as you, I don't think I should want to go near another horse again. That must be terribly hard for a man of your station." Recalling something Lady Belgrave had boasted about at the dining table, she drew a breath. "It must be terribly hard for the most gallant rider, who was, until now, always at the head of the hunt."

Crossing the threshold, she went to shut the door behind her. As she did, she saw the his shoulders twitch as Benjamin Belgrave choked back a small, inaudible sob.

The following morning, the air felt crisp and the temperature had dipped considerably. It would not be many weeks until the first snowfall. In the winter months it was hard to keep Thornycroft Hall warm. Rachel had been sent to chop firewood, a job that was usually reserved for the younger male staff, but with some having left, the task had become part of Rachel's long list of chores.

She picked up the first of the logs and yielded the axe, bringing it down hard. Splinters and shavings sprayed in all directions as it split cumbersomely down one side. Most of it would be wasted thanks to the flimsy pieces that had come away. It would be too difficult to salvage as anything other than wood chippings.

Her heart pounded hard in her chest as her arms ached and her body quickly fatigued. She had barely touched the log pile and the task ahead of her seemed arduous and impossible.

"Your posture is all wrong." The voice came from behind and she started, almost dropping the axe on to her foot. "It is none the wonder that you are tired already." The figure of Benjamin Belgrave hovered in the opening to the woodshed. He was leaning on his stick and his hair was hanging in front of his face, a dull and dirty curtain of blonde. He had come to watch and mock her, to gloat at her plight of uselessly chopping firewood in the cold.

Pushing down on the wave of anger that was threatening to rise up inside of her, Rachel ignored him and swung the axe again, catching the log off centre and sending it crashing across the little shed.

"I could show you if you like?" The click-clack of his stick sounded out as he edged closer.

"You are a guest of Lady Cecily's, she would be furious if I was to hand this over to you." She glanced at his hobbling form. "Besides, you are injured."

The comment stopped him short and he straightened, his face colouring. "I am not an invalid," he grumbled, swiping for the axe with his free hand.

She watched as he rested his weight on his stick after positioning himself in front of the log that she had placed ready for her next attempt.

With an expertly executed swing, he brought the axe down so that its blade slipped clean through the log, which fell into two almost perfect halves. He gestured for her to fetch another from the pile. Once again, he brought the axe down with such ease and precision that he made the task look ridiculously easy. "See, it is all in the technique," he said, making good his aim once again. "We are working very well together. We shall have this pile finished in next to no time. I shall chop, you can stack."

Rachel watched him work effortlessly for a long time before she spoke. "Why are you helping me?" Her words were filled with suspicion. It was preposterous that a young man of his station should be helping a girl like her. If Lady Cecily found out, there would be trouble.

"And why should I not?" Affronted, he stopped, only to look at her through the curtain of hair that he kept in front of his face. It felt unnerving speaking to somebody who kept one eye hidden and the other only partially in view.

"As I said, you are a guest and Lady Cecily will be wild if she finds out."

With another swing of the axe, Benjamin grunted. "Tell me something." He struck the wood again, "What is your name?"

Rachel had no idea why he should care for a servant's name other than to report them for some wrongdoing or impudence. As it was, she told him anyway.

"Well Rachel, I think you will agree with me that Lady Cecily would do well to be a little more humble. That face of hers could sour the sweetest of wines, curdle the creamiest of milk." There was a neat crack as the next log split in two and Rachel tried not to smile. It felt good to speak to somebody who shared her opinion of Lady Cecily. Still, she had to remember her place and this young man could be baiting her for sport. Now that he knew her name there would be nothing stopping him from exposing her disloyalty and naming her to the Thornycrofts.

He threw some of the scattered logs into one of her baskets and helped her neatly stack the rest. "Well that should keep them happy for a good while." Stretching his fingers out in front of him, he flexed them. "I should think that I might quite enjoy coming and doing that again some time. Do let me know when Cecily barks her orders about the fires again. I should very much like to help."

They made no further exchange before he picked up his stick and limped from the woodshed, leaving Rachel staring after him.

Master Benjamin took dinner with the Thornycrofts that night. The atmosphere around the table was stinted but Rachel thought she sensed a new lease of life in him. He and Sir Edward shared polite conversation and as she served, Rachel heard the topic of conversation switch to the village.

"What news of the rest of the village?" Benjamin asked as he lifted his wine, moving his elbows so that Rachel and Hannah could clear the plates.

Sir Edward shifted uncomfortably as he waited for the serving staff to disperse from the dining room. With Hannah ahead of her, Rachel hovered long enough behind the doors to hear the dulled voices.

Sir Edward's answer was grave. "More than a score last month and still the death toll is rising."

There was an intake of breath and then a pause. "Will you stay?" Benjamin asked.

"We have little choice." His words were closely followed by a bang so hard that the crockery not yet cleared from the table shook. There was a clatter as something fell over.

"Why?" Lady Cecily was so shrill that Rachel almost dropped the plates. "Why must you keep insisting that we have little choice? What is keeping us here Edward?"

Sir Edward growled a warning at her but she would not be quietened. "What is it that keeps us here Edward? What is it that keeps you here?"

"Enough." He raised his voice far more than Rachel had ever heard. The weight of it boomed through the house. It was rare that any of the staff heard Sir Edward shout and Rachel could sense that the rest of the house was listening, waiting for what would come next.

"No Edward, enough from you. I am tired of hearing that we have little choice in the matter. It has been three long months now and we have other residences, yet you choose to stay." A chair scraped heavily against the floor. "You choose to put your wife and son, your heir, in mortal danger." She was verging on hysterical and Rachel hurried towards the kitchen, afraid to be caught listening outside the door.

Their voices echoed through the great rooms of the house, Lady Cecily's becoming more of a shriek and Sir Edward's booming like a cannon as he tried to silence her.

Anna was in the kitchen, helping herself to some supper before she would be required to help Lady Cecily to bed. She was pretending not to notice the tensions and shouts as she brought a fork serenely to her lips.

"Enough!" Sir Edward roared again and Rachel noted how the strength of it paled even Anna's face as she chewed on her food.

"It is monstrous. Monstrous." Lady Cecily refused to heed his warnings. "If you force us all to stay here and die, you'll be shown for the monster that you are Edward Thornycroft." There was a sharp smacking sound and then a thud.

Silence flooded the house. Nobody spoke. Anna dropped her fork.

A series of low mumbles from the dining room broke the silence and then there were footsteps.

Her heart thudding, Rachel didn't know what she should do. She had never heard Sir Edward so angry and, despite her erratic nature, she had never heard Lady Cecily so hysterical.

The sound of Benjamin's stick clicking against the floor was followed by heavy slow footsteps.

Rachel looked to Anna who was sitting stiffly upright, her face having paled. As the footsteps retreated up the great staircase, they waited and listened. Then, without saying a word, Anna left the room.

It was late by the time Rachel had finished clearing up. Anna had not returned and so she had been left alone.

The door to Sir Edward's study had slammed shut at some stage during the course of the evening and as far as she knew, it had not opened again.

Her body was fatigued with the day's work, but her head was still rushing with thoughts about the scene that had unfolded in the dining room and the scale of horror that had befallen their neighbours.

Rachel walked through to the blue parlour. Putting out the fire that she had lit in there earlier that evening would be her last job before retiring to bed.

The room was warm and the smell of apple wood, along with the gentle hiss and crackle of logs, invited her to take a seat in a plump cushioned chair, just for a moment. She was weary and her arms ached from heaving baskets of wood to each fire in the house. Her body was grateful for the soft padding as she sat down.

She closed her eyes, listening to the peacefulness. There were no strange noises that Thornycroft was so often accustomed to and Rachel felt her shoulders dip slightly. It would not do to fall asleep but to rest, for just a moment, would be acceptable. Her eyelids fluttered, tempting her with the black stillness of sleep. She did not see the figure sitting in the chair next to hers, as it was facing away from her, the chair positioned so that its vantage point gave a view out of the great sash windows.

"Love. It's a strange thing isn't it?" The question startled her. In the reflection of the glass, she could see the fractured reflection of Master Benjamin. He made no effort to turn to look at her directly but seemed content to converse with her reflection. "The more I think about love, the more I believe that I should be glad never to love, or be loved." He laced the word 'love' with poisonous discontent. "It is a messy, ugly emotion. Love seems to drive people to behave in the most vulgar of ways."

In the window, Rachel could see that he had relaxed further into the chair and crossed his legs. "I should be pleased to keep my dignity and never fall to the follies of love."

"I disagree." Before she had even finished her challenge, Rachel was wondering what on earth possessed her to do it, but Benjamin was not offended. Instead, he seemed interested.

If she could see his face properly, she would have noticed the amused smile upon his lips. "Oh? What do you know of love?"

Affronted that he should presume that she should not know anything of love, Rachel felt defiant. "I know what it is to be loved and to love back without condition." Her retort was pointed and she watched his reflection in the window as he flinched.

"And who loves you without condition?" He was not being rude or obnoxious when he asked her.

"Loved. I was loved." Rachel traced her finger across the material of the chair pensively. "Before he died, my father made it obvious that he loved me more than anything, and I loved him back just as much. He told me of how much my mother had loved me too before she passed." Warmth filled her from the inside as she reflected on how kind her father had been to her and how, even though he had not been a wealthy man, he had seen to it that she had an education and wanted for little.

"What did he tell you of her?"

"He told me that when I was born she would not leave my side. He said that I had been all that she had wanted in the world and that she had showered me with kisses and love every morning and night."

"And do you remember your mother?"

Something tugged at Rachel's chest as she shook her head. "No, I do not. I was very young when she died. My father's mineshaft collapsed. She was down there at the time." Biting her bottom lip, she glanced over at Benjamin. He still had his back to her but he was sitting keenly upright, unfaltering in his interest in hearing her story. "My father never returned to mining. That's when he settled on the farm. It was Sir Edward's land." She did not know why she felt so compelled to elaborate so much to this arrogant young man, who probably didn't have a care in the world for what had gone before in her life, but she did.

His reflection looked at her thoughtfully before he shifted in his chair and rubbed his chin. "That is a terrible tragedy Rachel. And what of your father?"

"He died a little less than two years ago. It was just the two of us. He and Sir Edward had become friends. Sir Edward was good to us. When my father died, he took me in to his care. He and Lady Cecily will teach me how to be a lady in their service and they have promised to find me a suitor."

"He took you in to his care? You are expected to be taught the ways of becoming a lady, as a servant?" The irony of his statement was not missed.

Rachel couldn't help but feel on the defence. "It is not so uncommon and besides, Sir Edward has been kind to me. He has treated me well."

"But Lady Cecily does not treat you well."

Turning her gaze to the fire, Rachel watched the flames lick and spit as she considered her answer. "No, she can be full of malice at times," she answered truthfully, instantly regretting it. What was to stop him running off and telling the Thornycrofts about how ungrateful and disrespectful she was being?

"Cecily is full of malice all of the time," he acknowledged bitterly, his earlier distaste for his host returning. "Much like my own dear mother. I feel much sympathy for little Samuel. If he survives this plague, he shall either grow up too pampered and babied to make a man of himself, or he shall be forever trying to prove himself to her. There will be no room for him to love another woman."

Rachel did not answer, but pondered his words carefully. She turned them over and over in her mind. She supposed he was right and it saddened her to think that poor little Samuel would be ruined before he had even been given the chance to carve out his life.

The conversation was becoming too deep and Rachel felt in grave danger of causing offence. Pushing herself up from the chair, she told him that she would turn down his bed and heat it with the warming pans. She advised that she would leave the fire until he was ready to retire, but he dismissed her suggestion.

"No need," he said. "I can sort out my own bed and I shall snuff out the fire here. You should go and get some sleep. I expect your day has been, like every other, long and arduous."

Grateful, she turned to hurry from the room before he could change his mind.

"Rachel?" When he called her name, his voice was gentle and soft. The sound of it tripping so elegantly from his tongue made something flutter inside of her.

"Yes?" She licked her lips nervously. Her body was rigid as she waited for whatever he was about to say next.

"Thank you. I have enjoyed your company this evening. You are indeed a fine lady to converse with."

Shocked, she stood, unable to move, as though her boots were weighed down with river stones. Nobody had ever referred to her as 'enjoyable company' or a 'fine lady' before.

Fighting the smile that threatened to curl at her lips, she bit down on her tongue to get a hold of herself. "Thank you," she said, and her fingers curled around the coolness of the door handle as she thought how much she would like to sit with him some more.

Silence had enveloped Thornycroft Hall and she looked back into the blue parlour just once before going to her room.

CHAPTER 12

Mid-November 1665 – Eyam

The walk to Riley farm was an arduous one, uphill and on uneven ground. Even on the coldest of days, the journey would leave a fine film of sweat on Rachel's forehead. Her boots crunched at the lacy layer of frost that was webbed across the ground. The early call of the birds that had not yet disappeared for the winter echoed about the otherwise still landscape. Her lungs burned with both effort and cold as she stopped to catch her breath.

Ahead of her on the path, a murder of crows cawed aggressively at one another, their charcoal beaks showing no mercy to the carcass of a fox that was sprawled across the track that split the fields on either side.

Rachel had never liked crows. Cook always said that to see a lot of them together was a bad sign. Doing her best to ignore the chaotic gruesome feast that they were making for themselves, she pressed on.

The roosts at Thornycroft Hall were not producing and she had been sent for more eggs, with strict instructions to be swift.

Tiredness blurred her vision and fogged her head as she took the path that led to the Hancock's farmhouse. She hadn't slept. Not for any strange, unsettling noises or Samuel's cries, but for thoughts of her unexpected encounter with Master Benjamin in the blue parlour.

Whenever she replayed the soft purr of his voice and the calm authority of his manner, something would stir inside her. Even with his injuries, his confidence in his assertions had not wavered. He defied the social graces that people like Lady Cecily so rigidly abided by and he cared not for her sex, nor her class, he simply wanted to hear her thoughts and opinion.

All night Rachel had been consumed by thoughts of him. It was unusual behaviour for a man like Benjamin, and whilst she could not stop herself from feeling suspicious, a greater part of her was beginning to feel trust.

She wanted so desperately to ask somebody else about Goody Brown, but she had not dared speak of her to any of the other staff for fear of their loose tongues. Sir Edward had made it abundantly clear to her that Goody's presence was to be kept a secret.

After one of her noisy episodes, that he had tried to pass off as a disagreement between Lady Cecily and the wet nurse, Rachel had seen the nauseated look on his face and the worried furrows on his forehead. Goody Brown was a mystery that she was desperate to solve.

The Riley farm was one of the bigger ones in the village, bigger than the croft she and her father had owned. Nestled amongst the magnificent beauty of the surrounding fields, the farmhouse proudly welcomed visitors with stone and wood that had been bleached by almost a century of sun and weathered by the northern elements. It held a rugged charm that always made Rachel feel at home and wanting to curl up and stay for longer.

When Elizabeth Hancock answered the door, it was a relief to be greeted by her friendly face, red from her efforts on the farm and the heat of her cooking.

Even in hard times, Rachel knew that Elizabeth would see to it that her family were kept as well as possible.

The smell of baked bread brought saliva to Rachel's mouth and made her stomach growl. There had been no breakfast for her before she had left Thornycroft Hall and she doubted that anyone would think to save her any.

Elizabeth smiled warmly and opened the door wider so that she could enter the kitchen.

Hesitating, Rachel looked over her shoulder. Lady Cecily would not like it if she were to go inside. She had been told by Cook to make haste and certainly not dally or mingle anywhere that the plague seed could be lingering.

Guessing the reason for her hesitation, Elizabeth gave an impatient click of her tongue. "Never mind what anyone has said to you." Pinching Rachel's forearm, she shook her head. "Just look at you, all skin and bone. You'd think that they would see to it that their staff were looked after properly. I don't suppose you've broken your fast yet?"

Elizabeth all but dragged her across the threshold, ushering her to take a seat at the table where bread, cheese and eggs were laid in front of her.

"Here you are lass." A pot of sweet purple jelly was pushed across the table so that it rested under her nose. "There was a glut of blackberries in September and I made so much jam that it will last us through until spring."

Hungrily, Rachel took a chunk of bread and cheese, devouring half of it before Alice came running in from outside.

Alice carelessly slung the basket that she had been carrying on to the table before rushing to give her a hug. "Oh Rachel, I've missed you." She grabbed a piece of bread for herself and playfully batted at her brother who had come in with her. "Can you stay long? We have so much to catch up on."

Doing her best to swallow her breakfast before answering, Rachel gave a doleful shake of her head. "Cook will be on the warpath if I don't hurry and Lady Cecily would have me out on the street if she were to find out that I had even come inside. She does not like us going anywhere, except for necessity."

"And she is right to be worried." Elizabeth swept at some soot that had blown from the hearth. "But you look like you haven't had a good meal in weeks and I couldn't just send you back there with nothing in your belly. It is quite safe here Rachel."

"Aye you're right mother," Alice agreed. "Besides, it takes longer for us to find the eggs in winter. Those hens are scarce laying them with this frost but I've managed to find just enough for us and with some left over for Rachel to take back with her. Cook would surely rather that you waited for the goods than go back without?" Alice pointed at the flagon of milk and gave her a conspiring wink.

The Hancocks had agreed to supply Thornycroft Hall with their dairy goods and meat for as long as they could, given that folk from the larger market town of Bakewell were no longer keen for Eyam dwellers to attend the Monday market. For families like the Hancocks, it was a way to keep ends meeting with the trade out of the village all dried up.

With a grateful smile, Rachel nodded. "Yes, I'm sure that under the circumstances, Cook will be pleased that I waited, and I doubt Lady Cecily will find out. Besides, she is too busy reminding Sir Edward of her success at giving him a son and heir, unlike his first wife."

Giving a snort of disgust, Elizabeth threw the ash and soot that she had swept up out of the door. She returned the sweeping brush to the fireplace. "That woman will never come close to being the lady that Rosamund Thornycroft was." Sadly, she looked down to the floor. "'Tis such a shame what happened to her. She was a beautiful and kind woman before she took so ill. She would have been devastated to see what is happening to families in the village."

"Did you know her well?" Rachel hadn't realised that Elizabeth had known Lady Rosamund Thornycroft.

"Nobody knew her well Rachel lass, she kept herself to herself and rarely ventured out, but we knew of her and she was always so generous." Her eyes twinkled as she recalled her memories. "A very charitable woman, was Lady Rosamund. Of Italian descent you know." She smiled, as she recounted what she remembered. "Back then the Thornycrofts always donated so kindly to anything going on in the village, but she would rarely appear." The smile dropped and her expression clouded. "I remember near the end, when she was pregnant with her last child. Whenever they attended service, she was always hidden inside her cloaks, which is a shame as she was a great beauty. It was as though she had been sucked dry of her spirit. She didn't look at anyone, wouldn't talk to anyone. Part of her illness I suppose."

"Do you think that it was the demon getting to her soul?" Rachel asked but Elizabeth dismissed the idea.

"Aye, I've heard that superstitious nonsense too. What happened to that poor woman was nought to do with demons. Lost so many babes, I think it ate away at her.

Still, it's shocking what they did. Sent her away for a long time. I daresay that's what broke what was left of her spirit."

"Rachel's seen her ghost, or at the very least heard it." Alice's younger sisters, Anne and Libby, had entered the kitchen and were helping themselves to some bread and cheese. Anne was recounting what she knew of Rachel's experiences at Thornycroft Hall. "It haunts Thornycroft Hall and frightens them all half to death." Crumbs flew from her mouth as she spoke and Libby looked horrified, yet eager to hear more.

"Anne!" Alice hissed before giving Rachel an apologetic look. "You know how she loves a good ghost story." Her face had flushed at the shame of having revealed some of what Rachel had told her of Lady Rosamund's restless spirit, but Rachel was too interested in what Elizabeth knew of the Thornycrofts to care.

"Did you know of a woman called Goody Brown?" Rachel fired the question, taking Elizabeth off guard.

Elizabeth paused and screwed up her face as she thought. Then she shook her head before getting back to skimming the butter that she was making. "I don't remember anyone of that name. Mind you, she had a few different maids, did Lady Rosamund. Unlike Anna, who has been loyal to the core to your Lady Cecily."

Libby was bouncing up and down in her seat, impatient to learn more about Thornycroft Hall's ghosts. "Tell us more about the ghost Rachel. What does it do? What did she look like?"

"Could you see the noose marks around her neck?" Alice added, joining in.

"Alice that is enough." Elizabeth scolded, dropping her skimming knife. "You're old enough to know better than your sisters. Any more talk like that will have you sent down from the table. That goes for all of you." She warned all three sisters, eyeing each of them sternly.

Libby went to protest but Rachel noticed that both Alice and Anne kicked her under the table. They ate in stunted silence after that, with only Elizabeth interjecting with snippets of polite conversation. It was a relief when they had all finished.

Wrapping her shawl tightly about her, Rachel readied herself to set off with Alice who was to help her.

As Elizabeth handed her the basket of eggs, she paused thoughtfully. "Do you know, I think I do remember a woman, turned up here once. She was the last maid to Lady Rosamund. Strange she was. It was near the end, before…." She shook her head sadly, a distant look on her face. "She was all a panic, looking for some particular herbs, although I can't recall what." She wrinkled her nose as she thought. "Anyway, all I remember is that she was all twitching and impatient. I'd not seen much of her before then, but I'd heard news of her and I think her surname was something like 'Brown'. Folk who worked at Thornycroft Hall didn't take to her, said she did things, conjured things, did the work of the Devil."

"The Devil?" Anne's attention had been caught again and she dropped her bread on the table.

Elizabeth's face changed and coloured with regret. "Never mind about that nonsense though. Nobody knew her. Not really. It was a strange time, a sad time for the Thornycrofts. Like Lady Rosamund, the maid kept herself to herself. Never attended service mind. At least, I never set eyes upon her there. Folk turned a blind eye though. See, after Lady Rosamund got sick everyone just left the Thornycrofts to their own business. People are superstitious. Nobody wanted to be touched by what was going on in that house." Her words drifted as she looked out across the glistening ground from the window. "That's all I remember Rachel lass and I've probably said too much." She frowned and turned back to face her. "Why do you ask?"

"I've just heard talk of her, 'tis all." Rachel's answer was hurried, too quick not to stir suspicion, but Elizabeth was distracted with all the worries that the pestilence had brought to the village to press her any further about her interest. She covered the eggs and gave Alice a basket loaded with some cheese, butter and jam before sending them on their way.

As they walked back towards Thornycroft Hall, Rachel noted that the morning frost had not even begun to thaw and the sky looked just as cold, smothered by a low hanging, impenetrable white cloud. Silver and white skeletal limbs of trees clawed out at them from either side of the path and their breath billowed in chilly puffs as thin frozen puddles cracked through to hardened mud beneath their feet. The air carried the bitter smell of frost and cold and Alice's cheeks were pinched red with exposure to the weather.

Rachel wondered how long the poor girl must have been up tending to the animals on the farm before she had arrived. She knew that work for families like the Hancocks was harder when the frosts arrived, their fingers and limbs stinging and stiff from the harsh bite of cold.

"How are you dear Alice? Really?" Rachel asked. It was hard not seeing the girl who she had thought of as a younger sister for so long.

"We are surviving and we are luckier than most, living on the edge of the village, like you." Alice answered, but it was hard to remain positive, especially for a girl so young.

Rachel knew that Alice would have news from the village and although she dreaded to hear it, she needed to know. Many of her friends lived there and it broke her heart to think of them in any pain or grief. "And what of the village? Have you heard any news?"

Alice looked haunted as she carefully picked over her answer. "The Bradshaws and Sheldons have left. Took everything but the staff. Folk are taking in those without any families here in the village. Tom Harwood's Ma turned him away, said she had to think of the littleuns."

Aghast Rachel turned to her. She didn't know Tom Harwood well but she knew his family lived in the neighbouring village of Stoney Middleton because his father was a saddler. Tom had taken work at the Bradshaw stables whilst his older brother had a position with his father. It seemed shocking to Rachel that the boy's family would turn him away. "Where will he go?"

"An old couple in Bretton have taken him in. That's what's happening all over. Folk are taking in folk when they have nowhere else to go if their employers leave. Or they head for the caves." Alice looked out towards the fields. "Some are fleeing there anyway. Say it's better out there. Less chance of the pestilence finding them. 'Tis alright for the rich with their other residences, able to take off whenever they please and escape this misery."

Rachel's stomach turned. What would happen if the Thornycrofts left too? There was every chance that they would. Lady Cecily had made clear her intentions the night before.

As though reading her thoughts, Alice took her arm. "Do you think that the Thornycrofts will leave Eyam?"

Rachel thought back to the heated exchange that she had witnessed between her employers. Sir Edward had been adamant in his resolve to stay. "There's been no talk of leaving Thornycroft Hall. Not for my ears at least."

With a heavy sigh, Alice dragged her feet so that their pace slowed. "They should. You should. Each day that passes seems that there is less and less hope... people dying... friends." With renewed urgency she gripped at Rachel's arm. "My family is stuck here but you're not Rachel. Promise me, if the Thornycrofts depart, you will take the chance to leave too? I can't stand the thought of anyone else...." Tears shining in her eyes, Alice didn't finish her sentence. It was as though there was something she wanted to say, but she couldn't quite bring herself to do so.

"Who else Alice?" Rachel's breath was an icy pillow between them as she pressed her friend to say more, but Alice simply shook her head.

"I'm being silly when I should just be enjoying spending time with my best friend. But promise me Rachel, promise you will leave if you get the opportunity?" They were approaching the house and she looked out across the fields that yawned down towards Stoney Middleton. "I wish we could."

Horrified at the idea of leaving her friends, Rachel shook her head. "I won't be going anywhere Alice."

"Ma says you ought to. She says that if the Thornycrofts leave they should take their staff. That it's as good as murder not to."

Shuddering, Rachel stared at the haunted look on Alice's face. She was suddenly older, no longer the little sister figure that she had been for so long. There were things she had seen and heard that no child should be privy to. "Your Ma said that to you?"

Glumly, Alice shook her head. "Not to me, to Pa. I couldn't sleep and I...."

"You were eavesdropping." She hadn't meant to sound so accusing.

Alice spun to face her defensively. "Doesn't matter what you call it, I know what I heard and ma was scared. We all are." Then the tears began to flow, fat and unabated as her shoulders shook. "I'm so scared Rachel."

Putting her basket down, Rachel pulled Alice in to a hug before stopping herself and pulling back. If anyone from the house saw what she was doing, she wouldn't be allowed to return. "God has sent us an early frost Alice. This winter will be a cold one, killing off the plague seed. You'll see."

Gently edging away so that they were at an arm's length, Rachel smiled. "Come on. I've got something to show you." She gestured for Alice to follow her as she arced around past the servants' entrance and to the gardens.

Teeth chattering, neither of them spoke as they hurried through the gnarled and twisted twigs that had bloomed with roses only a few months earlier. They rounded upon the shivering trees within the little orchard. When they reached the little mound just beyond them, they stopped.

Rachel glanced at her and saw the realisation light Alice's face. "This is Lady Rosamund's grave. This is where she is buried."

Alice's eyes were still shimmering with tears as she looked down at the uneven earth that was spun silver with fine threads of frost woven across it. "How do you know?" she whispered.

"I just do." Rachel knelt and touched the ground beneath her. It was hard and cold. She drew back her hand and looked up. "I come here when I can, to pay my respects. Nobody else does. It's like she's been forgotten. No mark of what life she had. Nothing to say that she was once loved. Her fate in death is like my own mother's…" she trailed off and looked back down at the ground. "Nobody deserves that."

"Have you heard or seen anything else? In the house?" Alice's voice was fervent with curiosity.

"Sometimes." Rachel made sure that she kept her voice low, lest anybody else was about. "There's a woman who came, just before the plague. She's still here now. She knows my secret. She knows that I stole into the room filled with Lady Rosamund's paintings. She hasn't told anyone mind. She stalks about the house in the shadows and sometimes, at night, she makes such a dreadful noise." Rachel noted the intrigue on Alice's face as all thoughts and worries of the pestilence were pushed aside for a few blessed minutes. She stood up and leaned closer, her voice little more than a whisper. "Sir Edward was so disturbed when she knocked at the door. She stood there bold as brass. Both he and Lady Cecily paled, as though they had seen a ghost."

"Who do you think she is?" Alice asked.

"Her name is Goody Brown. Sir Edward has asked that I do not speak of her to anyone."

"You're telling me all about her," Alice pointed out.

Rachel stood up and brushed away the icy damp from her skirts "You can keep a secret," she said. "I trust you."

Alice bowed her head. "I'm sorry I told Libby and Anne about your ghost."

Rachel smiled at her. "Well as long as you don't mention Goody. You would as good as lose me my job here."

Alice nodded. "Cross my heart." She drew a cross over her chest with her fingers. "Have you heard anything more of the ghost?"

"We hear her all the time, although it is hard to know which noises are made by Goody and which ones are the work of the ghost. It is like her presence has reawakened the spirit of Lady Rosamund."

"Or the demon," Alice added, running her tongue over the cracks and chaps of her lips.

"Catherine Mompesson thinks I should not speak of that."

"Ma would agree. She doesn't believe in any of it."

Rachel shrugged. "I've heard the noises, but I've been saying my prayers and it has not been as bad of late."

"Maybe the prayers are what keeps it away."

Turning back towards the barren hedgerows of the rose garden, Rachel gave a wistful smile. "I sometimes wonder if they are one and the same – the ghost and the demon. Nobody talks of it but we all know. Johnny, the lad who works in the stables, said that Lady Cecily's mare, the one that kicked Master Benjamin, well he said that it just went wild. Startled by something unseen, he said. We all know that Johnny thought it was something to do with Lady Rosamund's ghost. We thought the same ourselves, but Lady Cecily silenced him with the most dreadful punishment. Master Benjamin does not remember anything of the accident." At the very feel of his name on he lips, Rachel felt her face flush.

Too caught up in their supernatural conversation, Alice didn't notice. "That's awful." She looked thoughtfully at the ground. "Do you think you will find out who this Goody Brown woman is? Do you think she hears it all too?"

"I wouldn't know. I have only seen her a few times and she scarcely speaks."

"Well I don't know how anyone could abide to live in the same house as a ghost, especially not one with such a dreadful story attached to it."

"I have to live here though. There was nought much for me to choose from when Pa passed Alice. Ghost or no ghost, it's a roof over my head and prospects for me at the very least. I am to learn what it is to run a household and they shall find me a suitor, a merchant from the city perhaps."

Sometimes Rachel thought that, even for her young age, Alice could be quite naïve. How could she have turned down the opportunity? She had no money in her pocket, no skills beyond the farm and an education that would only serve a man well. "Besides, Pa wanted me to stay with the Thornycrofts. The croft belonged to Sir Edward. He and Pa were friends. Good friends at that."

"Pah! Folk like us are not friends with folk like the Thornycrofts." Alice exclaimed, screwing her face up.

They stopped as Rachel realised that they had meandered off the path and circled back towards the grave. "There she is again," she said softly and reached to touch Alice on the arm. "Lady Rosamund and her baby."

They both stopped and looked down. Alice reached down to lay a hand to the crystalline ground.

Neither of them spoke for some time, and when Alice looked up, her eyes were shiny once again. "Hannah Rowland passed at the turn of the month." The words were a burden to her and she stooped with the weight of them as they tripped from her tongue. "I did not know how to tell you."

"Hannah Rowland?" Rachel's throat constricted as she repeated the name. Surely she had misheard what her friend had said? Hannah Rowland was from the village. She was young like them, full of cheer. There was too much life in her to be gone, but Alice confirmed that she had heard correctly by nodding, her expression sombre.

Feeling her knees buckle, Rachel sank to the ground. Hannah Rowland had been another of her friends from the village. If Hannah Rowland had ever seen Rachel in the village with the kitchen girl, Hannah, she had always jovially referred to her as 'Manor Hannah' and it had always brought a smile to the little scullery maid's face. The very thought of never crossing paths, or exchanging light hearted conversation with Hannah Rowland again, weighed impossibly upon Rachel. "Why?" she cried out, but she needed no answer. The plague was cruel, paying no discrimination to age or status. It could strike any person at any time. "Is she really gone? Hannah Rowland?"

Alice's tears were free flowing, drenching puffy cheeks. She reached out to take Rachel's hands. "Hannah has gone," she confirmed. "So that is why you must leave if you can Rachel. If the Thornycrofts leave, you must go with them. You must secure your escape from here. Promise me?"

Nodding, Rachel stared at the pitiful mound in front of them and at the bleak landscape beyond the garden wall. Clouds, swollen with the threat of snow, were hanging overhead, their presence suffocating.

She used to think that, like her own parents, Lady Rosamund Thornycroft had been unlucky with her untimely death. Now she thought that it could be deemed a blessing. None of them would have to suffer what the rest of the village of Eyam was suffering. People dying, people in agony, people waiting to see who would be next, or who else they would lose from their lives.

******

There was no further talk of leaving Thornycroft Hall. Lady Cecily had remained in a sulk for days, snapping at everyone, even Anna.

Her mood had unsettled Samuel, whose cries disturbed the whole house. His wet nurse said that he had a problem with his stomach. That the way he twisted and writhed and brought his chubby little knees to his chest meant that he was in pain.

Rachel had been instructed to make up a tincture for the wet nurse, with camomile. With the knowledge that ginger root was good for the stomach, she had set about finding some and was about to pare it with her little work knife when a hand fell down on hers.

"Nay lass. He is too young to have ginger passed to him. He will be made sicker." Goody had entered the room soundlessly. There was a small package of herbs wrapped in rags on the table beside her and she was looking down at Rachel's work with concern in her eyes. "Here, let me," she offered, taking the knife and some of her own herbs from the rags.

Elizabeth Hancock's words rang a warning in Rachel's head and she went to grab the knife back. "No, Lady Cecily has instructed me to make up a tincture for the wet nurse. She will not be pleased if anyone else has touched it."

Without hesitation, Goody took the knife back from her. "Then she need never know. You'll see," she said, smiling. "The bairn will be soothed in no time."

There was something disconcerting about her manner, the way she held the knife and the way that her beady eyes searched Rachel's. Her words were kind, but that was not to say that her intentions were.

Rachel made to retrieve the knife again and this time, there was a fire in Goody's eyes when she looked up. "You'll do as I ask and let me get on with it, lest we all suffer more without sleep for the pitiful wails from that child." A smile appeared then, crooked and rotten. "You'll see. You'll see."

Without saying anything more, Rachel waited for her to finish and took the tincture, deciding that she would throw it away and start it again later, when Goody had disappeared.

She was fretting over the thought of Goody 'conjuring things' and 'doing the work of the devil' when Anna passed her, flushed from the stress of the baby and Lady Cecily.

"There you are." She snatched the bottle from Rachel's hand before she could protest. "God's teeth I need some peace and quiet, we all do. I shall rub this on his gums and belly, as well as give it to the wet nurse. Lady Cecily is already threatening that she shall need to use my breast should this wailing not stop. I won't be bitten and chewed red raw. I won't." She hurried off upstairs, still fretting audibly as she did so.

Rachel never saw Goody re-emerge from the stillroom, but it was empty when she returned.

She stopped, taken by surprise at the way Goody had left everything. The leftover herbs had been neatly chopped, pressed and crushed, ready for her to make the next tincture. Then she noticed that some more had been left for her: dill, camomile and fennel. There was a small hothouse where they grew herbs, but Rachel had not realised that dill or fennel grew there. It was pitiful in the winter months and she relied on other sources for her herbs, but Goody had managed to produce them – or conjure them, she reminded herself and shuddered.

Nevertheless, by nightfall Samuel's cries had calmed and Rachel used the herbs to make more. Three doses a day for the wet nurse and a little to rub on Samuel's little tummy. Even Lady Cecily appeared marginally grateful, or at least, she wasn't as rude as usual when her path crossed Rachel's.

She would need to find a way of getting more of those herbs. With the neighbouring villages shying away from everyone in Eyam, the only way of receiving any required goods would be at the boundary stone where supplies were being left by the neighbouring villages, in return for coins.

CHAPTER 13

Late November 1665 – Eyam

When the first of the snow clouds billowed over the village, a letter arrived at Thornycroft Hall. One of the staff had picked it up at the boundary stone. It bore the Belgrave seal and was addressed to Master Benjamin Belgrave.

The letter had been propped up by the empty vase in the hallway and had caused quite a stir amongst the staff. "Perhaps it is his parents begging him to return home?" Anna had mused as she had placed it on a silver tray with instructions that Rachel should take it to Benjamin at supper.

Benjamin had taken more to eating within his chamber. It had become custom as Sir Edward was always locked away in his study and Lady Cecily made no effort to socialise with him any further than she was forced to. She did not like looking at the ugliness of his injuries. She had never liked to look at anything that was less than pleasing on the eye. With her blatant refusal to offer him any company or personal time, and with Sir Edward being so distracted with other matters, Master Benjamin had begun to retreat back into his chamber, venturing out only when required. Rachel thought that it was like his transience was making him melt into the shadows of the grand house, so that he was just another ghost.

Lady Cecily's disgust for his injuries was no secret. On the rare occasion that he had accompanied them for breakfast or dinner, Rachel and the other staff had noticed how she would do all that she could not to look in the direction of his face. On her own, she wore a permanent expression of twisted horror.

Over the last few weeks, it had been enough to deter him from his recovery progress. In Rachel's opinion, it had even made him regress.

He wore his hair loose and his shoulders hunched, as though to hide himself. There was nobody to speak kind, consoling words to him and from the fleeting conversations that he had entrusted her confidence in, he had made it clear that he knew of how his mother had snubbed him.

On the morning of the Belgraves' departure, Rachel had overheard Lady Belgrave weeping to Lady Cecily about the fact that all of her plans for her handsome son winning the hand of one of England's most beautiful noble girls, with a fine dowry to her name, were surely dashed. She had cried that he was no longer her handsome golden boy, that he would be viewed as a monster and no woman would want to look at him, let alone wish to have children with him. Even Lady Cecily had appeared shocked at Lady Belgrave's appalling reaction to the situation.

When she had left, she had been noticeably fussing over Bernadette, significantly more than she had upon their arrival. There was no doubt in Rachel's mind that Bernadette would become the new Benjamin.

Now Benjamin was becoming akin to a shunned, mistreated animal; holed away and untrusting, snapping and snarling constantly.

The trust he had started to put in Rachel had been revoked. It was terribly sad and extremely frustrating, but over the weeks Rachel ignored his bad moods, choosing instead to take a seat in his room and read psalms to him until he would settle and sink back into his chair, lulled by the sound of her voice or simply pleased for the company that she brought him.

Sometimes his eyelids would flutter shut and his head loll forward or back with the gentle purr of his restful sleep. On occasion that he did fall asleep, she would always cover him with blankets and squeeze his hand for comfort, marvelling at how soft and smooth the skin was in comparison to her father's or Alice's father's hands, which had been roughened and aged with hard work and the elements.

Rachel held the silver tray and looked down at the letter with the Belgrave seal. It was surprising, she thought, how despondent and dashed of all happiness she felt as she considered what the content of that letter might be. If Anna's thoughts were correct, Benjamin would be leaving imminently to return to his family residence.

Despite the knowledge that he would at least be safe from the threat of plague, a surprising heaviness clutched at her heart as she treaded up the staircase to his chamber. It was the same feeling that had been gnawing away at her since she had first clapped eyes on the letter earlier that day.

Knocking gently on his door, she waited with the tray that carried the book of psalms and his meal.

There was a grunt from inside. It was a noise that she had come to recognise the meaning of, one that indicated it was acceptable for her to enter.

Keeping the tray expertly balanced, she opened the door and then placed it on the desk.

Hunched, with his long fair hair covering his face, he motioned with his hand that she could leave.

His dismissive gesture did not offend her. On the contrary, it had become custom between them; he would wave her away, indicating that she was not required to do any further work on his account, hoping really that she would stay and keep him company for a short while longer.

She paused. He had not noticed the letter, or at least if he had, he made no acknowledgement of it.

In a way she was glad and she decided that tonight, she would take him up on his gesture of dismissal as the thought of reading psalms to him, knowing that he was likely to be leaving any morning soon, was more than she could stand. So she nodded subserviently before busying herself with taking the warming pan to his bed whilst he ate.

When she was done, she turned to leave. From the corner of her eye, she noticed that something had fallen to the floor. Stooping to pick it up, she saw that it was the letter. She held it out for him. "Master Belgrave, you dropped this."

"Burn it." His throat sounded scratchy and raw from lack of speaking. When he addressed her, he didn't bother to lift his head to make eye contact.

"But it carries the Belgrave crest at the top." Tracing the wax seal with her nail, she assumed that he must have been mistaken as to who the sender was.

"The words on that parchment mean nothing to me. Burn it," he growled, keeping his face hidden.

"If you are sure Master Belgrave?" Folding the letter to keep its content private, she went to leave the room and then paused, still facing away from him as she looked towards the door. "I have brought a tincture. I heard that you had complaint of stomach cramps earlier today. I added some mint to soothe and cool."

Pulling the door open, she went to leave. "It is late, so I shan't stay to read to you tonight. I have left the book on the tray along with the tincture and your meal."

"Why do you care?" The question caught her off guard. It was not asked in a petulant way, more a genuinely intrigued one.

At the threshold that separated the bedroom from the corridor, she froze. "I'm begging your pardon?" Apprehensive to engage in further conversation of this nature, for fear of the lump in her throat catching her voice, she hoped that he would simply withdraw back into his silent world of misery.

"I asked you why you should even care? I am confoundedly rude to you every night and yet you stay to read to me, and here you are bringing me a tincture for my pains." His voice had an unnerving calm to it, as though everything could change any moment.

Running her fingers along the edge of the Belgrave mark on the letter, Rachel searched for the right words. She had no idea of what those would be. Instead, she settled on the simple truth. "You are a guest here Master Belgrave and under our care. It is my duty to care for any soul staying here at Thornycroft Hall. It must be hard for a man such as yourself…." There it was again, her loose tongue. She couldn't seem to help herself from saying exactly what was on her mind when she was with him, but she did not want to rub salt into the wound, remind him of his horrific injuries.

From behind her there was a grainy noise and she realised that it was laughter, building in the back of his throat, sarcastic and mean. "Tell me, what exactly must be hard for a man such as myself?" He placed such bitter emphasis on the end of his sentence that it was clear how much her words had offended him.

Swallowing hard, Rachel felt her mouth go dry. "All I meant was that your family is so far away and loneliness is a terrible thing."

The grainy rattle in Benjamin's throat exploded into a roar of ironic laughter. "My family cares not a fig for me any longer. I am to become accustomed to this isolation. Mother fears that I will no longer attract the great beauties of noble England, worthy of continuing the Belgrave name. It would seem that everyone is aware of that fact, even the servants. Do you not think that I have heard the whispers?"

Her eyes trained on the dimly lit corridor beyond the doorway as she floundered for an appropriate response and failed.

Benjamin continued with his rant, unable to disguise the emotion in his voice. "The grave fact of the matter is that dear old mother, who cares for nothing but appearance, money and status, is quite correct. Who should want to marry this? " He pressed an angry finger into his chest. "Who should want to wake next to a monster every day? Even you can not bring yourself to look at me properly."

Her mind racing, Rachel wished that he would just say something rude and shout at her to get out so that she could leave. Now she was required to reply. "That's not true." There was no conviction in her response because he was right, but for the wrong reasons. She couldn't look at him because her heart was breaking at the very notion that it might be the last night that she was to see him, the last night that she should ever get the opportunity to speak with him, serve him, be with him.

"Is that so? Then why can you not turn to look at my face?" There, he said it. He was as worried about the look of his injuries as Lady Cecily and his mother were. How could he not understand that, in the grand scheme of things, the way he looked was of little importance?

"Your face is never in plain view to be seen. How can I be expected to see something that my eyes are guarded from every day?" It was insolent of her but she didn't care. People in Eyam were losing loved ones and dying from unspeakable horror every day and this spoiled young man was complaining about the scars of survival. Rachel imagined that the Syddalls, Rowlands and Hawksworths would have happily traded places with the scarred remains of Benjamin Belgrave if it meant that they had time to spend living with their loved ones once again.

"Words. You can not even turn to face me," he hissed and even though her back was turned, she thought she heard him raise himself to standing as the sound of his stick finding purchase with the floor echoed about the room.

Pivoting, Rachel spun around to face him defiantly. She pressed the door closed behind her so that they were truly alone.

He kept his head bowed, eyes low so that she could not see his face. Bent over his stick, he looked withered and wasted, his shoulders all but dragging him to the floor. This was not the man that she knew him to be. It was not the man who had found her chopping wood, who had invited her to keep him company in the blue parlour. This was a broken man.

Forgetting herself, her voice was suddenly filled with confidence. "I should like to see your face."

Refusing to raise his head, he wobbled beneath his weight for a moment before speaking. "Just go."

"I should like to see your face." Testing him, she took a step forwards, her words firm.

"Leave."

"I - should - like - to - see - your – face," she commanded as she took another pace towards him.

Beneath the bitter façade of this man, she could sense the sensitive child who ached for the love and affections of his mother once again. It pained her to see somebody reduced to such hopelessness and self-loathing.

He did not respond and he did not look up, but her courage had taken on a new lease of life.

Reaching out, her fingertips grazed the thick curtain of blonde hair that was hanging loosely in front of him. She could hear the quickening of his breath as she approached and she feared him. Rachel was afraid of what he kept hidden behind that shiny golden veil. She feared the temper that might be unleashed upon her for having the audacity to approach him like this, and she feared the way her heart was beating wildly in her chest.

"Master Benjamin?" When she addressed him, her voice was little more than a whisper. "I should like to see."

At last her fingers found contact with the line of his jaw and she felt the peppering of stubble, a mixture of rough and soft.

He did not move.

Tracing along from the angular edge of his jawbone, she let her fingers work their way across, feeling the cushion of his cheek until the warmth of his breath was upon them.

Reason screamed at her to stop. This behaviour was stepping well beyond the boundaries of a serving girl's place. A voice in her head warned her that her position would be in jeopardy if she took things any further. Raw instinct compelled her to continue.

She pressed her fingertips against the plump softness of his lips. They were still wet from the wine she had brought him and she thought she could smell its sweetness on his breath. Allowing her fingers to explore further, she wondered if he was aware of how her hands were beginning to tremble as she reached the outer curve of his mouth.

Pausing, she held her breath, waiting for him to grab her by the arm and throw her out of his room, full of accusations and insults.

He didn't move. In fact, it was as though he too had started to hold his breath, waiting for her fingers to move across and upwards.

She began to follow the line of his cheekbone. Soft skin crowned the stubble and then there was a ridge, a jagged, raised line of flesh knitted cumbersomely together. Velvety softness mingled with a coarse leathery texture. Part of her wanted to pull her fingers away but instead, she spread her palm and placed it gently across his whole cheek.

Slowly, she eased his head upwards until she was looking into the clear brilliant turquoise of his eyes.

The kick to his face from Lady Cecily's mare had shattered bone and scarred him appallingly, but miraculously, the hoof had missed his eyes, which looked all the more beautiful as they shone above the ruined, once handsome face. There was kindness in those eyes and depth that she hadn't noticed before.

With her hand pressed to his disfigured features, she stared at him. She had no words. Rachel did not know how to describe the way she felt as she held the gaze of this angry and hurt young man, but the feeling that fluttered between her stomach and chest was not one that she had expected.

Neither of them spoke. Their faces were inches apart. Eyes locked.

It was the sound of Samuel's distant cry from the nursery that broke the moment.

Flustered, Rachel pulled her hand away with apology and hurried from the room, leaving Master Benjamin staring after her.

CHAPTER 14

Present Day – Eyam

Her exposed skin felt the cool tickle of grass blades as Kate stirred. Dusk was falling swiftly and she was alone and confused in the field that she had passed out in. Thoughts that seemed so familiar and yet so foreign to her, drifted in and out of focus.

This was Riley Farm. It was where the Hancocks lived and worked. She remembered that the ground beneath her had been frosted hard. If she looked across the field, she should see the farm just beyond where she was lying.

Turning her head, she rubbed the blur from her eyes. There was no farm, no animals, just fields.

With a groan, she tried to pull the memories back but they were disappearing in the smog that filled her head.

Then she thought of the bogwood box that she had found at Thornycroft. Something inside her bristled impatiently. The jewellery in that box was precious, invaluable. It meant something sentimental and she had to protect it, nobody else could find out about it.

Pushing herself up with a jolt, she had the urge to go and hide it from untrustworthy hands.

A woman's face flashed in front of her mind's eye. It was puffy and white with blotches of rosacea and watchful eyes. Somebody had told her something about that woman. She rummaged through her thoughts, searching, trying to remember.

'The Conjurer'. That was the term that somebody had used to describe the woman with the puffy face and watchful eyes. She was not to be trusted.

An imprint of the woman had been burned into Kate's brain. It was a face that made her heart plunge with devastating familiarity, although she couldn't quite place it.

Rubbing the back of her neck she looked around, trying to work out where she was. It was growing dark and the cold air of evening was coiling about her body, licking uncomfortably at any bared patches of her skin.

From somewhere not too far away came the excited whinny of a horse. A breeze ruffled her hair and she tried to stand, clutching her stomach as she did so, nausea and dizziness threatening to make her fall again.

Patchy images of people continued to float around her head, hiding in dark crevices, waiting for another opportunity to be discovered. Desperately, she rooted around her mind for them but they were hidden too well.

Spinning around, she tried to dampen the fear that was squeezing at her heart, making it pulse faster.

Things looked different to how she expected them to look. Where was she? How had she got here?

Off to her left she could see a distant trail of lights. Houses: warm, cosy, welcoming. People would be sitting nursing cups of tea or watching television, oblivious to the lonely figure lost in the fields on the crest of the village.

Her head began to spin and she pressed her fingers to her head, massaging in circular motions. She breathed. In and out. Inhale and exhale. Then it all came back to her.

Whirling around, she could just about make out the silhouette of the stone circle that formed the little graveyard.

She was in Eyam, staying at her Great Aunt Edie's house. She had taken a walk to the Riley Graves. It was one of the many tourist spots in the village, telling the tragic tale of when the plague hit.

There had still been plenty of daylight when she had made her way up the track, before she had passed out.

Another wave of nausea washed over her as she stumbled towards the wall that separated the field from the track leading back down to the village. There was no way she was going to waste time feeling along it to find the gap. She climbed, hoisting her leg up, catching her foot and grazing her knee on the stones as she did so. She didn't care. Despite its peaceful feel, it wasn't a place that she wanted to be alone when the heavy curtain of night completely fell.

Back on the pathway, she hurried down towards the village, straining to see through the opaque veil of black that was drawing in all around her.

There was a sharp cracking noise off to her left and she remembered the trees. Almost losing her footing, her feet skidded on the gravel. Telling herself that the noise was just a squirrel or a bird in the trees, she persevered. The path felt like it was dipping downwards forever. Silently, she prayed for the bottom to come.

There was another noise from the trees and the sound of little feet scurrying. With a frightened whimper, she picked up the pace, arms out for balance.

Kate didn't care how stupid she looked. She just wanted to get away from the hollow black hole that she felt she had been thrown into.

When at last the gravel path spilled into the top of the village, she gave a cry of relief, but she didn't stop running. She ran past the houses, new and old. She ran down the pathway that stretched on beyond an area known as the Lydgate graves, ignoring the unsettling sensation in her head that triggered more unwanted and impossible memories from hundreds of years before. She ran non-stop until she reached the gate of Thornycroft.

The faces of people who had been drifting on the periphery of her consciousness had completely hidden themselves now, and as she neared the front door, she doubled over, emptying her stomach into a bed of Dahlias.

CHAPTER 15

Present Day – Buxton Nursing Home

Edie was sitting in her room, her body as still as stone. The pale blue curtains were tied back, giving her the perfect view of the neatly manicured lawns and well-pruned flowerbeds outside. Soon an inky sky would enshroud the garden, hiding its prettiness from view so that shadows could dance across it and stretch into ominous shapes.

Blinking back the tears, she thought of Kate alone inside Thornycroft. At least Kate thought that she was alone there. That was something to be grateful for.

Curling her toes inside her dusky peach slippers, Edie thought about the long dark hallway and the top of the staircase that she had fallen down.

Something had been there with her when she had fallen.

Of course, they had all thought that she was confused at first, when she had said it. So she had insisted. Then they had taken her seriously.

The police had been called but she had known that they wouldn't find anything. It would all point back at either a senile old woman, or worse, accusations thrown at her good friends. So she had lied. She had told them that they were right, that she had been confused, the shock of it all getting to her, and that she had simply tripped.

Something in that house had wanted to stop her research though. As unorthodox as her methods had been, she had been getting too close to the truth.

There was nobody who could help her and she wished that she hadn't even started with the damned Ouija Board that she and Francesca had thought would be such fun to try. Now it would never stop.

At first she had thought that uncovering the truth of what had happened to those spirits, whose memories she had stirred, would be the only way to stop it. The more she had learned though, the worse it had become.

Francesca had wanted her to stop. Obsessed, Edie had deceived her, continued with what they had started.

Then there had been Nick. He had asked her if he could paint Thornycroft. Naturally, she had been delighted to accommodate his request. Only, Nick had become just as distant and as obsessed as she had been. He had been very private about what he was sketching. Then one day she had caught sight of his pad. The images on there had sent an unearthly shudder through her bones. He was seeing what she was seeing and it made everything seem so much more real.

Her insistence on finding out what had happened all those centuries before had meant that she had dragged him into the whole sorry mess too. It meant that he would be in danger, unless she did something to stop it all.

Squeezing her eyes shut, she choked back a sob. Because of her, her two good friends had suffered and now her great niece was involved. Her only saving grace was that when Kate had visited, she hadn't appeared to know anything. That, at least, had given her some level of comfort. Then Edie had seen something dreadful.

It had happened when Kate had visited with Francesca earlier that morning. How relieved and secretly glad she had been to see her best friend with her niece. Francesca would look out for Kate, she had thought. As long as Kate had no idea about what lurked at Thornycroft, she would surely be fine, she had told herself. Then behind her, in the mirror, Edie had seen the air moving, vapour like. Ever so faintly, a figure had begun to take shape. It had hovered for a few seconds, a spectral spiral of dust. Then it had disappeared, leaving her questioning whether she had even seen it at all.

Guilt pressed at her, weakening her arms and legs, making her hands shake and her head throb.

She was too frightened to return to Thornycroft and yet, she wasn't prepared to let Kate reside there all alone.

All she wanted was for Kate to get back in her car and return home, where she would be safe. Then the house could be sold and Edie could forget it all.

She knew that she had appeared unkind and harsh, but was certain that if her friends and Kate were distanced from her, then they would all be safe from the threat of whatever was waiting in the old house. There was conflict there, conflict, misery and death.

Edie had felt as though something had wanted to show her things, enable her to unveil the truth. There was a stronger force at work though. Whatever it was that was skulking amidst the shadows, it did not want to be exposed. It had resided there with its secrets for centuries and a silly old woman was no match for it. That much had been clear when she had fallen. She hadn't been pushed as such, but it was as good as.

In her waking moments she struggled to remember exactly what had happened, but in her dreams, the memory plagued her.

Since being in hospital, every morning she would wake from the same nightmare, sweat lining her top lip and the sheets damp from the fear that oozed from her pores.

Something had rushed past her on that staircase, a force that couldn't be seen. There had been the most unearthly stench and then she had lost her footing.

Before passing out, she had seen it at the top of the stairs, shadowlike: a woman tall and willowy, with eyes that looked through a knot of hair.

Those eyes were the epitome of death and horror. They had glared at her and she had thought that they had looked so empty and devoid of humanity. It was as though those eyes had been hollowed out.

With a helpless sob, Edie closed the curtains and turned to stare dully at the pine door. No matter how frightened she felt, she could not leave Kate alone in Thornycroft. She would have to go back and sort things.

"The day after tomorrow," Magdalena had said brightly earlier that evening, holding the promise of discharge papers. With a clean bill of health from the Doctor, she could be discharged in just two days.

Edie had been prepared to do anything to stay. Now she realised that it was in her great niece's best interests to go.

Picking up the brush from the dresser, she pulled the soft bristles through her hair. She would have to toughen up and find the conviction inside to bring the old Edie back. She would return to Thornycroft and she would make things right again.

CHAPTER 16

Present Day – Eyam

Pushing the scrambled eggs about her plate, Kate stared into space with bleary eyes. It was nearly eleven in the morning and she had slept in late after struggling to get to sleep for being so ill. Her stomach was still churning from being so violently sick.

It had been a difficult journey home from the Riley Graves, where the Hancocks were buried. Darkness had chased her every step, making her feel as though she would never make it.

The sickness hadn't stopped until the early hours, when at last, too exhausted to keep her eyes open, she had fallen asleep with the lights on.

When she had awoken, her stomach muscles were aching and her mouth felt as though it was full of sawdust.

Giving up on the eggs, she sipped at her tea and attempted some dry toast before her mobile burst into life in front of her. An unknown number made her hesitate before picking it up.

It was a bright and melodious voice on the other end. Magdalena.

The call was short but Kate's mood and physical state had greatly improved by the time she set the phone back down onto the table. Edie was coming home.

As the reality hit, it dawned on her that she was completely unprepared. She would need to sort out a temporary downstairs bedroom, get the shopping done, clean the house and cook a welcome home meal.

Less than an hour later, Francesca was on hand with an assortment of scented candles, flowers and a lavish looking cream faux fur throw. "I was sure I had some cushions to match," she said as she let herself in through open the front door. "I shall just have to rummage about in the loft when I get back home. Anything more than five years old, Graham chucks it up there or in the bin."

She let the bundle of accessories drop to the floor before pulling something out of her bag. "I brought a spare pair of marigolds. Where should I…?" With a melodramatic pause, she threw the gloves down and rushed over to Kate, who had appeared from the dining room holding a duster and polish. "What on earth happened Kate? You look dreadful."

Managing a weak smile, Kate couldn't hide how delicate she still felt. She wasn't at all surprised by the reaction her appearance had invoked. Heavy circles outlined the hollows of her eyes and her skin was still a ghastly grey pallor. "Just a bit under the weather last night. Don't worry, I don't think I'm catching."

Rushing to her aid, Francesca led her to the lounge. "A bit under the weather? Nonsense, you look bloody dreadful. Take a moment to sit down. Shall I get you a water?"

Shaking her head, Kate insisted that it was nothing a long hot soak wouldn't fix and so after they had finished the cleaning, collapsed the dining table and set up the sofa bed in the dining area, Francesca indulged in making the room look cosy whilst Kate had her bath. When she emerged half an hour later, she felt much more human.

With a sharp intake of breath, she ran an impressed eye over the room that Francesca had transformed.

Candles had been arranged in a staggered formation of height along the marble of the disused open fireplace. A vase of vibrant red and orange flowers was resting on the middle section of the folded dining table. A large lamp had been placed by the bed and the cream throw she had brought with her was neatly folded across the bottom.

Delighted, Kate hugged her. "It's amazing. Aunt Edie will be so pleased."

Shrugging, Francesca's smile faded. "I'm not so sure. She really wasn't very pleased with me yesterday."

"Aunt Edie hasn't been herself, but if she's agreed to come home, that's a big step in the right direction."

Agreeing, Francesca crossed her arms over her chest and hugged herself. "I don't think she can quite forgive me over the business with that Ouija Board." Her face crumpled and she turned to face Kate. "She's been such a good friend to me. I'd hate to lose her friendship. She's a truly wonderful woman."

Giving her forearm a reassuring squeeze, Kate smiled. "And you've been a great friend to her too. You have a heart of gold. Look at how lovely you've been with me and we've only just met. Come on, I'll put the kettle on so that we can talk about this party that you're planning."

Declining the invitation graciously, Francesca explained that she had to go and give her horse, Jack, some exercise.

Checking her watch, Kate decided that heading into Bakewell to get the big supermarket shop complete was probably the next priority anyway. Given the bath had much improved how she was feeling, it seemed like a wasted opportunity not to. Besides, it would be a good way to get to see a bit more of the surrounding area.

The nearby town of Bakewell was heaving with traffic and people. It had taken her a good twenty minutes to even find a parking space, and after she had put the shopping in the boot of the car, she decided to have a look around the town.

Novelty shops of all kinds were nestled amongst the bustling streets. In between them were coffee shops and tearooms, each of them promising the best Bakewell pudding or tart.

Children rushed passed her, holding their parents' hands and licking ice cream in the hot sun, whilst older tourists ambled along slowly, stopping every so often to view the gaudy window displays of china, patisseries, cheeses and kitchenware.

It was a pretty town, if not a little too busy for Kate. The irony wasn't lost on her though. Here she was, feeling like the place was too manic, and yet her flat had been in North London, where even in the early hours of morning, it was busy. Things had certainly changed. Maybe, she mused, she might think about moving her next contract up North and having a more permanent change of scenery.

Navigating towards a bridge that yawned right across the foaming frantic rush of water from the River Wye, she took in all the lovelocks that couples had clipped around it and felt the familiar tug of sadness that would always pull at her when anything reminded her of Richard.

It still felt somewhat surreal, but she had to put what had happened with him behind her.

Contemplating again about a fresh start, she toyed with a bright crimson lock and wondered what had happened to the couple that had put it there.

It was later than she had realised when she returned to Thornycroft. After packing the shopping away, she paused to think about the diary and the box. In the light of day, with enough distance between the events of the previous evening and an ordinary day, she felt brave enough to succumb to the intrigue. She hadn't stopped to really inspect what had been inside the box and she was keen to read more of what Edie had logged. It might give her a clue as to why she was so frightened.

After fetching them, she poured herself a smoothie and wandered into the back garden.

It was peaceful outside and she pulled up one of the disused wrought iron chairs. Large patches of green paint had peeled away to reveal a stark, cold looking grey metal beneath. Kate decided that during her stay she would reinvigorate the garden furniture and buy some cushions to put on the chairs.

Sipping her drink, she looked at the box, running her fingers along the grooves of the design. She paused at the lip. Opening it before had coincided with her passing out. She didn't want the same scenario to happen again.

Tapping her fingernail against the edge, she looked at it thoughtfully before setting it aside and reaching for the diary. She would be better off learning more about what Edie had been up to before the fall.

It fell open on the page Kate had last read from. In spite of the warmth from the dipping sun, she shivered as she turned it to reveal the next entry log.

As she read, her skin tightened, shrinking away from the bone beneath. The entries seemed so familiar. Memories pressed impatiently at her head, urging her to think back and Kate jerked her finger down the page, finding the next paragraph that Edie had written.

The house is cold. It is always cold here. Our breath can be seen in puffs when we speak. I need to fetch firewood but it makes no difference. Maybe it really is the spirit of Lady Rosamund, trailing her icy coldness about the place. Still, that is of little significance in the face of what we now endure, here in Eyam.

People are dying. My friends and neighbours are suffering from unthinkable horrors, yet here I am, still scared of spirits and demons in Thornycroft Hall. There is someone here who eases my burden though.

Benjamin.

With a sharp intake of breath, Kate read the name again, this time saying it out loud. "Benjamin."

A curtain had been lifted in a dark corner of her mind and a young man pushed forward, his face lit up.

Kate felt her pulse quicken. She had dreamed of that face when she had passed out up at the Hancock family's graves over at Riley Farm.

In her dreams she had looked upon his face through the eyes of another. Rachel.

The name was all around her, whispered on an unexpected chilly breeze. She looked across the garden. The summer evening air was still and muggy. Not even the edges of the cloth that she had discarded onto the patio stirred.

Turning her gaze back to the book on her knee, she studied the words that Edie had penned. They all described scenes that she had witnessed, albeit when unconscious and dreaming.

Impatiently, she turned the page and gasped. There was only one sentence scrawled across it.

A demon is amongst us.

Intrigued, Kate thumbed through the next few pages. There was no structured logging of the entries though. Instead, the sentences were rushed. Chaos seemed to flow from the ink of the pen. Not much made sense and it was not clear who Edie had made contact with. The same theme flowed from the ramble of blue and black ink, repeating itself, referring to 'a demon living amongst us' and 'evil'. The writing looked nothing like Edie's.

Flicking back to the earliest entry of its kind, Kate noted that the lettering appeared to be of the same hand. Taking another sip of smoothie, she leafed through two more scantily filled pages before finding one with something red smeared across it. With a shriek, she threw the diary to the ground. Blood.

Catching her breath, she glared at it and then reached inside her pocket for the crystal that Francesca had given to her. Even feeling the cool rough surface calmed her.

Inhaling deeply, she tried to settle her nerves. What had Edie and Francesca been getting into?

Francesca hadn't given away too many details, but it was no wonder that she had been so upset by it all.

Bringing a hand to her mouth, she noticed how much she was shaking. Had they really made contact with the spirits of people from the past? Normally Kate would have dismissed the very notion as ludicrous, but she had seen and felt too much since arriving at the house.

Compelled to look behind her through the glass doors that led into the dining room, Edie's new bedroom, she half expected a figure to be standing in the window watching her. Of course, the room was exactly as it had been left after she and Francesca had decorated it: cosy, pretty and serene.

By her feet, the diary lay in a tent shape, spine facing the sky, pages facing the ground.

Each of the names written on those pages were inexplicably familiar to Kate and each of them inspired a different emotion. With Rachel there was familiarity, with Rosamund a deep fear and with Cecily a terrible hatred. There was something else too. A demon had been mentioned again. Kate wondered if it represented another entity or a person.

"Still lives amongst us," she said, the sound of her voice taking her by surprise. It was deadpan and unrecognisable.

Shaking her head, she shut her eyes. She refused to get involved in the nonsense. There was enough going on in her real life without getting caught adrift with the waves that Edie and Francesca had created. Still, the names refused to budge from her head. Rachel, Rosamund and Cecily.

She tried to imagine what it must have been like for the people living at Thornycroft when the plague had struck. It must have been an impossible torture to gaze out over the open space beyond the gardens of the house and feel bound to remain there, waiting to see whether such an unforgiving disease would snake its way into their lives next.

Catching herself, she realised that she possibly could imagine what it had been like. She had been imagining a lot since arriving at Thornycroft. After all, she had remembered how it had felt when Alice had told her of Hannah Rowland's death and she remembered the tiny flicker of hope that had come over her when Alice had suggested that the Thornycrofts might take her away from Eyam, to a safer residence, a sanctuary where there was no plague, no death and no misery. Kate could remember it all.

Remember.

With a start, she jumped. The smoothie that she was still holding slopped dangerously close to the lip of the glass. It was as though her mind had started to blur.

Setting the glass down by her feet, she breathed deeply and steadily. Of course she couldn't *remember* any of those things. It was impossible. She reasoned with herself that it had to be her imagination running wild, inspired by the poignantly placed green plaques around the village, each of them telling of the tragedy that had bestowed itself upon the residents of Eyam centuries before.

Rewrapping the diary in its crystal bound cloth, she promised herself that she would bin it, just as Francesca had implored her to do. The evening was still glorious and she should be enjoying what was left of it.

Tilting her head back, she watched as thin wisps of clouds scudded across the sky, momentarily blotting the golden orb of sun. To think that she could remember anything of what those people had suffered during the time of the plague was a ridiculous notion. Remembering was quite different to imagining. Remembering was to recall memories.

A movement from the lane ahead caught her eye. She sat up straight in her seat. Squinting, she used her hand as a visor as she strained to get a better look.

A knot of anger tightened in her chest as she regarded the figure of a man, holding something that looked like a sketch pad under one arm and a fold up chair under the other.

He stood up and began walking away. Nick Delamere.

How had she not noticed him before? Had he been sketching her whilst she had been sitting there? After all she had said to him the other day?

Furious, she leapt from her seat and the toe of her shoe caught on the glass that she had set down on the patio. The shrill sound of splintering glass shattered the silence around her. Kate hopped to one side as purple liquid pooled thickly in the cracks of the old patio.

Swearing, she stooped to pick up a large piece of glass, setting it down safely so that she wouldn't stand on it, before running over to the wall.

He had disappeared.

******

Placing the sketchpad against the easel in the modestly sized stand-to conservatory, Nick snapped on the lamp and picked up his paints.

Scrutinising the image that he had been working on, he squinted and leaned closer.

The figure was there, as she always was, in each of his creations. This time she had been alone. Her expression had been pensive, staring straight through him, as though looking out towards the fields beyond the wall.

Everything around her had been covered in a hard frost. Behind her, smoke from the chimney of the large house was curling and licking at the stark white sky. Her cheeks were pinched crimson and her dark hair whipped about her shoulders in the blustery wind. She had looked lost in conversation.

With untamed strokes, Nick dashed the brush against the paper, recreating the image that was still fresh in his head.

A few feet behind her were some birds. They were pecking hopefully at the tangle of brambles with bright red fruit. To her left, the branches of a tree were hanging low, shivering in the bitter wind.

Even from where he had been sitting, he had been able to make out the shade of her eyes. Blue. Not an ordinary shade of blue. An electric blue.

As he worked, Nick picked up the smaller paintbrush and added flecks of violet around the iris. In the early summer, her eyes would have matched the bluebells that would rampage Edie's garden, an unabated crest of blue.

There had been a deep sadness in those eyes as they had stared across the empty fields into the bland horizon beyond. In his painting, the sadness was etched onto every part of her face, making her appear older than her years.

When he had finished, Nick stood back to appraise his work and turned slowly around the room.

Canvases were propped up all around him. There were seven in total now. Rubbing the dark stubble on his chin, he took a seat, suddenly exhausted.

It had only been since his eyesight had started to deteriorate further that he had been painting. The painting wasn't a hobby. It was an addiction.

Choroideremia. That's what they had diagnosed him with back in his twenties. No cure and eventually blindness, but nobody could tell him when that would happen.

It had started with the gradual loss of night vision. Then it had slowed, but in recent months he had noticed a difference generally and had returned to his specialist.

Tunnel vision. That had been another term the specialists had used.

One day, in the not too distant future, he would have to think about a guide dog. They had told him from the off that it was highly likely there would come a day when his vision would deteriorate enough that he would qualify for one.

There had been a time when he had wondered if the bottle of Jack Daniels, always out on the kitchen bench, would become his only companion. There had also been a time when he had thought about living too fast and too hard, so that he would die young and never know how much of his sight would be lost over the years to come. All of these things, he supposed, were his way of coming to terms with his diagnosis.

Then, in spite of his failing eyes, he had found that he had really started to *see*.

None of it made any sense. The things that had become so vivid were things that appeared impossible, but they were there all the same. It was as though the world had layers that could be peeled back, revealing a different time, marked out by subtle or obvious differences in the landscape, buildings and people.

It was so implausible, yet it was happening, and it was fascinating.

That's what had fuelled his painting. He had no explanation, but he knew that what he saw was somehow real.

With a clatter, the paintbrush he was holding fell from his hand. Groaning, he reached for the painkillers in the top drawer of his desk. That was another symptom of his obsessive painting passion, the headaches.

Dragging himself to the kitchen, he filled a glass with water and slammed back the tablets before heading for the sofa. He would have to lie down for a short while.

Grabbing a cushion, he settled on top of the pale tartan throw and put his feet up, closing his eyes. He tried to clear his mind of all thoughts, but they persisted on returning to the paintings that were propped into place around the conservatory.

They didn't all feature the girl but they were all focused on Thornycroft and they seemed to tell a story, although he had no idea how it would end, or what would happen next.

With a shudder, his mind trained to the window at the top of the house, just as it had appeared for the pictures. Something had been up there - a shadowy figure. It had been there in other paintings too, subtle but there all the same: hollow eyes set into a shadowy face, staring down at the girl - they always were when the shadow was in the painting.

Nick wasn't sure he liked where the story was going, but he almost longed for each new painting session, as though he was reading a book, desperate to turn the next page.

Even before his sight had started deteriorating so much, he was sure that he had never been able to see things with the clarity and colour that came when he had the mind to paint.

Outside, somebody sounded a horn. He pressed his palms over his ears, screwing his eyes shut even tighter. Why did the world always have to seem so especially noisy whenever one of his headaches kicked in? He supposed that was the folly of the cottage that he had chosen to live in.

Right in the heart of the village of Eyam, it was cosy, quaint and homely - a far cry from the house that he had shared with his ex-wife. That had been a home of a magnificent scale, set in rural Cheshire. It had been far too big for just the two of them, but it had played to the dreams that they had spun out over bottles of wine together, of hordes of children and several pets. They had lovingly referred to it as their castle.

Back then, as an architect, their house had been his design. They had commissioned its build shortly after the wedding. It had taken two years of living in a mobile home within the extensive grounds, but they had done it. Everything had been perfect. Nick had felt like the luckiest man alive - until his world had come crashing down around him.

It had happened when his struggle with night vision had become increasingly difficult to ignore. He had received the diagnosis shortly before they were married. Only, he had never found it in his heart to tell her. Like him, she had been so excited and he hadn't wanted to tarnish the happiness of their impending special day. It had been a secret that he had swept under the carpet for years, pretended wasn't really happening.

It was just after his thirtieth birthday that he had finally told her. She had seemed so understanding at first. Then, over the years that followed, as the prospect of middle age and further loss of sight loomed upon him, upon them both, the cracks had started to show. His mood swings, her distance, meals apart, or in silence, and a sex life that had become a monotonous attempt to try for the baby that they had both been convinced would bring the shine back.

Then at last, over another awkwardly silent dinner, she had cracked. Her confession had been swift and her expression clouded with deep shame. The affair had been going on for ten months. It was long enough to be serious and evidently, the gold band that she had been nervously fiddling with on her ring finger during her confession, had lost its meaning. The following day, she had packed her bags and gone. Just like that.

Even though the day had been a long time coming, it had all still felt so very sudden and Nick had been convinced that she would return. He had rattled around for almost a year in their castle that had become his ruins and then the divorce summons had arrived. Full of guilt, she had not taken a penny from him. For her, it was a clean break.

When he had sold the house, he had made a fortune. What good was a fortune without anyone to share it with though? A home for one was all that he needed. The cottage in Eyam served its purpose perfectly. It was pretty, cosy and tucked far enough away from where his ex had moved to.

He had not stayed in touch with any of their old friends. Or rather, they hadn't bothered to stay in touch with him.

With bitterness, Nick supposed that when it came down to the really tough times, people would always find out who their real friends were. It appeared to him that they hadn't really been his friends in the first place.

The experience had scarred him and he often found himself wondering if he could ever really trust anybody again.

Despite living in a house with neighbours either side, Nick chose not to speak to any of them. Things were better that way. It would prevent him getting hurt in the future. The only person who he really spoke with was Edie.

Even his friendship with the Warrens was built on a pure business arrangement. He had provided the plans for their house and they had remained friends, inviting him to dinners or special occasions, but he never really let the relationship develop into what he would term as solid friendship, not like the relationship that he had with Edie.

Edie was a dear woman, with an open mind and a heart of gold. He had met her during a walk that he had been taking, when he had first noticed something different about her house. It had been flashes of imagery that had come to him at first, and he had thought that it was quite possible that he was suffering with some form of mental illness.

She had been pulling up weeds, wearing a straw hat and all the gardening gear.

Nick thought that he must have seemed so rude staring past her, straight into the garden. She hadn't judged though, unlike her stuck up great niece, Kate, who was residing there now. Edie had simply struck up polite conversation and had invited him inside for a glass of homemade iced tea. Nick had politely declined the pleasant offer. Then the next time he had seen her, he had accepted and the two of them had become firm friends.

He had never told her about what he had seen at Thornycroft, although he had enquired about the history of the house.

Her eyes had lit up when he had showed an interest. As an avid volunteer at the village church and museum, she had been keen to find out more about her own house.

In truth, Nick thought that at the top of Edie's bucket list was the opportunity for a shiny green plaque to adorn her garden gate, providing tourists another snatch of the story that gave Eyam its prominent place in history.

She had started researching, burying her nose in books and tasking Nick with showing her how to use the iPad that she had bought to help her with her mission, but then she had changed.

Like his painting, her research had become an obsession. Then Edie had taken the tumble that had landed her in the home.

Apart from the accusatory statement that Kate had made at the dinner party, implying that Edie was afraid of somebody, that was the last that Nick had heard.

Shortly after the accident, the police had started investigating, asking questions of people, but that had soon come to a close. They wouldn't tell him anything at the hospital and visiting was limited to just family.

If she had been more approachable, he would have liked to ask Kate more about Edie's health. Unfortunately, she had made her feelings towards him clear and so to find out anything else would mean engaging in conversation, which was out of the question. Conversation would no doubt only end in conflict, so he would just have to wait. Edie was bound to return to Thornycroft sooner or later.

It was late afternoon by the time he awoke. The headache had subsided to a dull thud and his stomach was grumbling. Hunger was a good sign at least. He couldn't abide the thought of a lengthy migraine knocking him out for days.

After slowly taking the stairs to the bathroom, he freshened up, splashing away the grogginess of his afternoon sleep with cool water.

It was as he was rummaging through the scantily stocked kitchen cupboards that he was startled by the impatient knock on the door. Nobody ever knocked for him, not even the postman. There was never any need. Whoever it was had to be a cold caller. If he ignored them, he was sure that they would go away.

Reaching for some bread, he slipped two slices into the toaster before finding a pan for the tin of beans that he had found.

The knocking grew louder and more impatient. Irritated, he slammed the baked beans down on the worktop and stood behind the kitchen door, waiting for it to stop. Still it persisted.

Pulse quickening with anger, he stomped down the hallway, imagining the smarmy, patronising smile of the pushy sales person on his doorstep.

Preparing himself to give his unwanted visitor a piece of his mind, Nick threw open the door before taking a surprised step back.

Standing in front of him was Kate. She was the last person he was expecting to see.

Before he could muster a greeting, she was speaking. Two spots of colour were high on her cheeks and her eyes glinted dangerously as she stood on the threshold, arms crossed over her chest. Words were spilling from her so fast that he was unable to keep up. He got the gist of it though. She had seen him painting again and she was not at all happy.

There was little that he could do other than listen to her rant. When she paused for breath, he stepped to one side. "Perhaps you'd like to come in?" he asked, a hint of sarcasm in his voice. It did nothing to calm the situation.

Visibly smarting from the spiked comment, the spots of colour in her cheeks spread and deepened. "What I would like Mr Delamere, is for you to stop this strange fascination you have with sketching Thornycroft. It's unnerving and you are being incredibly obtuse by persisting after everything that I said the other night." Her lips trembled as she confronted him and in that moment, he was taken aback by how attractive she was with her feisty glare and skin slightly rosy, both from anger and too much sun.

Pushing away the fleeting distraction, Nick shrugged before forcing a smile. "Whatever you say. Consider it done. I'll stop the painting."

Expecting her to leave, he went to shut the door.

She stopped him, wedging her foot into the bottom of the frame. Instead of pacifying her, his agreement to do as she had asked had invoked her irritation even more. "What do you mean you'll stop? That's it? You're not going to argue?" Incensed, her arms moved from her chest to her hips as she placed a hand on each one.

An ironic chuckle escaped him and he shook his head. "You're unbelievable. You're not happy with that? You want an argument?" Standing his ground, he leaned closer to her, challenging her to a verbal battle.

She didn't move, didn't open her mouth to protest or continue her tirade.

Realising that it was pointless to expect anything more from her other than confrontation, he made to shut the door again, just as her shoulders caved forwards and the furious expression on her face crumpled.

Letting her hands fall loosely to her sides, all of her anger seemed to disintegrate. "I didn't want any of this. This wasn't supposed to happen. None of it. I just wanted privacy and time alone with Great Aunt Edie, not fights on the doorsteps of her neighbours." Cupping her face behind a palm, she broke down in front of him, shoulders shaking and knees almost buckling.

Speechless, Nick watched, his mouth agape.

From behind him the toast popped up, the noise breaking the spell of misery that had overcome Kate. "Look, just forget it," she said, defeated. "Paint all you like. All I ask is that you try to do it when I'm not about. I don't care what Aunt Edie might have said to you, but I don't like it and I have my own reasons, personal ones." With a deflated sigh, she gave him a wilted look. "I really don't have the energy for a fight."

He watched as she pulled her stature back to upright with some effort before wishing him a good evening and leaving.

Gawping after her, Nick thought about returning to his meagre supper of beans on toast, but there had been something about that change in her that he couldn't brush aside.

He stared as she marched away down the path. It was as though a mask had been removed, revealing a vulnerable, softer side to her. She had history and Nick sensed that it was a painful one.

In that moment he felt useless, incapable of helping her and yet, her reaction had unearthed a feeling that had been so deeply buried inside of him, he had forgotten that it had ever existed.

Nick wanted to reach out to her, to pull her back towards the house. He wanted to put his arms around her and tell her that everything would be okay. He wanted to protect her. The feeling was almost alien but there could be no denying that it was there.

Inhaling sharply, he could smell the remnants of her perfume. It lingered even after she had shut the gate behind her and disappeared down the street.

He knew that he should run after her but he couldn't. His mind was telling him to move, but his legs weren't obeying and he found himself immobile, stuck behind the threshold of the front door.

No matter how unbearable and argumentative this woman could be, she had reawakened something inside of him that he had thought had been lost forever. Kate, he realised, made him feel alive again.

CHAPTER 17

Present Day – Eyam

"I'm an utter fool," Kate said after she had recounted her visit to Nick. She had found Francesca grooming her horse, Jack, in the field a little way up from Thornycroft.

Francesca had remained uncharacteristically quiet throughout Kate's version of events. The late afternoon sun honeyed her hair and mud splashes flecked her otherwise flawless forehead. Jack snorted and shook his mane as she rubbed the white diamond on his nose.

Amusement twitched at the corners of Francesca's lips. "Why exactly do you have such a problem with Nick sketching Thornycroft?" she asked. Her tone wasn't accusing but the question caught Kate off guard.

Plucking at a tuft of Jack's hair that had become stuck in the barbed knot of the fence, Kate met her new friend's curious gaze. "Wouldn't you find it uncomfortable if a strange man was watching and drawing your house all of the time? Goodness only knows what he finds so fascinating? Regardless, I think it's weird and intimidating and I don't like the thought of him being there like that whilst Aunt Edie is alone. It's disconcerting to say the least."

Lifting the leather harness over Jack's head, Francesca secured it. "Edie and Nick are good friends. I really don't think Edie finds it a problem at all. In fact, I think she's quite pleased with the company. Nick's harmless."

Taking the grooming kit that Francesca handed to her, Kate went to open the gate so that he could be led out of the field. Jack's hooves stamped out a hypnotic rhythm against the dried mud of the track as they took him towards the stabling area. "Well I don't like it." Kate was painfully aware that she sounded like a huffy child. Short of pushing her bottom lip out as far as it would go, she supposed that she was behaving like one. Sighing, she pressed her hand to her forehead. "I don't know. Maybe I have overreacted. See, I told you, I've behaved like an utter fool."

Francesca swatted at a fly. "To be fair, Nick has been rather stubborn and foolish too. He should have taken heed of your warning at the dinner party. All he had to do was wait for Edie to get home. Maybe he has a soft spot for you Kate. Stranger things have happened." She was teasing, but the comment made Kate's face flush hot. Francesca didn't notice. "Seriously Kate, Edie always says that Nick hasn't had it easy. Can't you just let him sketch? Edie says that it's a passion of his and she always says that-"

"Passion should be admired and nurtured," Kate chimed in so that they finished the sentence in unison. "Yes, I've heard that one many times growing up. Good old Aunt Edie. She always sees the good in everyone." Her gaze drifted across the fields, up towards the sky.

She wondered what her Great Aunt Edie would have made of Richard. She had never met him but she would no doubt have an opinion. The thought of him made her shudder and her stomach knot.

Francesca pushed open the gate to the stabling area. Loose strands of straw shifted beneath their feet as they approached Jack's stable and he tugged at the harness, momentarily resisting being taken away from his fertile, green grazing ground.

After she had put Jack in the stable and unharnessed him, Francesca turned her attention back to Kate. "What's the real problem Kate?" Once again, she had caught her off guard. Francesca had a sharp insight that was on a par with Edie's. It was an uncanny likeness that the two of them shared.

Picking up a stray rusty nail, Kate held it out. "That's lucky, poor Jack could have stood on that."

Taking it from her, Francesca put the nail in the pocket of her gilet. "Probably from one of the horse's shoes. You're avoiding the question Kate. Tell me to stop prying if you like, but has something happened that's made you react this way about Nick?"

"I told you, I just find it disconcerting on behalf of Aunt Edie. That's it. Nothing more."

Appraising her for a few seconds more than could be considered comfortable, Francesca failed to look at all convinced. Taking Kate's hand, she squeezed it gently. "Forgive me Kate, because I am prying. Prying is a terrible trait of mine. But listen, Nick Delamere is no threat and Edie loves him to bits, although I tend to agree with you that his gruff, impetuous nature isn't all that appealing at times."

"What happened to him that was so dreadful?" It was Kate's turn to be nosey.

Francesca shrugged. "He's very private," she said, giving her a sideways glance. "Much like you. It was Edie who told me about it all. I don't know the nitty-gritty. All I know is that he had a bad time of it when his marriage broke down. I should think he hasn't even given Edie the full story. I'm just asking you to go easy on him. Underneath all that gruffness, he's really a nice guy."

Stuffing her hands in to the pockets of her jeans, Kate sighed. "Well I think I've probably burned my bridges now. I don't get the impression he's a very forgiving type of person."

"You're right, he's not but people can surprise you." Swooping to give her a kiss on the cheek, she placed her hands on her shoulders. "Don't worry too much about it. Edie will be home tomorrow and I'll be over to see her as soon as I'm finished here with Jack. I hope that's okay, I mean, I wouldn't dream of intruding on you. I realise you'll need some time with her first."

"You wouldn't be intruding," Kate interrupted, her heart lifting at the thought of a welcome home committee just for Edie. "It would be lovely to see you. I'd love you to come over. I imagine that Aunt Edie will be grateful too." She waited whilst Francesca gave some instructions to a girl in the yard, then she looked towards the direction of Thornycroft.

Upon her return to the house, she felt even more empty and alone than she had when she had first arrived.

******

When Kate pulled up outside Thornycroft with her Great Aunt Edie the following day, the house and its garden looked so different. The stifling and sinister atmosphere she had felt only the day before had been melted away by the pearly sheen of a late afternoon sun. Everything looked far more pleasant. She even noticed that Edie's shoulders had relaxed a little. Even so, Edie had not uttered a word for the duration of the journey. The distraction on her face had been obvious and Kate wished that she would confide in her.

It had been much later than intended when the discharge forms had been signed, and so her agenda had not gone according to plan. She supposed that given Edie's behaviour towards Francesca when she had visited the home, it would be no bad thing to give her a little space following her return to Thornycroft.

Cumbersomely, she lifted the wheelchair from the boot and fumbled to erect it. Edie was still quiet, staring towards the overbearing house, her lips pressed tightly together.

"Francesca and I have made a wonderful temporary bedroom for you," Kate said brightly, helping her into the chair with some considerable effort. For somebody so small and frail looking, it was a heavy task transferring Edie from the car to the chair.

"I'll be glad to be rid of this thing when this dratted foot can take some weight on it," she huffed as they bumped down the pathway.

"It won't be long and I'll be here until you're back on your feet," Kate replied, but Edie simply grunted.

Disheartened, Kate pushed the key into the lock of the front door. "I made a fish pie for tonight, plenty of prawns and salmon in there." She was determined not to let her Great Aunt's mood dampen the day.

Pushing open the door, the welcoming smell of cooking greeted them. "It's going to be another lovely evening. We could sit out the back and have a drink before we eat. What do you think?"

Edie didn't reply. Her face had paled as she looked into the hallway, towards the staircase. Kate thought she saw her bottom lip quiver.

Keeping her tone bright, she persevered. "We could have a game of chess if you like, although you'll have to remind me of the rules. I'm hopeless." Her cheery disposition was beginning to waiver as she watched Edie shrink into her chair. She looked smaller and more vulnerable. "Or we could just watch a film," she suggested hopefully, but her heart was rapidly sinking.

"A drink on the patio would be lovely dear. Gin and tonic would be most refreshing. They wouldn't hear of that in the home. It'll be a pleasant change. Fish pie for dinner sounds delicious too." The shadow vanished and her features lifted as she reached for Kate's arm. Once again, she looked like the vivacious Great Aunt Edie that she had always known. "You've been an angel Kate," she added warmly and Kate felt her shoulders drop with relief. It was good to see the old side of Edie return, the side that she had known growing up.

They kept the conversation light as Kate showed her the room that she and Francesca had decorated. Pleased with herself, she took in the cosy arrangement. It was basking in a cosy amber glow from the sunlight that bounced from the heads of Francesca's neatly arranged vase of flowers. The view from the glass doors onto the patio and back garden was beautiful.

"So what do you think?" Kate pressed, unable to hide her excitement at how nicely they had done the room up. "Francesca helped me." Despite her straight set mouth, Edie nodded gratefully, thanking her for the effort.

Leaning forwards, she kissed the top of Edie's head. It smelled of hairspray and lemons, reminding Kate of her childhood. "It'll be great, just the two of us. Mum says her and dad will be straight over when they finish the cruise. That's not for a couple of weeks yet though, so we have plenty of time to catch up. Now, how about I boil the kettle for some tea?"

Edie turned. Her expression had shadowed again. "I've had enough cups of tea at that home to last a lifetime. How about that gin and tonic you promised? It's close enough to supper don't you think?"

With a chuckle, Kate nodded. "That's more like it." Sorting through the fruit basket for a lime, she busied herself making the drinks and set the oven to warm. There was no chatter between them whilst she worked and she caught Edie eyeing the staircase warily again.

The kitchen was choked with silence. "Come on." Kate pressed the glass into Edie's hand. "Let's catch the last of that sun. It's been a beautiful day."

It was a perfect afternoon and the view across the garden towards the boundary stone path was magnificent.

"You know that there's something here don't you?" The question was quiet and unexpected.

Kate spluttered on her gulp of drink.

Edie didn't appear to notice. "Something is in this house. Watching." She eyed Kate carefully, waiting for her to respond. When she didn't say anything in return, Edie continued with her line of conversation. "Thornycroft used to be much bigger of course. A rather grand house back when the plague hit the village." Edie took a sip of her drink and stared out across the garden. "Hard to imagine isn't it?"

"Hard to imagine the house back then?" Kate followed her gaze to the far side of the garden.

Edie's eyes had glazed over and her voice had taken on a new tone, dreamlike. "The plague. Hard to imagine what it must have been like back then. Here, in Eyam. For them."

Disguising her alarm, Kate kept her expression blank. "Yes, I suppose it is quite hard to imagine. It must have been dreadful and terrifying. I don't suppose anybody can fully comprehend the horror of it all."

Something jarred at her mind and Kate shifted uncomfortably in her chair as a strange sensation began to drift over her. It felt like she was being hollowed out, happiness drained from her, until she felt nothing but despair, rejection and utter loneliness. A cloud drifted overhead, temporarily blocking the sun.

"They've gone." The words tripped off Kate's lips in a sob, taking her by surprise. She had no idea what she was talking about, but the feelings were there inside her all the same. People had left her. That's how she felt, abandoned, terrified. The nausea that she had been feeling days before returned. Its ferocity forced her to put her drink down and she noticed that her hand was shaking.

Edie cast her a suspicious glance. They sat in silence for a good minute, Edie quietly observing her reaction.

When she spoke at last, Edie's voice was steady but there was an unmistakable urgent edge to it. "Who has gone Kate?"

The sound of the doorbell trilled through Thornycroft and into the garden. It cleared the fogginess in Kate's head. Relieved for the diversion, she stood up. "That's probably Francesca. She said she wanted to see you. I didn't think she would come over so late in the day, but I know she was keen."

The question that Edie had posed before the doorbell had sounded hung in the air like an unwelcome guest waiting for acknowledgement. Kate didn't want to answer. She didn't know how. The words that had come from her mouth hadn't really been hers.

Grateful for the interruption, she went to answer the door and Edie turned her attention back to the garden.

Using the peephole, she frowned. It wasn't Francesca at the door.

The figure of a man was hovering on the doorstep.

Taking a step away, she contemplated not answering but the over enthusiastic chime of the bell rang out again, jolting her into action. Sliding back the main lock and turning the bolt, she attempted a polite smile.

Looking bashful, Nick was standing on the doorstep. Rubbing the back of his neck with one hand, he smiled awkwardly. "I didn't mean to upset you yesterday." In his other hand he held a bottle. Extending it, he thrust it towards her. "A peace offering. I remembered you telling Graham and Francesca that it was your favourite."

Taken aback, Kate opened her mouth to say something, only to find herself dumbfounded. Taking the bottle from him, she mustered up a mumbled thank you.

Crestfallen, he pushed his hands into his pockets, the uncomfortable chasm between them growing. "Well I just wanted to clear the air between us."

Kate felt guilt gnaw at her. She hadn't meant to sound rude or ungrateful, the gesture had just taken her by surprise, and as she looked at him, wondering how she could right it all, she found herself wishing that he wasn't so attractive.

It was only as he went to leave that she found her voice. "Aunt Edie's home."

Stopping mid stride, he turned.

"You'll come in to say hello won't you?" Kate asked. "I'm sure she'll be pleased for the extra company." Gesturing for him to join them, she held open the door.

Breaching the threshold with one foot, he hesitated. "I don't want to intrude."

In spite of her melting reserve, her tone remained clipped. "I'm sure Edie will be delighted to see you." Inwardly she berated herself for keeping her heckles up. The poor man had come to offer her the pipe of peace and here she was, holding an expensive gift of wine in her hand and throwing it back in his face. "Besides, it would be nice for you and I to start afresh," she added quickly, before ushering him into the kitchen. "Why don't you join us both for a drink? Let's say it's my side of the peace offering." Opening the fridge, she reached for the tonic water and then for the ice tray from the freezer. "Gin and tonic okay?"

"Sounds great." He nodded in approval at the open bottle of gin on the worktop. "Ah the pink stuff. You've got good taste."

"Oh it's not mine. Aunt Edie needs to take the credit for that. I found it in her drinks cabinet." Throwing a handful of ice into a glass, she added generous measures of liquid and they walked out into the garden.

Once again, she kicked herself. He had tried to give her a compliment and she had rebuffed him. It gave them nothing more to say. The awkwardness between them lingered as they reached the spot where Edie was sitting.

"Nicholas!" Forgetting herself, Edie went to get up. Her grimace of pain had both Kate and Nick dashing over.

Shrugging them both off, she tried to adjust her position. "Force of habit. Stupid old crow that I am. Over eighty five years of rushing around on my own two feet and now this." Slapping her hand onto the arm of the wheelchair, she let out a frustrated cry.

"But it's only temporary." Nick was swift to her side, taking her hand in his. "Then you'll be back on your feet bending the ears of all those tourists at the church again." He handed her the glass that was on the table and then took a sip of his own. "Nice kick." He raised his tumbler towards Kate.

"Oh Kate's an expert at fixing a good stiff drink." Edie drained her glass and picked out the lime. It was a habit that ran in the family. She made a sour face as she sucked at the gin infused flesh. "Why doesn't Nick stay for dinner Kate? There's plenty in that wonderful dish that you've assembled. It'll be lovely to have the company."

Giving her a scowl, Kate knew her Great Aunt too well. She was trying to play Cupid. Both she and Nick were united in their protest, suggesting that Edie would need her rest.

They were both silenced by the authoritative flick of Edie's wrist. "Nonsense. You're a long time dead and this fall has made me realise that I should spend as much time as I can doing the things that I enjoy with the people who I like to spend time with."

To Kate's relief, there were no more awkward silences and when the sun had dipped behind the Peaks, they had all enjoyed pleasant conversation over dinner and Edie had them all laughing and joking for the duration. The ambience had lifted considerably and Kate had to admit that she had actually enjoyed Nick's company.

She was making the coffee when the soft hum of Edie's snores challenged the sound of the kettle boiling.

"Out for the count," Nick commented, draping his jacket across her to keep her warm. It was a kind, gentle gesture that didn't go unnoticed as Kate reached for the mugs.

"I can help you take her through," he suggested and they moved Edie into her bedroom, managing to lift her into bed without waking her.

Nick finished making the coffees whilst Kate made sure that she was comfortable before drawing the curtains and pulling the door to.

"Edie's a real trooper you know. She'll bounce right back." He handed her a steaming beverage and added some sugar to his own.

Taking a seat, Kate stared into her coffee, watching the tiny bubbles of foam pop on the surface. "I just feel so awful that she was alone when it happened. It feels so wrong that she didn't have her family around. I wish she had moved down South. Mum wants her to. You know Aunt Edie though, stubborn as a mule."

Chuckling, Nick set his teaspoon on to a side plate. "I think hell would have to freeze over before she gave up Thornycroft and Eyam. She loves this place."

"Two weeks ago I'd have agreed with you, but she was all up for selling the house earlier this week." Kate wrapped her fingers around her mug, feeling its warmth spread welcomingly over her hands.

Nick shot her a look of both bewilderment and concern. "When we were at Francesca's dinner party, you said she was scared. Have you worked out why?"

Sighing, she pushed her mug aside. "I don't know." Testing his reaction, she gave him a side-glance. "Have you ever felt anything strange here, in the atmosphere?"

Taking a sip of his drink, he frowned. There was a pause before he responded. "It's an old house Kate, with history. Any house of this age has an atmosphere."

Shaking her head, she leaned against the surface of the table. "It feels like something more than that. I suppose you're right though. Aunt Edie says that the house was around at the time that the plague hit the village. That was centuries ago." Raising her eyebrows, she considered what Nick had said about old houses having an atmosphere. "Given its age, I suppose it would be stranger if there weren't any noises." She turned her head in the direction of the corridor that led to Edie's room. "I just want her to be okay."

"She will be. You're here with her and if you always cook like that, she's one lucky lady."

Throwing a tea towel across the table, she laughed. "You're just buttering me up now."

He smiled at her and she noticed how his cheeks dimpled. "Maybe."

Warmth flushed Kate's chest and neck. Was he flirting with her?

As though reading her thoughts, he looked away, drained the rest of his coffee and went to rinse his cup. "It's getting late, I'm going to call for a taxi."

Kate thought it was strange that he wouldn't just walk home. It wasn't that far to the centre of the village, but she supposed that it was a pitch-black walk down the track. "Don't do that. I'll give you a lift. Aunt Edie's probably going to be out for the count until morning anyway. It's no trouble." She didn't allow him to protest and was accompanying him down the path to her car within minutes.

They linked arms in a bid to guide each other through the darkness that enveloped them. Nick didn't speak, as though he was focusing all of his thoughts on something else. They walked slowly. "I should really get the security lights fixed here," she commented as she clicked the locking mechanism on her keys. "That's a job for tomorrow I think."

When they reached the car, the feeling of his grip loosening from her arm took her by surprise. She hadn't realised that they had been holding each other so close as they fought their way through the darkness of the garden. Flustered, she dropped her keys and made a show of picking them up in the hope that he wouldn't notice how awkward she felt.

Dropping him at his cottage, she didn't even wait for him to reach the gate before she released the handbrake and headed for home.

They had not spoken during the short journey. Nick had appeared distracted and she was worried that he had noticed how flustered she had become.

When she pulled up outside Thornycroft again, she raised her hands and hit the steering wheel, cursing herself for being so stupid.

The spot on her bare arm that he had pressed his hand against lingered as a burning heat.

Tilting her head back, she shut her eyes and groaned. The feelings she was experiencing were simply a product of loneliness, nothing more. She couldn't read too much into them.

Hauling herself out of the car and back to the house, she tried to push the silly thoughts aside. Nick Delamere was not the sort of man who she would usually find herself drawn to. Attractive yes, but she imagined that he could be quite moody and certainly stubborn.

By the time she pushed open the front door, fatigue was creeping up on her. The pile of rinsed dishes in the kitchen beckoned her to stay up a little longer, but she was far too tired to do anything more than brush her teeth and slip into bed.

As she stepped into her pyjamas she thought back to Nick's reaction when she had asked him about Thornycroft's atmosphere. Something had been bothering her about it. Even though he had brushed the whole thing away, after that point in the evening, he had become very quiet. It had unnerved her and as she lay in bed listening to the creaks and groans from the settling of ancient beams and wood, she couldn't help but wonder whether Nick knew something more about the whole situation than he was letting on.

A carousel of thoughts spun around her head as she waited for sleep to relieve her of exhaustion and she thought of the diary. Instead of binning or burning it, she had felt compelled to keep a hold of it.

Earlier that day she had tucked it under her pillow with the intent of reading more in the privacy of her room.

Reaching for it, she pulled it out and placed the cardboard Ouija Board to one side with a grimace. That was one thing that she would have to get rid of.

The diary fell open and she licked a finger, leafing over each page until she found the next entry.

Since Lady Cecily forbade us to venture out of Thornycroft Hall, it has become suffocating here. It feels like she is always watching and waiting. Goody too – from her places in the shadows. She is as much a ghost of Thornycroft Hall as Sir Edward's first wife, always drifting about like a dark cloud, seen by nobody but me.

I am sure that Lady Cecily is waiting for any of hint of the sickness to be upon me so that she can be rid of me. Then there are the noises here.

I have seen the marks on Goody's arms and I have heard more of the rumours of 'The Conjurer', the maid who lived here when Lady Rosamund Thornycroft was alive.

They say that Lady Rosamund was kept in chains at night, that things always changed when dusk fell.

Sometimes the rattle of chains can still be heard and I wonder if it was 'The Conjurer' who was responsible for Lady Rosamund's demise?

Something is not right. Goody is also always in such need of supplies from the wise woman in the village, Liza Thickett. Only the other day she was waiting for me outside of the privy when she pressed some coins into my hand and insisted I go to Liza's home for some herbs and plants.

I am suspicious that the errand was not intended for plague remedy ingredients, but something else. Something only for Goody Brown, our resident 'Conjurer'.

The words were a tonic, making the hoods of Kate's eyes heavy and coaxing a sleepy fog to her brain.

Under the light of a full moon, shadows moved and crept along the walls of the room, their motion hypnotic.

She began to drift off, the diary falling to her chest, its words pressing against the covers.

Kate stirred and woke several times with the feeling that she was falling. The final time it happened, she tucked the diary into the drawer of the nightstand and picked up her phone, illuminating it to check the time. It was gone two in the morning and her legs were leaden with fatigue but her brain was wired.

Closing her eyes, she tried to shut out the words that she had read earlier and practiced some deep breathing instead, visualising her 'happy place'. It was a trick that her father had taught her as a child and it usually worked.

When she eventually fell into a slumber again, it wasn't a peaceful sleep, but a fitful one.

In the corner of her room, a shadow lingered, waiting for the perfect moment to drift towards her and reach out for the hand that Kate had left above the sheets. In her dreams, she felt cold and shivered as her teeth began to chatter.

CHAPTER 18

Early December 1665 – Eyam

The streets of the village looked bleak. Goody had sent Rachel for some supplies from Liza Thickett, with warning that she must not speak with anybody else about who needed them.

Liza was one of the oldest folk in the village and the nearest thing to an apothecary outside of either of Eyam's neighbouring hamlets. Rachel had never liked visiting old Liza. With the plague upon them, the journey to her little cottage was even less appealing than usual.

To help prevent breathing in any of the plague seed, she had been furnished with a cloth that had been balled around rosemary, sage, mint and lavender. Goody had assured her that it was a plague bag, supposedly able to ward off any plague miasma that might cling to the air. Rachel pressed it to her nose as she hurried through the village.

It was a secret errand; one that Lady Cecily would not have approved of, but Goody was desperate and she had helped Rachel countless times in the stillroom. Rachel hadn't forgotten either, that Goody had never breathed a word to anyone about her trespassing in to the forbidden room of portraits.

Liza Thickett lived alone. She was a strange woman with a stoop and an eye that never looked in the right direction. Folk didn't like to trouble her much, but she had what Goody needed. Apparently she would be expecting Rachel's visit and would have everything ready.

Her house was a tiny thatch, situated in a stretch of the village known as Orchard Bank. When Rachel arrived, a flurry of snow had begun to settle. A glow came from one of the windows of the cottage, highlighting the dusting of powdery white on its ledge.

Impatient to finish her errand, Rachel gave three sharp knocks on the door. There was a long pause before it was opened.

Liza looked at her with her good eye and mumbled a greeting of sorts, ushering for her to go inside. Her breath smelled of onions and there was a pungent odour in the house.

Modest in size, the kitchen behind her was cluttered with herbs and pots. A wooden table was in the middle and a fire was blazing next to it with an iron pot simmering away. Liza gave whatever was inside a stir before turning to face her again. "'Tis a wicked thing, this pestilence. Brought here for our sins." She picked up a knife and rubbed it across a belt to sharpen the blade. "Too many folk have sinned here in Eyam. The Lady of Thornycroft Hall, for one," she added with a disapproving look, as though it was Rachel who was at fault.

"Lady Rosamund's actions were long ago." Rachel was quick to the defence. She didn't want any of the blame for the arrival of the plague to land at the doorstep of Thornycroft Hall.

Picking up a stray stalk of mint from the table, Liza put it to her mouth and began to chew. Not once did her keen gaze leave Rachel as she spoke, "T'other one is still with us though, gloating and floating about with that smug smile of hers." She made no attempt to cloak her distaste for Lady Cecily.

Wiping her hands on her dirty apron, she picked up an earthen pot from an overcrowded shelf and dipped her hand inside to pull out a pouch. "I know 'tis Goody Brown who has sent you. Tell her that this is the last. If she needs more, she'll have to place her order outside of Eyam. I don't want to risk bad seed being brought into my home."

Goody had warned Rachel that Liza might react in such a way and she had armed her accordingly. "There will be a higher payment for your troubles." Rattling a pouch filled with coins, she let it fall on to the table so that a few spilled out.

Liza's expression soured as she looked at the money and her stony reserve faltered. With a grunt, she swiped up the pouch. "More you say?" Her good eye was filled with suspicion.

Rachel nodded. "You have my word."

Liza thrust the little bag containing the herbs for Goody into Rachel's palm and then sat down to count the coins. She put one between her teeth, biting to test its authenticity.

"Goody said that you were to make up a tincture first too. There are more than enough coins there to pay for it," Rachel said.

Impatiently, Liza pushed the coins to one side. "Aye, I was counting to make sure. Can't take anyone for their word these days." There was a loud snorting noise as she brought a hand to her nose, rubbing it with her fingerless gloves. "Desperate times these. Brings out the worst in folk."

Rachel disagreed as she thought of Catherine Mompesson and the Hancocks and how other villagers had taken in the poor Bradshaw staff, kicked out of Bradshaw Hall when the family had left. "And the best in them too," she added.

Liza's eye roamed over her before she nodded. "Maybe. Still doesn't do to trust too easy. Mark my words child." She cleared her throat noisily before setting to work with a bundle of herbs and other things that had been set out on her table.

As Rachel watched, she felt her confidence grow a little. "What do you know of Goody Brown?"

Putting her knife down, Liza looked up at her. "I know enough lass. I know enough."

"I've heard that she lived in Thornycroft Hall before, when Lady Rosamund was alive. Did you know her then?"

Ignoring the question, Liza continued working until she had bottled whatever concoction it was that she had prepared for Goody. She held it out towards Rachel. "That'll be a strong one mind. Two thimbles full each time is all she will need. Should keep for a good long while, through the cold snap at least." Nodding her head towards the pouch of herbs, she licked her lips and coughed as Rachel pressed the plague bag to her nose and mouth.

Liza stood up, her shoulders hunched and she rubbed her nose with the back of her hand again. "There's enough there to keep her through spring too. Mind and tell her that. I don't like the intrusion." She waved her hands impatiently as she gestured for Rachel to leave. "Now be gone with you lass. Leave old Liza be."

On the quiet village street, Rachel felt relief to be out in the cold again, away from Liza Thickett with her grunts and accusing glares. The smell of smouldering smoke stung her nostrils. Thick grey ribbons coiled ominously against the otherwise stark canvas of cloud.

"They're burning what they can after the plague visits their homes." The comment from behind her took her by surprise.

A man stumbled in line with her step. When he spoke again, Rachel noticed his slurred speech and realised that he must have come from the one of the village taverns and likely the Kings Head, where many of the miners would meet. "More death," he continued, his eyelids heavy with intoxication as he looked across the village. "Makes me look forward to getting down that damned mine just to escape it all. The air is thick with it at times. Anything that they can bear to part with, they burn."

Rachel's stomach dipped and she coughed as the smoke scratched at her throat.

From Thornycroft Hall, she had seen the thick grey plumes licking at the sky above and she had smelled it on the wind, but she had not placed it into this context.

She watched his lonely silhouette stagger off. As he weaved across the empty dirt track, she wondered how many of his family and friends he had lost.

Suddenly Rachel wanted the safety and familiarity of Thornycroft Hall. Despite her unhappiness there, at least she was away from all the sickness and death that seemed to ooze from every pore within the centre of the village.

With a quickened pace, she found herself passing the rectory and paused. Even though her encounter with the inebriated man had put her on edge and filled her with anxiety, it was impossible to resist a quick visit. She hadn't seen Catherine for a long time and she missed her.

Everything was different to how she had remembered it from her last visit. Even the winter blooms had been neglected. The path leading to the rectory was now only lined with the naked limbs of shrubs and the withered heads and stems of once colourful flowers.

It was the Reverend Mompesson who greeted her. His youthful glow had become sallow and the flame from the tallow candle that he was holding cast heavy hoods above and beneath his brown eyes. The burden of death and hardship was etched into his face.

Conscious of the burning fires in the neighbouring gardens and what they signalled, she greeted him meekly as he nodded for her to go through.

William rested the candle on a small table and politely asked after her, the Thornycrofts and Master Benjamin. As was the good spirit of his nature, he took the time to ask about each of them by name. Despite his obvious distraction, he still found the time and good grace to acknowledge the dire situation that Master Benjamin faced following his accident.

"We are all surviving, even Master Belgrave. It is easier living on the edge of the village." She glanced out towards the still open door. "I miss people here though. If it was not for Lady Cecily fussing and fretting, I would be back more, to help, to see folk and see my friends."

William was quick to answer, "And she is right to fear it. Lady Cecily is right to keep you at Thornycroft Hall. You should get back Rachel." His tone was hard and unlike one she had heard from him before.

"I was hoping I might see Mistress Mompesson whilst I am here," she suggested quickly, but the shadow that had crossed his face darkened.

"Catherine is still out tending to the sick and the grieving. She has taken a plague remedy to the Rowlands. I have just returned momentarily for the children. It is rare that they see much of either of us these last months."

Bowing her head, Rachel felt her throat bunch as she thought of poor Hannah Rowland. "I heard of Hannah's fate. Are the rest of them well?"

Picking up an empty crate in the kitchen, he went to put it out of the way in a far corner.

"Are they well?" She prompted him again.

Propping the crate against the wall, he turned to face her, his shoulders sagging and his voice low so that his young children would not hear. "Mary Rowland took her last this morning."

Feeling as though somebody had squeezed the last of her breath from her chest, Rachel staggered as his words echoed through her head.

Mary was Hannah's younger sister and they often played with the Hancock children. "Mary Rowland is dead?"

"You should get back to Thornycroft Hall. You risk everyone there by coming here. I am with sickness every day." William was angry. Rigid and tall he stood, his back turned to her. She wondered if he was fighting the emotion that betrayed his voice.

Feeling her hands tremble, she backed away. Had she made him angry? She hadn't meant to anger the Reverend. "These people are my friends though," she said. "Is there nothing I can do to help?"

"Go Rachel." His voice remained steady and low but his face had paled considerably as he turned and gestured for her to go towards the front door.

A sob caught in her throat. Eyam was no longer the place that she knew. It was haunted by death and misery and frustration. Even the good and kind Reverend Mompesson appeared lost and stricken by the horrors that the plague had brought with it.

Opening the door for her, he avoided her searching eyes as he showed her out into the cold, smoky air. "Do not return to this house Rachel. Not until it has left us."

"Too many have lost their lives already." Behind her, Catherine Mompesson had appeared, snow flecking her hair. She looked as serene and beautiful as always, except if it was at all possible, she looked thinner, like she had been stripped of her summer bloom. "William is right Rachel. You must go. It is best that you do not put yourself or anyone at Thornycroft Hall at further risk."

"It does not feel right just leaving my friends to die." Rachel's hands shook as she spoke and she thought of the heartbreak that the Rowlands must be going through. She knew only too well what it was like to lose a loved one. "I should see them, to pay my respects."

William could not hide his impatience. "Don't be so foolhardy. It is not your place to walk into the homes of the sick. You put more at risk. Get home."

Touching her arm gently, Catherine looked doleful. "You are a good girl Rachel, with a good heart. My husband means only to protect you. Leave tending to the sick and the dead to us. It is our duty to God. Your duty is to keep those you live with safe from the contagion."

Her face red with frustration and her throat swollen with a horrible lump of sadness, Rachel turned and fled. She wanted to get as far away as she could from the thick smoke, the stench of death and the echoing moans of sadness and loneliness that had become commonplace in Eyam.

Through to the last of her chores that day, Rachel had remained quiet and solemn, lost in grief. She had not even been able to face Master Benjamin, and had asked if somebody else would take him his supper. Then she had retired to her room and reached for the place that she had hidden the trinkets given to her by her father and the pendant that Sir Edward had gifted to her.

As she picked through the various stones and precious things, her fingers caught the chain of the pendant. Turning it around in her fingers, she looked at it sadly, wondering how it was that so many should have to suffer.

With the numbers of folk sick or dying, there had been talk that Lady Cecily was to be disposing of the services of more staff. No wages, no notice, no words of regret to be offered.

Hannah had overhead Anna and Frimley whispering about it, their faces filled with worry. Lady Cecily wanted no risk of the pestilence finding its way across the threshold of Thornycroft Hall.

Circling the pendant in front of her, Rachel imagined it nestled against the warm olive skin of Lady Rosamund and wondered if she would have behaved the same way as Lady Cecily if she had been alive when the plague had struck. She doubted that anybody could be as vile as Lady Cecily, aside from maybe Benjamin's mother.

The pendant circled in front of her hypnotically. She pondered over whether Lady Rosamund's spirit was wandering through the halls, watching the horror unfold around them, or whether her spirit was too trapped in the grief she had felt at the time of her death to be anything other than oblivious to it all.

"Are you here?" Rachel surprised herself, whispering the question as she watched the jewels set within the stone catch in different angles of light. "Are you here with me now?" She paused, holding her breath, waiting for a sign that she was not alone.

Bringing the pendant higher so that it was circling right in front of her face, she whispered again. "If you are here, show me."

She listened intently to the noises of the house. The settling of beams, voices downstairs in the kitchen, the stir of the wind at the latches and shutters.

"Rosamund?" The name caught on her lips. A dead name. A name that had known such misery and heartache, that even uttering it could bring on a hollow, doomed feeling. Was it her imagination or had the pendant changed direction? As she stared, she thought she could see it picking up speed.

A monstrous thud came from above. The pendant fell to the woven matting beneath her, its chain gathering in a series of loops.

Rachel's thoughts turned to Goody, who had been waiting for her in the shadows beneath the staircase when she had returned from Liza Thickett's cottage. She had thrust the pouch of herbs and corked bottle into Goody's palm.

Without so much as a thank you, Goody had retired to her quarters immediately. There was nothing ordinary, nothing pleasant about the woman. Even when offering Rachel help in the stillroom, there was a glint in her eye, as though she was conjuring up thoughts that she shouldn't be. Conjuring.

Another thud made Rachel look up and then she heard a strangled shout from Goody. The woman was mad, Rachel was quite sure of it. Once again she asked herself what possible hold Goody had over the Thornycrofts; why they permitted her to reside there as a hidden guest?

The sound of heavy boots on the stairs outside her room caused her to start. There was another shout. Sir Edward's voice could be heard fretting as he headed up the staircase that would take him to the entrance of the top quarters.

Forgetting about the pendant, Rachel hurried towards her door, opened it a crack and listened. She heard the door to Goody's quarters being opened. The heavy boots sounded out again as they climbed up the forbidden staircase that was shut away behind the locked door.

Downstairs, Samuel was crying again. There were voices from upstairs and another shout. Then there was silence.

171

It was some time before Sir Edward returned to the main house, shutting and locking the door to Goody's quarters once again. He said something to Frimley, his manner flustered and distressed.

Hurrying back to the open box on the floor, Rachel scraped up the pendant on its chain and placed it carefully next to her mother's cross.

Guilt pressed at her shoulders, weighing them down. She had been so wrapped up in the mystery and intrigue of Lady Rosamund that she had not thought to bring her mother's cross to her lips, to whisper a prayer and kiss it.

The shutters rattled as the wind picked up outside and snow was blown from the sky against the house and to the gardens below. Rachel touched the cross to her lips, feeling both the rough and the smooth parts.

How she needed a mother figure now. She was near enough a grown up woman, old enough to take care of herself. Yet all she wanted was for somebody older and wiser to wrap their arms about her and tell her all would be well. If Lady Cecily's plans held true, she could be homeless and jobless, with nowhere to go in the thick of a harsh winter. She would be lost, vulnerable, frightened.

The painting of Lady Rosamund flashed in front of her eyes. Some of those pictures had said that she had been afraid. She had not just been miserable but she had been afraid. Had she been afraid of something in Thornycroft Hall?

Once, when Cook had taken too much cider, she had told Rachel and Hannah the story of Lady Rosamund's last and fateful confinement.

The top quarters had been her confinement and her screams had gone on for two days before she had birthed the last child. None of the staff had seen her, for Lady Rosamund had kept to her chosen quarters, but all had been reported as well and although they had not seen the child, the staff had rejoiced.

Cook had recounted the night with tears in her eyes. The quarters that Goody Brown now resided in had been viewed as a place for new life and new beginnings. Over time they had become a place of horror.

Cook had said that if there had been a presence of sorts, it must have fed off the misery that had permeated the walls up there. It had found its way in to the shadows, had waited as Lady Rosamund had become more withdrawn, sleeping in the day and wakeful at night. Then it had taken its opportunity.

In spite of a successful birth, she had still been so desperately sad. They had all heard her moans and some had stopped by to listen to her weeping.

Cook had said that it had been after Lady Rosamund's stay with the priest, a year earlier, that she had never been the same. The priest had been employed to exorcise the demon from her. "A shell, hollowed out," Cook had said. "The light gone from her eyes." That was how she had described her and that was how she was certain that the demon had found its way permanently into Lady Rosamund's soul. In the end, there had been no fight left within her.

Dropping the jewellery back into its box, Rachel felt appalled at the very thought of it all.

Tucking the box away, she climbed into bed and shivered. Hunkering down underneath her blanket, she attempted to wrap herself snug as she waited for sleep to come, listening to the occasional hoot of an owl or the mournful call of a fox.

It wasn't a shadow that woke her, or the foul stench of stale urine that seemed to linger in the air, but the sensation of something lightly tracing the contours of her face. Fingers, long and cold.

With a start, her eyes snapped open. Using her elbows, she pushed herself up, cowering back into the wall.

A flash of silvery, insipid looking skin retreated into the shadows of the room as a breath was taken.

Sitting very still in her bed, Rachel kept her eyes wide, trying to make out the shape that was slithering back into the darkness.

Holding her breath, she looked towards the door. It was open. She was sure that she had shut it, but she had been tired and may not have done so properly.

As her heartbeat began to return to a steadier rhythm, she wondered if, after all the thoughts of Lady Rosamund's madness, and with all the death in the village, it had perhaps been a nightmare.

She began to melt back beneath the blankets, but sudden movement from just beyond the open door caught her eye, revealing a flash of something pale. A hand, an ethereal glow shining from its skin, dragged across the wall in the moonlight.

Sitting to attention once again, Rachel swung her legs over the side of her bed and stifled a cry as her foot hit the chamber pot. Ignoring the sudden urgency to relieve her bladder, she hurried to the door and stepped into the cold night chill of the corridor.

Moonlight spilled through the shuttered windows so that fractured bands of milky white lit the innards of the house.

Her breath spun out in front of her, giving away her position to anything that might have been watching.

Then she heard it. Scuffling and the unmistakable sound of footsteps on the staircase behind the door leading to Goody's quarters.

Curiosity quelled her fear as she tiptoed towards it, guided only by the light of the moon. Reaching for the handle she expected the door to be locked, but with no effort, it swung open.

Rounding on the foot of the staircase behind, she looked up. Shadows danced above her, but there was nobody there. She had heard the footsteps though. Those couldn't be explained away as a bad dream.

Tentatively placing a foot on the staircase, she told herself that all those noises and things that had made her hair stand on end really hadn't been her imagination. There was something unnatural in Thornycroft Hall, watching them all, biding its time. Now it had touched her and the thought of it made her skin crawl. The cold dead caress of its fingers, or something that had felt like fingers, had been etched into her skin. Against her better judgement, she began to climb upwards.

At the top of the staircase, she caught another flash of movement, just in front of the door that led in to the quarters that had once been Lady Rosamund's.

Rachel felt the press of her bladder again. Part of her wanted whatever was up there to show itself and part of her did not. She was close. She just had to find the courage to keep climbing. Trying not to think about the waxy dead feel of the thing that had touched her face, she pushed on.

Her legs began to feel heavy and she placed her palm against the wall to steady herself. She could hear it breathing but, for the darkness, she could not see it. With a final thrust forward, she propelled herself to the top of the stairs. Her heart was beating so hard that it felt as though it would pound out of her mouth at any moment.

Movement shimmied through the murky light in front of her again. She could feel something closing in towards her, sour breath, cold skin. Then she saw it, a hand reaching for her.

Clawing at the walls, she scrambled backwards down the stairs, almost losing her footing. The door at the bottom had almost shut. As she pushed it open, a thin veil of light drifted in, illuminating the shape that was gaining on her. Gulping at the stale air, she drew breath to scream.

"What do you think you're doing, creeping about in the thick of night?"

The scream emerged as a whimper as Rachel's eyes adjusted and her mind placed the voice.

Dressed in her nightshift, peppery hair spilling from her cap in wiry tangles, Goody looked feverish. She was holding a tallow candle that had gone out, the stink of it smoking and festering in the tiny space that they were in. Rachel noticed how Goody's arm trembled and how wild her eyes were. A fine film of sweat shimmered against the skin of her forehead and top lip.

Rachel opened her mouth to speak, to answer the question that had been poised with such accusation. She stammered, only managing nonsense before closing it again.

"Well?" Goody pressed her for an explanation as she ushered her out of the tight space that housed the stairs to the top quarters.

Rachel waited until they had returned to the relative safety of the servants' quarters. Her eyes darted around to check that nothing was lurking. "I thought I heard something."

"What? What did you hear?" Goody's breathing had not yet steadied and Rachel realised that she must have given her quite a fright. Goody gave her a light clip around the ear. "That's the second time I've caught you up to no good. I don't take kindly to sneak thieves and you know as well as anyone what Lady Cecily would do if she knew of this."

Horrified, Rachel shook her head. "I'm not a thief. Please, I just thought I heard-"

"Thought you heard something." Goody finished the sentence for her, drawing out the words with a childish lilt. "Yes, so you say." She narrowed her eyes, sizing her up, calculating what level of threat or nuisance she might be. "Now the truth, lest I march down to Lady Cecily and tell her everything that I've seen you up to these last months."

Rachel was stuck. How could she explain that she had thought that the demon that had possessed Lady Rosamund had been in her room, touching her face? It was preposterous to even think it, let alone say it aloud. "I just thought someone was out there. I thought they had been in my room."

A shadow crossed Goody's face and she shrank back as though Rachel had shown signs of the sickness that was ravaging Eyam.

"But it was just a bad dream." Rachel was quick to give her conclusion on the night's events, clearly keen to exonerate herself from any suspicion of folly or fever.

"Did you see? Did you see the face?" If it was possible, Goody had paled to a shade lighter than her shift.

Shaking her head, Rachel assured her that she had seen nothing and that it had all just been a silly dream.

For a few moments longer, Goody sized her up, her breath still short. When eventually she appeared satisfied that there was nothing more to concern herself with, she muttered something about dealing with her in the morning before going back upstairs.

Throwing herself back into her little chamber, Rachel shut the door with a soft click. Had it been Goody in her room? There had been something in her expression that had been strange. At first she had thought that it was fear but now, on reflection, she thought it had looked more like guilt. What would Goody want with anything in her room? With a start, she thought of the trinket box hidden away.

Throwing the blanket back, she raced to find the box, her hands fumbling wildly for the right place in the darkness. As her fingers made contact with the smooth edges, she pulled it out and opened it. Everything was still in its rightful place.

Breathing a sigh of relief, she pulled the pendant out and fastened it around her neck before carefully pushing the box back into the space in the wall.

If Goody knew about Sir Edward giving her the pendant, she could be trying to steal it from her for Lady Cecily or even for herself.

Tucking it under her night shift, she vowed to find a different hiding place for the box the following day. There was something sly about Goody Brown with her secrets and threats.

Climbing back into her bed, Rachel remained on her side so that she could keep an eye on the doorway. She pulled her hands protectively to her chest.

Goody Brown was not to be trusted, prowling around at night. There was no way that Rachel would let her or Lady Cecily get their hands on what precious few possessions she owned.

******

It was too early to rise, with no hint of dawn, but Rachel could not sleep for worry. She worried for her friends in the village, she worried for the young, barely begun life of Samuel, she worried for her own life and she worried for the potential and likely departure of Master Benjamin.

They had not spoken of their exchange in his chamber, but he had once again come to venture out from his confines more frequently, sitting in the blue parlour whilst she cleaned and helping her with the firewood.

Their companionship had not gone unnoticed and Hannah had whispered of Cook's disapproval. She said that there would be trouble.

Rachel chose to ignore the warning. Master Benjamin needed kindness and support. He was not only recovering from a terrible accident, but from the pain of losing the affections of his parents.

Rachel knew what it was like to lose loved ones, although she could not imagine the heartache that must accompany being rejected the way that Master Benjamin had been. Whilst he was doing well to hide his bitterness, she could see it in his eyes. Even so young, they were hooded with the burden of heartache and Rachel could see that the sadness inside of him was in danger of curdling into something else. Without human kindness and companionship, he would be lost to bitterness. Rachel was determined not to let that fate fall upon him.

Creeping downstairs, she paused outside Lady Cecily's chamber. Candlelight illuminated the crack of the doorway and the dim murmur of voices told her that people were up.

Rachel leaned her head towards the door, her ear keen. Even with Samuel to consider, Lady Cecily never emerged until long after first light, so the fact that she was up was strange, although it was remotely possible that she was with her babe. Then she realised the lack of plausibility in that scenario. The wet nurse took care of Samuel's nightly feeds and grumbles. Just before Samuel's birth, Rachel had overheard Lady Cecily boasting to her friends over tea that she would not let a child deprive her of daytime naps or a full night of sleep and that a wet nurse was a necessity.

Gently pressing her cheek to the door, she listened. There were two voices, each little more than a whisper. They were arguing.

The louder of the two belonged to Lady Cecily. "We can not stay. For Samuel's sake, Edward we must leave. We have the means. We can take some of the staff."

There was a muffled retort, words spoken in a voice too deep and husky to decipher. Rachel pressed her ear harder to the wooden panelling.

Lady Cecily's tone was heating with her temper. "She can not come Edward. She stays. To even consider it shows me that your loyalties are wavering."

"Poppycock woman. What nonsense is this?" Sir Edward's retort was clearer this time.

"Don't think I haven't seen you, that gaze lingering when she is in the room. I shan't stand by and watch. Your loyalties should be with your wife and son. She can stay at Thornycroft Hall until this passes but I want her gone when we return."

Bringing a hand to her mouth, Rachel sucked in her breath. They were talking about her, she was certain. Her cheeks flushed as she thought of Sir Edward's attentions and the night that he had given her a gift. She had thought of his affection as nothing more than gratitude for the safe delivery of his son and heir.

Burning with shame, Rachel recalled the rumours of how the affair had started with Lady Cecily, right underneath poor Lady Rosamund's nose. Biting down on her bottom lip, she considered whether there had been something more to the gratitude and gift that Sir Edward had bestowed upon her.

Lady Cecily was insisting that they were to depart Eyam in haste and that they would be leaving her behind, but worse, when the plague had gone and they returned, Rachel was expected to leave their employment.

In Lady Cecily's bedchamber, they continued to argue. Their voices had lowered so that they were mostly muffled again. From the tattered shreds of conversation that she picked up, Rachel knew that the subject remained as her position in the house. Sir Edward refused to make her homeless and unemployed, whilst Lady Cecily was throwing suggestions for alternative arrangements for Rachel.

The heat in Rachel's cheeks soared, but now it was from the anger that engulfed her. Who did these people think they were to play God with her life and decide what her fate would be? When the time came, she would pack her bags. She would not accept their alternative arrangements. She was old enough to find her way in life and she would shock them all by holding her head high and giving *them* her notice.

There was an angry bang, like the flat of a hand smacking the wall as Sir Edward muttered something and then the sound of Lady Cecily sobbing.

Heavy footsteps began to pound towards the door. Her heart lurching, Rachel hurried down the stairs as swiftly as possible, hurling herself into the safety of the kitchen.

For the rest of the day, she scrubbed, cleaned and served, barely uttering a word to anyone. Too lost in concerns of their own, nobody noticed.

Lady Cecily was in the blue parlour asking for tea, but there was no more. Supplies left at the drop sites in the village were basic and tea was not a staple requirement. It would be preposterous to even ask.

Her glare as frosty as the wintry gardens outside, Lady Cecily glowered at Rachel when she explained the situation. With an expression of distaste, she turned to look out of the window. "We will surely starve if we stay in this place any longer," she complained to nobody in particular. "I won't sit back and wait to be starved to death." Pushing herself from her chair with her long spindly arms, she swooped past Rachel, her skirts swishing against the floor.

Rachel went to pick up the embroidery that she had dropped and in doing so, looked out of the window. Everything looked grey. It was as though the bulging clouds overhead had leaked some of their dullness onto the world, washing it of colour.

Beyond the rooftops of the cottages fringing the centre of the village, black smoke licked at the drab sky. Rachel wondered how many more had perished.

"They want to leave." Master Benjamin's stick clicked against the floor as he entered the room.

With a gasp of fright, Rachel spun around. She had not realised that anybody else was around after Lady Cecily had fled.

Benjamin stopped some paces away from her. His hair was hanging over his pale face. It looked a limp and dirty mess in comparison to the shiny glossy mane that he had adorned when he had first arrived at Thornycroft Hall with his family. "Edward asked if I would go with them but *she* can't abide looking at me." His voice soured on pronouncing the word 'she' and Rachel realised that he was referring to Lady Cecily. "She says that I should return to mother, father and Bernadette. Mother would not stand for it though. I am soiled goods. I am as good as vermin, full of poison. I read her letter before it was burned." His tone was flat. "Mother is adamant that my return would carry the risk that I breathe the plague seed into the family home." Sullenness dragged at his face and the brilliance of his eyes had ebbed to the shade of pond water.

With a pained groan, he dumped himself into the nearest chair, letting his cane fall with a clatter. Chuckling bitterly, he sank into the backrest of his seat. "She would rather take her chances and lose her son and heir to the pestilence than allow me home again. It would of course be a small mercy should the pestilence take me. Neither she nor Lady Cecily would have to abide looking upon me again."

Lacing his fingers together, he leaned forward and rested his chin on top of his hands. "Tell me Rachel, do you know what it is to be rejected?"

"As you know Master Belgrave, I have no family, if that is what you mean."

An amused smile played on his lips and Rachel cringed. He was bored and he was in one of his moods. "Master Belgrave? Rachel, I thought you and I were on first name terms now." The plum in his voice had intensified but in a way that marked him as superior to her. He sounded cunning, sarcastic and sly. It was not attractive and with his mangled face, as he sat there, lips curled upwards into a tormenting leer, she thought that perhaps he did resemble a monster.

"Having no family to speak of is not what I mean, no," he said. "Your family might have passed, but did they love you? Did your mother pluck you from her breast and cast you aside?"

"We have talked about this already Benjamin, or do you forget?" She made a point of speaking his name. "I was not fortunate enough to know my mother. She died when I was young."

"Such tragedy." There was no sarcasm in his voice and all of his attentions were focused on her, but it wasn't clear whether his sympathy was genuine. "Your father then. Did he love you? I mean, you have told me that he did, but was it genuine love? Did he care for you as a father should?"

"Yes. Yes he did. He loved me dearly and I loved him back. He said that my mother had loved me dearly too. I was very loved." A wicked sense of pleasure rippled through her as he visibly recoiled, her response wounding him. She would not allow him to torment her in his boredom, confusing her kindness towards him with weakness. "I am sorry that your mother has not been kind to you," she added.

"I suppose you will go with them when they leave," he said. It was a statement rather than a question. Was there bitterness in those words? A longing? Regret?

"I suppose." Rachel turned to the grey landscape again and tried to imagine what the Thornycroft's second residence might look like, if it would be grander than Thornycroft Hall or much more modest in comparison. As her eyes trailed the breadth of the empty fields beyond the gardens, she knew that she would never find out. She wasn't prepared to let Benjamin know what she had heard earlier that morning though.

"I will miss you." The words were barely audible and when she turned to face him, his head was bowed, his shoulders heavy with a burden that somebody so young should not have to carry. The monster had gone, a broken young man in its place. He didn't look up again and he didn't say anything more.

Silently, she placed Lady Cecily's embroidery on a side table and then left the room.

CHAPTER 19

Mid to late December 1665 – Eyam

Cheeks pinched with cold, Rachel pushed open the door to Thornycroft Hall and listened to the hollow echo of her boots against the bare flagstones. The sound of carriage wheels cracking the dawn frost was ebbing away to nothing. They had gone.

The Thornycrofts, Anna, Frimley, Cook, Hannah, everyone except for Rachel and Johnny, the stable hand, had been either taken or given their notice.

She was expected to keep the house and Johnny the horses that were too old to travel in the unforgiving bite of winter.

Johnny's sister lived in the village though and he decided that he would return home after tending to the horses, rather than stay in Thornycroft Hall.

Master Benjamin had been right; they had left him behind too, although Rachel wondered how much of it was his own stubborn pride. He bore a stubborn dislike for Lady Cecily and it was doubtful that he would have willingly left with them, even if Sir Edward had tried to convince him to join them.

Rachel looked around sadly. In the watery light of morning, everything was an echo of its former self. The beautiful rugs had been replaced with the same rush matting that adorned her room. No fresh herbs or scented water had been sprinkled and the usual buzz of the house was gone. It was as though only a dark foreboding shell had been left.

Master Benjamin had refused to wave the Thornycrofts off and was still in his chamber. He had even refused to join them for the farewell dinner. However, Rachel decided that it was no bad thing. She had little doubt that somebody hadn't spat in it or worse. What the Thornycrofts were doing was beyond unreasonable. Refusing to take some of their staff was as good as stating how worthless their lives were. Still, at least they had left her with a roof over her head.

Loneliness embraced her as she stood alone in the huge hall. It took her hand and led her around each empty room, pointing out the half completed embroidery that Lady Cecily had left, a discarded swaddling blanket for Samuel, the glass that Sir Edward had used the night before, still waiting to be cleaned.

The embers of the fire in the blue parlour were smoking uselessly, waiting for somebody to relight them and make the room glow again. There was no point if it was not to be used.

With a heavy step, Rachel took to the stairs and paused outside Lady Cecily's chamber. The bed was still to be made up. She would be expected to strip the sheets and launder them fresh for their return, but when that would be, Rachel did not know.

Lost in a sea of time that seemed to stretch on endlessly ahead of her, she went over to the window and drew the curtains before snuffing out the candles that had lit the way for the Thornycrofts to prepare themselves for a long journey ahead.

Outside, a gentle wind gathered the powder of fresh snowfall. It looked like it would only be a light dusting and Rachel prayed for the safety of the carriages to their destination. No matter what bitterness she felt towards her employers, she wished them no harm and to travel through a whirling white snowstorm, where the sky and road became muddled as one, would be treacherous.

She looked around the room, imagining that at any moment she might hear the impatient cries of Samuel or cross demands from Lady Cecily. No noise came.

There was much to do in the house and only Rachel to do it. The breakfast dishes had been left, lunch and supper were to be prepared for Benjamin, wood to be chopped and collected, laundry to be gathered for sorting, scented water to be made up so that she could scatter it over the matting and the upholstery to keep it fresh.

As she mentally listed what was required to keep the house running, something fluttered inside of her. This was as good as her house now.

Perching in the window seat, she looked out towards the village and dared to imagine what it would be like as the Lady of Thornycroft Hall.

For starters, she would have her room moved to the back of the house so that she might wake to the glorious views of the fields down to Stoney Middleton. Of course, she knew exactly why Lady Cecily had insisted on her chamber being to the front aspect; it was to save her looking across to the first Lady Thornycroft's grave. The rightful Lady of Thornycroft Hall.

A noise startled her from her musings. Skirts sweeping across the floor and the gentle tread of feet on the staircase.

Her palms prickling, she gripped the window seat ledge. With everyone gone, she was now alone with whatever wandered the maze of corridors and rooms at night. It was an unsettling thought and one that seemed to awaken the house from its slumber as a beam above her groaned and the sound of a disturbed floorboard creaked.

Standing up, Rachel's first thought was to head to the stables. At least Johnny would be out there, mucking out the horses, checking their shoes, petting their velvety noses. From outside the room, there was another creak, then footsteps.

She hesitated, her hand curled around the edge of the door. The footsteps had stopped, as though someone was waiting, listening out for her.

For what seemed like a long time she waited behind the door, willing herself to find the courage to open it. When eventually she decided that she could not stay there all day, she pulled it back.

With no candle in her hand, the darkness of the corridor threatened to engulf her. She went to the table where Lady Cecily had left her lamp burning and she picked it up. Holding the lamp high, she widened her eyes, hoping that they would quickly adapt to the dimmer light as she stepped out into corridor.

Ahead of her, something moved. A shadow. The whites of eyes. A flash of skin.

"Goody." Almost breathless, the name floated ethereal in the darkness and Rachel wondered if Goody saw relief or suspicion upon her face. "You have not gone with them?" she asked, surprised.

"And nor it appears, have you," Goody observed. There was an edge to her voice, one that mirrored how Rachel felt. "Sir Edward has entrusted me with the running of the house, to ensure that those fortunate enough to have been allowed a roof over their heads know their place and their role here." There was no disguising the poignant meaning of what she said as she ushered Rachel to shut the bedroom door. "There will be no invasion of the Thornycroft's privacy." Deftly, she reached behind Rachel and pushed a key into the lock. "I shall advise you when you need to carry out your duties in that bed chamber or any of the other private rooms." The flicker of lamplight lit her face. As she glared at Rachel, all fancies about being the Lady of the house went crashing down around her.

Goody smiled, her discoloured teeth flashing dangerously. "Now, I do believe that I missed out when the Thornycrofts broke their fast this morning and I daresay you did too lass. Shall we fetch ourselves some breakfast?" Like the wind, she had changed, warmth radiated from her as she placed a hand on Rachel's shoulder. "You must sit and eat something before doing any more of your chores today Rachel lass. I shall take my breakfast tray upstairs, but I insist that you fill up well before starting on anything else." She gave her a conspiring wink. "Besides, Lady Cecily won't need these hands overworking themselves whilst she's away will she?" She put Rachel's fist in her palm and rubbed gently at the blisters. "Later I'll give you a salve for these. You have fine hands lass, seems a shame to have them spoiled."

Rachel stared gormlessly at this mysterious houseguest who was evidently as much a permanent feature of the house as the oldest tapestries that adorned the hall.

Neither revered nor welcomed, but there all the same, Goody's position had been elevated. The dynamics had changed. She was no longer a mere shadow that walked with the ghosts of Thornycroft Hall. Goody was the new mistress.

******

Only days had passed since the morning that the Thornycrofts had left, but everything seemed as though it had been desolate and empty for so long.

Keeping up with all the housework on her own was impossible for Rachel. Despite Goody's hint that she should try and ease off a little, she had still persevered at keeping the place up together but the task was too great. Even in the rooms that had been left unlocked, dust had begun to gather in places that it wasn't usually seen. The house was too big and her heart too heavy to do a proper job on it. With so few people living there and Goody spending most of her time confined to her own quarters at the top of the house, she finally conceded that it didn't seem to matter so much.

Goody did not interfere as much as she had first implied and she certainly seemed to turn a blind eye to the chores that Rachel hadn't managed to get around to doing. In fact, whenever Rachel bumped into Goody, she was surprisingly friendly and pleasant.

One afternoon close to Christmas, Goody appeared in the kitchen when Rachel was plucking a wild duck ready to be trussed, parboiled and roasted. Benjamin had shot it and had returned home delighted with his contribution.

When he had produced the bird, her heart had sank as she thought of the fatty, greasy mess that cook would usually endure with duck or goose on the menu. Still, she could not dampen Benjamin's spirits. So all afternoon she had endeavoured to do her best with it.

There were feathers everywhere and her hands were already sore from it, not at all like the quick work that cook had made of such culinary preparations.

"We are to clean the blue parlour," Goody announced with authority upon entering the kitchen. "Master Benjamin has requested that I open the room up." The keys jangled noisily where she had attached them to her apron.

Both Goody and Benjamin kept mainly to their own rooms, and given the way that he had looked at her when Rachel had broken the news of Goody's presence, informing him that she was to remain residing there, it was a surprising request for him to have made.

"Well come on lass." Impatience was making her terse. "You're making a dreadful mess in here. I'll finish up the bird and you can clean up in there. He wants the dining table polished with beeswax too." She shooed her away and by the time Rachel was finished her work in the dining room and blue parlour, the duck was plucked, trussed and parboiling ready to be roasted.

It was the new way of working; she would unlock the rooms when she saw it fit to permit Rachel into them. The sound of her keys had become her way of telling when Goody was nearby.

Each hour of the days that were to follow passed by slowly and on Christmas Eve Rachel cast her mind back to the previous year at Thornycroft Hall. The other staff had said that it had been the first year that the Thornycrofts had celebrated Christmas. Evidently Lady Rosamund had loved Christmas and so Lady Cecily was even more rigid with keeping to the puritan rules that had banned the celebrations for so long.

When the Thornycrofts had announced that they would be celebrating Christmas again, it had been a wonderful surprise for many of the staff.

Rachel closed her eyes and remembered how the house had been green with holly and ivy draped from bannisters and across the mantels. Spicy aromas had wafted through each room and the Yule log had crackled and burned, its wood smoke mixing deliciously with the smell of apples roasting in ale, the cooking of meat and a glorious blend of nutmeg and cinnamon.

Christmas this year was a stark contrast. There was no fat roasted goose, all golden and crisp, to be brought to a well-decked table. In the staff quarters, laughter and singing, tainted by too much mead and hot cider, had been replaced by a silence that was smothered in dust. Instead of shouts from Cook, red faced, hot and cross in the kitchen, there was only the pitiful sound of logs hissing to help them keep warm, and Rachel had never realised how loud her boots could echo through the rooms of a now empty house.

"That fire needs more logs. Your dallying will be the death of us lass." Vexed, Goody appeared from the kitchen. Her brow knitted with irritation as she reached for the basket that Rachel had carried in. "Go and fetch another after this one. I was out chopping wood until dark yesterday so we have plentiful supply."

When Rachel returned with another basket full of wood, Goody had disappeared from the kitchen and couldn't be found anywhere downstairs. Sighing heavily with fatigue, she supposed that she should get on with the potage. There would be no rich meats or spicy sweetbreads this year.

In the kitchen it was much warmer with the fire blazing. The pot had been filled by Goody, but nothing else had been prepared. Hard work did not appear to be Goody's role, although she did roll her sleeves up when needed.

As Rachel reached for an onion, a bang from the hall startled her. She dropped the knife that she had been working with. The light from outside was fading and she had forgotten to keep some of the candles lit, so it was difficult to see beyond the doorway.

A dark shape appeared on the threshold between the kitchen and hall. It bulked in the doorframe and she tried to remember if she had bolted the doors when she had returned from fetching the wood. Sir Edward had warned them of looters. "Some will use any opportunity," he had boomed before leaving. "Especially after a drink," he had added. "Look after the place and don't let any wanderers from the village in. Not all folk are honest and decent."

Then his gaze had been cast upon Goody. "We don't want anyone stirring up trouble." It had been a poignant remark, the sentence loaded with some secret meaning and the thought of it made Rachel feel nauseous. In that moment, Sir Edward had as good as admitted that something wasn't right about Goody Brown. It wasn't a comfortable feeling to have been left almost alone with her at Thornycroft Hall.

"What are you doing scuttling about in here like a little mouse when it is Christmas?" The shape moved forward, revealing the golden sheen of blonde hair that was speckled with dusty flecks of snow. Master Benjamin strode into the kitchen and dumped a pheasant on to the table. "And there'll be venison on the menu," he announced, proudly. "I was fortunate to spot a young deer." He winked at her and there was an air of arrogance to him. "I've never missed a shot yet. I left the carcass outside. I assume you know how to handle an animal like that?"

Whilst Rachel was sure that he didn't mean to sound full of pomp, she didn't like the way he was barking orders at her. Still, she had to admit that having venison on Christmas Day was far more appealing than what they would have had otherwise.

Bristling, Rachel lifted the pheasant carcass. It had already started to stiffen. "Of course I do," she snapped. It wasn't that she wasn't grateful, but now she would be up half the night preparing the meat. The venison would last them beyond Christmas day, however. What they didn't use would need to be prepared into steaks and salted.

"I thought we could all have a civilised dinner together tomorrow. I'm not rotting away in that room alone over Yuletide." There was something more buoyant about him as he stood looking distinctly out of place by the large kitchen table. "I dare say that the cellar has some good wine gathering dust. We should enjoy ourselves."

Shocked that he could even suggest taking the Thornycroft's belongings, Rachel baulked.

His footsteps were heavy against the floor as he hastened towards her. "What troubles you?"

"It is not ours to take." Her retort was weak and she knew that it would fall on deaf ears. Benjamin Belgrave struck her as the type of person who would see to it that he would get anything that his heart desired.

The kitchen echoed with his laughter and she worried that his arrogant side was returning. "You are right Rachel, of course. It is not *ours* but let us not forget that I am still a guest here. I would expect that the Thornycrofts would want me to be comfortable during my stay." As he spoke, a shadow crossed his face. "I hope that you do not insult me and suggest that I am nothing but a sorner?"

A flutter of fear rippled through her. Despite the companionship they had shared over recent months, Rachel was no fool. Something dangerous simmered beneath the surface. The abhorrent way in which his mother had rejected him was ample grounds for something sinister, ugly and twisted to take hold of the poor lad. Taking a step backwards she shook her head. "Not at all."

"Then why won't you join me for a toast to Christmas?" A daring glint twinkled in his eye. "King Charles would surely want every loyal citizen to indulge a little during Yuletide. If we have the means, it would be an insult to our monarchy not to, would it not?"

Keeping her attention on the pheasant that she had already started to work on, she was all of a sudden ashamed of her status and angered by his blackmail. "But as you pointed out, I am not a guest here, I am simply a servant."

"Poppycock. The Thornycrofts left you here Rachel, to take care of Thornycroft Hall. In my eyes that makes you as good as the Lady of the house." He stepped around her poking at some herbs. "And I am your guest. Your guest wishes to drink wine." She could feel his glare upon her, daring her to rebuff his request. "I wish to drink my wine in your company and that means that you shall have some too. We must raise a toast to the King."

"There's supper to make and now pheasant and venison to prepare. Master Belgrave, I have so much to do in here to take care of everything and Goody has disappeared again. I can not imagine she would approve of me engaging in drinking Sir Edward's wine with you either."

"There you go again with all these formalities. I thought we were on first name terms Rachel?" Pushing away from the edge of the table, he marched towards the doorway. "And I have no idea why you care so much about Goody Brown's opinion? She is not even a real guest.

"I remember her from when I was a young boy, running around with her tonics and brews for Lady Rosamund. None of them worked of course. She was still completely mad by the end of it all. I don't think I ever saw Goody do much else other than fuss around that stillroom when we visited. Certainly not like Anna does for Lady Cecily, or Martha does for mother. That Goody woman is a lazy, good for nothing old…."

"Can I get you something Master Benjamin?" Goody appeared, wiping her hands on her apron. "Only Rachel is very busy and I believe I overheard you saying that we are fortunate enough to have venison on the menu tomorrow."

It was impossible to disguise the height of colour that had risen to his cheeks and Rachel stifled a giggle. Grumbling something, he left them to it and with a tight smile that invited no further conversation, Goody went to retrieve the deer.

"I'll sort the venison Rachel lass," she said. "Despite Master Benjamin's misgivings, I've handled many of them in my time. You just worry about finishing supper for tonight. That pheasant there will be lovely boiled up with some onions, neaps, parsley and wine." She reached for the largest knife she could find and stood in the doorway, the blade glinting ominously. "We shall have a feast tomorrow. I'll see to that."

Goody was true to her word and had prepared the venison in next to no time with expert hands that left far less mess than Rachel would have managed.

When everything was ready and Rachel had finished cooking the potage for that evening's supper, Goody didn't wait to eat with her or help to serve Master Benjamin, choosing to take her share away on a tray, up to her quarters.

Rachel filled a bowl with the potage and cut some bread to have with strawberry cheese.

Benjamin was waiting for her in the great hall. "I thought we could dine together this evening," he suggested and gestured to the doors that led to the dining room. "I have found the best silver and the glass goblets."

Rachel's feet and back were aching and the thought of sitting in a comfortable seat rather than the hard kitchen chairs was heavenly. She followed him through and set his tray on the table. It was only when she lifted her head that she noticed the transformation of the room.

When he had stormed off, leaving her with Goody in the kitchen, he had not retired to his chamber or put his feet up, he had been busy decorating.

Swathes of ivy trailed the mantel and the candelabras. The best silver had been brought out and polished and the fine crystal goblets sparkled. He had even taken the time to find the good beeswax candles, which were glowing beautifully so that they set off the extravagant shimmer of the chandelier above, its glass dripping like frozen teardrops.

Opening her mouth, words caught in her throat. Was it too presumptuous to think that he had gone to this effort to impress her?

"Do you like it?" Pleased with himself, he smiled. She noticed that he had tied back his hair and removed the beard from his face. There was something about seeing him standing there that made her heart quicken and her breath shorter.

"I love it," she whispered in awe and the thought of kissing him on the cheek glanced through her mind, catching her off guard. It was a gesture that felt so right between them and yet, it was so very wrong. She dared to wonder whether it would make him annoyed or pleased. The dilemma rendered her immobile as she stared at him stunned. Between them, the silence that was building was verging on awkward.

Stammering something unintelligible, she hurried to fetch her own food, uncomfortably aware that the pit of hunger she had been feeling had been replaced with a nervous fluttering.

Setting her tray down, she wondered how she could possibly eat in front of him? This was a young man who had eaten with the fairest of girls at the King's court. What if she was to chew the wrong way, or spill something?

"Well, aren't you going to sit Lady Rachel?" With a gallant swoop, he pulled out one of the handsomely carved oak chairs for her before gesturing that she be seated. Expertly, he positioned it so that it was the perfect distance from the table for her. He waited for her to oblige his request to sit before going to take his own place opposite her.

Still unable to speak, she watched him. Her fingers curled nervously around the scroll ends of the chair's arms as Benjamin prepared for grace.

Remembering how Lady Cecily behaved when grace was said, Rachel brought her hands up and forward, clasping them together and shutting her eyes, hoping that he hadn't noticed how much she was trembling.

His voice was gentle, the words filled with meaning. He gave thanks to God for providing them with nourishment in spite of the terrible hardship that had been brought to the village and he acknowledged others who were less fortunate than them.

When her eyelids fluttered open, he was holding out a crystal goblet filled with wine, waiting for her to take it so that they could make a toast.

"Let's forget about fear, grief and sadness tonight Rachel." Smiling, he raised his arm and a splash of ruby red hit the table. Rachel wondered if she had imagined it or if she had been right in noticing that he too was suffering from nerves. If he was, the confidence in his voice betrayed them. "I shall make a toast. To Christmas. And to you, Rachel, my good friend."

Lowering her gaze into her goblet, she sniffed the richness of the wine. It smelled spicy and rich, far too good for the likes of her to drink. Lady Cecily would turn blue if she were to see them now. "To life," she said, offering her own toast and the words hung in the air, poignant, significant. They caught him by surprise and a look of intrigue crossed his face, lighting it, showing off how handsome he was in spite of the angry ridged scars.

For a while they sat in silence, neither of them lifting their cutlery. When Benjamin spoke, there was a sad edge to his tone. "You think I am a spoiled, impetuous man, do you not Rachel?" Taking a hearty swig of his wine, his gaze never faltered from her as he awaited her reaction.

Keeping her head high and her expression sober, Rachel lifted her soup spoon to her lips as gracefully as she could and gently blew before answering. "I think that we are just so very different Benjamin. Your life has been full of privilege."

"Privilege does not vanquish great sorrow," he interjected, reminding her that the gloss of nobility could not protect even the wealthiest of folk from heartbreak.

"Aye, I know, but I too have known misery. What the Lord gives, He can also take away." She focused on delicately spooning soup into her mouth, thinking of the way Lady Cecily and her guests would conduct themselves. Not a drop was ever spilled.

Breaking some bread, shame darkened his expression. "I can not imagine what it is like to lose both your parents to death so young. Our worlds are so different and it is easy to forget that the things that drive us and hurt us can be just the same." Sympathy clouded his expression. "Nor can I imagine the hardship that you have endured living as you have had to."

Snapping her head up, she glared across the table. His words provoked a stab of anger that felt sharp and tight in her chest. With even the social intimacy of sharing a meal together, the sea of distance loomed between them. He pitied her upbringing, her station in life. The very idea that he pitied her put her on the defensive. "Living as I have had to? So that is your opinion is it? That I am just a serving girl born into hardship and misery?" Swiping up her wine, she took an angry gulp. "For an educated young man, you are foolish. How can you not accept that even those poorer than you can be happy? Happier even."

Once again silence clung to the air between them and she cursed herself for being so stupid as to accept an invitation to dine with him. Then the roar of hearty laughter filled the air.

Aghast, Rachel watched as he dropped his bread to his plate and clutched at his sides with merriment until his eyes leaked. Feeling herself grow red with both embarrassment and fury, she let her spoon fall with a loud clunk. "What is so funny?" She no longer cared for the social differences that ordinarily demanded subservience from her. "Am I merely here as your entertainment? Am I simply like one of the court fools you have no doubt seen when dining with all of England's greatest beauties?" She was shocked to feel the wicked ugliness of envy fuel her anger, but she could not stop.

"I imagine they were the perfect dining companions, dressed in all of their finery and not a word spoken out of turn?" Inwardly cringing, she realised how obvious her jealousy was. Crossly, she turned her head, but not before catching the way her words had dashed the smile from his face.

Straightening, Benjamin's expression had become serious and he shook his head. "On the contrary, I am not laughing at you. I would never do that. I am laughing because I have never felt so free." His arms reached up towards the ceiling in dramatic statement. "I feel so utterly free and full of joy. That's how speaking with you makes me feel. You are the voice of truth and reason. There are no fanciful words for self-gain or any webs of deceit with you. The girls I get forced to dine with, who I sit with and walk with are dull. They are moths in comparison to a gloriously colourful butterfly. There is no amount of tailoring or finery that can make true beauty shine. None. They are boring Rachel. With you I see the world as it is. You strip away the falsehoods and make me see everything differently. It is refreshing. I should never tire of listening to your opinions."

Her stony reserve softened and she felt an inner glow. Its warmth curled the line of her mouth upwards and smoothed out her frown. The gap between them closed and the atmosphere relaxed.

Benjamin was sincere in his feelings towards her and he expressed them freely without any hint of awkwardness. The compliment that he had given her was not one that carried any expectation of retort or gratitude.

They continued to eat comfortably, simply enjoying one another's company, exchanging conversation with such surprising ease that Rachel found it easy to forget her earlier doubts and frustrations.

The evening wore on and the richness of the wine tickled the back of her mouth deliciously, making her head spin a little.

After eating, he helped her clear the plates and she did not question it or try to stop him. They were equal, two people who had come together to survive. No airs and graces.

It was only when they had settled in front of the fire together in the blue parlour, that Benjamin probed her once again about her life with the Thornycrofts. "Do you like living here Rachel?"

It was an odd question to ask somebody with little choice in such a matter and she frowned. "As I have told you before, the Thornycrofts look after me well. Sir Edward took me in under his employ after my father passed. It was a promise to him."

His skin was incandescent against the flames that were licking and spitting in the fire and he leaned forwards in his chair. "That was a strange way to answer my question."

"It was a strange question to ask."

Crossing his legs, he tried a different tack. "Why do you suppose that Lady Cecily behaves so appallingly towards you? She singles you out with much more disdain than other staff and yet, you are under their employ with the promise that she will teach you how to become the lady of a house."

Avoiding his gaze, she took a sobering breath before carefully crafting another answer. "Lady Cecily is rude and obnoxious to everyone."

Sitting back in his armchair, he laced his fingers together and perched his chin on top of them. "But to you more than most, don't you agree." It was a keen observation. "You are a very attractive young woman and she is a jealous woman. You should take heed of that."

This time there was no response that she could think of. It was not a conversation that she wished to continue, so she simply nodded her head before standing. "I should take the warming pans to your bed before it gets too late."

A shriek from upstairs caught them off guard and Benjamin's goblet dropped to the floor. It remained intact but the dregs of his wine stained the good rug that had been laid. "God's teeth!" he exclaimed, tilting his head to the ceiling as though that would somehow tell him what the noise had been.

Ignoring her thudding heart, Rachel hurried to find some rags and salt to soak up the wine. "'Tis Goody, is all," she muttered as she returned to dab at the spillage. There was another shriek from upstairs and she shuddered as she thought of the rumours of how Lady Rosamund used to change at nightfall, as though the moon brought madness to her. She wondered how much of that madness had rubbed off onto Goody Brown.

"Mother once told me that the woman lost her mind, just like her mistress," Benjamin blurted out. "She said that Goody used to use chains to restrain Lady Rosamund and that she too would be tethered, for fear that whatever darkness that lived inside of Lady Rosamund might take hold of her too."

Rachel stopped dabbing at the spilled wine as he roughly took her hand. His palms were damp. "I do not like you sleeping so near to her quarters with nobody else in the house," he said.

Pulling away, she threw the red soaked rags into a pile. "Goody is strange," she agreed. "But she does no harm."

Benjamin wasn't ready to let the subject go. "I cannot allow you to sleep up there any longer Rachel." Laced with wine, his speech slurred as he spoke.

Folding her arms across her chest, she eyed him with suspicion. "And where would you propose that I take my bed? In your bedchamber like a common wench?" Once again, she found that she was cursing herself for being so naïve. Would a man of Benjamin's station really tolerate her opinions and thoughts without a hidden motive? How she had wanted to believe him over dinner, but along with Goody's cries from the top of the house, reality was settling in, unwelcome and harsh.

Pushing himself up, Benjamin grabbed his stick and wobbled, the wine and the accusation throwing him off balance. "No Rachel. I would never suggest that, but you must take another of the guest rooms, far away from her. You forget that I knew of her before. She is not clear of mind."

Defiant, she tapped her foot impatiently. "You can only have been a young child back then, so how can you possibly possess such knowledge? It is rather convenient do you not think?"

He raised the eyebrow that he was able to still move. The colour that the wine had given his cheeks deepened. "You certainly have a high opinion of yourself and for that matter, a low one of me if that is how you feel." Incredulously, he glared at her. "To use the madness of an old hag to lure you to my bedchamber would be a rather pitiful and underhand attempt to bed you. Has tonight not changed anything for you?" Hurt blazed in his eyes. "Do you really look upon me as such a monster?"

Pressing his fingers to the red ridge that cumbersomely knitted his face together, his lips quivered for a moment, threatening to destroy his authoritative reserve. With a sobering breath, his expression hardened again and he staggered forward, menace in his step. He reached for her chin, catching it with his forefinger so that her face was tilted towards him. "A monster would not use clever words or manipulative tricks to bed you. A monster would surely have the black heart, the inclination and the power to take you whenever he chooses." The finger remained curled beneath her, propping her head up, reminding her that it was he who held all the authority and control.

Her head was spinning and she felt sick. How could he be such a gracious gentleman one moment and then throw such deplorable threats at her the next? She was a fool to have ever thought that they could be friends. He was right, if he wanted to, he could do anything he liked to her, or at least he could try. She would put up a good fight if he dared move any closer.

Taking a step to the side so that his hand fell from beneath her chin, she moved past him steadily and calmly before she neared the door and ran from the room. From now on, he could put the warming pans to his bed himself and fetch his own meals. She would avoid him.

As she crossed the hall, her footsteps were even louder than usual amidst the emptiness. Putting a hand on the balustrade of the staircase that snaked upwards into the belly of the house, nearer to Goody and her strange noises, she hesitated. Behind her she could hear the urgent click-clack of Benjamin's stick.

A heavy thud sounded out from above and she lost her footing as the hem of her skirts became entwined with her feet. Hitting the staircase with her knees and palms, she winced as pain shattered across her left knee.

Another thud was accompanied by another shriek and it was as though icy liquid trickled through her veins. How could it even be possible for a person to make such a noise?

Alice's words ricocheted against her skull. "I don't know how anyone could abide to live in the same house as a ghost?" she had said.

What if it wasn't Goody? What if the rumours of Thornycroft Hall were true and it was something else?

Rachel felt tears pricking at her eyes as she winced with pain. Now she was living with a ghost, a demon, a mad woman and a monster.

"Rachel wait." The sound of Benjamin's stick followed her, as did his laboured breaths as he struggled to catch up.

Using the palms of her hands, she pushed herself up and reached for the smooth curve of the balustrade so that she might continue to climb away from him, but something had caught her ankle. The area around her foot was being squeezed.

"Please Rachel?"

She turned to see his eyes imploring her to stop and listen to what else he had to say. It was enough to stop her from kicking out.

"You need to listen. Something happened here when I was just a child visiting this house." With a grimace, he limped closer. "Everyone was asleep when it happened. I must have been all of four years old."

Satisfied that she was no longer running from him, he slumped on the stair beneath her and took a moment to catch his breath. "It was the dead of night but something had disturbed me. I felt something on my cheek. A hand, fingers stroking up and down. At first I had thought it to be mother, only mother would never have troubled herself." Bitterly, he pursed his lips before continuing. "It was a woman, not mother but another woman. Goody Brown. I cannot know for certain whether she meant me any harm. I was just a boy and I was terrified. Of course, I shrieked and howled."

"And what happened next?" she asked breathlessly, part of her not wanting to know and the other desperate to hear. "What did she do?"

His face twisted as he recollected the childhood horror. "She disappeared from view. It was as though she had melted into the walls, but she didn't leave my chamber. Try as I might, I could not make out any shadow or outline, but I could hear her, shuffling around, panting like a dog and scrabbling about as though she was looking for something. There was a dreadful rumpus. Lots of shouting and footsteps and all the while she was still in my room."

"How do you know that it was Goody?"

Snapping his head back, his shoulders stiffened and his eyes were glassy. "I know because it was her name that they were calling. It was Goody who they were hunting for. Mark my words it was Goody Brown who stole into my room that night. Sir Edward had sounded furious with her as he roared her name."

As he remembered, he looked pained. "Waiting for someone to come to my room and take her away was terrible. All the while that they were calling for her, she was scuffling around like an animal. I wanted to shout to them, tell them where she was, demand that they hurry, but I was too frightened to do anything other than clutch the blankets to my chin and hold my breath. Then the noise was gone. She had left. Swift and nimble, like a cat. Nobody saw her leave though and to this day I do not know how. Within moments, Sir Edward had entered my chamber. Frimley was holding a lamp for him so that his face blazed orange and twisted with rage."

Benjamin paused, shifting uncomfortably on the step. He turned his head to glance upwards and keeping his voice low, he continued his story. "As he searched, Sir Edward never uttered a word, but his expression was one that I should never want to see on a man again. There was fear in those eyes and I could smell it on him too. Then I noticed him carrying something. A strap, a belt, a rope, I do not know which, only that it had been meant as a restraint."

Rachel thought of the marks on Goody's skin when on rare occasion she had rolled up her sleeves to make decoctions, infusions or tinctures in the stillroom. It made sense that they could be the result of rope bindings. Breathless, she cowered on the staircase, looking towards the direction of Goody's quarters. "Then what?"

Shrugging, he propped his stick against the wall and adjusted his position again, stretching out his leg with a pained groan. "Mother had rushed to my room then. There had been more shouts and then they had found her. There was a confrontation of sorts, before they took her back upstairs.

"I had been ushered away by mother and we cut our stay short, leaving at first light. It was a long while before we visited again. Mother said that after that night, they made Goody pack her bags and leave. There was no point to her staying with Lady Rosamund dead, especially if she was going to be causing the Thornycrofts so much trouble. Mother said that she had always thought there was something not quite right about Goody Brown. She believed her to be mad. Madder than Lady Rosamund if you were to ask my mother."

"Mad? I cannot believe that Sir Edward would keep a mad woman under his roof. What about baby Samuel? Surely they would not have willingly put him in harm's way?" Rachel asked, appalled.

"Mother says that after the death of Lady Rosamund, Goody was only kept on here because she knew of a dreadful secret. She described it to be a misplaced loyalty on the Thornycroft's part." He chuckled ironically. "If mother had known that the woman had been living under this roof at the same time as she was visiting earlier this year, she would have been horrified."

"You know that in the village, they used to call her 'The Conjurer'?" Rachel kept her voice to a whisper, terrified that Goody would be skulking about and listening.

Benjamin's face paled considerably and he nodded. "Even though I do not care to admit it, Mother's instincts are often right."

"But she hasn't been here for years. Surely there can be nothing so terrible about Goody Brown that they would still be so scared of her?"

Benjamin looked at her in earnest. "Why do you think that they have welcomed her back, given her a roof over her head, despite turning some of their most loyal servants out? It is because they still fear her and the secret that she carries." In the dim and fractured light, his eyes looked hollow and shadowed and he bit down on his lip as though ashamed of the confidence that he was about to betray.

"What secret Benjamin?" In her heart, she thought that she already knew.

"I overheard mother complaining about Lady Cecily shortly after the events of that dreadful night. We had returned home and she had been whispering with her sister. I had been playing hide and seek with Bernadette and had hidden in the orangery. Mother had brought her sister in for cake and she had been moaning as usual. It is no secret that she and Lady Cecily are not fond of one another and that Lady Rosamund had been a friend to mother, but I cannot imagine her to lie over something so awful."

Impatient, Rachel shook his arm to hurry the story along. Benjamin had such a flowery way of getting his point across at times and it was frustrating. "Please Benjamin, just tell me what this secret is."

Bowing his head, he gave a frustrated sigh. When at last he looked up, he stared her straight in the eye and she saw the seriousness that was etched into his face. "Lady Rosamund did not take her life. She was murdered." His voice had fallen to barely a whisper but the words knelled loudly in her head.

"Goody murdered Lady Rosamund Thornycroft?" She leaned closer to him so that they could speak without fear of being overheard.

"No Rachel. Mother meant that either Lady Cecily or Sir Edward committed murder and that Goody was privy to it, forced to bury her body and carry the burden. Don't you see? They do her bidding and allow her to stay here to protect their dark secret. That is why she is back and allowed to stay even now. Mother always said that is why Goody Brown is mad, because of the ugly truth of what she has witnessed. Mother may be many things, but she is no liar."

Sinking back into the staircase, Rachel felt lightheaded. It all made sense. Lady Cecily had been Sir Edward's mistress long before Lady Rosamund's death. That was common knowledge. She had only been a maid at the time, a maid who was bedding the husband of her mistress. Without the death of Lady Rosamund, it was doubtful that she would have been catapulted to the dizzy heights of Lady of Thornycroft Hall.

Shakily, Rachel pulled herself up and without another word, she climbed, her legs shaking. She did not stop her ascent until she neared the top of the house and was looking up towards the landing where the forbidden door to Goody's quarters was.

The banging and the cries from Goody had quietened. If there was any truth to Benjamin's words, then Goody Brown had been part of a murder conspiracy.

Nauseated, Rachel fumbled her way back to her room and shut the door, placing a stool against it. Then she thought of Lady Cecily languishing in the safety of the Thornycroft's second residence with her baby boy and noble position. It was a status that had been forged in blood.

CHAPTER 20

Present Day – Eyam

Over three hundred and fifty years later, the ethereal light of dawn was beginning to seep through the inky sky and a hand hovered over Kate's face as she slept fitfully. The sound of a creaking floorboard came from the staircase that led to the top of the house and the hand withdrew.

There was a gasp as a shadow flitted in and out of focus in the corridor. Something tall and spindly. It mingled with the veil of night that was slowly being lifted from Thornycroft, eyes searching, probing each room.

Kate's eyelids fluttered slightly as the shape that had been hovering over her retreated. There was fear in the room and Kate could feel it as she slept. She whimpered, her voice lost in the far folds of the house, carried away by the shadowy figure that slowly retreated back into the night, satisfied that certain secrets still lay dormant.

CHAPTER 21

Present Day – London

After he disconnected the call, a slow smile spread across his face. His efforts to find out where Kate had coveted herself away were beginning to bear fruit.

The owner of the bed and breakfast in Eyam had been extremely keen to get his business. A last minute cancellation had meant that luck was on his side. Twenty four hours was all that she had said was needed and the room would be ready from three the following afternoon.

The smile stayed with him as he reached for the leather holdall from the top of his wardrobe. As he pulled it out, his hand brushed past one of her cardigans. It was the angora one, the one that she had worn the night that they had first met.

Kate treated her clothes like she treated her men. It had been so easily discarded by her, unnoticed and unworn for so long.

Slipping it off the hanger, he held it to his nose and inhaled deeply. He could still smell her. Soon he would be reunited with that familiar scent and he would make her see sense.

A ripple of anger threatened to break his calm exterior. It was abominable, the way that she had treated him, after everything that they had been through together.

Neatly placing the cardigan into the case, he began to pack his clothes, folding everything and stacking it in impeccable order. There was no need for much, just enough for a few days. He was confident that a few days would be all that he needed.

It had been remarkably easy to find out where Kate had gone and he kicked himself for not having had the common sense to perform the last number redial at her parents' house earlier.

The residential home answering the redialled call was located in Derbyshire. When he looked it up on a map, the penny had dropped. He remembered her talking about her Great Aunt Edie who lived in Eyam. She was old and even though the residential home was located in Buxton, he had no doubt that it was something to do with her. She had never said that her Great Aunt lived in care. In fact, she had almost proudly boasted about her fierce independence and deceptive youth, so the home had to be a new event and one momentous enough to send Kate running to be with her. If that was the case, then Kate had to be staying at her Great Aunt's house whilst she visited.

Leaving the case open, ready to pack his toiletries the following morning, he went to the bathroom to brush his teeth. Pausing to look in the mirror, he scrutinised the reflection that stared back at him.

Splashes of stubble peppered his chin, flecks of grey beginning to show. He would have to shave and smarten himself up before his trip. The ripple of anger returned, welling into a wave in his chest. She had broken his usually smart, clean-shaven image, reducing him to the sorry looking man who stared back at him from the glass.

Clenching his fist into a ball, he banged it on the marble unit, barely wincing as the edge flayed the skin off his knuckles. After all the effort he had gone to for her, she was destroying him. Ungrateful cow.

Gripping the edge of the vanity, he steadied himself and took a deep breath, reeling in his thoughts. Getting angry wouldn't help the situation at all. He knew only too well how she responded to anger and he didn't want her running away again.

Squeezing the toothpaste on to his brush, he turned on the tap and let it run for a moment. By the weekend, he would have her back in his arms. That's what he had to focus on now.

CHAPTER 22

Present Day – Eyam

Kate snipped at the last of the flower stems and gently tucked them in to join the other shockingly bright blooms in a large vase.

The house was empty again. Francesca had arrived unannounced at the crack of dawn and refused to take no for an answer when she had insisted on taking Edie out for breakfast. They had only been gone twenty minutes, but to Kate it felt like hours. She had hoped to get some quality time with Edie and she had been surprised at how easily she had been swayed to disappear off with Francesca after the frosty reception she had given her at the home.

Taking the vase into the lounge, she fretted over where she should place it before deciding on bringing it back into the kitchen and putting it in the middle of the large oak table.

Rubbing her eyes, she groaned. Despite eventually falling asleep the night before, she had woken up exhausted. She'd had another strange dream during the night and it had been so vivid.

Her head pounding, she went to the bathroom to seek out some painkillers. Finding a packet of aspirin, she swallowed two before splashing cold water on her face.

The atmosphere in the house was thick and suffocating and she was sure that it was getting worse. It constantly felt like she was being watched.

Leaning against the sink, she pressed at her temples. She was probably overthinking everything after finding the diary and jewellery box. Still, it would do no harm to wear the crystal that Francesca had given her.

Finding it tucked into her jacket pocket, she sought out a silver chain and removed the pendant so that she could swap it for the crystal. Fastening the clasp, she relished the coolness of the stone against her skin. Either the crystal was working, or the tablets were kicking in, as her headache had begun to subside and she felt a little more like herself.

Returning to the kitchen, she tutted as she remembered that she had forgotten to buy coffee. She would have to go out for it instead. The fresh air, she decided, would do her good.

Outside, the temperature had cooled considerably and it was a relief not to be sweating. The walk down the track into the village was a pleasant one and she inhaled the summer sweetness of the air as she admired the beauty of her surroundings. Eyam was certainly a beautiful place to live. She thought back to the sleek lines of her cosy modern London flat and the hustle and bustle that she had become so accustomed to over the years. A move wouldn't be such a bad option. That was the beauty of contracting she supposed.

Richard's face flashed before her, crestfallen, frustrated, angry. How would he react if she did move? He would be bound to find out at some stage. Would he follow her? On more than one occasion, Chris had said that he would put nothing past Richard, that she shouldn't take chances with him.

When things had settled, she would get back in touch with Chris, confide in him with her plans. She had nobody else after all, not with all her old friends being so out of the loop. How could she have been so stupid for so long? She berated herself once again. Chris had become her best friend, her only friend and all because of her relationship with Richard. Never, she vowed, would she allow herself to be so naïve again.

The track opened out where the Lydgate graves were and the village sprawled beautifully in front of her. Brushing thoughts of her past aside, she hugged her arms about her chest and smiled as she crossed the road.

As appeared to be the status quo, the coffee shop was heaving, both with tourists starting out early and parents who had young children clinging to them.

"Oh hello love." A familiar voice challenged the trill of the welcome bell in the shop door. Edie's friend Lindsay was standing at the counter with another woman and a man. All three were smiling warmly at her. "How's Edie getting on? Any word on when she'll be back?" Lindsay asked, clutching a brown paper bag filled with baked goods in one hand and a steaming beverage in the other.

"She's just got home actually," Kate responded brightly, wondering whether Edie would mind her broadcasting that information to the rest of the village.

A look of relief fell across all three faces. The woman next to Lindsay pressed a hand to her chest. "That's wonderful news." She looked up at the man who seemed just as pleased. "Isn't that wonderful news Roger?"

Roger nodded and enquired as to whether Edie had given any indication on when she planned to get back to her volunteering.

"Steady now Roger, one step at a time," Lindsay cautioned him before adding, "I hear that Francesca Warren's having a Well Dressing party. Do you know if Edie will be up to it? It would be so lovely to see her."

Laughing, Kate stepped aside to let a lady with an impatient small child out of the shop. "Evidently she's the guest of honour. Francesca is insisting that she's going to marry it up with a welcome home celebration for Edie."

"Oh I am pleased," the other lady chipped in. "We'll be there, won't we Roger?" Kate assumed that Roger was her other half.

Roger gave an enthusiastic nod. "Last I heard most of the village are going." He pulled open the door to the shop so that the bell tinkled noisily again.

Lindsay offered another warm smile. "We'll see you there then. Give our love to Edie won't you?"

Promising that she would, Kate waved them off and ordered a Danish pastry with a flat white before sitting down at an empty table in the corner by the window.

Looking through the glass into the street, she found her mind drifting, thinking about the plague. It was hard not to given that the village did so much to keep its history front of mind. Many of the buildings and features within the village had retained their authentic appeal, with the stone built cottages, unspoiled Delf with the Cucklet Church and more traditional features such as the stocks and even the old water troughs. It was easy to imagine what everything had looked like back then, and as she waited for her coffee, her mind began piecing together a different image of the street.

The voices around her merged into a buzzing noise and she watched as the tarmac turned to an uneven surface and cars faded to animals nosing the ground for scraps of food or giving short chase to the odd scrawny wandering hen. A brown dog lolloped past the window. Its head was hung low and tongue out. She could see the sharp contours of its ribs poking through its scant fur.

Where children had once played, women pulled carts with goods, carefully keeping their distance from each other. Young faces peered from windows hopefully, waiting to see what their parents or older siblings would bring home from the various boundary drops, where goods would be left by neighbouring villages in return for coins, or as supplies from relatives living outside of Eyam. Their faces were paler than they had been the year before. They had been told to wait inside and not go out and play as they had once been accustomed to doing. The streets appeared virtually empty of normal life, like a ghost town.

"Can I join you?" The voice seemed far away and at first it seemed surreal, like an echo from another time. "Kate?" Somebody was calling a name. Kate. Somebody was looking for a person called Kate. A hand touched her shoulder.

Startled, she jumped, her elbow knocking over the cup of coffee that had been placed in front of her. She hadn't even noticed it had been put there. How long had she been staring into space like that and why hadn't she recognised her own name being called?

There was a flash of movement from behind the counter as a waitress sprung to the rescue, carrying over a handful of paper napkins and a cloth. Stuttering her apologies, Kate felt herself blushing.

Beside her, Nick was picking up the fallen, but thankfully undamaged cup, and helping dab up the mess.

Reaching for a clump of napkins, Kate joined them and apologised profusely once again, realising that the whole shop had gone quiet and was staring at the mess.

The waitress insisted that she would finish clearing it up and Nick insisted on buying her another one.

"I didn't mean to startle you." He took the empty cup and handed it to the waitress before sitting in the seat opposite and flashing her a look of concern. "How is Edie? I'm surprised she's not with you. She's not gone back to the home or hospital has she?"

Realising how forlorn and sorry for herself she may have looked, sitting alone staring blankly into space, she shook herself from her daydream. "No, no, nothing like that. Francesca dropped by first thing and whisked her off for breakfast. We're out of coffee and I needed a decent caffeine fix." She leaned back in her chair as two fresh cups and saucers were placed onto the table. Taking her knife, she cut through the shiny apricot in the centre of the pastry she had bought and gave him a cheeky wink. "Plus, I've quickly learned that this place is great for anyone with a sweet tooth." She offered him half on a folded napkin.

"You've got that right," he agreed and accepted the other half of the pastry. "Thanks."

"Edie's doing far better than I thought, considering she didn't want to come home," she said.

Taking a generous bite of his breakfast, Nick studied her carefully as he chewed. "And how are you doing?"

"I'm doing fine. I'm not the one who has had a fall." Hiding behind her cup, she took a sip of her coffee. Were her uneasy and unsettled feelings really written all over her face?

Licking some stray crumbs from his lips, he leaned across the table. "You said last night that there was something about Thornycroft. Kate, have you seen something?"

The direct nature of his question caught her off guard and the pastry slipped from her fingers onto her jeans. Grabbing a napkin, she pressed at the buttery stain. "I'm not having much luck today," she joked but failed to inject any humour into her tone of voice.

"Don't change the subject." His voice was a quiet purr but his expression was stern and searching. Not for the first time, she noticed how dark his eyes were against the velvety brown of his skin and how his cheeks dimpled with certain expressions. "Kate?" he prompted her, pushing for an answer.

The intensity of his gaze made her look away. She felt stupid and like she was allowing her loneliness to create romantic feelings that weren't really there, but at that moment she wanted to tell him everything that had been happening to her since arriving in Eyam. She wanted to tell him all about the dreams, the visions, the fainting spell at the Riley Graves, where the Hancock family were buried, and the strange feeling that she was seeing the village through somebody else's eyes.

Opening her mouth to speak, she paused and then shocked herself as she told him all about what had happened between her and Richard instead. "My ex partner was stalking me before I arrived here and I'm always on edge that he's just going to reappear at any moment." Biting the inside of her cheek, she took a deep breath as a weight lifted from her shoulders. She hadn't intended to impart any details of her past to anybody, let alone a man whom she had only just met, but the situation had clearly been bothering her far more than she had realised.

Sinking back in his chair, he looked surprised. "Wow. I wasn't expecting that."

With a nervous chuckle, she shook her head. "Neither was I. I mean, I hadn't meant to tell you. I'm a private person usually."

"I would say I'm privileged, but it's not really appropriate." He raised an eyebrow and a short silence prevailed until he spoke again. "Do you want to talk about it?"

Picking at some crumbs, she began to relay how Richard had changed like the wind and how his jealousy over her friendship with Chris had spiralled out of control. "He wouldn't even stop after we broke up. He was following me everywhere, turning up and checking in on me with the excuse that he was worried for my welfare. It got so disturbing that I had to call the police after he broke into the house." Picking at her napkin, she sighed heavily. "Of course, he came up with excuses, claiming that he was trying to protect me from Chris. Chris hadn't even been there. I was on my own, so Richard must have been watching me and waiting for the right time to pounce - when I was alone."

Tatters of red fluttered to the table from between her fingers, as she nervously ripped at the napkin. "It was terrifying if I'm honest."

"And that's why you were so upset with me when I was outside with my canvas." With a whistle, he shook his head. "I have to say that I did come around to your point of view but now I know the whole context, I feel terrible for being so stubborn and pig headed about it all. You must think I'm a complete bastard."

"Past tense. I *thought* you were a complete bastard, but you've just bought me another coffee and listened to me witter on about my problems, so you're forgiven. Besides, I was pretty off with you, far more prickly than I should have been. So for that, I apologise too."

Raising his cup, he offered a toast. "Truce?"

"Truce." The sound of china chinking together invited a ray of sunshine into her, lighting her from the inside. There was something in that toast that felt more significant than a truce, and she didn't think that she was imagining the twinkle in his eye that caused her pulse to quicken.

After they had said their goodbyes and she had returned to Thornycroft, it was far nearer to lunchtime than she had realised. Turning the key in the lock, she pushed open the front door and called out to Edie. Her voice echoed hollow and singular inside the house.

Throwing the keys onto the hall table, she checked her mobile and frowned. Two missed calls, both of them from Chris. Checking her voicemail she was surprised that he hadn't left any message, but then again, she had been clear that she had wanted a bit of space whilst the whole situation died down. Nevertheless, she wished that he would stop calling until she was ready. She wouldn't put it past Richard to be keeping tabs on any contact they were having.

With a frustrated tut, she threw the phone back into her handbag. Richard's behaviour had made her so paranoid that she often found herself second guessing what he might be doing or about to do. That was probably half the reason why she constantly felt watched inside Thornycroft. She had to remind herself that he had no idea where she was and so she didn't need to worry.

Thinking back to her conversation with Nick, she smiled. It had been so easy talking to him and it was as though a whole new person had emerged from beneath his moody exterior. She had enjoyed his company once again and his reaction to her history had put her at ease.

Hanging her bag up, she went to head upstairs, glancing momentarily into Edie's makeshift bedroom and catching sight of a pale arm draped across the top of the duvet. Poking her head around the door, she called her name softly but she was snuggled underneath the blankets, the material rising and falling with her steady breathing. She was obviously sleeping soundly. The morning with Francesca must have tired her out and it didn't seem fair to wake her, so Kate pulled the door to before setting about neatening the house up whilst she waited.

After tidying the kitchen, she toyed with the idea of calling Francesca to check on how Edie had seemed during their morning out together.

In the hall, she reached for her phone from her bag, but the crunch of tyres on the parking area beyond the front garden interrupted her.

Moving into the kitchen, she looked out of the window and saw Francesca's car coming to a halt. She frowned. Much as she enjoyed Francesca's company, she had been keen to spend some time on her own with Edie during the course of the afternoon.

Opening the front door, she waited for Francesca who was teetering down the path in a pair of killer heels, a great big smile on her face.

"Did you have a good time earlier? Was it a success?" Kate called out.

With a wave of her hand, Francesca pushed her oversized sunglasses on to the top of her head. "Just like old times. I'm afraid we got carried away and took a little shopping trip into Bakewell. I really need to head back in a second as I've got to get a whole mountain of shopping in for the party tomorrow. There's a real buzz in the village at the moment. Shame the forecast isn't so good, but no matter as we'll have a great time and Edie will love it." Her hazel eyes glinted with excitement. "Remember not to let on. She'll be so surprised. I've rounded up lots of the village too. I've got quite a party planned for her."

Fumbling in her bag, her heavy bangles jangled and then she pulled out a brown pot of pills. "Here. It's Edie's medication. She forgot her bag and so I was carrying them for her. Anyway, I don't quite know what to do with her as she fell asleep in the car on the way home and it felt a bit mean to wake her. I thought if you could help me get her back into the wheelchair, we should be able to do it without causing her too much fuss or discomfort." She gestured towards the parked car where Kate could see the outline of somebody slumped against the window of the front seat.

Something twisted in her gut and Kate felt herself pale. "Edie's with you?"

Oblivious to the wave of horror that had washed over her, Francesca breezily led the way back to her car. "Well of course she is. Do you think we can do it without disturbing her too much? It would be nice if she could have a bit of a nap as I'm afraid I probably tired her out a little."

Kate stared at the red of the soles of her shoes as she tottered down the path ahead of her. Her mouth felt dry and her head had begun to spin, the familiar dull throb returning.

Holding open the gate, Francesca called out to her for assistance before noticing that something was wrong.

Eventually, Kate found her voice. "So if Edie's in the car with you, who the bloody hell is lying in her bed back in the house?"

CHAPTER 23

Present Day – Eyam

The village was vibrant as the preparations for Wakes Week were underway. Amidst the flock of colourful tourists and sightseers, locals were setting up, organising, making plans and getting everything ready for what promised to be another fun filled week of events. The mood was bright and was nowhere near a match to how Nick was feeling as he walked back to the cottage from the coffee shop.

Still floored by the news that Kate had confided in him, he couldn't shake the tight ball of anger that had pressed itself against his chest. How one human being could do that to another was beyond him.

As he walked home he berated himself for his behaviour towards Kate when she had asked him not to sketch near the house. He had only managed to make things much worse by behaving so bloody minded about his paintings.

Nick pushed open the gate to his cottage and with a startled shriek, a blackbird bounced from the little wall that framed his garden. It landed on his neighbour's fencepost and cocked its head, watching him as he made his way down the path.

The light in the house was dreary. Even in the daytime, it was becoming too dark for him and he flicked on a light before heading into the makeshift studio that the conservatory had become. It had the advantage of being swathed in light for the best part of the day but the air could be stifling. Throwing open the doors before taking a seat on the chair in front of his easel, he closed his eyes and listened to the soft coo of wood pigeons.

He felt compelled to look at the paintings again, to line them up into the story that they were shaping, but he was worried that looking would feed the insatiable desire to return to Thornycroft and paint. Even though he and Kate were on better terms, it would be wildly disrespectful and insensitive to do such a thing after what she had told him about her ex. Resisting, he kept his eyes shut and tried to tune out the strange humming noise that was ringing in his ears.

The longer that he sat there, the more vulnerable and exposed he felt, as though hidden eyes were upon him. The hairs on his forearms bristled and he wasn't sure if it was the feeling that he wasn't alone or the light breeze that had danced through the open doors, licking at his exposed limbs.

With determined stubbornness he refused to open his eyes. One day he may lose his sight forever and this feeling of being immersed in total darkness would be one that he would have to get used to.

Over the years, he had been trying to hone his other senses. Sounds, touch, tastes, smell. Everything seemed to come with a flourish of colour. In his mind, he could conjure a rainbow palette to anything that he touched, tasted or smelled. Noises were sharper and clearer. Food was tangier, sweeter and saltier. He found he could even taste differences in the air between rooms. When he touched things, he would linger and feel every crevice and curve, constructing the image of its beauty in his mind. In fact, since he had been trying to focus in that way, the world seemed a calmer place.

As the breeze tousled his hair, he sank back into the chair, allowing his shoulders to drop.

Then he sensed it. Subtle but noticeable, there was a shift in the air around him. A hood of iciness glanced over his head. A small, barely audible sigh drifted into earshot. It was only fleeting, but his eyes snapped open at the sound of it.

Shifting in his seat, he scanned the room. Nothing was out of place or out of the ordinary. Still, he could feel her. He knew that it was *her*, the girl from his paintings. She had followed him. She wanted him to create more.

The easel was within his reach and the pencils were in their tin on the table next to him. It was all too easy.

Fixed in a trance like state, he watched his hand reach for his craft tools and the tip of his finger stroked the first pencil before lifting it from its resting place. Then he watched the first outlines of the lead against the page.

His arm began to move in rapid skilful strokes, but he felt as though he had no control. It would only stop when it was ready to.

First the fine blades of grass rustling gently against a warm spring wind. Then the trees and the seductive curves of the river, wending its way through what he knew would become vivid greenery.

When the time came, he knew exactly what shades on the palette he would mix. His pencil vigorously continued its assault across the canvas.

For the first time, the girl was turned away from the picture, her frame thinner and her dark hair tucked into a cap so that only a few wisps strayed to the wind. Her attention was focused on something out across the river and a hand rested on her back, between her shoulder blades.

A small bird was taking flight, beating its wings rapidly so that it would gain upon the land sitting beyond the river.

Before even finishing the sketch, Nick knew exactly how the finished item should look, the image planted firmly in his head. He no longer needed to be adjacent to Thornycroft to craft his paintings.

Tirelessly his arm worked and when he reached for the paints, he barely registered the dull ache that was growing in intensity in his wrist.

Behind him the air was vapour like, moving to and fro like the gentle motion of waves. Times overlapping and every now and then, the dark silhouette of a woman could be seen.

CHAPTER 24

March 1666 – Eyam

Rachel stood looking across the peaceful beauty of the Cucklet Delf. The winter had been a hard one and when the last of the frosts had thawed, she was not alone in her hopes that the cruelly cold months would have helped stifle the contagion, but almost every time she went to service, she would hear of another death or sickness. Still, it was possible that the disease was slowing, and both Rachel and Benjamin spent their evenings and mornings praying together.

Too ashamed of his appearance, Benjamin could not be persuaded to accompany her to service. Rachel could not understand it. Unlike so many in the village who had suffered at the mercy of the pestilence, Benjamin had been given the good fortune of a second chance to live. Besides, in Rachel's eyes, he was still handsome. When he smiled, his whole face glowed and his eyes always twinkled when they indulged in conversation.

There was something more to his persistence of barricading himself inside Thornycroft Hall though. He was even more terrified than most of falling victim to the plague.

It had been at the turn of the season, during a walk in the garden together, after she had turned another year older, that he had confessed his fears. "I've had my blessing Rachel. The Lord has looked kindly upon me once, it is unlikely he shall spare me so readily again if the plague should breach the walls of Thornycroft Hall." Then he had taken her hands in his and stared at her with such intensity that she had felt her knees grow weak and her mouth go dry. It had been as though he had wanted her to promise him that he wouldn't fall sick and that he would live a long and happy life.

Rachel could not promise any of those things. She had no idea what the future held for any of them. All she had been able to do was reassure him that by being God fearing and following the word of the Reverend Mompesson, the Lord would look kindly upon them.

Earlier that morning, having travelled alone to service once again, Rachel waited and watched as people dispersed, their heads bowed and their shoulders heavy with the despair that they continued to carry.

After the last of them had tailed off, she looked for sign of the Mompessons, but both Catherine and William had disappeared to attend pressing affairs within the village. So slowly, she had walked to the Delf, paying attention to the gently sloping hills of the meadow that were dotted with the delicate yellow and white petals of daisies and buttercups.

As she stood, reflecting on all of the events that had recently come to pass in Eyam, her shoulders weighed heavily with the burden of when and where the pestilence would strike next.

Stooping to snap the stem of a wild flower, a sickening wave of loneliness and fear washed over her. It was at times like these that she wished that her father were still alive. He would have known the answers to the questions whirling through her mind. He would have known what to do to see things right. She needed to feel the comfort of his strong embrace and the roughness of his palms stroking the back of her hands, the way they so often had when she had cried as a child.

Despite having the company of Benjamin and Goody back at the house, Rachel felt so alone. Even though she had many friends and the good fortune of knowing a family as generous and caring as the Hancocks, since the death of Rachel's father, Catherine Mompesson had been her only true confidante. She was needed elsewhere now though and with good reason for it. As the death toll had increased and people had needed to stay away from one another, Catherine's time for Rachel had become understandably scant. Besides, Rachel reminded herself, Catherine had her own children to worry about, not a girl who was as good as a grown woman herself.

As she picked another flower, she noticed that the first of the daffodils were proudly swaying in the spring winds. The sight of it gave Rachel hope. In spite of all the death that had come to the village, life was still a part of Eyam.

She looked out across the meadows. Come the summer, the fields would be awash with waves of pink and purple from knapweed, mallow and marjoram. It was, she pondered, one of the most beautiful places to exist and it seemed to make the horrors of the last six months fade away.

From the branch of a chestnut tree, a chaffinch eyed her with caution, its orange chest puffed out in a state of staged grandeur. Bending to pick one of the daffodils, her movement startled the bird into flight.

Rachel straightened and watched it bounce on a current of air across the Delf until it became a tiny dot in the distance. As its tiny body tumbled further away from her, something caught her attention.

Against the pale blue backdrop of the sky were two figures. On one side of the river was a young man, tall and thin. A short distance from him, but perfectly opposite, on the other side of the river, was a girl, not much older than Rachel. Emmott Syddall.

Emmott was betrothed to Rowland. Everyone in the village knew of it.

"The fairest lass in the village. She'll make a bonny bride," Cook had commented when she had news of the young lovers.

Rachel had wondered what it would be like to be so much in love and afterwards, when she had met Alice in the orchard, they had gossiped and giggled, imagining the possibilities of one day being in love with handsome suitors of their own.

Rachel held the daffodil to her chest as she watched the pair, neither of them speaking, simply looking across the river to one another.

It would be frowned upon, this behaviour. Emmott was putting Rowland's life in danger and Rowland putting the lives of his family in Stoney Middleton in danger too.

A knot of anger began to grow inside Rachel's stomach. Like a clenched fist it squeezed. She wanted to shout, to take Emmott by the shoulders, tell her to stop being so selfish. Then she stopped as she thought of Benjamin and how devastated she had been when she had thought that he was leaving Thornycroft Hall. If it had been Benjamin who was so near and yet so far from her, would she have arranged secret meetings with him?

Rachel caught herself as another thought struck her. She wondered if this was what it felt like to be in love?

Turning on her heel she ran. She didn't want to feel the giddiness or the ache of longing in her heart. It was preposterous to even associate her relationship with Benjamin with love. They were two people from such different walks of life, that only a year ago, the very thought of it would have made her laugh out loud.

She was breathless when she returned to the house and she almost knocked Benjamin over as he was returning from a walk in the gardens. In his hand he held some flowers and he offered them to her, suggesting they might look pretty in a vase in her room.

A deep blush blazed from her chest up into her cheeks. Snatching the flowers from his grasp, she uttered a brief word of gratitude before hurrying away.

CHAPTER 25

April 1666 – Eyam

As March slipped into April, Rachel ventured out to watch the young couple, undetected from a safe distance. She was fascinated by their dedication to one another. Rowland's loyalty appeared to be so strong that he would risk the pestilence just to see his true love. Never touching, yet their bond unbreakable, every day they stood either side of that river, sometimes calling across it to each other and sometimes just gazing at one another.

They were to be married later that year, in the summer. Rachel considered the possibilities of what they might do if the plague was still rife, whether they would be allowed to hold a ceremony from across the water, delivering their vows of love, honour and obedience in the eyes of God? Then she dared imagine that by then the plague may have passed, and how vibrant the celebrations would be.

On a fine morning near the end of April, Rachel returned to the Delf after hearing a rumour that Emmott's mother had just remarried after losing her husband, John, in the autumn. She wondered if the marriage would have reawakened the hope in Emmott, that one day the pestilence would be gone and she would be able to reach out and touch her beloved Rowland.

Rachel imagined how it would be for them, the tips of their fingers grazing, their hands linking together, pulling them closer until they could lose themselves in a long awaited embrace.

As she strolled across the grass, Rachel lost herself for a moment in the daydream. Then she stopped, her brow knitting in confusion. Rowland was there. Emmott was not.

Crouching behind a tree, she waited. It was a possibility that Emmott's mother had required something of her that was making her late.

A long time passed but Rowland's gait did not falter. He stood on the other side of the river, hopeful, unwavering in his wait for his true love.

Emmott did not turn up and when Rachel returned to Thornycroft, she was vexed.

The following day, she set off early, determined to see if Emmott would be at the spot that she had unfailingly ventured to every day to see Rowland.

Rachel waited. Even Rowland wasn't there when she arrived and so she knelt in the grass, picked some flowers and dozed in the warmth of the sunshine. When she awoke, she looked towards the river.

The lonely silhouette of Rowland had returned. He was standing on the opposite side of the little river, looking towards Eyam from as close a vantage point as he could get. There was no sign of Emmott.

Rachel returned to the village, running towards the rectory, only to be stopped by Thomas Stanley.

Thomas was leaving the rectory and so must have been visiting the Mompessons. He regarded her curiously with his jaw set straight and serious, as though he had come from a sombre meeting. "What is your haste lass?" He addressed her sternly as he brushed at the part of his arm that she had knocked into.

"Do you know of any news over at the Syddall household?" she asked, hoping that his morose expression would break into a smile and put to bed her fears for Emmott Syddall.

Giving her a cursory, grave glance, his gaze drifted up the road that led to a row of cottages, where the Syddall family lived. "Aye, it is a sad business. That is near on all of poor Elizabeth Syddall's children taken now, aside from young Joseph. Catherine is over there. William and I have said prayers for the protection and health of young Joseph." Sadly, he shook his head. "Seeing the youngsters suffer, that's the hardest part." For a while longer, he stared out towards the Syddall cottage, its location opposite Mary Hadfield's home, where the plague had started with the death of George Viccars. Then he bid her a good day, wished her good health and walked away shaking his head.

The news hit Rachel with a wave of nausea. In those days that she had watched Emmott and Rowland at the Delf, her hopes had been lifted as she had dreamed of their wedding, imagining the joy with the plague gone and two lovers reunited. Witnessing the unyielding hope in the lovers as they had met in secret each day, had given her something to cling on to. It had helped her think of a brighter future. Her heart heavy, she returned to the Delf.

A cloud had obscured the sun, its shade doing away with any hope that had been poured into her soul. Ever loyal, ever patient, Rowland was still waiting.

Rachel took care not to hide herself this time as she walked amongst the meadow grass and flowers. The golden daffodil trumpets had not long been replaced by cowslip, the drooping heads brushing sadly against her skirts as she walked.

Rowland either did not notice her, or chose not to, as she drew nearer.

She would not venture as near as Emmott had done, did not dare to go any further. Finding her position, she waited for him to look in her direction. As she waited, she thought about love.

To Rachel, the idea of being in love had once been one of the most perfect beautiful things to imagine, but as she watched the lonely figure of Rowland Torre waiting patiently for a girl who she knew the Lord had recently taken, she thought that love was in fact the cruellest and hardest of things a person could endure.

A fat tear slipped down her cheek as she looked across to the distant figure. His Emmott was gone. Whilst he was too far away to make eye contact, she was certain that he could see her. Slowly, she shook her head, hoping that he would understand, but the likelihood was that he would not believe it until he could see for himself the mound where her body lay, no doubt in the field near the Syddall home.

He remained rigid, unmoving, waiting for his Emmott to appear.

A hand pressed gently between Rachel's shoulders and she turned to see the kind eyes of Catherine Mompesson. "I had heard that you have been venturing up here Rachel." Her voice was soft and comforting, its gentle lull bringing more tears to Rachel's eyes. She sniffed them back and nodded her head gratefully.

"I know we don't talk much these days," Catherine continued. "But I still pray for you. I thought I would keep you company today, on your walk back." She gestured for Rachel to follow her out of the Delf. She didn't acknowledge Rowland in the distance and neither of them mentioned it as they walked back towards the village.

They kept their distance as they journeyed, but Catherine's words were carefully chosen to comfort and soothe. "I see the sadness in your eyes Rachel, every week at service. I know that Thornycroft Hall must be a lonely place to be without the Thornycrofts there and it must pain you even more not to have your father with you at a time as testing as this. I know how much you miss him."

Rachel didn't say anything. Compared to others in the village, her path had been an easy one. They walked in silence for a short way until Catherine spoke again. "How is Master Belgrave?"

With a shrug, Rachel straightened her cap. "His moods can still be melancholy. He has more good days than bad now. We walk together a lot, but he refuses to come to Divine Service." She couldn't disguise the crimson that flushed her cheeks as she confessed on Benjamin's behalf. "He doesn't want folk to see his face."

Lacing her fingers together, Catherine nodded. "It will come. Keep supporting him Rachel. It is a strong and good-hearted person who can help another through hard times. Your father would be proud, I am sure." Her kind smile faded and she looked into the street beyond Rachel. "My duties take me elsewhere in these sad times, but you are doing well. You must have faith. Now get home. It is not safe to linger out for so long with so many falling sick." A shadow darkened her lily white skin as she pressed her lips together and looked back towards the path that led to the Cucklet Delf, where Rowland was likely to still be standing all alone. "Too many have been lost already."

Rachel watched her walk away, feeling the loss of not having her by her side. Being near Catherine was always a great comfort and she had such a gift for saying the words that would bring solace.

Not for the first time, Rachel thought about how lucky Catherine's children were to have such caring parents. The Mompessons were good people. She thought of them both working tirelessly to tend to the sick and the grieving and her feet began to drag on her walk home.

Being stuck inside the dark walls of Thornycroft Hall made her feel so useless. People were sick, dying and grieving and she was no help to any of them.

The air was thick with an unnatural silence. No children played, no women called to one another from their doorsteps, or chased away the strays and no journeymen rattled through with their horses. It all seemed so very wrong. It was, Rachel pondered, rather like looking through a thin veil into a different world.

The silence filled her with unbearable loneliness and she wrapped her arms about her chest: a solitary figure walking the stark streets of a once thriving village.

CHAPTER 26

May 1665 – Eyam

Weeks passed in Thornycroft Hall and Rachel chose not to venture back down to the Delf. It was a fruitless and heart breaking exercise to watch Rowland Torre waiting for something that would never happen. Instead, she filled her days cleaning and trying to ignore the behaviour of Goody, which seemed stranger than ever.

Catherine had visited with a recipe for another plague remedy, but Goody was less interested in helping her in the stillroom than she had been on previous occasions. Distracted, she fidgeted and fussed, jumping with every groan and grumble that came from the beams, walls and rafters of the house. Then, quite unexpectedly, she had gone from being withdrawn and distant, to joining Rachel and Benjamin more. The haunted look, however, remained in her eyes.

Rachel often felt Goody's gaze lingering on her and a knife's edge was between them, words unspoken, lines uncrossed but waiting to be. It filled Rachel with so much unease that she found herself making excuses of unfinished chores so that she could leave the room. She had even taken to finding odds and ends of furniture to barricade the door of her chamber with at night. The story that Benjamin had told her about Goody venturing into his room, shuffling about and watching him, was too similar to her own experience. There was something so unsettling about the woman. They knew her and yet, they did not. Nobody did.

'The Conjurer'. Every time she recalled the name that Elizabeth Hancock had used to refer to Goody, she shuddered.

One late afternoon, when the sun was guttering behind the cooling clouds of evening, the three of them ate together. Rachel had invited her to join them for a rabbit pie that she had baked.

Goody hesitated, fighting some internal battle before making the decision to join them.

As they sat around the table, the atmosphere between them was choked, rather than the usual easy flow of conversation that Rachel had become accustomed to with Benjamin at mealtimes. The three of them kept conversation to observing the obvious facts. Rachel advised that she had it on good authority that Bakewell Market was closed to anyone who ventured from the direction of Eyam. The same went for everywhere else, Tideswell, Stoney Middleton, Grindleford and all of the neighbouring or nearby villages and towns. There was word that some folk would resort to violence if anybody venturing near the surrounding villages were suspected to be from Eyam.

All of them skirted around the fact that they were three strangers thrown into a situation wherein their lives were at the mercy of where the pestilence would strike next.

After dinner they retired to the blue parlour and Rachel brought through a flagon of the latest plague remedy to pour into their cups. Their faces soured with the taste and Goody advised that adding some rosehip and crushed raspberries would have sweetened the unpleasantness.

Benjamin snapped something in retort and for the rest of the evening Goody took to nervously wringing her hands. Beads of perspiration gathered on her top lip and the constant jarring of her knee was bothering even Rachel.

It was Benjamin who impatiently broke the silence. "Is something ailing you?" he demanded, his irritation plain.

Goody's knee stopped wobbling. She jerked her head towards him. The vague, empty look remained in her eyes.

Rachel shuddered. Whilst Goody's gaze appeared fixed on Benjamin, it was as though she was looking straight through him, at something nobody but she could see.

Benjamin's tolerance was running low. "Well?" He frowned. "What is it? You have been quivering and sweating for quite some time." He eyed her greasy skin suspiciously. "Have you a fever?"

The question made Rachel recoil and she noticed that Benjamin had sunk back into his chair, shrinking away from Goody, expanding the distance between them.

Mutely, Goody kept her gaze steady, but her lips quivered.

Impatient, Benjamin slammed the palm of his hand down against the chair's armrest. "Where is your tongue? You make enough noise when you are shut away in those God forsaken chambers of yours, so why the silence now?"

Still she refused to answer, but her face had paled and Rachel watched as she once again began twisting her calloused hands against one another.

"Answer me!" Benjamin raged, pushing himself to standing and cracking his stick against the floorboards.

Rachel winced. Goody appeared unfazed. Despite the ungainly stoop that he had gained from his accident, Benjamin was tall and he towered above them both as he rounded on Goody. "Answer the question. It is simple enough. Do-you-have-a-fever?" He pronounced each word as though she were an imbecile and marked the floor with a second strike of his stick.

Goody's eyes shifted and flickered. A small whimper escaped her lips.

Rachel held her breath, waiting for what was to come next. She felt herself beginning to tremble. Was this the moment that they would learn the plague had crossed the threshold of Thornycroft Hall?

"No fever." Goody shook her head and she seemed more focused, like her mind was back in the parlour room with them. "Nay, I am not ailed. Not the way you think. The pestilence has not breached these walls. Not here. Not this house. Not yet."

Tempering his anger, Benjamin spoke softer, encouraging her to elaborate. "Then what is it? You sit there sweating, stinking of fear, twitching and twisting as though you are tortured. These are not times for secrets Goody. I implore you to tell us what troubles you."

There was a pause and Rachel felt her own knee shaking and wobbling with the tension. Then Goody parted her lips to speak. Her voice was raspy, the words barely audible. "We are not..." she hesitated, glancing towards Rachel. "We are not alone."

Outside, the sun had begun to embark upon its nightly descent. The watchmen on duty would be preparing for their shift at the edges of the village. Rachel swallowed down the familiar taste of fear. "What do you mean, 'we are not alone'?"

Goody didn't respond and Benjamin's face went pink with anger. "Answer her Goody. Stop speaking in riddles." It was not helping the situation.

Goody's beady glare was first fixed on him and then on Rachel. She looked suddenly dangerous. Those eyes reminded Rachel of the crows that would wait for the demise of a vulnerable animal before swooping, snatching and fighting for the pickings. Goody saw the fear on their faces, smelled it on their breath, and her lips curled in malice. "We do not walk the halls of this great house alone. There are things that live amongst the shadows. Dark things. Secrets." She leaned forward, pushing herself closer to Benjamin, who began to look shorter, his presence waning. "Things a boy like you could never understand."

The clatter of Benjamin's stick resounded against the floor and Rachel jumped. At the same time, all three of them looked up, as though afraid that they had alerted whatever else was in the house to their whereabouts.

"She speaks nonsense," Benjamin concluded, keeping himself steady on his good leg, but his words were betrayed by the quake of his voice.

If it was possible, Goody's smile broadened. It fell from her face as quickly as it had appeared, leaving her looking stricken at the words that had tumbled from her lips. She had said too much. What secrets had she been about to impart?

Rachel frowned, willing her to continue, to share with them what she knew, what she had seen or heard, confirm that she was their ally, just as troubled as they were and not someone to be afraid of.

They paused. Even the house seemed to hold its breath, waiting to see whether Goody would betray its confidence. The troubled expression returned and she turned to Rachel. "You should run from this place. Leave. Never come back."

Hurrying towards her, Rachel knelt by her side and took her hand. It was clammy, her fingers trembling. "Goody, tell us what you mean, please? Benjamin is right, there should be no secrets now."

Slowly, Goody turned her head and Rachel noticed how the folds of her skin were beginning to sag, she had lost that much flesh over recent months, with the rationing of food and pacing with worry. She reached out with her free hand so that she could stroke Rachel's cheek. "Some things should stay buried in the past. Does no good to talk about them. Don't think I haven't heard you two whispering. I know what you say. I know what they all say," Goody said, looking around the room nervously, as though afraid that they were being watched. "Even the walls have ears here. But mark my words lass, the ghosts of the past should stay there. That's where they belong."

Leaning in closer, she tightened her fingers around Rachel's hand, grasping it until she wanted to cry out in pain. "So stop looking child. Stop searching for what lives beyond the darkness and the shadows of this God forsaken place. Stop whispering of it with him in the thick of night, 'cos you are only stirring up the dead from their graves and the demons from their slumber."

"Demons?" Rachel stammered, trying to pull herself free from Goody's sweaty, tight grip.

"You're a mad woman. Mad. Leave her alone." There was a snap as Benjamin, who had retrieved his stick from the floor, brought it down across Goody's arm.

Retracting her hand, she held her arm to her chest, her eyes narrow slits. "You're not the master of Thornycroft lad," she sneered at what could be seen of his face. "You are the pitied guest. You have no claim upon what I do or what I say. You just leave me to my business and I'll leave you to yours. 'Tis best for all concerned."

"Get out," Benjamin growled, but there was no need as she had already pushed herself from her chair and was heading to the door.

They listened to the sound of her slow footsteps retreating to the farthest reaches of the house.

Everything else in Thornycroft Hall was unsettlingly still. It felt as though whatever else was locked inside the great walls with them was listening, waiting for their next move, waiting to eventually pounce.

CHAPTER 27

Present Day – Eyam

The paintbrush slipped from between Nick's fingers and he clutched at his head as the familiar pounding returned. As quickly as it had come, the view into the past was gone but it had left him giddy, reeling, sick.

Next to the palette and water pot was a packet of painkillers. He reached for two and dry swallowed them, almost gagging on the chalkiness. Then he looked back at the canvas in front of him.

The girl was turned away from him, the picture giving away no emotion on her face, yet he knew all of her thoughts. He knew the reason why she had been standing there and he knew of the events that had followed on from the moment that he had so exquisitely captured in that painting. It was beautiful, one of his best yet. The fine lines, the reflection of light against colour, creating dimensions that made it seem so real, like one could touch her and she would turn.

Exhausted, Nick slumped in to the old rocker in the corner and wiped his palms against his jeans. His head continued to pound and he shut his eyes, pressing his thumb and forefinger either side the bridge of his nose, rubbing at the pain.

The painting had become a dangerous pastime, he knew that, but he still longed for more. It drew him to Thornycroft and its many shadows.

He thought of Edie and Kate rattling around in the old house. It was a pitiful size compared to what it had once been, but the shadows and secrets were still there, stalking the place, flickering in and out of focus, showing themselves to him when it suited them.

The throb in his head dulled and he got up, reaching for the picture. The paint was still wet. His fingers hovered just above it, longing to touch the girl who was gazing into the distance. The story that had been painted in his mind was fading fast but he remembered with distinct clarity an important message.

Rachel. The girl's name was Rachel. And she was not alone.

CHAPTER 28

Present Day – Eyam

Francesca's slim frame glided down the pathway to the front gate. Trailing behind her, Kate felt a growing feeling of unease.

Francesca attempted to gloss over the fact that Kate had thought she had seen somebody in Edie's bed. When they had run into the room minutes earlier, it had been predictably empty with no sign that anybody had disrupted the neatly turned covers.

"It's just because you were expecting her to be there Kate." Francesca was keen to dismiss anything strange or mysterious about the situation as they returned to her car. "There won't be any more to it than that. The mind is a funny thing," she insisted.

The words did nothing to reassure Kate.

Conscious of the amethyst she had fastened around her neck, she wanted to remind Francesca that it had been she who had insisted that Kate wear the charm for protection.

"You should keep that necklace on." As though reading her thoughts, Francesca turned to gesture at the amethyst on the chain.

Kate's fingers were instantly drawn to it. "If there's nothing to be concerned about, why is it so important that I keep this on?" She couldn't disguise the sarcasm, but she was frustrated. Frustrated and scared.

With a sigh, Francesca reached for her shoulders. "The amethyst isn't just a spiritual charm used to protect people from paranormal energies Kate. It will protect you from any negative vibes and thoughts that other people, either knowingly or unwittingly, project on to you. I just get the sense that you need it right now."

The edges of the stone rubbed against the pads of her fingers as she held it and turned to look back at Thornycroft. She desperately wanted to tell somebody about the visions, thoughts and dreams that she had been having. There was no sense to them, no warning. They would simply accost her at any given moment and she felt out of control. Every time, it was like somebody else's thoughts were spilling into her mind. They were beginning to consume her everyday life, but to consider talking about it to anyone made it all feel so far fetched. She imagined her own reaction if somebody had confided in her with such a story a couple of months earlier, especially somebody with her chequered recent past.

With a wistful smile, she reached for Francesca's arm. "Thank you. You hardly know me and you've been a very good friend. I'm grateful for all you've done for Aunt Edie too."

Francesca's eyes clouded. "You did get rid of the diary, didn't you?"

"Of course." The lie tripped lithely off her tongue before any guilt could set in. "All gone." She wondered how terribly transparent she must appear, but Francesca seemed satisfied. Jangling her keys, she was already heading to the car, preparing to open the door.

Edie's head flopped to one side and her mouth opened as she shifted her position. It took a lot of effort to get her into the wheelchair without disturbing her sleep.

Before she said her goodbyes, Francesca made Kate promise to call her if anything was troubling her.

Knowing full well that she would probably dip out of doing so, Kate agreed and gave her a swift peck on the cheek before taking Edie back indoors.

The house seemed emptier, like the aftermath of a party where the buzz of people parting company leaves a hollow void.

Manoeuvring Edie into the living room, Kate decided to use the time to prepare the vegetables for dinner. As she peeled and chopped, a wave of homesickness washed over her.

Reaching for her phone, she hovered over the number for her mother before thinking better of it. Her parents were on the holiday of a lifetime and there was no way that they would stay put if either of them thought that anything was wrong. Flicking through her contacts, she felt despair as she reminded herself once again that the only person who she really had to turn to was Chris.

Something she had once read came back to her. Emotional abusers did that. They isolated their victims from friends and family so that they became dependent. It dawned on her that this was probably what Richard had done, only she couldn't recall when, or at what point. He had seamlessly integrated her into his life so that by default, her only friend had been Chris.

When Richard's behaviour had changed, at first she had been too surprised and bemused to confide in anyone. She had closed down. Nobody would have understood and why would they? Richard had been the archetype of perfect: attractive, generous, funny, warm hearted and charming. The switch had been so out of character. He didn't have many friends, more acquaintances. There had only been Chris, and of course, Chris had become the focus of his obsession.

If it hadn't been for Chris, Kate would have had nobody to turn to, nobody to listen and believe her side of things.

She thought of the missed calls from him. There had been no voicemails or texts to follow up. Understandably, he would be peeved that she had snubbed him. Guilt weighed her down and she decided to send him a text, let him know that she appreciated his looking out for her, but she had to try and get through the summer independently. Leaning on him now could only do more harm than good.

She sent the text and waited for it to show up as 'read'. It didn't take long. There was no reply, nothing to reassure her that he was okay with that and understood.

Glumly, she turned to look out of the window in to the front garden. She wondered what Richard was doing, whether he had forgotten about her and moved on, or whether he was still stewing over everything. Even thinking about him brought on anxiety, tightening her chest and making her heart beat too fast.

She thought back to their last encounter, when he had turned up at her parents' house banging at the door and insisting that she let him in. His features had been wild, almost unrecognisable, as he had shouted at her to be reasonable and to stop being so blind. He had become angry and thrown out all the usual accusations involving Chris. Then the air had been rent with the sound of breaking glass. That was when the police had been called.

Of course, according to Richard it had been an accident. He had slipped and put his hand out. His arm had been cut. It had missed a major vein by millimetres, but there had been no sympathy as he had been taken away, protesting over Chris and how he had played them all.

Chris had been there, consoling, comforting, a shoulder to cry on. He was a better person than her. He had pitied Richard and made excuses for him, but Kate had been furious. Chris hadn't deserved any of the abuse that Richard had hurled his way.

Now she had rebuffed him, but she had to. Friendship was all that they had and there could be nothing more. He couldn't be her saviour, her hero, her 'go to' when the going got tough. They could be nothing more than friends.

Gripping the edge of the table, she allowed the past to replay through her mind. Chris had been kind, patient, understanding and empathetic.

"I'm an idiot," she had said one evening after another pointless row with Richard.

Chris had bumped into her in the supermarket as she had been deliberating over ready meals for one. He had seen the look on her face, ushered her back to his place, insisted that they get a takeaway, his treat so that she could have a good old sob in private. She had taken him up on the offer, accepted one too many glasses of wine and allowed the tears to fall until she had felt a dishevelled, unattractive mess.

Chris had told her that she had to try and think about it from Richard's point of view, that she couldn't let go of the good times just because they were going through a rough patch.

She had tried her hardest to rekindle the feelings of the good times with Richard; the way they used to laugh so easily together, fall in to bed exhausted but not too exhausted to enjoy one another's touch, the way he used to tuck her hair behind her ear.

None of it had worked. The bad times had put too much of a tarnish over the good memories. So she had shaken her head, said that she couldn't, that she'd had enough and if that made her a bad person, then so be it.

Then Chris had taken her hand in his before reaching up and tucking the stray strands of hair from her face, just like Richard had done in the good days. He had brushed away her tears with a curled finger and told her how beautiful she was, even when her face felt puffy from crying. He had held her close, whispered in her ear what a good person she was.

Her head had been giddy with wine and upset. He had caught her off guard and then their lips were touching, their bodies sliding together, his hands slipping down her back. For a moment, she had indulged herself, welcomed the feeling of being loved and wanted but not owned. Then she had pushed him away.

With a lusty look he had tried again, but she had insisted that it was wrong, wriggled away from him and grabbed her coat.

He had apologised, said that he understood, but there was no disguising the look in his eyes. She had hurt him. He had called her a taxi and they had never spoken of the kiss again. Not until her and Richard had truly split up.

Her decision not to see Chris over the summer was the right one. She wasn't stupid and she knew that he couldn't gloss over that one kiss. Even if it had made her pulse quicken and body shake a little at the time, to allow it to ever happen again would be utterly wrong. They would be proving Richard right and giving his insane behaviour some justification. Besides, Chris wasn't her type.

At that moment, her mind flashed back to Nick. Nick angry with her. Nick forgiving her. Nick calling a truce. Nick's hand accidentally touching hers. His eyes. His smile. The way he had listened to her, so intently and without judgement, when she had confided in him over coffee. Kindness had been etched on to his face, replacing the cold façade that she had seen in the beginning.

Beneath her ribs, her heart pounded a little faster and she felt a nervous shiver pass through her body. Catching herself, she shook her head and stood up, but she was unable to wipe Nick from her mind or rid herself of the feeling that had invaded her body.

With a groan, she leaned against the kitchen window and told herself that she was just confused after allowing the past with Richard and Chris to creep up on her like that. Romantic feelings of any kind were the last thing that she needed fogging her life any further.

CHAPTER 29

Present Day – Eyam

At the other end of the village, the owner of Honeywell Cottage and Guest House opened the door to a gentleman with a Southern accent. Richard. With a disarming smile, he insisted that they should adopt first name terms for the duration of his stay.

He had arrived earlier than she had expected, but thankfully his room was ready and a casserole was on the stove just waiting to be heated.

Despite it being the busiest time of year for Eyam, the gent would be her only guest that week which was disappointing as she had hoped that she would fill her rooms for Wakes Week, given how many tourists it could attract. Still, beggars couldn't be choosers and she had not long opened.

"Come through, come through." Ushering him over the threshold, through the lounge and up the stairs, she was keen to show him the newly decorated guest room. She'd had all the wallpaper steamed off and selected a more neutral shade of Warm Buttermilk. Everything in the bedroom was neatly pressed, even the curtains looked wrinkle free and the smell of beeswax polish clung to the air.

The man surveyed the room, narrowing his eyes critically as he scanned every detail. He was clearly a perfectionist. Just as she thought he was about to express his dissatisfaction about something, he turned around. "It's perfect," he said, flashing her another extremely charming smile.

Breathing a sigh of relief, a hand fluttered to her chest. "Oh good, I am glad. Well you settle in and freshen up. Dinner is at seven but I can bring it forward tonight if you would prefer? Or I can prepare a small snack. Some bread, a sandwich perhaps?"

With a wave of his hand, the man shook his head. "No need, no need. Seven is just fine. I should like to take a walk around the village first. It's been the most diabolical journey. Traffic all the way." He adjusted the collar of his shirt, seeming to relax somewhat. "Still, I'm here now."

"Well of course. The bathroom is right next-door and there's a washbasin in your room, right here by the fireplace. Now, can I fetch you a cup of tea?"

A flicker of impatience crossed his face and his tone sharpened. "No really. I don't need anything. Just tell me how to get into the village."

Slightly taken aback by his abrupt change in demeanour, she gave him directions before hurrying back downstairs to finish off in the kitchen.

Washing her hands, she looked out of the window at the heavy clouds that were closing in overhead. It was a shame that rain was forecast when the gent had just arrived but still, Eyam and all of its antiquities was enchanting in all weathers.

CHAPTER 30

Present Day – Eyam

The day had rumbled on quietly for Kate. Edie, who had barely spoken a word after she had woken up, had retired to her room to read, leaving her alone with the emptiness of the house and the chaos of her thoughts.

Kate felt as though she was losing her sanity. Snippets of memories that didn't belong to her kept flashing into the forefront of her mind. All it took was a cursory glance out into the garden or to catch herself staring at something in the village.

Everything was familiar, but not as she knew it. It was like her landscape had been glossed over with a new coat of paint. The roads were smoothed out with tarmac instead of undulating with mud cracks. Cars were parked where hens and geese had once pecked for food. Worst of all though, green plaques adorned so many walls and houses in the village, the words on them cruelly reminding her of all the friends and acquaintances whom she had lost to such unspeakable suffering.

Kate shook her head, trying to free herself of the thoughts that were clearly someone else's. All of those things, the tarmac on the road, the plaques on the houses - they were normal, of her time. She sat down and felt the edges of her mind blur again.

Earlier that day, she had happened across the sign telling of Hannah Rowland's death, as well as others in the Rowland family. Hannah had been her friend – the thought had struck her hard, but it had been Rachel's, not her own.

The plaque was nailed to the wall of the café where people buzzed in and out, smiling, happy and oblivious to the horrors that Hannah and her family had suffered, that *she* had suffered.

Kate caught herself again and cried out. It was happening again, just as it had done outside the café when she had read that plaque. An inexplicable ball of rage had grown inside of her as she had stood outside, noticing how those words were only distant facts to these tourists who bustled carefree, in and out, clutching full stomachs or cakes and ice-cream to take away. Then she had come around, shaken the cobwebs that had been woven across her brain and hurried home.

The thoughts weren't normal. They weren't even possible. Those people had lived over three hundred and fifty years ago. She was beginning to wonder if this was what they called post-traumatic stress disorder and the impossible memories were a product of what had happened between her and Richard. Was it possible that she was trying to lose herself in another life to forget about her own? She was contemplating calling her GP when she thought of the bogwood box.

The box was where she had tucked it away. Kate took it out of its hiding place and sat down cross-legged in the living room, staring at it, hesitating to lift the lid.

For the best part of an hour she remained like that, until a noise from behind startled her.

"What have you got there?" Edie was perched on the threshold of the doorway, her hands poised against the wheels of her chair.

Flustered, Kate attempted to rewrap the box and shunt it beneath the fringe of the sofa.

Edie was too quick. With surprising deftness, she manoeuvred herself into the lounge, gaining upon her before she could finish the job. Her face darkened and she pursed her lips.

It was Kate who broke the silence. "Aunt Edie, I was just sorting stuff, trying to help and-"

"Snooping. You were snooping." The cold edge had returned to Edie's voice.

A frisson of shame shot through Kate. "No, I wasn't snooping. It wasn't like that, I just-"

"You were snooping Kate dear. I should have known of course. You are your mother's daughter and she is my niece after all." Holding out her hand, she gestured for Kate to return the box to her.

Feeling like a berated school child, Kate placed it in her outstretched palm.

"Where did you find it?" Edie demanded.

There was no point in lying. Kate supposed that she had been snooping, just not with the intention of finding anything untoward. "I was in the top of the house, looking for some old photos, trying to find a bit of family history. It was quite innocent. The box is clearly very old. How did you come across it?"

Tight lipped, Edie looked her up and down. Kate knew that she was trying to assess just how much she had found up there. "I found it one day when I was laying some poison up there. There'd been a lot of scrabbling and scratching. Rats. Nasty things. It had been hidden away behind some of the old beams." Suspiciously, she glared at Kate. "Who else knows about this?"

"Nobody. I haven't told anyone about the box."

Edie's keen eyes were boring into her, checking for any hint of deceit. When she appeared to be satisfied that Kate was telling the truth, she allowed her shoulders to relax a little and traced her fingertips across the lid. "The contents are probably of some value but I really wanted to find out a little more about the owner, so I've kept it for the time being. I know I should really hand it in to the museum though." Licking her lips, she leaned forward, a glimmer in her eye. "Have you seen inside dear?"

As she watched Edie's hand hover over the lid, Kate felt pressure in her chest and her skin go cold. "It's really quite wonderful," Edie continued, oblivious to the rushing of blood that was pounding through Kate's head and ears.

Her tongue felt too thick for her mouth and she looked to the doorway. The corridor beyond it was darker than it should be at that time of day. It was as though shadows were blotting away the light that was streaming in through windows. Something was waiting on the periphery, desperate for the box to be opened.

Kate thought of the jewellery inside of it. She remembered the cool roughness of the precious stones in her palm and she remembered Sir Edward's steely gaze as he had handed the pendant to her, cautioning her to keep it a secret from Lady Cecily.

No. It hadn't been her whom he had handed the pendant to. The memory was made up, a fabrication, a fantasy. She wasn't going to go down this path again.

The darkness beyond the doorway billowed and contracted. Kate tried to speak, to warn Edie off lifting the lid.

"I think it must have belonged to the lady of the house," Edie mused. "I want to get it properly dated of course." Her voice was growing distant, a small noise against the rushing of Kate's pulse and something else. Moaning, scratching, thuds. Something was desperate to get to her, to get to them.

She watched Edie's fingers play with the lip of the lid and the air in the room grew close. The rush of Kate's adrenalin became a whooshing noise, like a wind tunnel, and she felt like she was being pulled away from the spot that she was kneeling on. Her fingers clawed uselessly at the pile of the carpet and the drone of Edie's voice faded further away.

A bell began ringing. Persistent. Growing louder, its noise began to dominate everything as it disrupted the reverie that Kate had found herself in. A strange tinny tune played out, drowning out the whooshing noise, overpowering the pulling sensation. Kate felt herself fall forward. The noise persevered, an annoyingly jolly chime. Then everything was still.

The shadows in the doorway had dissipated and once again, the hallway looked as it should.

Shockingly oblivious to Kate, Edie had turned her attention to where the chiming was coming from. "That surely can't be Franny again?" she exclaimed. "She said she was busy for the rest of the day."

Kate tried to swallow and catch her breath as the room came back into full focus and she started to steady.

"Quickly Kate dear, you answer it and I shall put this out of harm's way. I'll show you another time."

Feeling a little shaky, Kate went to answer the door. On the doorstep, a red haired youth with a shock of freckles patterning his nose and cheeks glowered at her. "Delivery." There was no attempt to hide his impatience.

For a moment, Kate stood slack jawed, scrambling for the memories of her own life to slot back in place. Then she recalled the online order for a chest of drawers to go into Edie's makeshift bedroom. Holding the door open for him to pass, she gestured towards Edie's room as he struggled through, not bothering to remove his shoes.

"Where do you want it?" he asked and grunted with effort before she grabbed the other end, making lighter work of the load.

"Just in front of you. That room there." She nodded towards Edie's temporary bedroom and with a final grunt he let it rest against the wall before going back to where he had left his scanner for signature.

"Thanks." She scribbled a signature with her fingertip before closing the front door. Her shoulders sagged as she considered the flat-pack assembly work that it would require.

"What's this?" Edie was giving the packaging a suspicious glare. "I hope you haven't gone to any expense on my account Kate?"

Shrugging, Kate tried to feel more optimistic about the daunting task ahead of her. "It's just some drawers. I thought it would add to the temporary bedroom. We can move them into one of the rooms upstairs when you're back on your feet again."

Gratitude twinkled on Edie's face but she kept her expression firm. "Well I shan't hear of it. You tell me how much and I'll give you the money."

Hurrying towards her, Kate took her hand and gave her a meaningful look. "Aunt Edie, it's a gift. It's the least I could do. You've been unendingly generous to me all of my life, just let me offer something back." She glanced uneasily at the slightly battered looking box. "The box looks a bit worse off for the journey but hopefully it will be a nice addition to the room, a useful one."

Edie smiled. "It's very kind of you. Thank you." She looked through the door of her room and to the patio that was benefitting from the last of the sun as it continued to wink through the heavy patches of foreboding cloud. "I think I should like a breath of fresh air on the patio dear, do you mind? I'm quite happy managing to get myself out there if you wouldn't mind opening those doors. They can be quite stiff and awkward at the best of times."

There was no more talk of the box of old jewels and Edie had tucked them away again. It was like it had never happened.

Relieved, Kate nodded, sweeping away the guilt and fear creeping up on her as she helped her outside.

******

Pinning the last of the bunting up in the orangery, Francesca slumped into a loveseat and sighed. The decorations were up, Graham had called to say that he was on the first flight back to Manchester in the morning and the caterers were sorted.

Some of Edie's friends from the museum had taken a break from setting up the village ready for Wakes Week, in order to drop over a beautiful welcome home cake for her. The party wasn't due to start until the following afternoon, after the Well Blessings, and so Francesca was more than organised. Everything was perfect and usually, she would have felt on a dizzy high with the excitement of it all. Francesca loved Wakes Week and Edie enjoyed it even more, but this year was different. Too much had happened and her shoulders were heavy with the burden of guilt.

Her morning with Edie hadn't been the wonderful picture that she had painted for Kate's benefit. The whole time Edie had been down in the mouth and quiet. When she had spoken, there had been a bitter edge to her tone.

Francesca was certain that she held her responsible for what had happened and she was right to. It had been Francesca who had enthusiastically joined in with the idea, actively encouraged the Ouija Board evenings; a bored housewife looking for a bit of spice, she had thought it would just be a bit of fun, but everything had got out of hand. Edie had taken it too seriously.

Picking up a stray ivory balloon, she noticed the crystal that she had placed in the far corner of the room and gave an involuntary shudder. Turning away from it, she tied the balloon back onto the wall sconce behind her and then picked up the loose ends from all her decorations.

She wandered through to the kitchen only to notice another crystal that she placed next to a potted orchid on the window ledge. Francesca had put it there after trying to convince Edie that everything they had experienced had been down to their overactive imaginations, that she should forget it all and move on.

She chewed nervously on the inside of her cheek. If that was true, then why had she taken it upon herself to so very carefully place all of her crystals in strategically sourced corners of the house? Kate had been right, why had she insisted on giving her the amethyst necklace for protection too?

With a shudder, she recalled how their Ouija Board sessions had unfolded. The atmosphere had all but crackled and Thornycroft had felt suffocating. One of the entities they had thought they had made contact with either couldn't reveal itself or it refused to. It was the latter that sent shivers through Francesca.

They had asked and asked but the only response they had received was an instruction to leave. Something dark and evil had been clinging to the air that night. Francesca had felt it crawling over her skin, raking at the roots of her hair and permeating the blood in her veins. It was as though it had been feeling its way for a route in to her body. She had felt violated, dirty and like she was about to be shown something that she didn't want to see. Then the lights had gone out.

They had fumbled for candles and after lighting the tapered ends, their breath had billowed in front of them in great icy puffs.

None of it had been natural and she had begged Edie to leave and stay with her for the night. She hadn't refused. They had both spent the night at Francesca's house and Edie had agreed to no more dabbling.

They hadn't spoken of it again in weeks. The diary had been tucked away and Francesca had shown her how to wrap and bind it with a crystal to ward off any negativity. She had told her that the mind was a powerful tool, that even though it was likely their imaginations were culpable for what they thought they had witnessed, that it was still a good idea to use the crystal that way.

Then one day, Edie had shown Francesca an antique jewellery box that she had found in the upper part of the house and the exquisite old jewellery inside. They had both been nursing a second Bloody Mary, laced with an extra shot of vodka at Edie's insistence.

"It's cursed," Edie had announced with surprising nonchalance as Francesca had lifted a beautiful ornate pendant from the box. "All of it is cursed." Her voice had twisted and when Francesca had looked at her, there was a sour expression on her face.

"Put it back," Edie had said, her voice gravelly and her eyes full of accusation.

It had taken Francesca by surprise and she had dropped the pendant with a clatter so that one of the tiny stones had fallen out. Apologetically, she had gone to retrieve it, to insist on having it fixed, but Edie had been gruff and quick to temper. "Just put it back," she had snapped, almost catching Francesca's fingers as she banged the lid shut. That had been when they had heard the heavy thump from the top of the house.

Startled, they had both jumped and looked at one another.

The strange twisted mask had slipped from Edie's face and she had appeared to be her old self again. "You heard that too?" Her voice had reverted back to the one that Francesca was familiar with.

"It would have been a bit hard to miss," Francesca had joked, but she had felt the familiar uneasy bristle of hairs on the backs of her arms as they had both strained to listen for anything else.

"It's been happening a lot. Creaks, groans, moans, thuds." As Edie had lifted her drink, Francesca noticed her hand shaking.

Francesca had watched her slurp impatiently from the glass, as though willing the alcoholic concoction to calm her nerves. "It's an old house," she had reasoned, but had been unable to shake the feeling of dread that was snaking its way up her spine and coiling itself about her shoulders, neck and scalp. "Surely you're used to the noises here?"

Knocking the rest of her drink back, Edie had pointed to the box. "More so since I found that. It's a jewellery box."

With a furrowed brow, Francesca had looked on with concern. "Yes, you said."

Resting her empty glass on the wooden table, Edie had lifted the lid of the box. She looked – different. "Would you like to see what's inside?"

"You've just shown me." There was a note of hesitation in her voice as Francesca had tried to work out what her friend was playing at, but Edie had seemed confused.

"No, I haven't," she had insisted with a frown. "You'll love the contents. I found it after having a clear out upstairs. I think this is very old. I'm sure it is something to do with the spirit we made contact with." She looked at her with wicked delight and licked her lips. "Or maybe even connected to another one," she had added with a conspiring whisper.

Another thud had sounded from directly above them and then there had been something like running footsteps. In the dimly lit house, with all the talk of spirits, it was impossible to differentiate the noises from the banging of the old pipes that ran through the walls.

"Let's go outside." Francesca had suggested quickly, her voice as bright as she could muster. "You're supposed to be able to see the Seven Sisters in the sky tonight. We should take a look."

"Let me show you this first Franny. Really, it'll take your breath away." Edie had already started fingering the chain with its beautiful pendant and was carefully laying it in her palm as though she had forgotten what had happened only minutes earlier.

"You've shown me, remember Edie? You didn't want me to touch it."

Edie had shaken her head and pointed out the intricate details before whisking it back and closing the lid to the box protectively. "Nobody can know," she had whispered, leaning forwards. "Not even Nick."

Francesca had not understood quite why she should be conspiring about a jewellery box, but in that moment she had become concerned about Edie's mental state. It had been like she was lost in another time.

Then it had been obvious, despite her agreement to leave well alone, to put it all down to their imagination, Edie had continued with her mission to dig up the secrets of Thornycroft and its dark, hidden past.

Francesca had pulled her up on it but Edie had put pay to her interference. She had been convinced that she would find something useful and of note in her research. There had been no reasoning with her.

When they did see each other, her demeanour had become more frail and scared, but still she refused to discuss any of it with Francesca. The topic had become the elephant in the room whenever they had coffee or a walk. Her behaviour had become akin to a person with an addiction - hiding the truth from those around them.

Then one day, Francesca had found her staring into space, a stagnated cold cup of tea in front of her. The milk in the jug by her teacup had soured and curdled. It must have been off for days and Edie hadn't noticed.

As she cast her mind back over everything that had happened with Edie, Francesca felt the familiar prickle of unease on her skin. She climbed the stairs to her bedroom and slumped onto the bed before pulling a cushion protectively to her belly. She should have spoken out then but she hadn't. Dementia was a word that she had avoided using.

Guilt spread dark wings about her body, encasing her in its hollowness. If she had said something back then, Edie may have avoided her fall. Sniffing back tears, she reflected on the fact that she hadn't pointed any of this out to the police or the home, but some deep instinct had stopped her.

Even after her time with Edie earlier that day, she couldn't come to the conclusion that her mental health was an issue. Despite her sombre mood, she had appeared lucid and with her wits very much about her. Nevertheless, something was simmering beneath the surface. Francesca could feel it. Much like one could sense an impending thunderstorm with that impatient stifling stillness in the air.

Usually outspoken and brash, Edie had barely uttered a word during their trip to Bakewell. When she had, she'd skirted around anything to do with the fall or the events leading up to it. There had been times when Francesca had noticed pure terror in her eyes; when she had stirred her tea with a shaking hand, mindlessly cut her fruit scone into tiny squares and stared dismissively at the wonderful array of cheeses in their favourite cheese shop.

She would have mentioned it upon their return to Thornycroft if she hadn't noticed that some of the same symptoms that Edie had been presenting were becoming evident in Kate; the latest being her insistence that she had seen Edie in her bedroom when she had been asleep in the car.

All of Francesca's deeper instincts pointed her towards something else. That was the truth behind why she had set about placing the crystals in all of the important corners of the house. If there was some dark force at work, something that her and Edie had stirred up when they had dabbled with that Ouija Board, she had to keep herself cleansed if she was to be of any help to her friends.

Reaching for her phone, she sent Graham a swift text with the perfunctory declaration of love and kisses, informing him that she was going to get an early night.

A good night of sleep would see her straight and she would be able to think more clearly about how to deal with the situation in the morning.

Whatever her decision though, there would be no point in ruining the party that she had planned in Edie's honour. Until that was over, everything else could wait.

CHAPTER 31

Present Day – Eyam

Edie grumbled and groaned to herself, stirring as a breeze tousled her hair, the threat of rain overhead. Opening her eyes and shifting her weight in the cumbersome wheelchair that the home had provided, she winced. She must have drifted off, although she had no idea for how long. The medication she was taking was terrible for making her feel so drowsy and she was getting irritated by all the sleeping she seemed to be doing, it wasn't in her usually active nature. She reminded herself of the terminology they had used at the hospital and home. It was all a part of the recovery 'process'. As she rubbed her stiffened neck, she wished that the 'process' would just hurry up.

Blinking away her grogginess, she looked around, the confusion that comes between sleep and waking upon her. There didn't appear to be anyone else around. Kate was nowhere to be seen, probably still battling with the chest of drawers indoors. At the home there had always been somebody buzzing about the gardens or hurrying past her room. Her heart dipped as she considered the possibility that she was in fact alone in Thornycroft and she stared dully at the cracks in the weather beaten patio. Thornycroft was no longer a place she wanted to call home. The atmosphere that had gathered like a huge threatening cloud was hanging heavy about the place.

Panic took hold. Was she really on her own? Had Kate gone out and left her? She wanted to cry out for her great niece but something stopped her. It was as though the house was listening, waiting for her to give her position away.

She thought of the shape on the stairs the day that she had fallen and she thought of the words that had been scrawled in the diary she had been keeping. Even though she had been holding the pen, those words had been written by another hand. They warned that she was not alone. They warned of something else that resided at Thornycroft.

When she replayed it all, it seemed like utter nonsense, but Edie knew how very real it all was. That was why she was now recovering in a wheelchair, dosed up with pills that were making her so unbearably drowsy rather than helping with the Wakes Week preparations and talking to tourists about the rich history of Eyam.

Miserably, she turned to look back up at the house. There were secrets locked away in the bricks and mortar, secrets that she had started to uncover.

Regret weighed heavily on her shoulders. She had gone about her research in an impatient unorthodox way, not the way they did things in Eyam. She had bypassed the historical archives that had been so cleverly and painstakingly combed through by her neighbours and acquaintances, the true historians, and now she was paying the price.

The house watched her. Shadows beyond those dark mullioned windows watched too. An involuntary whimper caught in her throat just as Kate appeared.

"Ah so you're awake. I've finished the chest of drawers." Rubbing dust off her hands, her demeanour was spritely. She hadn't picked up on the horror that had overcome Edie. "It didn't take too long actually. I noticed you had drifted off again. I hope you don't mind that I didn't wake you? I just thought that your body probably needs the downtime to recover properly after the fall." Fussing with a cushion that had fallen to the floor from one of the garden chairs, she plumped it. "They say that sleep is the best healer. How are you feeling?"

Edie swallowed down an unpleasant taste. "Parched. I should love a cup of tea. I'll make it if you can help me out of this thing." Bored of feeling constrained, she went to push herself up. A gentle hand on her shoulder stopped her.

"No Aunt Edie. The hospital said not until your next visit and only then if you can manage with the crutches. They said that it's important you don't push yourself."

With a cry of frustration, she balled her fist against the hard arm of the wheelchair. "I'm sick and tired of being told not to push myself all the time. They're treating me like a frail old woman."

Smiling apologetically, Kate went to take her back inside. "It's only temporary and it's not as if you're handcuffed to a post. The whole idea is that you're mobile. I know they were supposed to provide an electric powered wheelchair, but we'll have to make do for the meantime. They were very positive that you will be back on your feet in no time anyway. It's only a bad sprain. Besides, if you actually use this one the way you're supposed to, you'll have arms to envy soon."

"Muscles on a lady are unsightly," she said with a haughty sniff, as Kate found a good spot at the oak table in the kitchen.

Filling the kettle, Kate chuckled, her laughter tinkling through the house and noticeably lightening the atmosphere. "Not any more they're not. It's the in thing now. Strong not skinny." She reached for the biscuit tin that had been recently filled with an assortment of teatime favourites. "Or something like that anyway."

Edie looked at her quizzically. "And how are you faring with that one dear?" The pair of them laughed as Kate feigned a pose to show off her muscles. Edie gave a nod of approval. "Not too shabby," she remarked, feeling some of her humour return. "I should imagine Nick's noticed too."

The comment sent an instant flush to Kate's face and Edie noticed the brisk way that she turned away to find the teabags.

"I don't think Nick Delamere has the slightest interest in the state of my arms." Her voice was too high, too indignant.

Raising an eyebrow, Edie smiled wickedly. "I dare say not dear. He seemed rather taken with your face last night." She fluffed up her hair. "Still, you are from a line of natural beauty and rather nice legs too. You know what my nickname used to be of course?"

Grabbing the milk from the fridge, Kate was shaking her head in mock protest. "Aunt Edie, if you tell me that story one more time, I think I'll be able to recite it word for word." It was a family joke that Edie was particularly proud of her teenage nickname 'Spindleshanks'. The nickname had been awarded to her in her younger years by virtue of her long legs.

Kate placed some bourbons and custard creams on to a plate and winked. "But you have got a great set of pins. I'll give you that. Uncle Joe was a lucky man." She set a cup and saucer in front of her.

Dunking a biscuit, Edie eyed her with amusement. "Let's not avoid the subject. It's quite obvious that you are rather taken with the dashing Nick Delamere yourself. You're still blushing."

Kate's colour deepened and her expression went from one of amusement to one of irritation. "Please let's drop it about Nick. I'm not interested in any kind of relationship and believe me when I say that he does not have the slightest bit of interest in me. I assure you."

Edie was quietly amused. Kate was being overly defensive and the flush to her cheeks was very telling. Knowing better than to argue with her though, Edie didn't push it. She continued dunking her biscuit in between bites, silence hanging between them. Kate appeared to be distracted by something and it was some time before either of them spoke.

"Has the house always seemed so…?" Kate paused as she searched for the right word. "Has it always seemed so alive?"

The question took Edie by surprise and she sank back in her chair. "Well you surely remember your visits as a child, Kate?" Guarded, she avoided catching her eye.

Wrapping her arms about her chest, Kate persisted to press her about the house. "I don't remember it feeling quite like this. There's a lot of atmosphere here, isn't there? Not that it's a bad thing," she added quickly, as though worried she might have struck a nerve. "I suppose it was just a bit disconcerting when I was staying here on my own."

Reaching for the teapot, Edie helped herself to a top up. "Well you were used to that poky London flat, Kate dear. It's bound to feel different." Without looking up, she could feel Kate's careful, searching gaze upon her, looking for clues or hints to aid her line of enquiry.

Uncomfortable, Edie shifted in her seat before using her need for the bathroom as an excuse to break the conversation. As Kate pushed her to the downstairs bathroom, Edie's mind raced. Had she found the diary when she had found the box? She couldn't have, otherwise she surely would have mentioned it? Still, she couldn't dampen the flurry of panic that had awakened inside of her. Shutting her eyes, she tried not to think about it.

She didn't want to think back to that day on the staircase again. Someone or something had pushed past her. She wasn't senile and she wasn't mad, she had felt it, seen the air moving in front of her. She had even seen the vapour like curtain hovering above when she had been lying helpless at the foot of the staircase. Whatever had been in Thornycroft on that day was still there, only hidden. It always had been, hovering behind a thin veil that separated the living from the dead. The Ouija Board with Francesca had brought it nearer and made its presence felt.

She hated the idea of Kate alone, afraid, just as she had been night after night in the weeks leading up to her fall. Was it possible that Kate had witnessed something herself? How she wanted to know, but talking about it would surely only serve to make matters worse?

When she had freshened up in the bathroom and they were back in the kitchen, Edie suggested that they take an early evening walk to see how the Wakes Week preparations were getting on. "I don't know about you, but I'm in dire need of some more fresh air."

Kate nodded enthusiastically, but her bright demeanour did nothing to disguise her obvious relief at the suggestion that they leave the house for a while.

Edie knew then that Thornycroft was putting her on edge. The walk would do them both good. Even more, it would be a good opportunity to pop into the church and the museum to let them know that she was back.

Dark rain clouds were gathering fast and thickening when they set out on their walk. They choked what was left of the sun so that they were lined with an electric looking edge. Rain was imminent, but the air felt warm and close.

The walk into the village was challenging, with the wheels of Edie's wheelchair bumping over the rugged terrain of the track and the mugginess making her skin feel sticky.

"We should have driven," Kate grumbled as she felt a film of perspiration freckle her chest.

"Nonsense. I always walk this route." Edie twisted her torso so that she could give Kate one of her looks. "Twice a day I'll have you know."

Kate heaved her over onto the road that spilled from the track. "Except for the fact that when you do it, you don't have your heavy Aunt to push about."

Chuckling, Edie fell back into her old self. "Just think about those fashionable muscles Kate."

They took the road through the village at a pleasant stroll. The air smelled sweet, as it does just before a torrent of summer rain. As they passed the last dribble of tourists, Kate thought how beautiful and peaceful the place was. "Museum first, or church?" she asked.

"I should think the museum will be shut now dear. They'll all be preparing for tomorrow." Kate noticed how Edie's whole demeanour had lifted since leaving the house. "Do you remember how your mother and father used to always bring you for Wakes Week? There's always such a wonderful atmosphere." The sparkle had returned to Edie's eyes.

"It dates right back you know. The family who lived at Thornycroft back in the seventeenth century will have enjoyed Wakes Week just as we do now." She chuckled to herself. "Of course, the celebrations were quite different back then."

Kate said nothing as Edie continued to tell her about the somewhat more macabre nature of the Wake Festivals in those times. She knew all of this, or rather, could remember it all. She remembered the crackle and spit of roasting mutton, the jaunts and cheers at the bullring, the smell of ale on the breath of revellers and the heat of bodies as they danced merry into the wee hours. Of course, she was even able to remember that bitter sorrow when the summer was promising to be a long and hot one, but in place of the merriment to be had at the Wakes Festivals, the plague had ensured only grief and desolation.

Edie was quite lost in her reel of facts to notice Kate's despondence. "Let's just head straight to the church," she suggested. "There's usually somebody in there."

The pavement curved around towards the rest of the village on a gentle incline that wound past the primary school and towards the church.

Kate glanced to her right to see the rectory and mused that, aside from the cars lined up along the road, it wasn't all that different to how it had once been.

She stopped. There she was again, unwrapping layers of memories buried in a part of her brain that she had not known existed before. It was an impossible thought. She could have no memory of what the village had been like in those times. Still the images rushed at her unabated, despite her internal struggle to stop them.

Roses. Catherine Mompesson had kept a beautiful bloom of roses that summer. They had scented the walk to her front door so pungently that she had one day feared she was falling foul of the pestilence when she had wandered up the path. A sweet smell was, after all, how they said the symptoms of plague often began.

No. Kate shook her head. She had to keep her cool. She was just letting her imagination wander.

"Kate? Kate dear? Is everything alright?" Edie's voice sounded distant. "Kate?" The name echoed through her mind. "Kate? Is something wrong?"

A roaring noise rattled her head and with startling clarity, Kate found herself staring at the street ahead and the bright red streak of a car going far too fast through the village.

"Kate? Why did you just stop like that? Are you not feeling well?" Edie's concern shook her back to reality.

Kate tried her best not to appear as absent as she felt. "Not at all. I was just taking everything in. I've not been out much since I got here, so it's nice to just stop and look. It's so pretty."

If she had noticed anything to the contrary in her behaviour, Edie didn't comment further. She nodded in agreement. "Oh I love living in Eyam. It's where my heart is." She turned, her face animated. "Have you seen the view from Francesca's house? Stunning."

Stepping over the threshold to the churchyard, Kate navigated the flagstones and stopped again.

Edie had moved on the conversation, was saying something about a mistake in the engraving of the tombstone they had paused next to. Kate couldn't hear her properly. Her vision had blurred and somewhere deep inside she felt an old wound rip open. Through her tears, it was impossible to see the name carved into the stone. There was no need for her to read it though because she knew. She had mourned in this place before. The feeling was an echo from the past, bouncing against the walls of her mind, bringing its rawness into the present.

Turning her head, she tried to focus on the huge sundial that had been placed against the church and she focused her breathing, choking back a miserable sob. Once beautiful pale skin would have now long wasted away. Only bones would be left. Bones still enshrouded in the rotting shreds of the sheet that the fragile body had been wrapped in after it had taken its last laboured breath.

Kate continued to stare at the sundial, willing it to bring her back to her own time, to stop the awful hole of despair that had opened inside her gut, but everything around her was spinning and her knees were buckling beneath her weight.

She looked up to the sky and wanted to frown. The ominously thick cloud that had been hanging over them had dispersed quite impossibly. There was no longer any threat of rain and the muggy thundery air had given way to a dry heat. Her nostrils tingled and itched. She could smell something sweet. Roses.

"Stop it." Kate pressed her hands to her temples. She wasn't going to allow this to happen again. Not in public, especially not in front of Edie.

The scent of the roses was quite giddying. She put her hand out, feeling for something solid to stop her falling, but the air was thin beneath her weight and it felt as though the earth was opening up, swallowing her whole.

Opening her mouth to cry out, she had no idea whether any noise escaped her lips, whether anybody had heard the desperate cries for help that were resounding inside her head. With each fraction of an inch that she fell, the cries grew more distant.

Then rough hands were taking hold of her, rescuing her from the dreadful falling sensation, taking her by surprise.

CHAPTER 32

June 1666 – Eyam

"Rachel?" The dark eyes of William Mompesson were looking down at her. Concern was etched into them, so that the early onset of lines wrinkled the surrounding skin. His hands clutched at her arm, keeping her upright from where she had stumbled upon her walk home. In her right hand, she gripped at the handle of the handcart, filled with a sack of flour, milk and other supplies. She was returning from another ration drop, having placed her coins in the running water there, to ensure that they were washed clean of any plague seed.

The gates to the churchyard were shut and the stonework looked lonely and stark beneath the hot haze of the sun. Usually, fresh flowers would be laid on graves. People had far more to trouble themselves with now though and the place was desolate.

Rachel stopped to look at the wilting stems of the last flowers she had left for her father at his grave. Their heads dropped and what petals were left had started to brown and curl.

The smell in the air continued its pungently sweet assault on her nostrils and her mouth quivered as she looked back at William. Wasn't that how it started, a smell so sweet that would later lead to a fever? A faint ripple of panic caught her so that she wobbled again and his grip tightened. She sniffed. What else? What else was a sign that the pestilence had at last caught up with somebody? Fever, sickness, a headache, or a sore throat? She wasn't certain that she could remember.

"Rachel, are you unwell?" he pressed, helping her to stand upright again.

Finding her balance, she let go of the little cart and held on to the curve of William's elbow to steady herself. Allowing herself some time to breathe, she looked around, swallowing hard. With surprising force, she pulled her arm away sharply as she realised how close their bodies were. If she was falling foul of the pestilence, she should not be near any other person.

He frowned at the gesture, her intent misunderstood. Then she wrinkled her nose and rubbed it. "Begging your pardon Reverend Mompesson, but that smell, it's so-" Rachel was interrupted by the appearance of Catherine, holding a basket laden with the early bloom of roses.

"Do you need to sit down?" Catherine asked, her concern a reflection of her husband's. "I was just cutting back the roses which are growing wild now as the petals can be used for plague bags. Would you like to take some?"

The sweet scent of the roses that Catherine's basket carried was unmistakable. Rachel felt the panic subside a little. Her relief palpable by the slope of her shoulders, she accepted a bundle and added them to her cart before being advised that service was to be held elsewhere that Sunday, at the Cucklet Delf.

The two young Mompesson children were playing in the garden behind Catherine, their childish delight over soil and fallen petals showing off their blissful ignorance of the severity of the situation around them. Catherine and William must have taken good care to protect those children but their minds, though still young, must have had some acknowledgement of the horror that they were facing daily.

The earlier hopes of May had plummeted as the death bell tolled through the diminishing village more and more frequently throughout the month of June.

No longer did Rachel need to be hurried along home by William and Catherine. She knew the dangers of staying on the streets too long and as she bumped her cart back along the dirt track that led to Thornycroft Hall, she hoped she could persuade Benjamin to join her at the Delf for Divine Service. Being in the open air would surely make him feel safer from the threat of the plague seed.

News of just how many more had perished had not arrived at the doors of Thornycroft Hall. They had heard the unwelcome peal of bells, all mingling into one long knell, telling them that there had been death, although they were losing count of how much.

The knowledge weighed heavily on her shoulders as she went about her chores and used the petals that Catherine had given her to make up more plague bags. They would need them when attending service.

On the morning of service, they were in the garden, Rachel and Benjamin, amongst the untamed waves of grass, hidden behind the wall that led to the boundary stone. In quiet contemplation they watched the dawn break with clouds that blushed peach and gold against a wan sky.

Birds chirped from the safety of their nests high in the spangles of gold and green leaves, oblivious to the misery that had befallen the land beneath them. A squirrel dashed across the wall, its tail a curled brush as it darted up the nearest elm.

Benjamin had found her wandering outside alone when darkness was still cloaking the landscape from view. Neither of them could sleep after a night of creaks and moans that had flooded through the house.

After heeding Benjamin's warning about Goody so many months before and her strange behaviour in the blue parlour, Rachel had eventually taken to permanently bedding down in one of the guest rooms near to his. It wasn't just Goody's strange ways that frightened her. The words she had used in the blue parlour had stuck. "We are not alone," she had said.

Rachel was growing increasingly certain that a restless spirit was residing in Thornycroft Hall with them, wandering the corridors and drifting in and out of rooms.

Part of her wanted to run into the village and tell Catherine, to seek words of comfort from the Reverend Mompesson. In ordinary times, they would have been able to help her and hush her troubled mind, but they had their hands full, so it felt indulgent, selfish and churlish to darken their door with fears of restless spirits.

"You're troubled," Benjamin noted as he stood beside her, the backs of their hands grazing against each other now and again.

"These are vexing times Benjamin and you refuse to come to service with me, even though it has been moved to outdoors." Her tone was flat and her answer obvious, but it was not the only reason for her troubles. She sat down on the grass, bringing her knees to her chest.

With a heavy sigh, he joined her. "Do not ask that of me yet Rachel. I can not." Self-conscious, he turned away as she looked him hard in the face, challenging him.

"People are dying Benjamin." Unable to keep the bitterness from her voice, her words were pointed and accusing, making him flush with shame.

"All the more reason to stay safe here, inside Thornycroft Hall, away from the contagion. The death rate slowed last month. You said it yourself only a few weeks ago. There is hope now, hope that all this death and sickness is soon to be behind us. It will not be too long now, I am sure. Then I will come to Divine Service. Not before." Despite the mournful clang of the death bell, he did not know about the others. Either that or, like Rowland Torre, he was in denial. She had not the heart to tell him of the death count sharply rising again since the beginning of the month.

With a clipped retort, she shook her head and plucked at a blade of grass. "We have a duty to God. He will know those who go to service and those who do not."

He was angry. "Do not cast this upon me Rachel. That is not the only worry that keeps you from sleeping. It is not my absence from Divine Service that troubles you, is it?" Quick to pull her up, to remind her of the truth behind her worries, it was Rachel's turn to colour. "What else Rachel? What else preys upon your mind night after night?"

Combing the grass with her fingers, she cast her eyes downwards as she recalled the growing list of names of neighbours who had been taken to their graves in the last few weeks.

There had been something in Catherine's expression when she had handed her the rose petals; it had been something of despair and then she had looked so sadly upon her children, as though it would be the last time she was to lay eyes upon their innocent play.

"Rachel?" He took her hand and sat closer, encouraging her to speak. His palm felt warm and comforting and in spite of herself, a tingle danced up the length of her arm.

Biting her bottom lip, she deliberated on whether or not to tell him. Benjamin had been filled with hope only a month earlier when there had been news that the death count had slowed. It was that hope that had been keeping him going. To dash it from him would be cruel, but he would find out eventually. Better it came from her rather than some other way.

The sun had climbed higher and shafts of light danced in his golden hair, lighting his eyes and making his skin glow so that he looked almost angelic. It was in that moment that she took a breath and told him the plight of the village and her shoulders collapsed inwards as the reality hit her. There was no more hope. The situation was worsening. Now they were waiting. Waiting for pain, waiting for death, waiting to see who would be taken first in their household and left to the rough, careless hands of the sexton as he dragged them to a grave that had not even been consecrated.

It all came tumbling out, her fears, nightmares, the pent up worry and frustration that dragged at her like chains every single day as she scrubbed, cleaned, cooked and polished, wondering what the point of any it was. Exposing her inner most feelings to him felt so right and such a relief.

In those moments, she laid herself bare to his judgement. Then she cried, ashamed that she should be so selfish when they had not even been touched by plague and they lived far enough from the heart of the village to at least have some level of protection.

For a time, he said and did nothing. Then he leaned toward her and kissed the top of her head before reassuring her with words that she needed so desperately to hear.

She asked if he was scared, but he simply smiled, his scar making his features twist awkwardly. It was an expression that Rachel had grown very fond of. Then he shook his head, said he had changed his mind, promised that he would take her to Divine Service that morning and that they would stand together in front of God.

As he looked upon her, his face filled with a fierce passion, alight from the golden hue of the sunrise, Rachel thought that she had never seen anyone look so beautiful.

Their eyes locked and warmth radiated between them. The intensity of his gaze made her feel as though he was searching her soul, reading her every thought. She felt exposed, naked, like he could see every part of her. It made her head spin and her pulse quicken.

Moistening her lips, she drew nearer to him, feeling the tickle of his breath upon her skin. Then they were touching.

Their faces brushed together, gently at first, hesitating, the moment drawn out so that time seemed to stand still. She felt the soft cushion of his lips as they trembled against hers.

Rachel had never kissed anyone before and her heart raced as he gently drew her into an embrace, pulling her closer to him so that the kiss became deeper and more urgent, his mouth exploring hers with delicious impatience. Then, just as she had begun to relax into the natural feeling of being locked so tightly against him, he pulled away, an appalled look upon his face. "I am so sorry Rachel." He hung his head, ashamed. "I should never have presumed to-"

Reaching up to press her fingertips against his lips, she hushed him.

It was enough for him to know that she felt the same as he did. Tenderly, he took her hand, raising her to her feet. For a blessed few minutes, the both of them forgot what it was to live with the unrelenting dread of death and devastation.

As expected, Goody refused to join them at service and so they walked down the track together into the village beneath a sky that had earlier promised glory but was beginning to threaten rain.

The Mompessons had told her that Divine Service would be held in the meadowland of the Cucklet Delf and Rachel couldn't help but ask herself, would the lonely figure of Rowland, Emmott Syddall's lover, be there, waiting and looking, hoping to glimpse his true love amidst the dwindling numbers of parishioners? It was a horrible thought and she tried not to look for him, keeping her head bowed as they walked towards the large bowl shaped meadow.

They stood in clusters, each group far enough away from the next so that the plague seed could not be passed from those possibly infected to those who were not.

As Benjamin gripped her hand, Rachel noticed the stares. People would know of the unfortunate accident. As the women had shaken linen out on their doorsteps and the miners had collected in the tavern at sundown, they would have spoken of Benjamin's mixed fortunes; the handsome young nobleman who had been saved from death, but with injuries that would scar him hideously for life.

Squeezing her fingers around his hand, Rachel held her head high, giving those who stared for a little too long a look of defiance.

Even in times as hard as these, she had no doubt that tongues would wag. The orphaned serving girl with nothing much of a dowry to her name, standing with the disfigured gentleman from a family as noble as the Belgraves was one thing, but their hands intertwining like lovers was a scandal and one that would never have come about if it hadn't been for the tragic circumstances that surrounded it.

Some looked away hurriedly when Rachel's eyes caught theirs, some continued to stare, intrigue or disapproval upon their faces. Rachel couldn't blame them, not really. There had been a time when she would have wondered too, but it was strange how class and circumstance no longer mattered when thrown together by tragedy.

A hush fell upon them all as a tall figure took his post on top of the great jutting limestone rock that weather and time had fashioned into an ivy and lichen tangled arch.

The Reverend Mompesson was not the only figure raised above them. Next to him was Thomas Stanley, his stance sombre.

It was a strange sight, these two figures of authority, so opposed in their practice of old and new religion, standing together, unified as one.

Rachel's gaze drifted towards Catherine, whose head was bowed, as they opened with a prayer.

The villagers were pitted in a semi circle around the rock. Catherine was positioned directly opposite Rachel's line of sight. Even with her head bowed, Rachel could tell that her natural glow had dimmed. Something was missing. She looked around the semi-circle, each family cluster, one at a time. There was no sign of the Mompesson children. Rachel's heart lurched in her chest. Had something happened to them?

Without her children by her side, Catherine was smaller and more fragile than usual and something else had caught Rachel's attention. Catherine's hands, although clasped tightly in front of her, were shaking. It was a subtle tremble, but Rachel had seen how steady she normally was, how reserved and graceful.

Above her, William stood, a black silhouette against the sun as it appeared from behind a rain cloud. Like Thomas Stanley, his face was in shadow. It was impossible to read either of their expressions.

Rachel's insides twisted as she lowered her head to pray and give thanks to God for keeping her safe and with courage.

When William Mompesson addressed them, he spread his arms out so that they were like the wings of a great black bird. The death count was still rising. Rachel did not want to hear the next list of names that were to be prayed for. She could not help but think that one day her name or Benjamin's may be on that list. They would become lost souls, like Lady Rosamund and like the Gabriel Hounds, who were said to have swooped across the white peaks, portending the death of George Viccars and countless others after him. It felt hopeless, pointless and utterly distressing.

Closing her eyes, she wondered where the Mompesson children were and prayed that they were safe and not taken to their beds. Surely Catherine would not have come had they been sick?

She thought of how the walls of Thornycroft Hall had become a prison and how tormenting it was to look out onto the rest of the world. Her throat bunched as she questioned why they had stayed when they could have run.

The thought struck her with astounding clarity. It all seemed so simple. She and Benjamin could start again. They could take the horses that had been left behind and flee. Nobody would need to know from where they came. Together, Rachel was certain that they could do it.

The Reverend William Mompesson's words thrummed in her ears, penetrating her traitorous train of thought and shunning her back to the gently dipping field that she was stood in. "My refuge and my fortress; my God, in whom I trust." His dark hair billowed about his shoulders as he spoke and she wondered how he could remain so stoic, not a single crack in his words.

"Let us pray for the beloved whom we have lost here on God's earth. Let us pray for the safe passage of their brave souls." He had adjusted his position so that his face was no longer shadowed.

As he paused, Rachel shifted her gaze, only to see his dark eyes searching the crowd and then they rested on her. With shame, she turned her head, worried that he would see the selfish, disloyal thoughts that she had entertained.

"Each and every one of them," he continued, nodding in the direction of one of her neighbours. His words were unfaltering. They were intended to give them the comfort, strength and conviction needed to stay, and yet Rachel found herself unable to stop fantasising about her escape.

Lowering her eyes, she bit her lip until she tasted the metallic notes of blood on her tongue and her head began to spin. Taking a breath, she steadied herself, feeling the coarseness of the grass beneath her feet and reminding herself that she had a duty to God to remain strong.

The Reverend's words continued to echo through the countryside. "You will not fear the terror of the night, nor the arrow that flies by day, nor the pestilence that stalks in darkness…"

The idea of the pestilence stalking her in the darkness made her shiver and she thought of the dreadful noises that would rattle through Thornycroft Hall in the dead of night.

"You will only look with your eyes and see the recompense of the wicked."

At those words, Benjamin's revelation some months earlier hung in front of her. Goody was privy to murder. If there was truth to what he had said, then could the fact that she was caught up in a dark conspiracy concerning the death of Lady Rosamund Thornycroft be enough reason to weaken the walls of Thornycroft Hall against the plague seed? Could the demons that haunted Goody bring the pestilence to all of them?

Lifting her face to the sun, Rachel contemplated how she could convince William Mompesson, so committed to leading his flock through such dark times, that she needed his help whilst so many were sick and dying every day? No, there could be no way of convincing him or Catherine of the help that they really needed at Thornycroft Hall. It would be up to her and Benjamin to continue enduring what happened behind the walls of the house. Nobody else would be able to intervene.

It was down to choice now for her and Benjamin. Do they stay and wait it out, or do they leave the comforts of Thornycroft Hall with no safe place to run to? Benjamin would be shunned from any of the Belgrave residences. Lady Belgrave would rather him dead than put any of the rest of the family at risk. It was a harsh decision to make, but Rachel was growing more convinced that they should take their chances and leave.

A cuckoo called out as the sermon ended. For a moment, the Reverend Mompesson paused, his head bowed in a bid to hide the emotion that had suddenly overcome him.

On top of that limestone arch he was a black shadow, an unnerving silhouette against the aesthetic backdrop of fields awash with waves of purple thistle and golden buttercups.

A pregnant silence filled the Delf whilst they waited for William Mompesson to begin speaking again. Save the nervous repeated twisting of Catherine Mompesson's fingers, nobody moved. Their breath held, each of them waited for whatever had moved the Reverend so very visibly.

For a fleeting moment, his unwavering authority weakened before he slowly raised his head and regained his composure. Then his chest appeared to puff out and he became taller and more prominent as his authority reigned over them. He was the man to put their trust in, the messenger from God whom they should listen to, heed and follow. Once again, his voice did not falter as his words echoed around the Delf, sealing the fate of each villager in front of him and even those who had chosen not to come to service that morning.

"And so here we are, disciples of the Lord, following His path. Just as the Lord Jesus Christ sacrificed himself for our souls, God is asking that we in Eyam do the same, for the souls of others. We must find courage in our souls and pray to God for the strength in our hearts to lead us on this journey, for it is our turn now to do as Jesus Christ, our Lord did.

"Your strength and prayers have brought us this far. Now we must take an oath. We must take an oath to confine ourselves to this village. No soul must enter and no soul must leave. It is God's will now. Have faith and He shall protect us. He will guide us on our journey. For those who follow his path, there will be salvation at the end. God bless us all."

Tensing, Rachel felt her hand slip from Benjamin's as the significance of his words chilled the blood in her veins. There would be no escape plan, no brave new start. Their struggle for survival would continue and probably end in Eyam.

Bereft of any wind, even the trees had appeared to stop moving. Rachel noticed a single bead of sweat trace its way down Benjamin's face, leaving a thin salty trail. Her palms were damp and clammy and her mouth as dry as bone. For all of these many months they had kept themselves confined and so it should be no different. But it was, it was very different.

Now they were bound by the word of God to stay. Their prison walls, although transparent, had become solid. A Holy prison, wherein they had the word of their Reverend that he would see to ease their suffering in return for their sacrifice. To breach it would be to breach the will of God.

Some had sunk to their knees, others had begun to pray. Rachel simply stood and stared into the horizon, through the invisible wall of their prison.

It was indeed a blessing that her parents had not survived to see the past year, or this fateful June day when their only daughter was as good as condemned to a dreadful, painful death.

She thought of Lady Cecily's little Samuel and the way his fat little fingers had curled around her own when she had held him. He would never know of the girl who had helped deliver him on a stormy night and Rachel would never know what it was to have a baby of her own stare up at her, full of need and unconditional love. The secrets of Thornycroft Hall and Lady Rosamund's unfortunate and untimely demise would remain buried with her bones and with Goody Brown's. Thornycroft Hall's walls would remain forever muted, coveting away whatever dreadful dark crime had put Lady Rosamund into an untimely grave.

William climbed down from the great stone that would serve as their new altar for service. He appeared engaged in earnest with Thomas Stanley and then they too parted one another's company, ushering their congregation back to their homes.

Not everyone followed. Those with surviving family members clutched at their loved ones for dear life, their hands clawing at one another, using one another to prop themselves up. For those who were alone, or who had lost so many, they began their lonely journey back to their homes and the place that they would take their final rank, diseased breath.

A flicker of anger ignited somewhere in the depth of Rachel's stomach. She wanted to be sick. She wanted to scream. She wanted to cry. Instead she stood, statue-like, watching and listening to some of the villagers whispering. The Mompesson children had not been at service, not because they were sick, but because they had been sent away. William and Catherine had sent them away from Eyam before the decision was delivered. Rachel rocked back on her heels, shocked.

Why should the Mompessons save their own flesh and blood but ask that everyone else stay to die? Why should they have to cower in the dark corners of their homes, waiting to see when the pestilence would lay its claim on them? How could the Mompessons, her friends, have been so callous as to send their own children away without helping others to escape?

Rachel thought about balling her fists and pounding them against William Mompesson's back. She thought of telling him that she wouldn't do it, that she wouldn't resign herself to certain death. Then she saw Catherine, a beautiful air of calm radiating around her as she continued to hold herself with great dignity and courage, and her anger dissipated.

Catherine could have left with the children. She could have chosen to go with them and turn her back on her neighbours in Eyam, but she hadn't. She had chosen to stay. Catherine Mompesson had chosen to remain by the sides of all of those who had been forced to stay behind so that she could comfort them, care for them and stand tall with them.

Rachel felt a small flame begin to glow inside of her and she felt a strength that she had not known before unfurl itself.

God had spoken to them using the mouth of William Mompesson. He had asked them to make a sacrifice and stay, but in doing so, he had not bound their hands or fenced them in like cattle in a pen. There was still a choice to be made for her and Benjamin. That was both their gift and their curse.

To stay would mean that their bodies would likely surrender to the destruction of the pestilence, but to defy the cordon sanitaire and leave would mean that whatever life they would get to live, they would be handing their souls to the Devil.

Taking a step forward and then another, Rachel walked beyond the great limestone arch, leaving the echoes of grief and fear behind her. At her feet, a single dandelion swayed in the breeze, its seeds a puffball of off white. With a neat snap, she plucked it from the ground. Milky white liquid gathered around the end of the stalk.

As she gently blew the seeds into the warm summer air, she silently made her choice.

CHAPTER 33

Present Day – Eyam

Arms were under her head, supporting its weight. There was a stinging sensation against her cheek, accompanied by a slapping noise. Her eyes flickered but all she could see was dandelion seeds dancing on a current of warm summer air. Somebody was saying something to her. Benjamin? No this voice was different, older, a lilt of tongue that was quite unlike the plum accent of Benjamin Belgrave. She tried to look up. The dandelion seeds had blurred and the sky was different. It had been replaced by a darker, moodier colour.

Speckles of wet began bouncing from her forehead, wetting her lips. She licked them, tasting the raindrops and tried to open her eyes again. The movement caused a flurry of excited voices.

"She's stirring. I think she's coming around," said a woman whose voice she didn't recognise.

"Stand back, don't crowd her," another woman said. This one was a familiar voice, one that reminded her of home baked rock cakes, lemonade made from real lemons, too sour but great on a hot day, and warm hugs. A feeling of homesickness washed over her.

"I've got her Edie, don't you worry." A man's voice next, self-assured, kind.

Kate coughed and her eyes began to open. Rainclouds were gathering above, already splitting at the seams. She coughed again, wheezing for air. The sensation of her lungs opening and letting in fresh air brought her to.

"Kate? Kate dear? How are you feeling?" the familiar voice asked and bright blue eyes were staring down at her. Edie. Kate knew her as Great Aunt Edie. Everything was coming flooding back to her at a dizzying rate and she shut her eyes again.

"We should get her inside," the man suggested. "Here, can somebody help?"

"You should fetch Nick," Edie added.

"Delamere?" The other woman asked and Kate assumed that Edie must have responded with a nod as hurried footsteps disappeared down the pathway.

Kate clenched and unclenched her fist. She was inside her own body again. It felt right and familiar, not like before. Using the man who was holding her as a way of leveraging herself to an upright position, she insisted that she would be fine. "I'm okay really. I think it's this heat. I just came over a bit funny with the air being so close and muggy."

"Aye well, the storm should clear off this atmosphere. You should really get yourself to a doctor, mind lass. You just crumpled there on the path."

Kate recognised him to be one of Edie's friends, Roger, the man whom she had met in the café. "Honestly, it's nothing a good night of sleep won't fix." She had managed to set herself to kneeling and was preparing to stand up.

They were interrupted by more quickened footsteps. The woman, who Kate now recognised as her Great Aunt's friend Lindsay, was with Nick who was hurrying along beside her.

"Kate?" He took her hand and helped her up. "What happened?"

"Really, I'm fine. I think I just gave everyone a scare. I fainted, that's all." The fuss and attention was making her feel self-conscious.

"You gave us all quite a fright Kate dear. Don't just brush it off." Edie could come across quite firm when she wanted to. "Roger's right, we should call a doctor."

Frustrated, Kate slapped her hands against thighs. The dizziness had worn off and she felt perfectly normal again. "People faint Aunt Edie. It was nothing, really. I'm fine now."

"Come on, I'll get the kettle on." Nick was insisting on helping her back to his cottage, but Kate was already pulling free of his grasp.

"Listen, I'm really grateful for everybody helping but I'm not an invalid. I'm fine now. Honestly." She gave them an apologetic look as she registered their concerned faces. Whilst she in no way wanted to appear rude, she didn't want any more fuss or questions.

Nobody looked entirely convinced.

Stuffing her hands in to her pockets, she sighed. "Thank you," she said sincerely to Lindsay and Roger. "It was good of you to help."

"Aye, well you should at least take him up on that hot drink," Roger insisted sternly. "Plenty of sugar. Not too milky." He rubbed at his bulbous nose, before turning back to the church. "I'll be in there if anyone needs me, just putting things back in order for the evening."

Kate nodded gratefully as Lindsay suggested that she and Roger would take Edie back to Thornycroft whilst Kate got her strength back with a strong brew.

Curled up with a cushion on the sofa in Nick's front room, she listened to the sound of a kettle boiling and the clanging of cutlery and cups. The room was quite different to how she had expected it to be, with a vast bookshelf being the focal point. Several pictures were hanging on the wall behind her, all of which appeared to be sketches and photographs of some interesting looking buildings. A modestly sized television adorned the top of a cabinet in the corner, as though it had been an afterthought. The house was cosy, simple and put together in a way that made it homely and interesting without being cluttered.

Nick appeared carrying two mugs and a plate of ginger snaps on a tray. He set it down on the wooden coffee table and handed her the tea. "I thought I'd let you add your own sugar," he said, pointing towards the bag on the side. "I'm afraid I don't do the whole jug of milk and china bowl like Edie. It's the basics with me." He reached for the bag and opened it. "You should really have a spoonful though. Good for the shock of fainting, or so Roger says anyway."

"Thanks." Kate wrapped her fingers around the mug and sank back into the sofa. "I'll pass on the sugar though."

Laughing, Nick shook his head. "Just like Edie. Stubborn. I bet you'd refuse a bandage even if you were bleeding to death. You really don't buy into the damsel in distress persona do you?"

Indignant, Kate glared at him. "Absolutely not. I don't make a habit of fainting in front of people or needing to be rescued. Don't get me wrong, it was great that Roger and Lindsay were there and thanks for swooping in to help out, but I was bloody mortified. People were looking too."

Again, Nick laughed, flashing perfectly straight, white teeth. "Oh they'll all be talking about it for weeks on end, the woman who fainted in the churchyard."

Eyes wide she bit down on her bottom lip, causing him to erupt into even more laughter.

"Well I'm glad you find it so funny," she huffed before going to take a sip of her tea and wincing at the heat against her lips. Then, in spite of herself, she found her mouth stretching into a smile.

"Yep." There was a glint in his eyes as he took the mug from her and put it down next to his own before he took her hand in his. "You're too good to tease, you get so uptight but look…" He touched the side of her face, the gesture intimate, catching her off guard, making her blush. "I made you smile."

"I suppose you have. That's something I haven't done in a long time." She realised with a sudden sadness that she really hadn't laughed or enjoyed herself for so long, that she had almost forgotten how to. Nick had made her laugh effortlessly when he had stayed for dinner the night before and now here he was making her smile again.

Conscious of what a bedraggled mess she must look, she pulled her hand away and pushed it through her short blonde hair.

The grin slipped from his features, replaced by another look, one that was more intense, making her catch her breath as her pulse quickened. "Me neither," he said. "Not since…" He looked away.

"What? Not since what?" Kate was aware that she had exposed some of her deepest secrets to him, but he had barely given anything away about himself, not that she expected him to. Nick Delamere appeared to be one of those men who could never share their feelings or fears. He seemed impervious to emotion, like he had created an impenetrable shell as a form of self-preservation.

Taking her by surprise, he pulled her up off the sofa and led her out of the lounge, along the short corridor to the kitchen and through a glass door into another room.

The evening was drawing in earlier than usual, with the storm clouds still gathering as the rain drummed down on the roof. Nick fumbled for a light. They were in a conservatory. It was several degrees cooler than the rest of the house and a number of large rectangular shapes were gathered around the edges.

With a popping noise the main light, by way of a floor lamp hung from a tall hook shaped brass stand, was flicked on.

There was a gasp. Kate realised it had come from her. Several rectangular canvases had been propped up around the perimeter of the room, with another still on the easel. They had all been finished to the most astoundingly beautiful detail.

A huge foreboding looking house appeared in all of them except for the last. The artist had created hard lines of shadow, making it seem all the more eerie and disconcerting to look at.

Every one of them featured a figure too. It was the same subject in each. A girl with brilliantly blue eyes and long dark hair, mostly pinned beneath a white cap, stared out from all but the one that he had painted last. In that one, the girl was turned away, gazing out across a beautiful meadowland that stretched lazily towards a river, where the silhouette of a man was stood alone.

Kate knew exactly whom that silhouette belonged to. Rowland. The memories were all there, tucked away in the farthest reaches of her mind, clamouring to make their way to the surface again, just as they had been doing ever since she had arrived in Eyam.

Turning to the other paintings that seemed to be propped up in order from left to right, she took a step forward. She reached out with her fingertips and gently touched the first canvas. He didn't try to stop her.

The girl was placing the single stem of a rose against a mound in the ground. "Lady Rosamund's grave," Kate whispered as her fingers tingled with the heat that was emanating from the painting.

The red of the budding flower's head was a brilliant scarlet, the colour of thick blood. It matched the tiny scratch on the side of the girl's forefinger, from where she had been cutting the flowers to place around Thornycroft Hall. Above her, the sun was rising high, starching the sky. "It had been a hot summer. One of the hottest I'd known," Kate whispered, barely aware of the words that were coming from her mouth.

Her focus then turned to the building behind the girl in the painting. It was unmistakably Thornycroft, only a much larger, grander, menacing version of the house. The walls were as grey as the most overcast of days. Shadows from trees crept across it and the unabated clamber of ivy snaked its way up the dull brickwork, bringing Kate's eyes to the blackness of the windows at the very top of the house. The hidden, forbidden quarters. Goody's home.

Like soulless eyes, those windows glared back at Kate, daring her to look further into their blackness. Kate felt herself drawing even closer to the picture, taking in every detail, recalling every taste, smell and touch of that day and then she recoiled.

From one of the windows at the top, a pair of hollow eyes looked out. They were empty, void of all humanity. It was hard to see much else beyond those eyes, which although a minor detail in the painting, were in fact the focal point. They glared at the girl who was standing over the mound. There was a frightening hunger in them, as though nothing could sate the owner's desires.

Kate had seen those eyes before, both in the present and the past, but she couldn't put her finger on who they belonged to.

In the picture there was nothing human about them. They were filled with darkness and unspeakable horror. Thoughts of Gabriel Hounds and of superstition reeled through Kate's head and then the words from Edie's diary.

We are not alone.

Those were the words Goody had used when they had been in the blue parlour.

Kate stopped herself, corrected the train of thought. It had not been her who Goody Brown had said those words to. She had said them to somebody else, to Rachel. Kate was not Rachel.

Taking a step backwards, she tore her focus away from the painting and turned to face Nick. His face had paled from watching her study his work. Her reactions had not been lost on him.

"You painted these?" she asked. "All of them?"

The look of concern did not leave his face as he nodded. "It all started earlier this year." He took a nervous breath, "It started when I'd been visiting Edie. Around the time I'd been back to my specialist."

"Specialist?"

With a sigh, he leaned back against the wall, his shoulders sagging. "I have a vision impairment. Choroideremia is the clinical term."

Kate's blank look prompted him to elaborate. "My vision is deteriorating and has been for a long time."

"That must have been a shock to the system." She didn't know how else to respond and kicked herself for stating the obvious, but Nick only shrugged.

"I suppose it was. At first, I just couldn't see as well at night. It's worse now though. I can't see anything if it isn't bright enough, so at night, I'm as blind as a bat, as they say. Nobody can tell me for sure when I will lose my sight altogether, but this year it got a bit worse. It was around then that I started painting. I couldn't help it, I needed to capture what was happening."

"What do you mean?" Kate was confused.

There was a pause as he eyed her carefully, judging how trustworthy she was and how much information he should impart. "In spite of losing some of my vision, I'm starting to see things."

He sighed, as though resigning himself to sharing everything. "It's like a film just comes down over my field of vision, a screen if you like. When it lifts, I'm seeing people who can't be there. And it's not just the people I'm seeing, it's the period of time that I'm seeing them in. I don't now how to describe it. Time travel?" He shrugged, "Whatever it is, it all seems completely impossible when they appear in front of me, but they're bloody well there." He gave a bitter laugh. "Obviously I've not told my specialist about that part. She would have me carted off if I did. I told her about the sensation that a film of something seems to warp my vision. I've had tests, but they're drawing blanks."

He glanced anxiously at the paintings. "They thought it could be cataracts at first. There's nothing else to suggest the vision has deteriorated further since my previous visit. I think they're putting this sensation of a film going over my eyes down to a neurological impact, my brain's way of registering the vision loss."

Folding his arms across his chest, he tilted his head back against the exposed brickwork of the wall. "I thought I was going crazy, but I didn't care, I wanted to see more. It was like a story was unfolding. That's where the paintings are coming from."

"That's why you hadn't seen me that first day isn't it?" Kate exhaled slowly, the facts coming together in her mind. "You were painting everything that you could see." She paused and her voice became a grainy whisper. "You were painting Thornycroft's ghosts."

"Thornycroft's ghosts," Nick repeated, slumping down the wall until he was sitting with his knees to his chest. It was as though the relief of confiding in someone had allowed him to relax.

His eyes drifted across each of the paintings. "Go on, tell me I've lost it, that I need to find professional help."

"Why would I say that?" Kate asked, although she knew perfectly well why he would expect her to. She had omitted telling anybody about her experiences for the same reason.

"Well it's hardly normal, is it? I mean, people don't just start seeing things appear in front of them that can't possibly be there." He gave a bitter laugh. On his face, he wore a torn, broken expression. Embarrassment tilted his gaze to the floor.

"Don't they?" she asked.

The question took him by surprise and he jerked his head up, his gaze falling upon hers. In the bright flicker of the lights, his dark eyes twinkled with unasked questions.

Sighing, Kate took the chair from in front of the desk that held paints, white spirit and brushes and sat down in it. The expectation on his face intensified as she hesitated, trying to work out how she should admit to her own recent experiences. It was impossible to find the right way of explaining that it had been happening to her too, but she didn't have to.

"You were whispering things when you were looking at the paintings just now." He eyed her suspiciously. "What is it that you were saying Kate?"

"Everything here," she said, arcing her arm around in a semi-circle. "I've seen it all before, or at least I've had dreams about it, if you can call them dreams."

She hesitated before sighing with resignation. "They don't just happen when I'm asleep, these dreams."

Eyeing him cautiously, she looked for signs to suggest that he thought she was losing it, but Nick's expression remained neutral. "It's like I can be just getting on with my day and boom, I see something that can't possibly be there or something tweaks at my memory."

Raising his eyebrows, Nick nodded over at the paintings. "I'm inclined to say that anything is possible now." He shot her a look. "Is that what happened at the church earlier? One of these dreams?"

Nodding, she licked her lips. She longed for another cup of tea, but she was desperate to unburden herself of what she had been going through since arriving in Eyam. "I feel like I'm being stalked, watched. I've felt that way before of course, with Richard, except this time it's different. The person or people doing it have been dead for hundreds of years." Taking her head in her hands, she shook it as though to free herself from the preposterous scenario that she had described. "It feels so ridiculous when I say that. Only, when she gets hold, it's as though I'm here in Eyam except that everything is...different."

"She?" Nick pressed her to elaborate.

"The girl in your paintings, I think it's her memories that I'm reliving. I recognise them all." She pivoted to avoid his gaze, turning her own to the chipped paintwork of the window ledge. She knew that she should stop talking whilst she still had a shred of credibility left. Getting it all off her chest felt too liberating though, too much of a relief. "Things in front of me fade into an entirely different scene. The place might be the same, but there will be something there that isn't there now; a carter on the uneven track into the village, hens pecking for any food they can find in the street, the older houses, as they once were." She felt lighter, as if a weight was lifting from her shoulders. "And I can't stand to look at the plaques around the village. They remind me of what was lost. The names, I knew so many and grieved for them-" She stopped herself, glancing at him from beneath her lashes. "Or at least *she* did and she's showing me how it was for her, the girl in your paintings, Rachel. I am seeing and feeling exactly as it all was for Rachel."

"Rachel." Nick repeated the name. It hung in the air between them as though it had been given substance.

For a few minutes, the monotonous patter of rain against the roof was all that could be heard. "Why do you think she's doing it? What happened to her?" he asked eventually.

Defeated, Kate looked out the window at the thick sheets of rain descending upon the village. There was no sign of respite. "I don't know, but I think she's trying to show us."

Pushing his hands through his already tousled hair, Nick began to swear. "Shit! Shit, shit, shit!" Frustrated, he rubbed his fingertips vigorously against his scalp. "This is crazy. We're crazy."

"We can't both be crazy." Kate was quick to the defence.

"True. What about Edie? Do you think she's seen anything?"

Kate hesitated, unsure whether to tell him everything but he was looking at her with such earnest that she felt it was the right thing to do. Taking a breath, she indulged him in the knowledge of all that she had found out since arriving in Eyam. She told him about the diary, about the Ouija Board and about everything that Francesca had told her.

As he listened his expression remained blank, until there was a pause and he rubbed at the stubble on his chin. When he spoke, his tone was deadly serious. "She did all of this shortly before the fall? And Francesca too?"

Nodding, Kate felt a stab of guilt. She was as good as throwing her new friend under a bus as she watched the emotion build in his face.

His jaw tightened and he clenched his teeth. "What was she thinking? What had either of them been thinking to do something like that? I thought it was just silly kids that messed around with that kind of stuff, not two mature women."

"I don't think you can really lay too much blame on Francesca."

Anger flashed across his face. "No? I suppose it was Edie who supplied the damned board and invited Franny over for an evening with restless spirits was it?"

Kate nodded, but not to be calmed, he continued his rant. "She should know better, but she's always doing something with those crystals, pushing them on to people, filling Edie's head with nonsense…"

"Nick that's a bit harsh. Francesca isn't solely to blame. Yes, it was a silly thing to do in a bored moment maybe, but I don't think she ever thought that anything would happen. After they made contact, she begged Aunt Edie to stop. It's Aunt Edie who persisted. It's her who wanted the plague story for Thornycroft."

"Well she got her story alright." Nick was wild with accusation as he grabbed one of his paintings, "Only I'm not sure the main plot is about the plague is it?" He shook the canvas, almost hitting it against the corner of the table. "Is it Kate? Haven't you noticed what's in all of the pictures that feature the house?"

A shiver passed through her, freezing her bones as he pushed the canvas in front of her, forcing her to look again.

Kate didn't want to look. She knew what it was that he was driving at. She had lived through it, knew what it was to be scared of it, to hear it and smell it but never quite see it. "Stop it Nick."

Nick wasn't ready to stop. He threw the painting to the floor and grabbed another. It was one of Rachel sleeping. Slices of moonlight carved her chamber into sections of light and dark as the elongated gait of a shadowy figure hovered at the threshold of her door.

"No Kate, I won't stop." Thrusting the painting towards her so that it was a fraction from touching her nose, he was intent on making her look at it. "This is what they've done. There's something else in Thornycroft and whatever it is, it's determined to show itself."

Discarding the picture, he pressed his palm to his forehead. "You hear about this sort of stuff, people messing about with the supernatural and making contact with things that they shouldn't." He gave a sardonic chuckle, "Not that I gave any of it much thought until now."

"What do you think it is?" She felt relatively calm in the wake of Nick's sudden outburst.

"I have no idea." His voice was level again, but when he looked at her, he was wearing an urgent expression. "We can't leave Edie on her own there though."

Reaching for her hand, he guided her past the upturned paintings and towards the door. "Come on. It's dark, so I'll need your eyes. We have to get back to Thornycroft now. I'll stay in one of the spare rooms and in the morning, we'll work out where we go from here."

Pulling the front door shut and locking it, they braced themselves beneath the onslaught of rain.

Kate held his hand, guiding the way, neither of them aware of the shadow that had emerged from the back of the house: a figure hidden amidst the storm, watching them.

CHAPTER 34

Present Day – Eyam

Anger twisted at his insides as he replayed images of Kate's betrayal in his head.

"I don't want anyone else. I just need to be left alone," she had insisted the last time he had seen her, only now she had shown him her deception. He had been right to follow her and to check up.

As he had been taking his walk through the village, he had seen her, walking out of the graveyard, leaning on a tall lean man with dark hair and skin. She had followed him with such ease into the cottage. To a stranger it would have appeared as though they had known each other for years, but that couldn't be right, could it? She couldn't have known that man before, could she?

He had stayed to watch them both. Creeping through the gate and crouching by the window just behind a rhododendron bush, he had ensured that he was obscured from the view of any passers by.

The thought of their hands touching, their eyes meeting so intimately as they sipped tea and talked, sharing such intense conversation, made his heart clench with rage so that the blood pumped hot through his veins and pulsed at his temples. Then they had disappeared together into the conservatory at the back of the house.

How could she do this to him? With a cry of anguish, he doubled over as his stomach muscles tightened. He spat into the grass and stood up, watching the two figures slipping off down the road hand in hand. Her hand so casually and easily linked with someone else's.

Pulling the hood of his kagool further over his head, he licked at the rain that had gathered on his lips. He had to find out where she was going, where she was taking this strange man.

The sick hollow void that was threatening to swallow him whole, loomed like an abyss inside his body. Part of him wanted to return to the guesthouse, pack his bags and go home, get on with the rest of his life and put her behind him once and for all, except he couldn't. Not without really knowing. Besides, he reminded himself as he began the walk down the gentle incline that took him past the church and school, he had come to Eyam to get Kate back in his life, not to leave her to live out a completely new one without him.

Determination pushed him on as he trailed behind them. They crossed the road opposite a coffee shop and headed up a track. Keeping a safe distance, he followed, just a shadow in the darkness.

It was a long walk to the big house that was nestled comfortably within a large plot of land. They stumbled down the pathway together, their hands never once separating until Kate fumbled in her pocket for a key. When they had disappeared inside and shut the door, he stood for a while, watching more lights snap on, bringing life to the various windows.

Raindrops gathered on his lashes and pooled at his feet. It was as though she had plunged a knife into his chest, the handle twisting with every minute that the door remained closed behind them.

It was a long time before he turned to leave and began the dreary walk back to the guesthouse.

On the way, he detoured to the village local, The Miners Arms. The pub lounge was a cosy and busy contrast to the wet streets outside.

He waited his turn at the bar, his mind distracted by plans on what to do next and he barely noticed the double whisky that had been placed in front of him, until a woman politely asked if she could squeeze in to place her order. Ignoring her, he lifted the tumbler to his lips and drained it in one go.

He leaned towards the man behind the bar, speaking above the clatter of merry voices. "Do you happen to know this woman?" The photo he kept in his wallet had a neat fold down the centre, but it didn't obscure the pretty face with its carefree smile.

Eying him cautiously with gruff reserve, the man hesitated before glancing down at the photo and then shaking his head. Even if he did know Kate, there was going to be very little this tight-lipped fool was going to give him.

Pushing down on the waves of anger that were swelling in his gut, he ordered another whisky and looked at the photograph in despair. She smiled back at him, happy, laughing, those green eyes twinkling with thoughts that amused only her, mocking him, goading him, deceiving him into thinking that she was his. The anger had returned and he snatched the photo up from the bar.

"What are you doing with that picture of Edie's niece, Kate?" A woman with cropped grey hair and a friendly face was standing next to him, her neck craned to get a better look. There was no accusation in the question, merely friendly interest.

Slipping the photo into his pocket, he turned to give her a disarmingly charming smile. "Oh, you know Kate?" He noted the almost empty glass of orange juice in her hand and ordered another, dismissing her polite protest as he pushed it towards her.

"Lindsay Warner." The woman stuck out her hand and gave his a confident shake. "I know Kate's Great Aunt Edie. In fact, I saw Kate only a couple of hours ago." Her expression faltered and the smile slipped from her face. She chose not to elaborate further. "How do you know her?"

"She's my partner. I prefer that term to girlfriend. Girlfriend always sounds so flippant, don't you agree?"

Lindsay looked confused. Either the finer nuances of labelling a lover had no resonance with her, or she was aware only of Kate's latest conquest. He suspected the latter and began to enjoy the discomfort that his presence might cause. It would go a little way in serving some manner of retribution if he was to highlight her infidelity, at the very least. "Richard." He extended a polite hand. She didn't take it.

"Oh." Lindsay pressed the flat of her hand to her chest and took a step backwards. "Richard you say?"

He faltered but didn't let the smile slip away. What had Kate said? What had the imbecile whom he had seen her with earlier said? The waves of fury swelled further, great big crests forming, preparing to thrash whatever was to cross their path.

A look of recognition lit her features. "Well, I must say, it's a pleasure to meet you Richard. Edie talks about Kate a lot and she has told us all about you too. Edie's been chomping at the bit to meet you for months. She must be delighted that you're here in Eyam."

So Kate hadn't been mouthing off to anyone. At least she had maintained some shred of decorum. "Actually, she doesn't know. Neither of them knows." He gave her a conspiratorial wink. "So how about we call it our secret? I thought I'd surprise her tomorrow."

A cloud shadowed her features and she took a nervous swig of her orange juice.

He frowned. "What?"

"Well I'm not one for gossip and I'm sure everything is just fine, but you should know that Kate had a little turn earlier in the village. It gave us all the fright of our lives, but last I saw of her she was insisting that she was fine and she certainly seemed well enough, so I don't want to worry you."

Slamming his drink down on the bar, he feigned his concern. "Is she alright? Where is she?"

"Oh she really did seem quite alright afterwards. She's ummm, she's…" Now that she was stuck, tripping over her words, unsure whether to divulge where Kate had really been, it was enough to convince him of her deception.

"You should go over to Thornycroft now," she suggested. "And see for yourself. Our friend Roger was over there but he sent me a text about a half hour ago confirming that Kate was back and all was fine." She was smiling again. "So it really was nothing to worry about," she added quickly. "The mugginess was probably just getting to her."

"Probably. Even so, I can't stand to think of her in any distress. Well I think that's my cue to head off. Lovely to meet you Lindsay."

"Do wish Kate well for me when you see her. Lovely to meet you too Richard," she called after him as he embarked on picking his way through the crowd to the door.

Waving his hand to indicate that he would pass on her well wishes, he left the pub with a cunning smile playing on his lips.

Of course Kate was okay. She had been far more than okay when he had seen her snuggling up to her new fancy man.

The plan was already playing out in his head as he turned the corner to head back up to the top of the village. That nosey woman in the pub had been of far more help to him than she could realise.

His smile broadened, in spite of the heavy rain lashing against his cheeks as he pushed on through the village. Kate really would be surprised and it was high time that she let him back into her life, whether she wanted him or not.

CHAPTER 35

Present Day – Eyam

Lindsay had needed to get back to finish the preparations for Wakes Week, but Roger had stayed on at Thornycroft whilst Kate was with Nick. He had still been insisting that Kate go to A&E when he left, and advised that he would be calling in the morning to check in.

"He can be an old fusspot but he does mean well Kate and you should at least take heed of some of his advice and rest up," Edie said sternly when he had left. "You gave us all a terrible shock," she added when Kate rolled her eyes.

"Come on." Nick nudged her gently towards the lounge. "She's right."

Edie had a new lease of life. She had stopped grumbling about the wheelchair and insisted that Nick help her with making some of her famed hot cocoa whilst Kate put her feet up.

Perched on the edge of the sofa, she half listened to the noise of Edie and Nick clattering about in the kitchen.

Tension began to pull at her neck and shoulders. The house felt alive again. Upstairs, floorboards and beams shifted whilst the rain thrashed at the windowpanes.

On their way back to Thornycroft, she and Nick had discussed how they should broach the issues at the house with Edie. They had come to the decision that they were better off leaving it until after Francesca's party. Nevertheless, the knowledge that the jewellery box, diary and Ouija Board were still all tucked away in the house, like an ominous stack of games, made her nervous and on edge. Throwing any of it out felt wrong, even the Ouija Board, as though doing so would cause some irreversible shift that would anger whatever was in the house with them.

Tapping her foot impatiently, she looked around the room. Everything was so normal looking, yet the hairs on the back of her neck and arms were raised. Goosebumps peppered her skin and the feeling of being watched was making her feel stripped and exposed. She felt as she had done when Richard had been stalking her.

Suddenly she wanted to check on Richard's whereabouts, call Chris, get him to confirm she was safe. She reached for her phone and hesitated. That would be unfair.

Guiltily, she chewed on her lip, the memory of his lips against hers, just that once, paling into insignificance in comparison to the wild erratic way her heart beat and skin tingled when she was near Nick.

She didn't want to give Chris the wrong idea by calling him, but what else could she do? Nobody else would be able to reassure her of Richard's whereabouts. A swift phone call was all it would take and if Chris was to bring up the idea of visiting her again, she would just have to remain firm with her decision.

She pressed her thumb to his name and waited. Her chest felt constricted as she silently willed him to pick up. It rang out to voicemail. She took a breath, readied herself to leave a message and then cut the call.

Standing up, she swept the damask coloured curtains closed across the large bay window and folded her arms across her chest. Something didn't feel right.

She hurried over to where the diary was stowed. Edie had put the box elsewhere but she still didn't know that Kate had hidden the diary away behind some mats in the cabinet.

Quietly, she opened the cabinet door and her hand hovered at the back of the pile of mats, her fingers desperate to feel the leather binding and the fine leaf of the pages. There was a story to be told and she needed to add to it. The urge was irresistible.

Reaching for it, she took it out of its hiding place and tiptoed upstairs.

No lights were on in the upper part of the house and the air was significantly cooler. Kate barely noticed the plummeting temperature as she followed the corridor along to her room and opened the little dresser just beyond the foot of her bed.

She stood for a moment, relishing the darkness that covered everything in shadow. At night she was able to keep her eyes open and recall how the house used to look, how it should look. Her mind began to wander. Fingers needled at her brain, poking somebody else's memories into it.

This room, this had been Benjamin's chamber. It had been the place that she had first traced her fingers along the ridges of his scars and felt the beautiful curtain of golden hair tickle her skin.

"Kate?" A voice broke the obscure memory, shocking her into the present. She dropped the diary into the drawer and slid it shut.

The corridor was bathed in light and Nick was standing at the door, fumbling for the light switch to her room. She reached for the switch herself, flooding the room with a bright glow so that he could see.

"What are you doing up here? Are you okay?" He was holding a steaming mug of cocoa.

"I was just going to find some blankets for you. Make up a room," she lied, feeling her face flush with the shame of the fib. It didn't feel right to hide any of her truths from him.

Waving a dismissive hand, he gestured for her to go back downstairs. "Don't worry about me, I'm happy with the sofa. Come on, Edie's made that famous cocoa of hers." He winked as he handed the mug to her. "Laced it with a good measure of Bourbon."

"That's Aunt Edie for you." She tried to keep her tone light as she followed him downstairs. It was impossible to push away the thought that the atmosphere had shifted again though.

None of them spoke whilst they nursed their drinks and Kate wondered if both Edie and Nick had also noticed the static that seemed to be buzzing in the air around them.

It was Edie who broke the silence, announcing that she was going to turn in for the night.

After Kate had helped her, she returned to the living room where Nick was busy plumping up the cushions. "All good?" he asked, noting her return.

She nodded and went to help him. "I wish I could just go to sleep. It just feels like an impossible task tonight." She checked her watch. It wasn't late and the night stretched on ahead as an arduous unlit road.

Silence filled the room once again. Thoughts of the diary, the jewellery box and the hidden portrait of Lady Rosamund that Edie had first mentioned in her notes were distracting her.

Glancing at Nick, she decided that she couldn't hold back. "I want to show you something." She motioned for him to follow her up the stairs where she slid open the drawer containing the diary.

The smell of its leather binding pleased her. It was the sort of smell that promised intrigue from the moment the front cover was folded back. "This is what I found in the top part of the house."

Offering the diary to him, he took it. They sat down together on the edge of the bed. She was aware of how much her heart was hammering in her chest. Was it him, or the fact that she was about to show him the diary, share Rachel's world with him?

The back of his hand glanced against her thigh as he set the book on his lap. Something electric sparked her insides and she looked at his face as he regarded the diary with interest. She thought of how Rachel had looked upon Benjamin, of the kiss that they had shared and she desperately wanted to reach out to Nick, to feel it all again. Could that be Rachel's feelings for Benjamin, or were they her own feelings?

Her mind began reeling as she watched him thumb through the pages to the point that she had marked with the paper turned back.

The passage on the page began in Edie's handwriting but the cursive letters quickly became smaller and far more slanted.

Nick frowned as his fingertips brushed against the imprint of the writing. "What is this?"

The question brought her back to her senses. "As an uneducated guess, I'd say psychography." Saying it aloud didn't sound as ridiculous as she had imagined.

He licked his lips, tracing his fingers across the words. "I'm going to struggle to read it in this light, the writing is too small."

Gently she took it from him and began to read the extract.

It is God's will that we are to remain here. No man, woman or child is to leave and none are to enter. It is not as though things are much different to before I suppose.

They stopped letting anyone into the Bakewell Market last month and venturing anywhere beyond our boundaries would lead to stones being thrown and people crying out as though a murderer was amongst them.

I suppose we are fortunate that the Earl of Devonshire, from the Chatsworth Estate, has agreed to keep us in supplies. It is a bitter irony that the poorest families in the village will eat better now than they had eaten before the plague contagion came.

Catherine called with a plague remedy. Goody is far more skilled in the stillroom than I, and so together we have created more tinctures to fortify ourselves with. Still, the numbers are rising and the pestilence is more rampant than ever. And amidst all of this, there are the noises and the shadows here in Thornycroft Hall.

Aside from her help in the stillroom, Goody's distance has grown ever since the day that she almost confessed something to Benjamin and me.

I wonder if it is fear that keeps her locked away, or whether it is guilt for her part in the death of Lady Rosamund Thornycroft?

When Nick put a hand on her arm, worried by the change that had come over her as she read to him, she didn't notice.

The impatient scrawl of words were filling black and white memories with colour and inflating the images in her head.

As she read on, the temperature dipped and the rustling of material against the corridor floors drifted through the otherwise silent house.

I find myself fearing that it is only a matter of time, but I am ever grateful that Benjamin has at least taken to attending Divine Service with me. It may be too late for Goody Brown's soul, but may the Lord look upon us favourably for the sacrifice that we are making.

People within the village are split in their religion, with many still of the old way, before the restoration. None of that matters now. The Reverend Mompesson and Thomas Stanley put their differences aside and stood together during Divine Service at the Delf. We have too, in order that we might survive and prevent the spread of sickness.

It is strange to think that something so dreadful can unite the old and the new clergymen.

In its enormity, the pestilence here in Eyam overshadows and pales into insignificance the new law that was supposed to keep Thomas Stanley at least five miles from our parish.

The pestilence makes a mockery of any punishment served to those who harbour a different set of religious beliefs to the King's, because it has brought forth a common purpose for us all, no matter what our beliefs may be.

Survival.

I shared this view with Benjamin once and at first he looked to me as if I was mad, but then in his solemn, sad way, he agreed.

It gives me some solace to think that even in these miserable times where fear of pain, death and loss can be tasted upon your tongue, that we stand together as a village, united with the Reverend Mompesson and Thomas Stanley leading us, and with Catherine comforting us, tending to us, reaching out to every soul.

Alas, as time passes so slowly here, in this long, unforgiving heat, it has never been clearer to me that our destiny is not ours to control...

CHAPTER 36

July 1666 – Eyam

Days drifted past and they were like feathers being blown in a gale, their direction at the mercy of a far greater force.

Goody had not cared about the news of the cordon sanitaire. When Rachel and Benjamin had told her of the Reverend Mompesson's sermon, she had simply stared blankly at them, nodded and returned to her quarters. She was like a ghost, hovering in the shadows, emerging less and less, the only evidence of her being the hollow moans and ominous thuds that would come in sporadic waves. The more that she isolated herself, the more Rachel thought that it was like observing somebody lose all threads of sanity that connected them to the rest of the world.

There was both a coldness and wildness to her, in her appearance and mannerisms. Every time she caught sight of her, Rachel's skin would prickle.

Goody no longer wore her cap but allowed her peppery hair to tumble down her back like dried grass. She cared nothing for appearance, manners or adhering to the rules of etiquette as a guest in somebody else's home. Her curses in the stillroom could be heard all through the house and her howls at night seemed to be heightening.

It was on one particularly trying day that Rachel, unable to cope with the noisy despair that was emanating from Goody's quarters, bolted from the house.

The day was miserable, muggy, with air that was too close, too stifling, making the material of her clothes lay damp against her skin. All she wanted to do was scrub her body clean. They hadn't fetched enough water to fill the tub, so she was left with no choice but to head to the river if she wanted to wash properly. Besides, escaping the suffocating confines of Thornycroft Hall was what she really needed.

Her flowers had finished for the month and the abhorrent cramps had this time come with headaches and a smell that she couldn't stand. Goody's noise was making her feel even more unclean and she wanted some peace.

The river that ran through the Cucklet Delf had some good shaded patches and the water was clean, flowing and fresh.

Clutching a bag filled with a clean shift, pomade and rags for washing, Rachel hurried through the village, hoping that there would be nobody down there and no sign of the ever optimistic Rowland, who insisted on fruitlessly waiting for his Emmott.

As she had hoped, it was quiet at the Delf. Save the chirrup of birds and the song of crickets, she was alone.

Finding a spot behind a tree, she checked again before peeling away her outer garments and wading into the water in only her shift. The river was cold, startlingly so, but it felt good and she plunged herself in, crouching low to save her modesty.

Rubbing the rags across her skin, she looked out across the meadowland, wondering how many would turn up for the next service and how many more would be taken to their sickbeds? She scrubbed harder, determined to get every grain of dirt from her skin and under her nails.

When she was done washing her body, she shook her hair from beneath her cap and dipped her head into the chill freshness of the river. Then she took a bag of rosemary and lavender, cupped her hands and relished the scrub of herbs against her scalp.

Afterwards, she sat a while on the riverbank, leaning back on her elbows and allowing her head to dry in the patches of dappled sunlight that the trees and patchwork of cloud would allow.

The smell of grass and wild flowers made her nose itch and when the bright orb of sun burst through cloud and tree canopy, her eyes watered. Filling her ears was the relentless chatter of wildlife.

In those precious moments it was easy to let her mind wander, to try and forget the tragedy that was living, breathing and dying all around her.

Rachel closed her eyes. She thought of Benjamin, of the way that her heart would leap if their hands should accidentally brush against one another and of the way that he always managed to bring a smile to the corners of her mouth with his conversation and opinions, even on the dreariest of days. It was obvious that Benjamin had those feelings for her too, that she was more than just a maid to him.

Then her happiness plunged. Things would be different when the pestilence passed. If they were to survive, he would return home eventually. There would be no reason for him to stay, nor any reason for her to stay with him. A maid could have no place next to a man of his noble standing.

Thinking of it made her chest feel as if it were cracking, preparing to be split into two halves and never put back together.

Sadly, she found the clean dry clothes and hiding behind a tree, replaced her still damp shift with another.

The words that Benjamin had once used to describe his view of love resounded in the air all around her, mocking her feelings, chiding her for believing that it was acceptable to feel anything other than subservience when it came to him.

"I should be pleased to keep my dignity and never fall to the follies of love," he had once said to her.

When it came to the subject of love, he had made his intentions clear and it would do no good for her to think of him with every heartbeat. Besides, despite what he believed his mother thought, there would no doubt be plenty of beautiful girls of his own standing, waiting in line for a potential marriage. One day he would find love with one of those girls, a great beauty of wealthy blood and with a fine dowry to offer.

The very thought deepened the crack in her chest, threatening pain like she had never felt. Scooping up her bag of clothes, she hurried back towards the village, trying to focus her mind on something other than Benjamin.

Walking through the village was like walking through a ghost town. Barely anybody was out and if they were, they didn't dally. People still had their business to attend to, but for the most part, they kept their heads down, concentrating on whatever they needed to do before barricading themselves away once again.

A girl whom she recognised as Jane Abbett was sweeping the doorstep as Rachel walked by. Rachel didn't know the Abbetts well. She recalled that the eldest lad had briefly taken employment with her father, on the farm. His employment hadn't lasted much more than a month due to his idling. The Abbetts had not taken kindly to the fact that her father had not kept him on, but that was all in the past. What did it matter now that they were all suffering a far greater worry?

Jane looked up from her work and Rachel nodded politely. Her gesture was returned with a scowl.

Looking away, Rachel shook her head. It seemed silly that the Abbetts should still hold a grudge after all that had passed, especially as her father was now cold in his grave.

"This is your doing I shouldn't wonder." The words were little more than a hiss but they stopped Rachel in her tracks.

Jane put down her brush and pointed an accusing finger. "Everyone knows about you and what goes on in that God forsaken place."

Something twisted in Rachel's gut. People liked to lay blame when something terrible happened, but not in her village, they were good people. Jane continued with her allegation. "Aye you might well look at me like that Rachel Craven. Butter wouldn't melt, but I know. We all know."

"What is it that you think you know?" Unable to help herself, she challenged her. How dare Jane Abbett point a finger of blame at her?

Jane's face contorted into an expression of hatred. "That house is full of sin, always has been. Now you are parading about with that, with that…" she paused, trying to find the appropriate words to convey her disgust.

"That what?" Rachel dared her to say it.

"That monster." Jane didn't even flinch at the horrible insult that she dished out.

Rachel felt the colour drain from her face and then rise back up again in an angry wave. What were people saying? How could they be so cruel? "I presume that the monster you are referring to is Master Benjamin, Lord Belgrave's son?"

"*Lord Belgrave's son.*" Jane mimicked nastily. "Status means nought to none of us no more. Not here, not now."

"Then why are you even troubling yourself to pass judgement?"

Jane lurched forward. "Because we saw, we all saw. You held his hand and flaunted your sin at Divine service. 'Tis not right, none of it." She lowered her voice again and looked around nervously. "Ma says that bad things have happened in that house since the day it was built. And everyone says that monster should never have lived. 'Tis the Devil's work that he did and there you are holding his hand and standing by his side, as bold as brass in front of us all. Nay, 'tis not right. None of it."

Shaking her head sadly, Rachel observed the fear in Jane Abbett's eyes. It clouded her judgement, tainted her view on things, bubbling away until she knew not what to do with it other than throw it out in anger. The anger was directed at Rachel but another day, it would be directed at some other poor soul.

People were being forced to live together in what was swiftly becoming a mass graveyard. Rachel could smell the fear on the street, on the sweat of her neighbours. Fear was manifesting itself, making them all react in different ways.

Rachel wanted to run and never look back. Instead, she had to continue walking towards Thornycroft Hall, where she was to stay put, wait it out until the end, whatever the end would be.

Responding to Jane would be fruitless and it would do no good to antagonise the situation. She knew very well how it appeared, she and Benjamin.

Pivoting, she turned to head back, but coming towards her was a line of men, their faces slick with dirt and sweat. None of them walked together, but all a safe distance apart. There was no laughter, no cheerful greetings to children playing, no playful comments intended to make the younger women blush and the older ones click their tongues, no clapping one another on the backs or suggesting a drink in the tavern. It was not like before. The scene looked so wrong. It did not belong in Eyam. It did not belong to the usual light-hearted ambience of summer.

Rachel did not want to pass them. She did not want to see those faces eyeing her suspiciously, scrutinising her relationship with Benjamin and forming opinions on how their relationship may have had a part to play in angering God and bringing such a dreadful sickness to the village.

Abruptly, she turned on her heel and hurried back up the road, Jane Abbett still muttering something behind her.

She took the upward curve that led past Mary Hadfield's cottage, where it had all started. The road took her past the lonely abode of Jane Hawksworth, who had lost all of her family and who appeared a shell of the gregarious woman she had once been. She passed the desolate sadness of what had once been the thriving home to the Thorpe family, now a mere hollow space, all of them gone.

She found herself hunching her shoulders, covering her mouth and nose with her hand, as she passed the row of cottages that had been hit so badly.

Not once did she look up as she hurried on, keen to turn up towards the Orchard Bank that looped up and around, back to the track that led to Thornycroft Hall. All the while she chastised herself for being so stupid. What had she been thinking to come in to the village with no real need for it?

Angrily, she thought of Goody. It had been her fault. Goody's noise, her madness that had driven Rachel from the house. She had needed to escape the confines of the oppressive walls, but the decision had burned her. Now all she wanted was to hide within those walls. Her heart pumped hard, hammering at her chest as she propelled herself forwards.

As she turned up towards the bank leading to the water troughs, a stout woman ran past her. At first, she was a blur of white, until Rachel focused her vision to see that she was half naked, shrieking and running towards Liza Thickett's tiny home.

Mesmerised by the strange, unexpected sight, Rachel stopped and watched, her jaw slack as the woman pounded at Liza's door with balled fists. Her red hair was loose and wild, sticking up at all angles from sweat and filth. She wore only her shift and it looked to have been cut or ripped at the thigh, exposing bare flesh.

Even from a distance Rachel could make out the ghastly lumps that ravished her limbs like rotting apples, bruised and shiny like they were fit to burst. The rest of her ample, exposed skin was scarlet with livid spots and rings, some tinged already to black where the blood had pooled, stagnant and diseased beneath the sallow flesh.

"Liza Thickett, let me in," she shouted, her voice as wild as she looked. "I need a potion. My children are gone because you wouldn't help, and now this pestilence is upon me." Her fists rapped at the door and the wall, unhindered by the bloodied mess that each blow was creating. "You can not keep it all for yourself. If I die, on your head be it Liza Thickett, on your head be it!" Spittle sprayed from her mouth as she screamed, but Liza refused to answer.

Rachel recognised her from market days, although she could not remember her name. For a moment, she thought that the woman would collapse as she laboured to breathe and wobbled with the fever, but some deep need for survival spurred her on. With two swift kicks, she had broken the shoddy hinges of the little door and stumbled into the house.

Running forwards, Rachel considered stopping her, but this woman was rife with plague and she didn't dare go near.

A man, who in comparison was half the size of the crazed woman, hurried past. He followed the woman into the little house that belonged to Liza.

There were more shrieks and a terrible cry before he dragged the woman out, limp and useless. One of the boils on her arms had burst, putrid yellow liquid that was tinged with red spilled from it in a thick stream. It had trickled over the man's hands.

Horrified and disgusted, Rachel felt her stomach lurch.

The woman was still alive, her breathing shallow. All the fight had gone from her and she was barely able to hold herself up to walk. A rotting lump in her husband's arms, she hung limp as he all but dragged her away. Her eyes were open, bloodshot. They were misted with a glassy gaze, burdened by the certain knowledge that she would soon be gone, wrapped in sheets and buried in her garden or the fields nearby. Her head lolled in Rachel's direction and she stared listlessly at her.

What, Rachel wondered, could be going through her mind? Was she completely insane with sickness, or was there still a part of the woman she had once been left inside her?

Rachel remembered how she had seen her at last market day, exchanging gossip with Elizabeth Hancock, calling for her children to hurry along. It was a far cry from what was left of her now.

Her husband's sobs of distress clung with an audible ugliness to the air all around them as he took her into their home.

Rachel turned towards Liza's cottage. She should check on her, make sure that the old woman had not come to any harm.

As she got closer to the cottage, a figure appeared. It was just beyond the open arch of Liza's broken door. Liza. She moved into the light, giving Rachel a better view of her.

Liza was pressing her fingertips to her face, touching the raised scarlet tracks that the woman's nails had left behind on her cheek and neck. Her eyes were wide with fear and shock.

Running forward, Rachel went to help but Liza called out to her, her voice a vicious rasp. "Get away. Do not come near. I said it to her already and I'm telling you, I want no one near me. You can keep yer filthy money too. No more potions or tinctures, teas or possets. Not for you, not for that damned 'Conjuror' of yours and not for any amount of money."

Liza regarded the battered remains of her door. "That mad woman broke down my door and it was doing a good job of keeping the pestilence out. I'll need to make another tincture now. For meself this time mind. Get gone. Do not come closer." She hissed like a cat and Rachel took a step back. The scratch on Liza's cheek was deep and it was enough to make Rachel wince.

Nin Thomas. That was the name of the woman. Rachel suddenly remembered as she took stock of what Liza was saying. What state of mind must Nin have been in to harm an old woman?

"I said be gone with ya lass." Liza raised her voice, startling Rachel into taking a few steps backwards. Though her voice was fierce, Rachel could see that her teeth were chattering from the shock of it all. Then she spat on the floor and made to chase Rachel off.

Breaking into a run, Rachel did not look back. She ran up to the orchard, not stopping, even when her lungs were on fire and it felt as though there was no breath left in her chest.

When she reached Thornycroft Hall, she slammed the door shut behind her and slithered down it weakly, clutching her head in her hands.

"What's troubling you lass?" Goody had emerged from her quarters and was staring at her from the staircase. There was no emotion in her voice but her eyes betrayed her, making Rachel believe that perhaps she did care after all.

"Nought. Got a headache," she lied, but in spite of the distance she put between herself and everyone else, Goody was no fool. With a withering look, she suggested that a brandy was in order.

"I know where they keep the good stuff. Don't you worry lass," she said, before disappearing down the corridor, her large bunch of keys rattling noisily. When she returned, she was holding a crystal cut decanter filled with amber liquid.

Rachel followed her into the kitchen, where Goody filled two cups, passing one to Rachel and taking a deep drink of her own.

"Go on lass. Take a good glug," she encouraged and Rachel brought the cup to her mouth.

"Now can you tell me what troubles you?" Goody's tone had softened and her eyes had grown kind.

The liquid burned her palette in a deliciously spicy way and Rachel felt her shoulders relax a little. How she wanted to tell Goody the truth about what Jane Abbett had said, and about Nin Thomas with all her diseased boils who had attacked Liza and made her bleed. She couldn't though. Liza had said there were to be no more supplies for Goody.

Even worse, if Benjamin was to find out what Jane Abbett had said, that the village had branded him as the monster who never should have lived, she could only imagine what it might do to him.

Sadly, she shook her head. "'Twas just some heartbreak I witnessed passing a house in the village." Raising her head sharply, she only told half of the truth. "Poor Nin Thomas. The pestilence has evidently made itself known to that family."

Rachel glazed over for a moment, thinking about the putrid river of yellow and red running slow and thick down Nin's husband's arm and the flecks of Nin's spittle on his cheek. "I imagine that her husband Ned will be next," she reflected. "They have no kin left. So within the week their house will be empty."

She looked Goody straight in the eye. "'Tis the horror Goody. It gets you here." She pressed a fist to her chest.

Draining the remainder of her cup, Goody slammed it on the table. "All this death and grief. Shouldn't be for one so young to see."

"We all have to go at one time Goody. This might be ours."

With sudden gusto, Goody pushed her chair back. "No lass!" There was a fierceness that had ignited the spirit inside of her. "It can do no good to think like that. It won't last, this pestilence." She spat the word out, her tone dripping with disdain, as though that alone could fight the disease off. Then she reached for Rachel's shoulders. The gesture was unexpected, bordering on affectionate. Rachel could see determination in her eyes and something else. Fondness maybe?

273

"We can outdo it lass." She squeezed her hand again and pressed it to her chest. "We're made of strong stuff you and I. I know you are. I see it in you." She smiled. "It's in your spirit, in your lineage. Any fool can see that just by looking at you."

Rachel battled with the queasiness that threatened every time she thought of Nin, Nin's husband and the frenzied wounds on Liza's papery skin. It made her realise how shockingly delicate humanity was in such tragic situations.

The whites of Nin Thomas's eyes had been flecked pink and red and her fingers clawed, like an animal ready to pounce. Poison had bloated her, thick and putrid, building in her body, rendering her into an uncontrollable rage. Rachel did not want to end up like that.

"How? How do we outdo it?" Her bottom lip quivered.

Goody remained solid in her reserve. "Lass, we stand strong. We wait for it to pass." She turned her head to look into the flickering flames of the fire as they licked at the brickwork. "It will pass. Eventually. We just need to survive."

Goody appeared thoughtful for a moment, as though considering whether or not to disclose something else to Rachel. She looked her straight in the eyes. "My grandmother was said to have thwarted the sweating sickness as a child, even when it took her neighbours, friends, parents and all of her kin. Seven year old she was." There was pride on her face and motivation. "A child. My Grandmother was just a child when the sweating sickness rampaged through York and left her with nobody. She had to learn to survive, even before it had passed through York. Just a bairn," she reiterated again, her accent thickening. "She carried on though. She just got on with it, with life, without them. It can be done. Do not be disheartened by what you have seen today. Some folk just aren't as strong as others."

Abruptly, she took her hands from Rachel's shoulders and picked up the decanter of brandy, ready to return it to its rightful position in the study. The whimsical look had left her. "I should go now." Her coldness and distance had returned.

"No wait! Goody, wait. You'll have dinner with us tonight?" Rachel reached out for her. The tips of her fingers grazed only the air between them.

Goody was already retreating back into the shadows of the house, to her quarters, where she could make her strange noises, be alone with her grief, her madness, or whatever it was that made her that way.

That night Rachel returned to the modest room that she had been appointed when she had first arrived at Thornycroft Hall. She did not tell Benjamin. He would not understand what could have possessed her to move closer to Goody's quarters. He would only worry for her, but her encounter with Goody that afternoon had confirmed, that in spite of everything she had heard of the woman, in spite of what she and Benjamin had witnessed, she meant no harm to Rachel.

When she had placed her hands on Rachel's shoulders, there had been genuine warmth in her touch. It defied the coldness and hardness that seemed to surround her.

Goody Brown was a strong woman, one to be feared but respected. Her presence, all of a sudden, made Rachel feel strangely safe. She wanted to be closer to her. The things she had said to her had brought her comfort, hope, an unexpected sense of safety.

As she lay awake in her bed recounting the words Goody had used to comfort her, Rachel realised something quite poignant. Not once had Goody mentioned God.

CHAPTER 37

3rd August 1666 – Eyam

In the passing weeks, news of more sickness was rife in the village. The threat of plague suffocated them. It was their gaoler, forcing them to wait for the death sentence that would eventually come to pass. At any time it could come looking for them, find its way into their bodies, put them into early graves. It was evident to Rachel that Goody feared it as much as Benjamin, because despite the brave words of wisdom that she had imparted in the kitchen, there were days when she would not emerge from her quarters except in the dead of night.

Rachel would lie awake listening to the shuffle of Goody's footsteps and laboured breaths as she crept about. She would hear Goody's curses as she worked in the stillroom on remedies with all kinds of odd things in them that she would take back to her quarters. Remnants of strange herbs and plants would always be found on the work table after she had finished her work in there.

Often, Rachel found her mind wandering back to Nin Thomas, recalling her twisted, ugly expression before she had attacked Liza Thickett. It was something that she wished she could erase from her memory and yet it was an image that she knew would haunt her forever.

Nin would be long gone, wrapped in her own fetid sheets and buried, her clothes burned. Shuddering, Rachel considered the likely possibility that Nin's husband would be buried now too, their corpses rotting and their house yet another left empty for the sexton to loot and ravage. She hadn't seen Nin's husband, Ned Thomas, at Divine Service since that terrible day. Then again, she hadn't really been looking. The thought of their fate was a resounding echo in her head, waking her in the still of night and hounding her as she worked throughout the day. It was a constant reminder that none of them were safe and it kept her from carelessly wandering into the village as she had done before.

On the occasions that Rachel bumped into Goody in the kitchen or the stillroom, she was on a permanent mission to find the right ingredients for another concoction. The memory she had of Goody, comforting her when she had returned from the village so shaken and upset, was swiftly becoming a distant one. She was a woman possessed. The stillroom was chaos and it was impossible for Rachel to keep up with tidying it. Rachel wondered if Goody was even eating. The effect was dramatic. Her once plump bosom sagged into her shrinking stomach and her cheeks dragged downwards, as though something was sucking the life out of them.

"She let the demons in," Lady Cecily had once said about Sir Edward's first wife. The words rang in Rachel's ears whenever she saw or heard Goody.

One morning, Rachel was in the kitchen seeking out the clay pot that had been filled with coins, when Benjamin stormed in complaining. His mood was black from the hunger that had set in. There had been no eggs from the hens again and their rationed supplies were thin. Supplies from the boundary stone could not come soon enough.

After breaking a wad of stale bread for himself, he disappeared into the main living area of the house, leaving Rachel with her thoughts. Slipping the coins into a pouch, it dawned on her that Wakestide was nearing.

Only a year ago the whole village had celebrated and danced, whilst children played games and feasts were spread. This year there would be no reason for celebration and no bright smiles or happy laughter. Sadly, she pondered what the Reverend Mompesson would say to them during Divine Service on the Sunday preceding it.

"I'll come with you to the boundary stone." Benjamin had returned to the kitchen, his sulk having lifted. "You'll need a hand and I can't imagine *her* being of any assistance." Unable to hide his disdain, he motioned to the ceiling, making it clear that he was referring to Goody, who was locked away at the top of the house.

Her spirits dampened, Rachel gave him a weary look. "I am grateful for the help. After I have fetched the supplies, I have so much to do. 'Tis wash day. I should have risen earlier. 'Twas unwise not to do it all before going out to collect the supplies."

"Pah. Who says wash day has to be today?" Benjamin was in one of his rebellious moods again. Whilst it was a trait that Rachel loved, sometimes it could be tedious.

She sighed heavily. "This is the day it always has been Benjamin."

Folding his arms across his chest, he smiled with amusement. "And who is to say that it can not be tomorrow, or the next day, or the day after that?"

He had a point. She chuckled, an impish feeling lifting her spirits. There was nobody to reprimand her for slacking on her duties. Why not take advantage? "You are right, I suppose."

He gave her a boyish smile. "Of course I am. What do you say to taking a walk with me after we have been to the boundary stone? We can take the guns and find some game. Sir Edward left me the key to the case, said we might need them if there were any intruders. I'll take mine and you can take one of his. There are no rules we need to follow here any longer."

"None, except that we must stay here, behind invisible walls," she corrected him.

"Maybe so, but we will not stray beyond those walls to shoot rabbits, or if we are lucky, some fowl, although that will be trickier without the hounds to hunt out where they land." He sniffed, letting the air fill his lungs as though they were outside in the fields already. "It is a fine day for it. You will enjoy it."

His passion and excitement were infectious, but Rachel hesitated. "I'm forbidden to even polish Sir Edward's guns, never mind take one to shoot. Besides, I wouldn't know the first thing about how to. Even Lady Cecily is not permitted."

Waving his arm, he led the way into the great hall where the rifles took pride of place behind locked casing. "No rules remember," he insisted. "You have a fine arm for it." His thumb and forefinger squeezed the top of her arm. "I can show you."

"I don't know…" Rachel watched as he pushed the key into the lock and swung the doors open to reveal the line up of Sir Edward's prized weapons.

Benjamin's change in mood was not to be thwarted. "Come on, let's make the most of nobody being here to impose their rules and regulations on us. Let's stop looking inwards and start enjoying what we can whilst the days are still long and lazy."

There was to be no arguing with him. After he had shut the cabinet again, without the slightest of qualms, they linked arms on their walk to the boundary stone.

Benjamin helped her douse the coins in vinegar as Thomas Stanley ushered them to hurry and take their supplies before heading back.

"I shall make a feast for tonight if we are lucky enough to shoot some game," Rachel said as they walked back down the track. Benjamin's suggestion had enthused her.

Two women from the village glared at them as they passed. Rachel held her breath. One of them was Jane Abbett, the other her mother.

There was no nod of greeting or polite words from either of them. They were too caught up in watching the spectre that passed them.

Rachel prayed that they would not say anything to spoil Benjamin's happiness. She could read their thoughts on their faces and it saddened her. Even in the midst of such hardship, there appeared to still be room for judgement. She could imagine just what they were thinking.

Lips pursed and cheeks spotted with colour, their gaze lingered over Benjamin's face. Either he had forgotten to cover the angry pink scars and ridges, or he no longer cared.

Rachel was pleased. She felt giddy with pride walking with a man like Benjamin and she wanted to show him to the world. Those scars were testament to his strength, his courage and his ability to survive. Holding her head high, she glared back at them, daring them to say something out of turn. Neither did.

After they had returned with the supplies and Rachel had made a knot of bread to take out with some cheese, they agreed to take the track that led towards the Grindleford Road.

Benjamin was bursting with excitement at the idea of teaching her to shoot game. She felt her chest swell as she admired his enthusiasm. It was just another part of him that she was growing to adore. She thought how very wrong she had been about him when they had first met, assuming him to be the spoiled rich, petulant heir to the Belgrave title. In contrast, he was gruff but gentle, pensive but light-hearted and he held such deep and intellectual opinions. Above all, he respected her mind and treated her with kindness. "Should we eat first and get our strength up?" she asked.

"Whatever you wish. This is your afternoon," he appeased, squeezing her closer to him and she dared to feel happy. There were moments when being with Benjamin made nothing else matter. The rest of the world could fall away around them and she wouldn't care. It was easy to forget about everything when her hands fell into his and their lips explored one another's, tenderly at first and then with hungry passion.

The sun was high and hot when they found an opening into a field, and they found a suitable spot to sit, amongst the brilliance of red poppies. It was a glorious day, hot and balmy, the sort that was too warm to work overly hard. Rachel was pleased that Benjamin had convinced her to leave the washing.

She began to spread out the modest picnic she had packed. Everything around them was peaceful and tranquil. Birds were singing and the untamed grass tickled her skin as Rachel unwrapped the bread. Benjamin had thought to bring some of the spicy wine.

"As there are no rules any longer, I shall pay the Hancocks a visit later," she said as she broke two chunks of the still warm loaf. "'Tis a shame we missed them on the way to get the supplies. They usually always use the boundary stone for the supplies, but they may have ventured to the well or the waterfall instead."

"They have been good to you since you lost your father?" Benjamin poured some wine into one of the cups.

"Yes. Alice and I have always been close. She is akin to a younger sister to me. Her mother and father, Elizabeth and John, have always taken the time to ensure I'm still well fed and looked after. Elizabeth won't see me leave the farm any other way than with a belly so full that I fear I'll topple over on the way back home. It has always been that way. They are kind people and I miss them." As she sipped from her cup, a thought struck her and she turned to Benjamin with excitement. "You should come with me."

He looked hesitant.

"Please Benjamin. They are good people. They do not judge and they would love you."

"Rachel, there may be no rules when it comes to the chores and the housekeeping, but we can not ignore the rules that should be obeyed when trying to stop the spread of sickness. It would be foolhardy to go knocking on doors for the mere pleasure of socialising."

"But the Hancocks live on the fringe of the village, as we do. There can surely be no harm?" She knew she was whining, but she missed her friends terribly and she wanted them to meet Benjamin so much.

Ignoring her protest, he lay back and folded his hands behind his head. "I think the heat of this sun is melting away your sense. Scores of people are dying here every month Rachel. I won't have you put our lives in danger just because you miss your friends. Leave the matter be until at least the cooler months arrive."

Even though she knew he was right, his arrogance tweaked at her nerves. This was the side of Benjamin that she did not care for so much, the side that so confidently expected everybody to obey his every command. It made her want to get up and stomp off, just to show him that he couldn't boss her around. "And what will you do?" she asked defiantly. "Lock me up in those awful top quarters with Goody Brown I suppose? Make her my keeper?"

Shutting his eyes, he chuckled, refusing to take her seriously. "Possibly."

Chewing on her bottom lip, she tried to read his face. It was impossible to tell whether he was joking or not. She finished her drink and her bread, but her appetite was waning. The frustration that she sometimes felt around Benjamin made her react like a petulant child, but his easy dismissal of her suggestion hurt.

As though sensing her mood, he got up abruptly. "Come on. We should look to make use of our time up here now. A rabbit stew would be a fine change and if we chance upon a pheasant it will be as good as Christmas."

Reluctantly, Rachel followed him. She had heard of the terrible and fatal injuries that could result from inexperienced people loading guns. They could backfire. Sir Edward had talked about it once after news of the death of an old acquaintance had reached Thornycroft Hall.

Benjamin busied himself with seeking out a good spot for them to stand before instructing her to position herself in front of him. "Posture," he began saying, pulling at her shoulders. "Posture is everything. You don't want the blast to knock you over or destroy your shot."

When he was satisfied that she was standing correctly, he let go of her and insisted that she watch him first.

Watching him rest the butt of the gun against his chest, she noted how he carefully stalked the horizon ahead of them, the gun barrels slowly arcing in a semi circle. "Follow the line and look ahead for any movement, track it and…."

Rachel had been moving slowly in sync with him, mimicking his posture, holding her breath and keeping her eyes trained for a streak of brown when she stopped.

Above them, up and over the track that led to the Riley Farm, where the Hancocks lived, a figure was stooped, labouring to drag something along the ground.

"Benjamin stop," she said, squinting as she attempted to get a better view. Through the balmy screen of haziness, she could see the outline of a woman who was of lean but strong build. The woman was visibly hunched by both the burden of her load and despair.

Something cold slithered beneath Rachel's skin. The sun no longer felt pleasantly hot on her neck and face. Sweat that had been tickling her hairline ran in cold drips down the nape of her neck, pooling at the base of her shoulders. Beside her, even Benjamin appeared to be holding his breath.

She knew that figure. Her gaze tracked along the outstretched arms to the hands that were carefully clutching an ominously sized shape wrapped in sheets.

Silently they watched, as with difficulty, the woman heaved herself and her load toward the field next to the Hancock's farm.

"Elizabeth." The name escaped Rachel's lips as nothing more than a whimper. Her eyes remained locked on the abhorrent truth that was unfolding in front of her. "It can not be, surely it can not be?" Rachel took a step back as she saw Elizabeth Hancock stop just ahead of the little orchard within the field and gently lower the swaddled body of a child into an open grave. Elizabeth's shoulders shook uncontrollably as she took hold of a shovel and poured soil over the top. Then she paused for breath, but she did not discard the spade, instead she began the labour of digging again.

The cold slithering sensation coiled its way about Rachel's body and the taste of bile built up in the back of her throat.

"She's digging another grave," Benjamin said.

Rachel wanted to run and call out to Elizabeth, to demand that she tell her what was happening, but she was struck dumb and rooted to the spot. They waited, not uttering another word as Elizabeth disappeared into the farmhouse only to re-emerge some time later with another much smaller bundle.

Rachel swallowed down the sour taste and then found her voice. "No! No! No!" she cried out, the words scraping against her throat. It was impossible to tear her eyes away. She felt compelled to watch the horrific scene unfold in front of her. "I can't let her do it. This can't be happening. 'Tis a mistake."

Before she knew what she was doing, she had broken into a run. "Elizabeth no! It cannot be! Elizabeth!" Her screams echoed, futile and hollow amidst the empty fields as she pushed forward, tearing at the dried grass that whipped at her legs.

"Rachel stop!" Benjamin was behind her, clawing through the air to catch her arm. Wild with the hysteria that she felt growing inside of her, she threw him off. "Rachel!" he called after her, his limp hindering him from gaining on her again. She could hear his grunts of pain as he fruitlessly attempted to reach her. Tears blurred her vision as she pressed forward, her screams unabated.

All the while, the figure of Elizabeth Hancock did not flinch or turn as she walked with solemn pace, holding the small child who she had birthed only five years earlier.

Rachel's head was swimming. It had to be little John who she was carrying. The bundle was the right size. The first could have been either of her daughters, who were closer in age, Anne or Libby.

"Please don't let it be true. 'Tis a mistake, just a dreadful mistake," Rachel repeated through tears as she watched her stop again: a mother so carefully and gently holding her little boy, cradling his swaddled head to her heaving bosom. Then she descended to her knees, holding the little body above the hole in the ground.

As the second child was lowered into the soil, Rachel tumbled hard. She hit the ground awkwardly. The pain in her shoulder and arm were dulled by her instincts to scramble back to her feet and keep going. She had to reach Elizabeth and find out which of the children had been buried first and if any more were sick.

Lifting herself to her knees, she felt warm, strong arms wrap around her torso. Fighting, she tried to wriggle free. Despite her determination, she was no match for Benjamin. The firmness of his chest pressed at her forehead as he pulled her towards him, preventing her from continuing her pursuit.

Frustrated and angry, she struggled, pounding her fists against him until her energy was spent and grief began to weaken her resolve. With a final cry, she collapsed and let him fold her into an embrace so that her tears could fall.

His hands gently stroked the locks of hair that had fallen free of her cap and she felt his lips, warm and comforting, grazing the top of her head as he held her and hushed her.

Squeezing her eyes shut, she tried not to think of the sight of Elizabeth Hancock alone, without help, interring the bodies of two of her children into their graves. Two innocent lives - dead. Where was Elizabeth's husband, John? Where was Alice? Where were any of them? Why was it only Elizabeth who had shouldered the burden of the task?

The thoughts and questions whirled around in her head like a snowstorm as Rachel clung to Benjamin. Her fists were balled tightly, the material of his shirt locked between her fingers. If she did not keep clinging to him, it felt as though she would fall from the face of the earth. She buried her face deeper and pressed the flats of her hands against her ears, but there was no escaping the dreadful sound of Elizabeth Hancock calling and howling from her door for somebody, anybody, to help.

In those moments, with a sense of miserable anguish, Rachel realised that the two freshly filled graves would not be the only ones Elizabeth Hancock would be digging in the field by the orchard that week.

CHAPTER 38

10th August 1666 – Eyam

The rations in the kitchen had been untouched for days. Eating and sleeping were no longer of significance to Rachel and she refused to speak with even Benjamin. Now she was his prisoner and he was her guard.

All she wanted to do was run to the Riley Farm, find Elizabeth, ask her what was happening and offer her some comfort. She knew how it was to be alone in the world and watch loved ones grow weaker until their last dying breath was taken, but she could not imagine how that could be for a mother.

Each morning, she would slip out at sunrise and return to the spot where she had witnessed Elizabeth enduring the sickening ordeal of burying more of her family. A week had passed and Rachel had watched in mute horror as she had dragged the bodies of John, her husband, and then William, her teenage son, from the house. Then she had heard the desolate screams from a throat raw with crying, before Elizabeth had emerged with the tiniest bundle of all.

Within a week, she had watched her bury most of the Hancock family.

Rachel waited each day, praying that she would see somebody other than Elizabeth emerge from the house. She had become certain that none of those who had perished had been her dear friend Alice and she prayed that she was in good health, that she would be spared and no more of the Hancock family would come to harm. Rachel knew that it was only Alice and one of her younger sisters left. Over the days that passed, she had also become certain that Anne, Alice's younger sister, still lived.

Then, the evening before, as she had been standing and praying at dusk, Elizabeth had appeared again and the sight had caused Rachel's knees to buckle.

Weighed down with despair, Elizabeth had been removing another of her precious children from the house. It had been the unruly yellow curls tumbling from the sheet that had given it away. Alice.

Alice, dear sweet Alice with her mischievous smile and tinkling laugh. At that moment it had felt like Rachel's broken heart could never be mended. On her knees, Rachel had watched Alice's body fall hopelessly into the ground.

She had not slept that night as the solemn lonely funeral of the girl who had been as a little sister to her, had played over and over in her head.

The inkiness of night was still hanging over the village when she arose from her bed, the morning still to break. Caught in a nightmare that seemed like it would never end, she drifted to her usual spot to watch over the Hancock home and pray for Elizabeth and Anne.

She prayed that there would be no more bodies wrapped in sheets and that Elizabeth could sit down and take the time to grieve, that she and Anne could take comfort in still having one another. She prayed that the plague would pass and that she could run to the farm to provide them both with the comfort that she had been unable to give over the past week.

As she whispered her prayers over and over, a red dawn began to bleed out above the line of trees behind the Hancock home. She willed the door to remain closed, for nobody to appear with stained bundles of sheets. She tilted her head to the crimson sky, a reflection of the poppy field behind her. As she did, the door opened.

Elizabeth. Her posture had crumbled considerably. She looked older and weaker and her gait was burdened with what she had come to endure over the recent days that had passed. Each movement looked pained as she stooped to dip her hands in the water trough. When she was done, she turned so that she was facing outwards, her line of vision directed straight towards Rachel. They were too far away for their eyes to meet, but nevertheless, Rachel felt her gaze rest upon her.

For a long while they stood like that, until Elizabeth gently raised her hand. A sombre gesture of gratitude that said she knew Rachel had been there each and every day, praying for her and her family, offering solace from afar.

Rachel raised her arm, spreading her fingers. The silence all around them was thick. Then, her tread heavy, Elizabeth returned to the house, only to appear some minutes later with the final lifeless bundle of a child that she was to take to the small graveyard by the orchard.

Pressing her hand to her mouth, Rachel felt her heart shatter as she watched the final trip poor Elizabeth Hancock would make to that small makeshift cemetery. This time her pace was even slower and her shoulders even more stooped.

As the scarlet sunrise began to burn into a brighter morning haze, the last of the soil was turned and Elizabeth sank to her knees. There would be no more foreheads to press cool flannels to, no more quivering lips to try and drink the useless plague remedies and no more anguished cries to comfort. She was alone.

Falling to the ground, Rachel felt the damp of the morning dew soak through her skirts and a sense of hopelessness engulfed her. They had all gone. All but Elizabeth. Her friends, who had been like siblings, were all dead and buried. Their father, Elizabeth's husband, John, who had been so jolly, full of jokes and rambunctious laughter, would never speak again.

Alice's infectious smile burned like a fever in Rachel's brain. Memories of laughter, of sneaking off on market day, of hot broth and warm bread in the Hancock kitchen were all that she had left.

Rachel pressed her palms into the damp dewy grass, her tortured cries joining Elizabeth Hancock's as they blotted the morning chatter of birds and shook the air above the otherwise empty fields.

When there were no more tears left to shed, slowly, her shoulders slumped, Rachel returned to Thornycroft Hall.

******

"Rachel you have to eat something." Benjamin placed a plate of food on the floor by her bed. Goody had joined him and Rachel noticed how the skin underneath her eyes was sagging even more than usual.

"Please pet," Goody begged, wringing her hands together nervously. She had emerged from her quarters to help look after her. Both of them were worried. "It won't do nobody any good if you don't eat." She picked up the plate and offered it to her. "You'll waste away."

Waste away. Rachel thought about how each of her friends was wasting away beneath the soil at the Riley Farm. How could she eat when the Hancocks had suffered so much and she hadn't lifted a finger to help them?

Taking the plate from Goody, Benjamin waved it near Rachel's nose. The rich, sweet smell of rabbit and onion turned her stomach. She couldn't think of anything other than Elizabeth – alone at the Riley Farm, possibly succumbing to the same fate as her family, but with nobody to look after her.

When she refused to respond, Goody and Benjamin exchanged a look. Her grief over the tragedy that had befallen the Hancocks had united them both in their efforts to help her.

"It's good Rachel. I caught the rabbit fresh today," Benjamin said, persisting with his effort to convince her to eat.

Rachel didn't care how fresh the meat on the plate was. Neither of them seemed to understand that she could eat none of it knowing that Elizabeth had nobody left.

She stared blankly at them. Nobody else could know about what had become of the Hancock family because the sexton from the village hadn't helped with the burials.

The atmosphere changed and there was a rattling sound from somewhere in the heart of the house. Benjamin's eyes widened and Goody visibly paled. Rachel was beyond caring.

Again the sound rattled through the house and above them was the ominous creak of a floorboard.

The candles in the room flickered. Goody pressed a hand to her chest and then rubbed at her wrist, turning it over to reveal the red raw marks that were there. Her eyes misted over as she rubbed at them. "I must go now," she said quietly. A hint of reluctance haunted her voice. "It is time."

If Rachel had been in higher spirits she would have questioned Goody's demeanour, but she felt no level of alarm or concern. She felt numb.

Goody disappeared from the room. Rachel wished that Benjamin would leave too. All that she wanted was to be left with her thoughts and the punishing pain of starvation in her gut. The pain was a reminder of how she had allowed her friends to suffer, how she had done nothing but watch and wait for each body to be dragged from the house.

The Hancocks had meant so much to her, been so good to her. They had deserved better than she had been able to give in return.

Turning away from Benjamin, she stared at the wall in front of her, silently willing him to leave her alone. She needed to get out of the house, to go to the Riley Farm and check on Elizabeth. It was sheer cruelty to leave her, except she knew that Benjamin wouldn't let her go.

"Rachel if you don't eat, you'll weaken, you'll…" He was unable to finish the sentence without the words cracking.

Rachel felt her bottom lip quiver again as he laid a hand on her arm. She couldn't speak. She didn't know how to express the emptiness that was inside her, how it felt as if somebody had taken a huge spoon and hollowed her out, leaving nothing but a shell.

He whispered her name, his voice shadowed by tears. His lips grazed the side of her head and the warmth of his breath danced over her skin. "I love you."

The words hung between them, a glowing beacon in a place that had become so bleak and dark.

When she turned around, he had already left.

CHAPTER 39

Present Day – Eyam

"Morning sleepy." Nick was in the kitchen, his hands around a mug of coffee. He was wearing the same clothes from the previous night but his hair was wet from the shower he'd already taken.

Kate glanced at the clock on the far wall. She had overslept. Raking her fingers through her hair, she tried to piece together the events from the night before. She had no recollection of going to bed. When she had woken up, she was fully dressed beneath the duvet.

"You were out like a light," Nick said. "Does she always sleep so well?" he joked, smiling across the table at Edie, who was regarding them both with great interest whilst enjoying a thick slice of toast and marmalade.

He didn't appear to notice how dishevelled Kate looked, or if he had, he wasn't showing it. "I thought it best to just put a blanket over you and leave you rather than wake you up."

"You must have needed that Kate," Edie interjected before taking another bite of her toast.

Kate brushed under her eyes with her fingertips, hoping that she wasn't sporting panda rings from remnants of day old mascara. "I must have." She couldn't remember falling asleep. All she could recall was reading the diary with Nick and then everything was a blur.

The diary.

Panic hit her. What had he done with Edie's diary?

As though reading her thoughts, Nick stood up and motioned for her to sit down. "I tidied everything away after putting you to bed, so that you would wake up to a neat room." Reading between the lines of his comment, she knew that he meant he had tidied away the diary to keep it safe.

Edie nodded in approval. "I do like a tidy man. A tidy man won't leave his underwear strewn about expecting you to pick it up after him Kate. They're keepers, the tidy ones."

Kate opened her mouth to protest at her Great Aunt's lack of discretion, but already Edie had started to expertly steer the conversation back into calmer waters. "So did you sleep well Nick? I can't imagine the sofa was the comfiest choice."

Rubbing his neck, he nodded. "The sofa was far comfier than I imagined it to be. Thanks Edie."

"It's a shame. You could have had one of the other rooms upstairs. You didn't need to wait to be shown." She averted her concentration back to her toast and waved it at Kate. "Would you like some dear? We've got a lovely doorstop of bread right there. Freshly baked yesterday. I bought it on the way back home with Roger and Lindsay last night."

Declining the offer, Kate hurried back upstairs to shower and smarten herself up. She needed the time to take stock of what had happened the night before. The fact that she had passed out in front of Nick was a distinctly uncomfortable notion. Even though she trusted him, he was still pretty much a stranger and she had been vulnerable, unconscious.

When she emerged from the shower, she returned to her room, looking for the diary before dressing.

Nick had tucked it under her pillow, leaving it open on the page that they had been reading from.

With force, the dream hit her, sending her reeling into the armchair by the nightstand. A deep emotional pain tore through her chest and she felt a sense of loss like she had never felt before.

Faces were swimming through her mind and then the circle of graves that she had seen only days earlier. The Riley Graves. Only, the name they had been coined with, by virtue of their location, seemed so detached. They were the graves that belonged to the Hancock family. Her friends. One week they had been there and the next Elizabeth had buried them all.

"Stop!" She pressed her hands to her ears, feeling the tears sting her eyes. Thinking about it was sending her head into a spin again. She looked up, trying to focus on something in the present and saw the curtains. They were still closed. Their pale yellow ropes were slung casually from the hooks either side. Gently, the curtains billowed and she watched as the paisley pattern puffed in and out.

Gripping the arms of the chair, she desperately tried to maintain her hold on the present. Then she noticed that the curtain material had stopped billowing. One of them had puffed outwards as though something behind it was keeping it there. Her eyes followed the outline. A shape was pressed against the material. Was it her imagination, or could she make out a head, an arm, a knee and then....

Kate's gaze was pulled towards the shifting light in the small gap where the edges of each curtain were not quite touching. Something was moving behind them. Slowly. Deliberately. Long fingers trailed against the material, feeling for a way out.

Kate wanted to scream. She opened her mouth. The shaft of light spilled out across the room as the gap widened, and an indent that looked like the shape of a head turned.

She opened her mouth, felt the scream building in her chest.

Fingertips curled around the material's edge, sliding up and down. Kate's voice caught in her throat, no sound came out. She was glued to her seat, unable to move.

Her gaze moved downwards to where the hem rested, just above the floor. There was the unmistakeable rounded toecap of a boot. It shifted as the hand began to drag the curtain back.

Kate wanted to stand up, to run down the stairs and into the kitchen where there was coffee and toast and real living, breathing people.

All of a sudden the most putrid smell invaded her nostrils, accosting her lungs, causing her to cough. The room was getting brighter. Soon she would see what was hiding there. Had it been there all night? She didn't want to see. She wanted the curtains to remain closed, for it to be dark again. She didn't want to…

"Kate? Kate, are you okay in there?" Nick's voice brought her back to her senses. The smell had gone. She found her breath, stopped coughing and tilted her head. The curtains were properly drawn shut again, the light filtering through only a small gap. There was no billowing, no shape, no fingers and no toecaps belonging to boots.

With a rush of air, she felt like she had been released and she sprang from the chair, racing towards the window, pulling the curtains back with such force that the curtain rail rattled noisily.

"Kate?" From outside the closed door, Nick's voice was filled with concern.

"I'm fine, just had a bit of a tickle in my throat." She looked out of the window at the garden below. The allotment was thriving, birds were flitting about, swooping to the ground to look for fallen fruit or pecking for worms before taking flight again. Everything was normal. As swiftly as the strange feeling that somebody had been in the room with her had arrived, it had gone again.

She turned back to her bed. The covers were rumpled, her clothes in a messy pile on top. Things couldn't be more normal. Pulling her robe from the back of the chair, she slung it on before answering the door to him.

His face was full of suspicion. "What took you so long to get to the door? Are you sure you're okay?"

"Had to make myself decent. I do have some self respect you know." She tried to smile. Her attempt to come across as light-hearted wasn't washing.

He peered over her shoulder in to the room, seeing the unmade bed, her clothes and towel strewn across the floor. She felt immediately embarrassed by the state of it.

"Come on," she said in an attempt to change the subject. "Aren't you getting involved in all this activity that's kicking off today?" She guided him out, pulling the door shut behind her. "I've got so much tidying to do," she added in a hurry, keen to demonstrate that she wasn't the slob she probably appeared to be.

"Kate," he said, reaching for her shoulders and turning her to face him. "I know something isn't right. Did you see something just now?"

Shrugging him off, she went to carry on towards the staircase. "Everything is fine. I'm just a bit jaded. That's all."

"No!" His arm shot across her line of direction, blocking her from going further. "Don't shut me out. Something happened to you last night, when we were reading the diary. I saw everything. You didn't just fall asleep. It took ages to get to that point."

Appalled that he had witnessed whatever state she had been in, she brushed away his arm, feeling her face heat up. She didn't want to know how she had looked, what had happened. Avoiding the subject was the preferable option. "Please Nick, not here. Can't we just get on with the day?"

Not to be deterred, he put himself in front of her. "No, we can't. Why won't you tell me what was going on in there? I mean, aside from anything else, you look like you've seen a-"

"Don't even go there!" Fuming, she pushed past him but he grabbed her arm, pulling her back towards the bedroom. "Nick!" She was seething with him for openly discussing it all in the corridor, with Edie potentially within earshot downstairs. The sound of the radio drifting up from the kitchen and the clatter of crockery suggested that she was busy stacking the breakfast dishes ready to be washed.

Refusing to entertain her protests, Nick pulled her back into the bedroom so that they could speak without the risk of being overheard. "Where's the diary?" he asked as he shut the door.

"You know where it is."

"You've looked at it this morning?" Lifting the pillow, he saw that it had been moved.

She shook her head just as he spotted the diary lying where she had discarded it on the bedside table.

Pouncing for it, he began to thumb through the pages. "Look," he said, finding the entry that they had started reading together the night before. He pressed down on the centre fold, flattening it. "Kate, everything stopped. Edie hadn't written anything more after the page that we read up to, but then you started talking." He flipped the page over and the handwriting changed. "This is everything that you said to me last night. I gave you a pen and you wrote it all down as you spoke."

Sucking in her breath, Kate read down the page. The words were familiar, the Abbetts' disapproval and judgement of Benjamin, the attack on Liza Thickett and the tragedy that had fallen upon the Hancock family. "Oh, I..." She couldn't finish for the lump in her throat. Her head was swimming, threatening to drag her back to a time that she didn't want to witness any more. Nick's hands were on her, grounding her, anchoring her in the present.

"I think we need to seek some professional help," he concluded. "This has got to stop. We don't know what happened to Rachel, but it's likely that she perished too. What if that happens when you're in one of these trances?"

"Professional help?" The idea seemed impossible to Kate. "Who could we possibly approach?"

"Someone who deals with this sort of thing, someone with experience. In my opinion it's not really a case of what if something bad happens, I think now it's just a matter of when. We don't know what we're dealing with here. The supernatural? A ghost? Something else?"

Kate thought of what Edie had originally claimed had happened on the day that she'd had her fall. Somebody had pushed her.

She bit down on her lip. What if that was true, if Edie really had been pushed? Kate had felt the energy, she had seen it start to materialise into something of substance. Instinctively she knew that if this was a genuine haunting, then it wasn't just Rachel that they were dealing with. There was something malevolent lurking within Thornycroft, stalking them all, something that was trying to stop Rachel telling her story, and it was dangerous.

Still, who would believe them? It all sounded like complete drivel. Besides, she still had to deal with the very real threat of Richard. If she started confiding in people that she thought a ghost was stalking her, they would be likely to question everything she had said about Richard's behaviour. "Nick, I really don't think it's a good idea."

Not to be put off, he clicked his fingers, the light bulb moment animating him almost comically. "What about the church? Surely the church can help with this sort of thing?"

"No!" Her retort was vehement. "I don't want people knowing about this. It's utter nonsense."

Nick's patience was thinning. "It's dangerous Kate. If you could have seen yourself last night-"

"I'm not getting anyone else involved." Throwing the diary onto the bed, she stormed across the room. "I've had enough interference and unwelcome intrusions after everything with Richard. Please, I just want to leave it for a while. Just let things settle."

Pulling open the bedroom door, she stopped dead in her tracks as she faced the impossible.

Eyes like flint, Edie was standing outside the room, her expression cold, cruel, calculating.

Kate felt her jaw drop open. There was no explanation of how Edie had got herself up the stairs with no stair lift or any other form of assistance, let alone to be standing, unsupported, as though the accident and injuries had never happened.

"Aunt Edie?" Kate reached out to touch her and it was as if she had broken a spell. With a gasp, Edie's face twisted into a look of complete shock as her legs gave way beneath her weight.

Like lightning, Nick was by Kate's side, the pair of them somehow managing to catch her as Edie began to crumple.

CHAPTER 40

Present Day – Eyam

Opening the window, he leaned out into the fresh air. He couldn't remember the last time he had slept so well - like a baby.

The morning had an earthy smell to it - the sort that comes after the ground has had a good soaking from warm summer rain. It was hot and humid. The rain had done nothing to clear the air. In London that kind of weather would mean shirts sticking to backs and sweaty angry motorists swearing at each other. Up in the Peaks though, it seemed different, full of anticipation.

It was almost ten and the owner of the guesthouse had promised breakfast up until half past. Smirking to himself, he imagined her pacing between the kitchen, dining area and then to the bottom of the stairs, wringing her hands, wondering whether she should knock, or whether she would risk upsetting her only guest.

With an impatient growl, his stomach begged him to go downstairs, but he wanted just a moment longer to reflect on his plan. It seemed strange to think that by nightfall he and Kate would be reunited.

The road through the village sprawled out in front of him, tailing downwards into the centre, towards the cottage that he had seen Kate in with her new fancy man the night before.

Angrily, he shut the window with a bang. It was more than he could stand, imagining that pervert's hands on her. Shutting out the image, he picked up his phone and went straight to the photo bank, finding one of them laughing together on the boat. He had cropped it so that their faces were tucked snugly together, side by side in the perfect close up: happy, alone, just the two of them. The picture was as exactly as things should be.

Throwing the phone on to a chair in the corner, he then grabbed the large fluffy yellow bath towel that had been left for him and turned his nose up in disdain at the fact that he didn't even have the privacy of an en-suite.

When he at last headed downstairs, half an hour after breakfast was supposed to have finished, his mouth began to water as the smell of sausages and bacon wafted into the hallway.

"Good morning." The lady who owned Honeywell Cottage greeted him with a bright smile. "I didn't like to disturb, so I waited until I heard you up. Come through, won't you?" With a sweeping motion she gestured to the little dining room where she had laid the table with neatly pressed linen, a glass of freshly squeezed orange juice, a variety of fruit, yoghurts and cereal and a cup and saucer ready for his choice of hot beverage.

He brushed aside the stab of guilt when he saw how pleased she was to entertain, reminding himself that he was paying good money to stay and that he would leave a good review.

"Tea or coffee?" She hovered with a pot of each and he opted for the coffee.

"Big day in Eyam today," she began, handing him a jug of cream. "It's the start of Wakes Week. Will you be visiting the Well Dressings?"

"I certainly will." He had no idea what the Well Dressings were but he didn't want to give anything away.

She continued talking as she went to fetch his breakfast. "It's always a grand affair, Wakes Week. Well worth a visit. There's so much going on in the village. I've heard the Warrens are having a party too. An open invite to the whole village you know." She placed the plate in front of him and brushed at a splash of coffee that she had noticed on her otherwise pristine tablecloth. "A lovely house. Amazing views." Giving him a sheepish look, she giggled. "I've often wondered what it's like inside that house after driving past. Everyone knows of it because there was a lot of fuss when it was built. Some arguments over boundaries and some of the neighbours were cross with the noise."

Picking up a mug of tea for herself, she shook her head. "It's a shame because the Warrens are a lovely couple. I bump into them sometimes in the shops, always very warm and friendly."

The sound of her voice dulled into the background as he chewed thoughtfully on his food, wondering whether Kate and her new boyfriend would be making an appearance at the party. He hoped so. It would be his perfect opportunity to catch her red handed and expose her for the slut that she clearly was.

CHAPTER 41

Present Day – Eyam

"Will you stop fussing?" Edie chastised Kate for the umpteenth time. They were sitting in the kitchen, nursing another cup of tea. Nick had left after both he and Kate were satisfied that Edie wasn't injured. Since then, Kate had been trying to persuade her to concede to going to the hospital, just to be checked out. "I'm not hurt, I'm absolutely fine," she insisted stubbornly.

Neither of them had queried how Edie had actually managed to prise herself out of the wheelchair and climb the stairs. The very idea seemed a total impossibility as Kate regarded how awkwardly she was shifting her position.

"I should call Francesca, tell her that we'll bypass meeting in the village this afternoon and just head across to her house instead." Kate was conscious that the party was a surprise and was careful not to give anything away. They were supposed to meet Francesca at the Well Blessing ceremony, which was to mark the start of Wakes Week.

"You'll do nothing of the sort," Edie objected without hesitation. "I am perfectly well and I look forward to this every year." She sniffed, giving her a haughty look. "Besides, it's you we should be worried about, what with all this fainting." Cocking her head, she looked at Kate with scrutiny. "How are you feeling now?"

"Like you, I'm just fine." Kate rinsed the cups, avoiding Edie's watchful gaze, but she could feel her glare burning a hole into her back.

It seemed preposterous that neither of them were bringing up the elephant in the room. "Aunt Edie, something's going on." Kate moved away from the sink and rested herself against the kitchen counter, waiting for the predictable response, the denial of any knowledge that strange things were happening.

Edie's reaction was dramatic and unexpected. Tears filled her eyes and her features melted back into the fearful expression she had worn back in the home, when Kate had first discussed her return to Thornycroft. "Oh Kate, I don't know that I can stand it any longer. It's like Thornycroft is no longer home. Everything's changed." She brought her hands to her face.

Rushing to her side, Kate wrapped her arms around her shoulders. "We can sort this out Aunt Edie. I know we can." She was making commitments she couldn't promise to keep, but she didn't know what else to do. "Just tell me what's been happening? We both know that things aren't right and refusing to talk about it is futile, dangerous even."

Pulling a tissue from her pocket, Edie blew her nose and straightened. "Very well." She glanced around the room nervously. "Not here though Kate, somewhere else."

They found a table for lunch in the rear garden of the Miner's Arms, and Edie relayed everything that Francesca had already confirmed, filling in the gaps about the diary and what she had taken to doing in private. "At first I'd thought it was a good way of doing some research, that I could back it all up by asking for access to the archives, searching online, but then it got out of hand." Dropping the crusts of her sandwich, she looked deflated. "There's a force in that house. Something doesn't want the story to come out. I thought it had to be my imagination running riot, that somehow I'd been making it all up, writing what I wanted to hear. I thought that it just couldn't be real, but there's a physical presence Kate. I've seen things. Felt things. The fall…"

"You said you were pushed."

"I know how it sounds." The tears were threatening again.

Kate thought of the boots at the hem of the curtain, of the ghastly pale hand peeling back the edge, threatening to reveal what she really didn't want to see. "I think that you were pushed Aunt Edie."

Edie's obvious relief was infectious. Kate felt it too. "It's not just you. This fainting spell yesterday, it's all linked." She relayed her own experiences and Edie recoiled in horror, putting a hand to her mouth.

"I'm so very sorry dear. What have I done? If only I'd listened to Franny's warnings but no, stubborn as a mule, I always have to carry on with every pursuit, see it through to the end."

"Nick thinks the end can only be bad."

"Nick knows?" Accusing, Edie glared across the table, her lips twitching as she waited for an answer.

"Nick has experienced things too."

Edie flinched. "I thought as much. I saw him sketching once." Exasperated, she sighed. "It's getting out of control. We can't stay there any more. Let's just go back to Surrey. Your mother will be delighted, I'm sure."

Kate felt furious on Edie's behalf. She couldn't allow her to be pushed out of her own home. It wasn't right, wasn't fair. "No! We won't be forced to leave." She reached across the table. "You have Francesca, Nick and me. Together, we can beat this. I mean, if I can deal with a real live stalker threatening me, I can surely deal with a ghost?"

The words slipped out before she could stop them and Edie stared at her incredulously. "What did you say?"

There was no point in trying to brush it all under the carpet. Kate's shoulders dropped in defeat as she let everything spill out, from how things had kicked off with Richard, to the way he had continued to stalk her, to threaten Chris and then all about the restraining order that had been issued. "So you see," she said, trying to appear nonchalant. "If I can deal with someone like Richard, a ghost should surely be a breeze?"

"I prefer to use the term 'paranormal entity'. Ghost sounds so childish and silly, but Kate, this man sounds positively dangerous. Why didn't you tell me? Why didn't your mother?"

Kate shrugged. "I suppose we didn't feel the need to worry you. Besides, how do you break news like that to somebody over the phone?"

"Oh Kate, I'm so terribly sorry that you've had to put up with all of this." A look of thunder darkened her face. "If only I could get my hands on that young man, I'd like to give him a piece of my mind, tell him what's what."

"You don't tell people like Richard what's what. Rational thought doesn't appeal to people like him," Kate said, but she loved Edie all the more for being so angry about it all.

"Well you're here now, with me, and he's far away. Stupid man. He had better not cross my path." She gave Kate a wicked smile. "It's a shame our ghost couldn't get to him."

Kate laughed. That was Edie through and through, able to find humour in any situation, even the completely dire ones. They got back onto the subject of Thornycroft and agreed that they would speak with Nick later on, ask if he would stay overnight with them again. Safety in numbers seemed like the best policy until they could work out what to do.

The crowds were spilling across the village even more so after lunch. In spite of the ominous cloud and stifling muggy atmosphere, there was a happy buzz. Edie appeared swept up in it all, delighted to be chatting to her friends again when they appeared through the sea of tourists.

Laughter was everywhere but Kate couldn't relax into it. She couldn't shake the feeling that she was being watched. Reaching into her bag, she checked her phone. No messages, no calls and she had disconnected her Facebook account long ago, so there were no notifications from that either. It made her feel alone, on edge and she wished that Chris would return her call, just to tell her that she was safe, reassure her that Richard wasn't hiding somewhere, biding his time, waiting to pounce.

The irony didn't escape her that this feeling of being watched, stalked and preyed upon was exactly what was happening to her at Thornycroft too.

If it was Rachel who was haunting her, or somebody else, they were always waiting, finding the most opportune moment to catch her off guard, when she least expected it. And for what? She mused over that fact. Was the purpose to tell a story? What was it that had happened that had caused this haunting? She felt certain that it was more than Rachel's experiences of the plague, that something else, something sinister had been at work in that house, veiled and overshadowed by the tragedy of the plague that had befallen Eyam. There was something hiding in the corners of the house, taking every chance it could to stop that story being told. That's what Edie had said too. She believed it was the reason for her fall.

Kate reflected on everything she had told her; how she should never have opened up the top part of the house and how, if she had known what had happened up there centuries before, she would have had it bricked in. They were jumping to conclusions though, reading between the lines of what Edie had written, of Nick's paintings and of the visions that Kate was experiencing.

What was it that Benjamin Belgrave had told Rachel again? Kate rattled her brains for the answer, searched amongst the pockets that held her own memories as well as those belonging to Rachel. Then she remembered. He had said that his mother had thought Lady Rosamund had been murdered and that Goody Brown had been involved. Elizabeth Hancock had said that Goody had lived at Thornycroft Hall before, in the days that Lady Rosamund had been there. The 'glory days', when furniture and tapestries had been shipped in from Italy and Lady Rosamund's gowns had been the talk of the village. Those were the days that Goody had resided there before, the mysterious maid who had helped Lady Rosamund through the loss of her babies and who had a reputation that had named her 'The Conjurer'. All of it made Kate shudder.

Then she thought of Nick. She would have to ask him if he would consider staying overnight again, let him know that she had told Edie everything.

She turned to see Edie surrounded by her friends, including Francesca, who had arrived in a flurry of excitement.

Explaining that she was off to find Nick, she ignored the knowing exchange that was shared between Edie and Francesca and started to walk away from the square, up the short incline that curved around towards the church and the Plague Cottages.

Most of the tourists had clustered for the blessings of the wells and the street was quieter than she had expected it to be.

Glad of some space, she opened the little gate to Nick's house and tapped on the door. When there was no reply she knocked harder before giving up. He could be off shopping. She would just have to catch him later or get his number off Edie. In the meantime, she decided to go and make up one of the spare rooms before heading across to the Warren house for Francesca's party.

******

Nick was sitting on the boulder so that he was on a diagonal facing Thornycroft. On his way down the track, he hadn't passed anybody. They were all too busy celebrating the start of Wakes Week.

Crossing his legs, he stared thoughtfully at the empty house. Its dark windows stared back at him, willing him to pick up his sketchpad. A trickle of sweat traced down his neck and he pulled at the collar of his shirt. The air was so close that he was almost wishing for a huge clap of thunder to roll across the sky above him. The clouds clearly hadn't dispelled themselves of all their rain the day before and another bout of it was due.

You need to hurry Nick.

He whipped his head around sharply. There was nobody around, but the voice had been there. Clear. Direct. Imploring him to get started.

The familiar tingling in his fingertips began to travel up his arm. It would get unbearable unless he began to draw, and then the headache would kick in. Impatiently, he threw open the sketchpad, feeling an ecstatic rush as his pencil hit the paper. Then he looked up.

The haze he had become accustomed to before painting was hampering his line of vision. A curtain falling, so that everything shimmered behind it: the house, the garden, the apple and plum trees. Then it was as though the curtain was lifted again.

Daytime had become night. Thornycroft loomed over him. Edie's apple and plum trees were now part of a much greater orchard, sprawling across the gardens. High in the sky, the moon was a silver crescent, and on a pathway leading away from the house was a figure. It was stooped, as though trying to shrivel into the darkness in a bid not to be seen.

As the nib of his pencil furiously drew lines, shading and shadows, he didn't notice the ache in his wrist that was building from all of the effort.

To any onlookers, it was a strange sight. He wasn't even looking at the page as he drew. His gaze was locked on something dead ahead of him in the distance, and his hand was busy creating what he could see - a scene from hundreds of years earlier, locked in time, waiting for life to be breathed into it again…

CHAPTER 42

Mid August 1666 - Eyam

The house was silent when she found her boots and carefully pulled back the bolts on the servants' door in the kitchen. Even Goody's cries, which had been particularly mournful and pained, had long quietened.

It was cool out, much cooler than she had anticipated, but there was no time to fetch a shawl, not if she didn't want to risk waking Benjamin.

Rachel had thought on Goody's warning about wasting away and she had made a decision. She had a duty to her friends. What would Alice, Anne and Libby think if they knew that their mother had been left alone and was possibly dying? What would any of them think?

Despite the nausea in her stomach, she had eaten her supper, just as Benjamin had asked of her, and then she had lain in her bed thinking hard. She had thought about what Catherine Mompesson would do. Then she had crept into the stillroom where she had spent time making up the latest remedy that Catherine had written out for them. It was all that she could think to do to be of any help.

Clutching a basket containing the bottle and a wrapped knot of bread in one hand and a lamp in the other, she hurried out into the night, shoulders hunched, afraid she would be seen.

The stony track up to the Riley Farm was a difficult one to navigate with just a lamp under a sliver of moonlight. With each step, her heart seemed to pound in her mouth. She knew that the night watchmen were still on duty to ensure that nobody left and nobody entered the village. It was a chance as to whether anyone on duty would stray as far as the Riley Farm. A lone traveller like herself would be suspicious and Rachel wasn't sure what would happen to anyone who was accused of attempting to defy the quarantine.

Noises from the trees and the undergrowth made her jump as she pushed on up the hill, her breath laboured with adrenaline and her bladder feeling suddenly full. Shuddering, she picked up her pace, hurrying on until she saw the outline of the Hancock's farmhouse.

Ascending the track, Rachel was aware of how isolated Elizabeth must have felt up there, burying her family. Their neighbours, the Talbots, had died only the month before from plague and so there really would have been nobody nearby to help.

There were no lights in the windows and no smoke from the chimney, but given that it was late, that was no surprise. Every step that she took sounded far louder than she had intended.

When she reached the front door, she knocked far too quietly to be heard. Raising her knuckles again, she knocked and waited for the light of a lamp to bring a glow to one of the windows. No light came.

Gingerly, she raised her hand to the door and pushed. It opened with a gentle creak.

The kitchen was swamped in darkness. Resting her basket on the table, she found her posy bag and held it to her nose. It wasn't wise to risk infection.

Holding up her lantern, she swept it across the length of the table. It was a mess. Even with all of her children and the upkeep of the farm, Elizabeth had always prided herself on a well-kept house. A stale half eaten loaf was in the centre of the table next to a pot of cold soup. It smelled rotten and old. Unwashed pots littered the room and there was an acrid stink to the air.

As Rachel wandered from the kitchen, she noticed the neat lines of boots, all empty of their owners. Alice's cloak was hung on a peg, as was Libby's and Anne's. It was a sad sight.

Placing a foot at the bottom of the staircase, she called up softly. Only silence answered her. Calling out again, she climbed upwards, dreading what she might find at the top.

Alice's room caught her attention first. She had shared it with Libby and Anne. The beds were stripped and the air still smelled foul. A pile of rags lay discarded on the floor, a pattern of rusty red and off yellow soaked dry into the material. Feeling her stomach heave, Rachel turned from the room, trying hard to erase the thoughts of Elizabeth trying to cut the poison from the swellings on her daughters' limp bodies.

Checking the other two rooms, there was no sign of life. In Elizabeth and John's chamber she could make out the silhouette of an upturned crib, blankets cast aside, as though somebody had thrown it. There was no sign of Elizabeth anywhere.

Calling Elizabeth's name, Rachel was relieved that at least she wasn't lying helpless and weak, her body struck with plague. There was only one place left that she could be. Hurrying from the house, she left the basket in the kitchen.

The grass was well trodden on the slight incline leading up to the orchard that fringed the field next to the farm. She was retracing those steps that Elizabeth had taken with the bodies of her children and husband. In the burning heat of the day, it must have made the dreadful task so much worse for her.

Nearing the trees that stood in tall staggered rows, their fruit already ripening, the scream of a fox startled her. The hairs on the back of her arms were standing on end. She could see no hunched form over the freshly dug graves and she could hear no woeful cries. All was still.

The irony of how much Alice would have loved a midnight adventure to a graveyard was not lost on Rachel as she stared ahead, trying desperately to see any sign of Elizabeth. She didn't want to tread any further, but her conscience wouldn't let her turn away. There was no way she was going to leave Elizabeth alone to suffer.

Something streaked past her, hopping through the hole in a gate and onto the track that ran parallel with the field. It was only a small animal, a rabbit or hare, but it was enough to give Rachel cause for fright. Her nerves were on edge. "Elizabeth?" she called, her voice trembling and weak. "Elizabeth?" There was no reply.

Then she saw them. Seven mounds had been formed in the shape of a circle.

With a sharp intake of breath, she stopped. "Alice."

A rush of emotion caught in her chest and she sank to the ground clutching at handfuls of grass as she said each of their names. Then she reached out and stroked the freshly turned earth. "Alice," she repeated her friend's name as she wept. "Funny, dear Alice, you were always like a little sister. Why did you have to go? Why did you have to leave?" An unexpected rage built up inside her. Throwing down the posy bag that she had been holding, she roared up into the navy blanket of night. "Why did you let this happen?" The scream that ripped from her chest took her by surprise. She could not temper it. "What kind of God does this? What kind of God takes such innocent lives with such cruel conviction? Why?"

Her breathing hard and shallow, she fell forward to her hands and knees. She didn't care who heard, or what they would do to her for such an outburst. All she cared about was the fact that her dearest friends had been taken. Everyone was dying. No household appeared to be unscathed. The whole village was succumbing to disease and death. Nobody was safe. Nobody would escape.

It was some time before she found the strength within herself to walk back to Thornycroft Hall. The whole place was still in darkness when she quietly slipped through the servants' door and into the kitchen, intending to heat herself some mead and take more of the plague remedy. Her cheeks felt sticky from tears and her face red with the pinch of the night air, but she felt calmer. In the morning, she would visit the Mompessons, tell them about the Hancock family and see if the Reverend Mompesson would bless the earth that they were buried in.

Placing her lantern on the worktop, she stooped to remove her boots and shake out her skirts.

"Where have you been?" The question was flat. She turned.

Benjamin was sitting in one of the chairs at the table, his bad leg stretched outwards and his arms folded across his chest.

"Walking." In an effort to disguise her guilt, Rachel busied herself with finding a flagon of mead and a cup. "I cannot sleep."

"Where?" His tone was accusatory and she shrank away into the scullery, making a show of looking for something.

"Just walking up on the fields. It gave me time to think." She brought out a pot to hang over the fire. "Stoke the fire Benjamin, I shall heat us something warm to drink."

Benjamin didn't move. His arms remained folded across his chest as he regarded her with suspicion. "Did you go to the Hancock place?"

"No!" Defiant, she went to pour the mead into the pot above the fire. "Of course not."

"Liar." He spat out his response as though he could taste poison. With her back to him, she could hear him getting to his feet. She couldn't turn to face him. "You went to the Riley Farm. What did you find Rachel? What was it that made you risk your life, my life and Goody's life? What possessed you to go there? They're all gone. You saw for yourself."

"Elizabeth is still there. She had to bury all of them. She did it by herself, alone. Or had you conveniently forgotten?" Pivoting, she faced him, challenging him, and she was shocked to see him take a step back. He was scared of her.

"You saw her?" Hesitation stalked his response as he took another cautionary step backwards. Then the realisation hit her. He wasn't frightened of *her*. He was afraid of what she may have picked up over at the farm.

Carrying on with her task, Rachel shrugged. "She wasn't there. I'm going to go to the Mompessons in the morning, ask if they can go up there, see if-"

"Why can you not just leave it?" he bellowed with rage. "Why put us all in more danger by roaming the streets like a stray animal? Do you not value your life, or mine, or Goody's? Do you not care what happens to us?"

"Of course I care," she protested, taking a step towards him, but he backed away, fear shadowing his features.

"Then why did you do it? Why did you do this?" He didn't wait for her to answer before stalking off, back to his room, slamming the door.

Rachel didn't even try to sleep that night. She was too frantic about Elizabeth Hancock's whereabouts. It had been eight days since she had witnessed her bury the last of her children and it was worrying her that she could not be found at the farm. Catherine and the Reverend Mompesson would know what to do.

At first light, she wrapped a shawl about her shoulders and headed out into the village. It was going to be another dry day, the sort that she would have once relished if she had been given leave to go and see Alice, or simply sit in the rose garden enjoying the rich scent of flowers and the unending views over the moors that yawned down towards Stoney Middleton, but nothing would be the same again.

The rectory was ominously quiet when she arrived and for a moment a cold wall of dread began to close in on her, but the sound of Catherine's welcoming voice came from one of the windows. "Come in Rachel, we have some freshly made jam and eggs for breakfast. That is on the assumption that you have not yet broken your fast?"

Rachel shook her head and waited for the latch to be lifted from behind the heavy door. Catherine pulled it open and gestured for her to go into the kitchen where the table was already set. They sat down opposite one another at the table and Catherine went about spreading jam across a slice of the hot loaf she had cut. "William is out early today. There are so many more sick and dying. This last month has been the worst." She pushed the bread across to Rachel. It was warm and inviting after going for so many days without eating much. "You look pale Rachel. Tired."

Feeling her posture curl inwards, Rachel looked away. "These are worrying times."

"Indeed they are, however, we must do what we can to survive." Catherine took a bite of her bread. She didn't appear to enjoy it.

Rachel put her breakfast down in front of her, untouched. "Are you not going to tell me to go, that I am putting the lives of those I live with at risk by being here?"

Catherine shook her head. "Not this time."

Taking her bread and jam, Rachel bit into it. The tang of gooseberry was sharp on her tongue. They ate for a while before speaking again. "The Hancocks have passed." Even saying the words didn't feel like the truth. It was too much to digest.

Placing the palms of her hands on the table, Catherine sighed. "I know. I suspected that was the reason for your visit."

"I went there last night, looking for Elizabeth. I was worried she might be-"

Pushing her stool back, Catherine got up abruptly. "I visited yesterday. I went as soon as I heard. Word was slow to reach us." A haunted expression glanced over her. "There are just so many sick and dying."

"All of them," Rachel said, her voice cracking. "All of them dead. She buried them herself. There was nobody to help." She watched as Catherine turned, steadying herself against the surface that was behind her.

"It was a great pity that such a pious woman should have had to endure such suffering." She kept her back to Rachel as she spoke.

"I made up a tincture for her," Rachel said. "I used the remedy that you gave us, but I couldn't find her. Oh Catherine, I'm so worried. What if she is sick? What if she can not get to it because she is lying somewhere with nobody to help her?"

"Elizabeth Hancock is gone." Deadpan in her delivery, Catherine's knuckles had noticeably whitened as she gripped the edges of the bench.

"Gone?" Rachel felt herself quiver as another onslaught of grief threatened to take over.

"She has left Eyam. Packed up. Left the village and run from it all. We think it likely that she has gone to Sheffield. She has a son there."

Rachel didn't understand. Elizabeth was devout in her religion. There would be no way that she would leave. "But what about our oath to God? William said that-"

"For some I should imagine that the burden of grief can break them." There was no judgement upon Catherine's face, no procrastinations over the damage Elizabeth may have done by breaking the village agreement, but the fears that had manifested themselves the night before came flooding back to Rachel. What if they were to seek Elizabeth out? What if they were to catch her? Would she be punished? What would the sentence be? Death? More pain, more suffering?

As though reading her thoughts, Catherine turned, her posture strong and steady once again. "Nobody will look for her, even after this is over. Elizabeth Hancock has suffered enough. No mother should have to…" She stopped and looked down to the rush matting beneath her feet. There was no need to say more.

"Finish up your breakfast Rachel and promise me that you will be vigilant in taking care of yourselves at Thornycroft Hall. The plague can breach any door. William and I had thought the Hancocks and Talbots would at least have some chance of safety being at the far reaches of the village, but in less than a month all of those lives were claimed."

"Catherine, I'm scared and I don't know what to do." She hadn't meant to sound so pathetic, but it was true. Every moment of each day, Rachel tasted the bitterness of fear. It was as though it would never end.

"You have to have courage Rachel. Say your prayers and keep your strength up. This will be over soon, I am sure. It can not last another winter, we just have to see ourselves through to the colder months."

Rachel didn't want to leave. She wanted to stay at the rectory. It felt safer with Catherine.

"I promise you that I'll visit before the month is out," Catherine assured her. "But for now, it can only be fleeting visits, to check you are safe and in good health. My services are needed with the sick and if you are well, I do not want to risk bringing the contagion to your door by coming too often or staying for too long."

"Promise you'll come Catherine?" Rachel knew that she sounded pitiful and weak, but she no longer cared. Benjamin had looked at her with such disgust when he had caught her sneaking back in from the Hancock house. He would never speak to her again, she was sure. Catherine was all that she had left.

For fear of passing any hint of the disease between them, Catherine didn't offer her the solace of an embrace. Her sober expression was enough. "I promise to come Rachel. You must simply wait."

******

A week passed but Catherine did not come. The village was rife with plague, too many were dying or grieving and in need of Catherine's help. So Rachel waited. She cleaned the rooms that were open in the huge house whilst listening to the gentle huff of sobs and whimper of moans from Goody's quarters. She watched Goody wordlessly take food and her own remedies to where she resided in isolation, and whenever she passed Benjamin, he simply glowered at her, avoiding her, punishing her for the risk that she had taken by visiting the Hancock home.

Rachel's chest felt heavy, as though an iron weight was in it. Benjamin's stony reserve had struck her hard. He was so very angry with her for what she had done and she understood why, but she wished that he would have the heart to think of what poor Elizabeth had been through. It was, however, likely he would avoid her for days, either for fear of the contagion being upon her, or to demonstrate his lack of forgiveness.

Sadly, she picked up a bundle of herbs from the kitchen and took them to the stillroom. The stillroom with all its wonderful fresh and vibrantly pungent scents had become a place that she liked to take the time to think.

Pulling open the door, she hesitated as she saw Goody pacing, panic in her eyes. She hadn't noticed Rachel as she brought a fist to her forehead, pounding at it as if trying to think of something. Muttering to herself, she inspected the poultice that she had been making and cried out in despair.

Rushing towards Goody, Rachel noticed how much her hands were shaking. "Whatever is the matter Goody?"

"We need more supplies from Liza Thickett. Here, I'll write you a list." Motioning for Rachel to follow her, she hurried to Sir Edward's study where she found a parchment and quill. Rachel didn't have the heart to tell her that Liza had told her there were to be no more supplies.

"Good lass." Goody's voice was steady enough as she pressed the list into Rachel's hand, but there was a shadow on her face. Something bad had happened, Rachel could sense it.

"Has something happened to Benjamin?" she asked, terrified that she had brought the plague back from her visit to the Hancock home. Goody shook her head.

"Are you unwell then? What is it?"

"Nought you need trouble yourself with, just get these things and all will be well. Please lass, there's not much time." As she moved away, Rachel noticed the blood on Goody's sleeve and how she flinched as she brushed her arm against the door on their way out of the study. Had she cut herself? There had been noise coming from her quarters in the early hours. It was plausible that she had cut herself, but a cut on her arm seemed like a strange place for an accident with a blade.

"What are you standing there for? Make haste." Goody's patience was wearing thin. As she chastised her for dallying, she sub-consciously held her arm. The edge of some makeshift bandaging stuck out from beneath her sleeve.

There was no need for her to tell Rachel to hurry for a second time. Determined to get what was needed, she ran to Liza Thickett's house.

"Liza?" she called out, banging her fist against the door. At first she did not notice the red cross that someone had daubed against the wood.

"Liza?" she called out again.

"Dead and gone." A man had thrown back the shutters of his window. He spat on to the street below. "Not long after Nin and Ned Thomas. I'd stay away from there. The pestilence lingers." He didn't wait for her to respond before pulling the shutters back into place.

Fat droplets of warm rain had started to fall from the sky. A cat meowed mournfully as it jumped off the wall outside the house, padding towards her, skinny from lack of food. Its fur was starting to get damp. A neglected animal, its owner no longer around to take care of it, Liza's moggy. Rachel backed away and then shooed it. It would do no good to stroke it or take it in, no matter how sorry she felt for the creature.

Gathering her skirts, she ran home, desperate to get away from both the rain and the threat of the miasma of plague seed that might still be lingering around Liza Thickett's empty cottage.

"This can not be." Goody grabbed her by the shoulders when she returned with the news of Liza. "I have done so much already, I just need the right supplies and I am certain that…" She hesitated and looked Rachel up and down, reading her expression, as though judging whether or not she had said too much. "No matter," she said, wiping her hands on her apron to clean them of the plant pulp and herb cuttings. "I know of a place."

Pushing her way past Rachel, she hurried up to the top of the house before emerging some time later, dressed to go out into the rain.

"Where are you going?" Rachel challenged her, stepping in front of her path.

"I'll be back by nightfall."

"You're not leaving the village. You can't."

Goody forced her way past. "Lass, I can do as I please. I know of a place on the skirts of Tideswell. It can do no harm. I shall be quick."

"They'll stop you."

"They won't know me. I'll say I'm from Orchard Bank if they ask."

Rachel was horrified. "That's not even a village, it's just the local name for a part of this village."

"Exactly." Goody was adamant that she was going.

"But you can't, you could be taking the pestilence with you. This sacrifice we are making Goody, it is sacred, an oath to God."

Goody laughed, but there was no humour in it. "I have made enough sacrifices over the years lass." Something flashed in her eyes. It was a certain knowledge that demonstrated she had seen things and done things that would have the hairs on Rachel's scalp bristling.

Rachel implored her not to go, thinking of any good reason she could argue with. "The Reverend Mompesson said that nobody must enter and nobody must leave. To do so would be breaking God's will."

"Aye, and you told that to your friend Elizabeth Hancock, did you?"

She faltered. How did Goody know about Elizabeth? She rarely left her quarters, and certainly never left Thornycroft Hall. How had that news reached her already? Goody glowered at her, daring her to make another challenge and get in her way.

Realising that her size meant she was no match for a woman like Goody Brown, she stepped aside. "Please Goody," she pleaded one more time, hoping that she would see some sense. "You must think about what you are doing."

"You follow your Reverend Mompesson's ways, I'll follow mine."

"Thomas Stanley stands by the decision too. 'Tis both of them Goody. If you won't listen to William Mompesson, then at least listen to Thomas Stanley."

"I listen only to what I know is needed." Sub-consciously, she traced her fingertips across the wounded area of her forearm and down to the angry looking ridges on her wrists. "We all need to make our own sacrifices. I need what I need and that is that."

"But Goody, this is unforgiveable. What can possibly be so important that you would go against the word of God?" Rachel knew her attempts to reason with her were proving futile, but she had to at least try.

Goody was already at the servants' door, poised to face the rain, basket over her arm. "I'm going on foot. Less likely to cause trouble. I hope you can one day understand and forgive me lass. You've much to learn, but you're a good girl." She opened the door into the rain, stepped out and swiftly shut it behind her.

Rachel wasted no time. For the sake of Goody's soul, she had to stop her and by any force or means necessary. She ran fast, sliding over the muddying track, her hair falling from her cap and sticking to her face and forehead. The Mompessons would help. Reverend Mompesson could ride after her, bring her back and talk her around. Or he could send for Thomas Stanley to do so. Rachel had no idea who Goody would respond to more favourably, but either man would do a better job than she had. Perhaps the Reverend would send men for her? She would ask them to ensure that they didn't use too much force. Goody was not a bad woman, just a bit strange.

Smoke curled from the chimney of the rectory, licking its way through the rain. The windows were still shuttered and, in the garden, the last of the roses bowed their heads, their petals already tinged heavily brown and folding inwards. Rachel raised her hand to knock sharply, but the door was already opening so that she almost fell inside.

The house was dark and quiet behind the Mompesson's maid who had opened the door to her. Her eyes were ringed red, the pouches of skin beneath them damp. Behind her, the silence was ominous.

"I need to speak with Reverend Mompesson as a matter of urgency." Rachel heard the hesitation in her own voice, some deeper instinct telling her that her need would not be fulfilled that day.

Slowly, the maid shook her head. "The Reverend is attending to some personal business. He cannot be disturbed. Not today." She went to shut the door, but Rachel held it with the toe of her boot.

"Catherine then." She tried to ignore the roaring in her ears as she spoke. "As it happens, I was supposed to see Catherine. She said that she would come to Thornycroft Hall."

The maid stared at her, the expression on her face telling her everything. Rachel refused to acknowledge it. "She is to visit us you see. I know she is busy, but if she knows it is me-" Her words were strangled by a wave of devastating emotion. Rachel didn't want to look at the fresh tears that had sprung to the maid's eyes, or listen to the deathly silence that suffocated the house.

"I will come in and wait," she insisted. "Catherine is always so pleased to see me. I could help you with preparing to break her fast this morning. She is always so good to me that I would be happy to help." Rachel knew that she was gabbling a string of nonsense, but it was as though her words could change things and alter the harsh reality that was glaring her in the face, ringing in her ears.

"Mistress Mompesson will not be returning." The maid's voice was low. "Not today."

"Tomorrow then?" Rachel asked brightly, fighting the weakness that was spreading over her body.

"Not tomorrow pet." There was pity on the maid's face. She had overhead the many conversations that Rachel had engaged in with Catherine, seen the way Catherine had been of comfort to her through the grief of losing her father. She had witnessed the motherly embraces and how she had given Rachel remedies to help keep her safe from the contagion. She knew of their bond and she knew what pain her news would inflict. "You should go home Rachel," she said. "There is disease here. Catherine would not have wanted you to be at risk. She is in her chamber now, with William. He needs a moment before she is…" Choked, she couldn't finish and Rachel didn't want her to.

Turning back into the street, for the second time that day, she fled back to Thornycroft Hall, hot rain pelting at her. She wanted to cry and howl with grief, but no noise would come out.

When she reached the house, Rachel looked up at the dark clouds in the sky, noting how they were fringed with the golden light of a sun that wanted to shine. Soon there would be a rainbow.

Catherine was gone. Catherine. Her friend. Her confidante. Good to so many. Selfless. Courageous. Kind. Gone.

Rachel stumbled as she threw open the doors to the great hall and her stomach lurched. Vomit spilled from her, seeping into the flagstones. She fell to her hands and knees, watching it pool in front of her. She wiped her face with her sleeve and then she opened her mouth. The sound of her grief echoed throughout the bleak solitude of the stone walls.

CHAPTER 43

Present Day – Eyam

Kate opened her eyes. She had fallen to the ground when she had seen Nick perched by the boundary stone, his arm working tirelessly to paint whatever it was that he could see. All around him there was a haze. Figures danced in and out of it, flitting about between present and past.

Somebody was standing above her, telling her to leave, to stop watching, threatening her if she was ever to return to Thornycroft. It didn't want her to see, didn't want her to feel the despair that was eating away at her insides, but she wanted to look. She wanted to crawl back into that haze. She needed to do so for the sake of her Great Aunt Edie and because she had to know the truth.

Lifting her head, she tried to push herself to standing and failed. So she began to crawl. The haze was getting bigger, throbbing like a beating heart, threatening to swallow Nick. It was creeping closer to her. She could feel it, hear it.

Reaching out, her nails dragged at the delicate fabric between times and her scream mingled with one that had echoed around Thornycroft Hall over three hundred and fifty years before.

CHAPTER 44

25th August 1666 – Eyam

Rachel was alone with thoughts of Catherine, of the Hancocks, of everyone who the pestilence had so cruelly taken. She had no idea how late in the day it was, but she was certain that William would have had Catherine's body interred into the ground already. He would be expected to get on with helping the rest of the parish. Rachel wondered how he ever would.

Catherine had been the backbone of the village, nursing the sick, comforting those who had lost loved ones and who were well aware that the plague seed was probably festering inside of them, waiting for its chance to bloom with its ugly red rings and blackened lumps. Everyone would feel Catherine's death. Even those who had not supported the Mompessons when they had first arrived in Eyam would suffer the loss of her.

Rachel walked through the house, her mind absent of any purpose. Nothing felt real. She wondered if she would wake up and find that it had all been a dreadful nightmare.

Realising that she had wandered towards the kitchen, she found herself in the doorway, listening to the return of the rain as it beat against the house. From the mullioned windows she could see that it was no longer a drizzle, but a shimmering curtain of water that was descending upon the village, quenching the fields and crops of their thirst.

Benjamin hadn't cared about the rain when he had stomped out earlier that morning. She had no idea where he had gone. His emotions were clearly clouding his judgement. Everything was as silent as it had been at the rectory. The silence made the threat of a bump, a moan, or the tread of an unseen foot on a floorboard all the worse.

Rachel tried not to think of the rumours about demons or Lady Rosamund's restless spirit. Catherine had crossed over into heaven, she would surely be looking upon her with distaste if she knew that Rachel's mind was even entertaining the idea that such entities walked the corridors and rooms of Thornycroft Hall. Rachel told herself that she needed to be more like Catherine, to take the courage that she had shown her and make it a part of herself.

All she could do was wait for Goody to return. Against the silence, she tried not to listen for any noise that would prove something other than Goody Brown's madness existed. As she did so, her gaze rested on what had been left on the table and she wondered how she had not noticed it before. An iron ring with keys fanning from its entirety was on the edge. Goody's keys.

Rachel allowed her fingers to curl around the coolness of the ring of keys. The metallic tang of them was strong, enticing her to pick them up and use them.

She drew a sharp breath. It was her chance to find out more about Goody, but the thrill was dampened by the thought of going into those quarters alone. Her palms beginning to sweat, she lifted them from the table.

One of the keys was shinier than the rest. It was the key to Sir Edward's study. She needed a distraction to take her mind off her grief, off Goody's betrayal and off Benjamin's contempt for her.

Finding information that might tell her who Goody Brown really was didn't necessarily only mean going up to her quarters. Sir Edward's study would surely hold some clues that might explain why a woman so strange, who almost let the Thornycroft's son and heir die at birth, should remain as a guest.

The darkening sky made it feel more like dusk and the diffused light creeping in through the windows did not push far enough along the corridors to make it possible to see everything clearly. Feeling her way along the walls, she found the intricately carved double doors that she knew led into Sir Edward's study.

Her hands shaking with both excitement and nerves for fear of being caught, Rachel found the key and cumbersomely went to push it into the lock, scratching at the surrounding panelling as she did so. The long awaited click echoed through the empty hallway. Holding her breath, she pushed the door open.

Thanks to the large arced windows lining the back wall, it was much lighter in the study. Everything was still, like a stage that had been set.

Seeing the room devoid of Sir Edward's presence, his high backed mahogany chair empty, was strange. It occurred to her that even Lady Cecily had probably never had the privilege of being alone in his study.

A feeling of power rushed through her body, dizzying her. Moving to the desk, Rachel pressed her palms against its surface. Where a layer of dust had settled, the imprint of her hands gave away her guilt. She would have to remember to clean everything that she touched.

Moving around the edge of the desk, she pulled up the large chair and sat in it. This, she thought, was what it must be like to be master of a grand house.

A glass with a trace of amber liquid that had pooled into the base was set to one side. She bit her lip as she recalled how kind Sir Edward had been when he had invited her into his office to pay her thanks for her part in the safe delivery of baby Samuel.

Reminding herself that none of that mattered anymore, she carefully pulled at a drawer. It opened seamlessly. Inside, a wad of parchment was piled next to an empty inkpot and a quill. She held her candle as close as she could to the inside of the drawer, to inspect further. There was nothing else to see. Rachel supposed that anything of a secretive nature would be locked away.

Surveying the room carefully, her gaze rested on the cabinet against the far wall.

Predictably the doors wouldn't budge and none of the keys on the ring were made to fit the lock.

Rachel looked around her, imagining she was Sir Edward. Where would he hide the keys to the place that no doubt kept all of his business, his secrets and anything else of note?

She upturned clay pots, pushed her fingers right to the back of every drawer in the desk, checked under the rug and looked for loose floorboards. There was nothing.

Deflated, she slumped into Sir Edward's chair. It was still raining hard outside and water droplets bounced noisily off the windows. Goody would be back soon as she would be hurrying to get in from the wet, and if she was caught snooping about the study, it was highly likely that the Thornycrofts would receive the message. No matter what happened, Goody's allegiance would always remain with them, or Sir Edward at the very least.

It dawned on her how very foolish she had been to let herself in. What had she expected to find? Why would Sir Edward keep any history on Goody Brown? She had worked at the house nearly two decades earlier.

Getting up, she berated herself for being so stupid. There was a noisy clatter as the collection of keys fell to the floor.

Kneeling to retrieve them, she banged her head against the edge of the desk and cursed. Her mood darkened. It had all been a waste of time. If she had wanted to find out more about Goody Brown, she should have had the nerve to go up to her quarters instead.

As she went to stand, something caught her eye. Underneath the desk there was a groove carved into the wood. It wasn't a natural part of the design and it was almost impossible to clearly make out in the light, but its surface didn't look even.

Reaching for her candle, she took care to hold it steady as she crawled beneath the desk, keeping her head low. The candle flame guttered, its acrid smoke catching in her throat and distorting her view. Tracing her fingers along the groove, she found its edge. Something moved.

Shocked, she withdrew her hand before feeling around again. Her fingertips brushed against cool metal. Huddled awkwardly, she grasped for it. A key.

Scrambling out from beneath the desk, she hurled herself towards the cabinet and pushed the key straight into the lock. A gratifying click released the latch and the door opened, revealing the cabinet's secret innards.

Rolls of parchment were stacked neatly and there were letters too, crisply folded, the seals broken, all bearing the same crest in deep red wax.

Pulling out a letter, she opened it.

The writing on the page was small, mean looking. The quill had been pressed hard to the parchment. There was no address and no polite formalities introducing the content.

Edward,

I am sorry that this letter will not bring you the news you have hoped for. Rosamund's condition remains the same. She cannot or will not speak, and respectfully, I have my reserves about your decision. You asked for my honesty before we embarked on our journey. I give you that now.

Baltazar, the Priest you sent us to, lives as a convict under shadow here, on the outskirts of Chester. I fear that since the siege of York there is no place for him, even where the King's army still has a hold. There are soldiers here and there is plundering. There are many things these soldiers do that go unnoticed or ignored.

We have met a friend, a good friend. She has said that she can help protect us from the plundering that goes on. She lives as a commoner but seems to have connections to the King, although I do not know how and I dare not ask. I am merely grateful for what she has done for us so far. She knows Baltazar, and from her own experience, she knows how cruel priests can be when they are put in positions such as this. She warned me that she has seen great cruelty from the hand of a clergyman, although she will not go into any detail. I trust her though Edward. She brings us salves for Rosamund's arms and they work well.

Last night, under the cloak of darkness, she brought a remedy for our Lady Rosamund's state of mind. It settled her but it did not last and Baltazar has threatened to bind her mouth if she continues with her noise.

I do not feel safe beyond the boundaries of our wonderful village. The war is far from over. You know that Edward. I beseech you to think upon it.

Baltazar has seen to it that our lodgings are as comfortable as they can be, but for a holy man pushed out from York Minster since the siege, comforts cannot be what they once were. I offer you some cheer in that we are well looked after, but I fear that if there is no improvement in Rosamund, he may change his methods.

The Priest Baltazar insists that Rosamund has a demon inside of her. As you know, I have been sceptical, but even I must confess that it is as though her mind has been taken. Baltazar says that the demon holds her tongue and that if it has the force to do that, it will have such force to take hold of other parts of her.

He is preparing to cleanse our Lady with Holy Water. He says to truly cleanse her will take some force.

You may choose to bring us home before he makes that decision. If your choice remains that we stay, know this - I will do my best to let no harm come to her.

At night we are both in chains. Baltazar says that if I am to insist on staying with her when the moon is out, then it is the only way to keep us both from harm. He says I risk the demon entering me. I am strong though and I will not allow that to happen.

I spend my waking hours praying to God, hoping he will hear and that he will save her soul.

Upon this letter you have my word, I will not leave her side, I will never leave your beautiful Rosamund.

Burn this.

The letter was signed 'G'. It had to be Goody. Unfolding the next, Rachel read on.

Edward,

Our friend has visited once again. She brought news that there has been some unrest nearby. She brought her son with her, a mere infant. He is a bastard child. She says her father fights for the Royalists, that he has the authority to send her word and move her to safety. Tomorrow she has safe passage to another part of the country. She has been moved before and so I trust the news she brings us.

She is guarded, but she has our best interests in mind. She thinks we risk our lives being here with this Priest. Rosamund knows this too. Even though she is not speaking, I see it on her face.

I write in the knowledge that I place myself in danger with every scratch of this quill. I risk my employment with you, but I risk my life being here, as does Rosamund, your wife. I will happily risk everything if it brings her back to safety.

The Priest Baltazar continues his experiments to rid our Lady's soul from the grasp of the demon and I fear it is breaking her.

She has started to speak, but only to me. At night she whispers, her tongue thick with grief, as she recounts how she is responsible for the death of the last child, your stillborn son. She believes that the demon put thoughts into her head that caused his death and she cannot forgive herself. I worry that she will repeat these words outside of these walls and we both know what that could lead to.

I believe that it is Baltazar who has put these thoughts in to her head, making her believe that she is to blame for the loss that you have both suffered. Baltazar means well, but I question his methods.

Please Edward. Bring us home.

Burn this.

G.

Her heart pounding and her limbs shaking with adrenalin, Rachel pulled out another letter and looked for the date. 1645. It looked to have been written by the same hand. The broken seal was of the same marking as the others.

Edward,

You have not replied to my last letter and Rosamund is weak. Her body cannot take much more of this torture. I call it torture because that is all I can report it to be.

We hear no news from you and with every day that passes, more of her blood is spilled.

Our friend has long gone with her son, escorted to an evidently safer part of the country. The Priest has all but drowned Rosamund in Holy water to within an inch of her life. Her blood has been let and then burned. None of this is helping.

She is begging Baltazar to put an end to her torment. Your wife wishes herself dead and I fear that Chester is under threat from this bloody war that rages across our country. We are both in danger. This cannot be the outcome that you hoped for?

Baltazar may write to you and tell you that all is well, that it is the demon that uses Rosamund's mouth to beg for mercy and for death. I can reliably inform you that it is her voice, no other.

It is dangerous here. I implore you Edward, bring us home.

Rachel inspected the pile of letters. They had all been placed in chronological order. The next was written a week later, advising Sir Edward that the experiments had stopped on the grounds that his wife was too ill. The Priest had shown some empathy at last and he had given Goody the means to make up salves, to bathe her in lavender scented water and to soothe her with the views of the city from another room.

The content of the letter still begged for Sir Edward to show his wife some mercy, to bring her home to the healing power of the majestic White Peaks and to try another way. Then there was a gap of time, indicating to Rachel that either Edward Thornycroft had burned the letters that had followed, or that Goody had ceased to write. In the next, Rosamund had regained her strength and there was hope.

Edward,

I bring good news. Our dear heart Rosamund has shown improvement. Her spirits are lifted, her eyes glint and there is a shadow of a smile that I have seen at the corners of her mouth. Baltazar has said that her beauty is returning.

She has told me that she feels lifted, as though the Demon has been wrenched from her. Baltazar agrees with me that there is a difference. He is blessing everything that she eats and drinks and I continue to pray.

I confess, for a while my faith in God threatened to waiver whilst seeing our beautiful Rosamund in such a state. However, she is now making good progress. Our faith has kept us strong.

It cannot be long now Edward. Things still do not feel safe here and I hear rumours and worrying news most days. Nevertheless, I shall await our carriage home with a lighter heart.

G.

Tears blurred Rachel's eyes as she read. Lady Rosamund had suffered so much, and all because she had lost her children before they had even been able to take their first breaths. To have been put through all of that, and with her life constantly feeling under threat from the war between King and Parliament, it was a surprise that she had survived at all. Rachel wondered if Lady Cecily had already been employed by then and whether she had already acted upon her motives to steal Sir Edward's affections.

As she stared down at Goody's words, she swallowed a lump of shame. Like so many others, she had assumed Goody to be of bad blood, just because she was different and because there were rumours. She had listened to what Benjamin had told her about Goody's part in the death of Lady Rosamund, but reading those letters only demonstrated how much Goody had loved and tried to protect her. Pausing, she opened the last letter again.

Your wife wishes herself dead. This cannot be the outcome that you hoped for?

The words snaked their way across the parchment, their accusation hinting at an ugly truth. What if the death of Lady Rosamund had been Sir Edward's intention? Time and again there had been no heir for Thornycroft Hall, and to have a wife whose behaviour suggested that she was possessed by one of the Devil's own would have been no excuse to nullify the marriage. If Sir Edward had wanted a legitimate child, the only way would have been for the death of Lady Rosamund, leaving him free to marry another. If she had died at the hands of a Priest who was trying to cleanse her soul of the demon, then so be it.

Rachel threw the letters down and looked back into the nook that she had taken them from. There were more there - letters to physicians and letters to and from a lawyer.

Reading the content, she gasped. So Sir Edward had sought to find a way to divorce his wife, only these were dated later than 1645. These were written the year that Rosamund had died, possibly just after her final baby had died. The lawyer's legal advice suggested that there were no grounds for Sir Edward to nullify the marriage.

Shocked, Rachel turned and stared accusingly at the painting of Sir Edward Thornycroft, his prominent nose, dark features and long swathe of fine glossy hair. Had her father known that he had befriended a murderer? Surely not, or he would not have entrusted her into the care of Thornycroft Hall upon his deathbed.

Picking up the letters, her hands shook with anger and shock at the revelation of what she had just read.

She decided that she would stay at Thornycroft Hall for as long as the plague kept her inside the village boundaries. Then, if she were to survive, she would leave. It did not matter where she went, but she could not stay living under the same roof as murderers who should have hung from the gibbet a long time ago.

Lifting her candle, she deliberated for a moment, contemplating whether or not she should confide in Goody. Her motivation for returning to Thornycroft Hall was still a mystery, although now it was clear that she would have played no part in the death of Lady Rosamund. Goody was a strong woman, a good ally to have and despite breaking the oath that they had made as a village, knowing what she knew of her past, Rachel could forgive her.

A sound from the hallway startled her. She withdrew her hand carelessly from where it rested in the still unlocked cubby of the cabinet. There was a soft thud as several rolls of parchment toppled out.

The sound of boots clicking against the floor warned her that somebody was back. It would do no good to get caught in Sir Edward's study, not even by Benjamin, especially given how angry he was with her.

Quickening to gather the misplaced documents, she noticed that one had uncurled at the edges, displaying part of its official looking content. She picked it up, aware of the footsteps that were echoing through the house. It would not be long before she was caught.

Shutting the cabinet door, she turned the key and made haste to press it back into its groove beneath Sir Edward's desk. Then, folding the slip of parchment that she had kept hold of, she tucked it down the neck of her dress and ran from the room.

The length of the corridor was in darkness and the footsteps had stopped. Rachel held her breath as she quietly pulled the study doors shut. She would need to leave them unlocked so that she could return the document she had found after reading it in the privacy of her chamber.

Tilting her head to one side, she kept her ears keen. She had definitely heard footsteps. It had not been her imagination or the creaking of the house. She went to call out for Goody but then stopped as she heard the soft breath of a moan from upstairs. It was like an echo in time. Had the spirit of Lady Rosamund stirred in the knowledge that Rachel had been reading the letters, their words scrawled across the pages, hinting at the truth of her tragic fate?

Her breath was short as she tiptoed through the hall, reaching to light sconces. From the kitchen there was a crash and the sound of a man cursing. It was clearly Benjamin who had returned.

The fire had died to embers and he was attempting to stoke it. On the table were two hares and a pheasant. He had done well. "We'll need more firewood," he grumbled, doing nothing more to acknowledge her presence.

Guilt still pressed at her for putting him at risk by visiting the Hancock home. Unable to bring herself to speak, she turned and made her way to gather more wood from the shed.

Benjamin had worked hard to chop more. It had been stacked neatly, the axe left upright and gleaming amongst the woodchips, and in spite of herself, Rachel couldn't help but smile. It seemed strange to think that a young man from a background like his had taken to labouring like her father, a tenant farmer, but that was part of what she loved about Benjamin.

After collecting the firewood, she left some in the kitchen before taking the rest upstairs. Goody would need plenty more in her living space if she returned soaked through from the rain. Placing a basket of it by the door that led to her quarters, Rachel pressed her ear to the panelling. Nothing. The house was silent again.

Returning to her room, she used the flame from her candle to light the others that she had placed in an arc on the little wooden dresser. Taking a seat, she listened to what was left of the rain gently pattering at the windowpanes and reached for the square slip of parchment that scratched uncomfortably at her skin beneath her clothes.

It bore all the markings of an official looking document and it had originally been rolled into a scroll. Forgetting herself whilst escaping the study, she had folded it in an unruly fashion before pushing it into her bodice. She would have to take care to flatten out the creases.

Placing it on the small table, she spread it out. The light from the candles was all that was left for her to read with. Their flames ebbed with every small draught that leaked through the windows, rattling the shutters.

Beneath the officious looking writing were signatures. Squinting, she leaned in closer, trying to decipher the lettering. The heat of the candle flames threatened to singe her hair and skin. She barely noticed.

One of the signatures belonged to her father, Oliver David Craven. It had been scrawled with prominence, beneath the flourish of words that clearly stated the terms of the generous legal agreement.

Perplexed, she read again, assuming that it was her own ignorance misinterpreting what was in front of her.

The croft of land had been gifted to him along with the promise of an annual sum, far more handsome than was usual for a tenant farmer's entitlement. Sir Edward's signature dramatically spread itself in blue ink above his name, giving no uncertain confirmation that he had agreed to provide the land and the salary, in return for a child to be raised as Oliver's own. The child should want for nothing and was to be well fed and clothed. An education would be necessary, with a Governess stipulated by Edward Thornycroft. The child would be loved unconditionally. The child, Rachelle Maria Thornycroft, was to be named Rachel Maria Craven.

CHAPTER 45

Present Day – Eyam

"You've captured it just as it was." Tears were rolling down Kate's face, the memories raw, not fading as they usually did.

Nick did not move. His fingers were still clasped around the pencil, its nib broken but the sketch finished to dramatic perfection. Heavy and light shades blended to create a dark, moody atmosphere that captured Rachel's trepidation as she had hurried towards the Riley Farm to search for Elizabeth Hancock.

Kate lifted her head to look away from the painting and beyond the wall that snaked its way around Thornycroft.

At the top of the house a shadow moved past a window, fleeting enough to be a trick of the light, but there was no mistaking its human like shape. "Did you see the rest?" she asked.

Slowly, coming around from his daze, Nick turned to her. His eyes were clouded. He licked his lips and nodded. "She's showing us something."

"Lady Rosamund Thornycroft was murdered." The words caught in her throat, causing her to cough.

"By her husband," Nick said, finishing the sentence.

"He had her tortured."

Nick nodded, his own voice catching with emotion. "And all because she was suffering with depression. Who wouldn't after losing all those babies?"

Kate could still feel the crispness of Goody's letters between her fingertips. "All of Lady Rosamund's hopes and dreams dashed away every time. People pointing their fingers at her, blaming it on the remedies that Goody had concocted to help ease her suffering. Instead of treating her with empathy and love, recognising how emotionally fragile she had become, they looked to blame her, to say that her grief was the product of a demonic possession." Kate choked back a mournful sob, the sickening revelation that Rachel had uncovered in Sir Edward's study, weighing heavily in her stomach.

"I suppose that's sometimes how it was back then." Nick shook his head as though ridding it of cobwebs. "This has really shaken you, hasn't it?"

Sniffing, Kate dashed at her cheeks with the back of her hand. "I'm sorry, the feelings are so strong. It's as though I'm living another life and there's this huge ball of despair just growing inside. I felt everything that she did, Rachel I mean. Arrrrgggghhh!" She pressed the flats of her hands to her temples, blotting at the pressure that was building. "I can't take it anymore. It's crazy. None of it can be real and yet, here I am, struggling to keep a grip of what is now and what was then." Her hands were shaking. "I'm scared that I'm losing my mind."

"Hey." Nick drew her towards him, pulling her into a hug. "You aren't losing anything. This is happening to me too and it happened to Edie. We can't all be losing it."

She didn't protest. His arms felt safe, strong and warm. She began to feel grounded. "I just wish I knew how to control it. Maybe you were right earlier, maybe we should try and get an expert in."

"Or we should just let her play out the story."

Pulling away from his embrace, Kate looked at him with uncertainty. "Earlier today you were saying that to allow it to go any further would be dangerous and now I'm inclined to agree." She wrapped her arms about her body, hugging herself protectively. "Edie told me that she thought she'd been pushed when she had her fall."

"Edie was pushed?"

"Yes and I believe her." She looked back over at the house. "Something bad is in there and Edie is right, it doesn't want the story to come out. I can feel it. It's malevolent."

"I can too." He gave a disbelieving chuckle. "If you'd said anything like this to me a year ago, I'd have laughed in your face, thought you were a complete lunatic." He shivered. "But it's so real and it's happening to us all. We should be looking for some external support here. How about we go inside, search online for some local expertise, a medium? We'll book someone to come out here as soon as possible."

Agreeing, Kate helped him gather his sketchpad and pencils before making their way back to Thornycroft.

As soon as they found the lady's website, Kate knew that she was the one who they needed. A Welsh lady with a long history of psychic cleansing, she agreed to make a window available in her diary first thing the following morning.

"Edie's not going to like this. You know how she is about people interfering," Nick pointed out the moment that Kate put down her phone.

She shot him a look. "We have to do something though. You're the one who suggested it in the first place remember?" Referring to their conversation earlier that morning, she felt her body quiver as she recalled the way Edie had been stood outside the bedroom listening, the hard, almost unrecognisable look on her face. "It's the best thing to do. I just want it all to stop."

"Have you been back up there?" he asked.

"Where?"

"The top of the house, where you found the diary."

Kate shook her head. "No. I've locked it and there's no way I'm going anywhere near there without a professional in tow."

He nodded in agreement, but was unmistakably disappointed.

"Come on." She wanted to leave it, stop talking about it all in the house. "Let's get your room sorted and then we'll hit the party. Francesca will go mad if we're late. She's worked so hard."

When they reached the Warrens' house, the air was almost crackling with unspent energy. "It's going to be one heck of a storm tonight." Graham greeted them at the door, his warm smile a welcome, normal distraction from the madness that they had been experiencing. "Franny's pulled out a whole load of candles in case we lose the lights. I don't think the worst of it is supposed to hit until well into the night though." He glanced up at the turbulent looking sky behind them. "Mind you, we could do with a good storm to break up this muggy atmosphere. Can I get you both a drink?"

He didn't wait for an answer and gestured for them to place the bottles that they'd brought over onto the table. "I'll take care of those," he said, leading them towards a bar area that had been set up in the Orangery. "Mojitos," he announced, waving over at a trendy looking male. "Franny's an absolute whizz at them, but they take so long to make that we decided to hire in the experts."

Two tall glasses muddled with mint and ice were thrust across to them both. "Looks great," Nick commented with approval.

Distracted by his job as host, Graham had already hurried off to meet some more arrivals.

"It seems like most of the village are set to come," Nick said as a girl dressed in a black and white waiting outfit offered them a tray of canapés.

"Wow, Francesca really has pulled out all the stops." Kate picked up a savoury filled profiterole.

The room dazzled around them with pretty fairy lights and vases filled with black and white ostrich feathers. At the far end, a table decked in gold and black had been set up ready for a buffet to be served, a neat pile of gold trimmed napkins and plates stacked at each end.

"That's Francesca for you," Nick said, sitting down at one of the cabaret tables that had been hired. Overhead there was a crackle and Kate noticed the speakers. Jazz music from the roaring twenties started playing out as more people began to file in.

"Edie's going to love this." She smiled appreciatively as she joined him.

Nick nodded in agreement. "Her favourite era isn't it?"

"The Great Gatsby is one of her favourite books," Kate said, admiring the canopy of lights that had been draped in neat lines across the ceiling, ready for nightfall. "She's lucky to have such good friends," she added, turning her focus back to him. "And I'm lucky too." The comment hung poignant in the air between them and Kate wondered if she had said too much, overstepped the mark.

Nick didn't respond. His expression was solemn and then she saw the look in his eyes, the way they twinkled at her. Without warning, she felt nervous, excited, filled with anticipation. Feeling a heat prickle its way over her chest, up her neck and towards her face, she brought her glass to her lips, ignoring the paper straw and taking a large gulp instead.

Feedback from the audio speakers screeched through the room, piercing their ears, before the jazz music was replaced by a voice. "Afternoon folks and thanks for coming." Graham addressed the room en masse. "I've just had word from Francesca, that she and Lindsay are bringing our guest of honour back to the house now. So if I could ask you all to remain as quiet as possible until they arrive. Then, when they come through, I'm under strict instructions that we should all shout, 'Welcome home Edie'." He gave his audience a playful smile before continuing, "We all know how draconian Franny is when it comes to these things and nobody wants to see me strung up." A polite rumble of laughter filled the room. "At least not until we've got this party in full swing."

Kate couldn't help but smile at Graham's humour. He was a good man and she loved how his face lit up when he acknowledged his wife. Theirs was a genuine love. The sort that would last and the sort that she hoped, one day, she would be able to find.

The room was animated with excited whispers, laughter and chatter. Everyone looked so happy, so pleased to be there for Edie. A swell of pride overcame her. Edie was clearly a dearly loved member of the community. It pained her all the more to think that she had been frightened enough to want to move away. Eyam was her home and Kate vowed that she would see to it that Edie would stay there, safe, secure, happy and loved by all of her friends.

Several people started hushing one another and above the quiet that fell upon the room, the sound of tyres on gravel could be heard. Kate's stomach made an involuntary flip and then hands were on her, pulling her forward to stand at the front with Nick so that she was one of the first people who Edie would see.

The handle of the front door started turning and then three figures were in front of them, silhouetted against what light was left of a swiftly dulling late afternoon.

"Welcome home Edie!" The chorus of voices chimed through the house, followed by the chink of glass and laughter.

Kate couldn't see Edie's face properly as Francesca wheeled her through, but she saw her bring her hands to her cheeks before a glass of champagne was thrust upon her amidst the merry haze of celebration.

Smoky undertones of jazz embraced the room as people moved forward to hug and kiss Edie, telling her how pleased they were that she was back, that she was okay, that they couldn't wait to see her back doing her part with the volunteering.

Amidst all of the attention, Edie looked up, caught Kate's eye and reached out for her. "Kate my darling," she cooed and turned to a group of women who were surrounding her. "Have you met my beautiful niece yet?" She gave her a warm smile and her gaze drifted knowingly to where Nick had casually placed his arm around Kate's waist. Kate hadn't even noticed. It felt natural, safe, right.

"And of course, you know Nick Delamere," Edie added, the remark making it appear as though they were a couple. Kate gave her a warning glance before engaging in a series of introductions.

The afternoon whizzed by with a buffet of Asian and Caribbean fusion being served. Kate had become separated from Nick, mingling with everyone, laughing and joking with Edie and joining in with toasts to Edie's good health.

By the time the canopy of lights was switched on, the cabaret tables had been pulled to the edges of the room and people were already dancing on the small, makeshift dance floor.

Kate watched as Edie threw her head back to laugh at something Nick whispered to her. Everything looked normal and happy; the way it should be. The strange events that had been going on since she had arrived in Eyam seemed like a distant memory, a dream even. Thoughts of Richard, and the awful months she had endured, of his obsessive behaviour and stalking, seemed distant too, like it was all shut behind a wall of glass.

She thought of the way it felt when Nick's hand accidentally brushed hers, or how it had been when he had put his arm around her waist, and she realised that in spite of everything, for the first time in a long time she was actually happy.

People were milling about everywhere. The merriment of the evening had definitely started to near its peak and she decided to take a two-minute breather.

There was a door from the kitchen that led into the back garden and she opened it, relishing the cool drops of rain that flecked cool against her face as she stepped outside. The area immediately outside was lit brightly for smokers. Kate hoped none of them would come out and interrupt her time alone.

Overhead, in the distance, there was a flash. A flicker of monochrome lined the lead grey clouds with hot silver. As she had so often done as a child, Kate started to count, "One, two, three, four, five, six, seven, eight, nine…" The sky was almost violet. "One, two, three, four, five, six, seven, eight, nine," she continued counting and the darker part of the garden was illuminated, just for a second or two. It was long enough for her to notice the figure standing over by the weeping willow. "One, two, three, four, five, six, seven, eight…"

A low but unmistakable roll of thunder preceded the next flash. The figure had gone. Kate ran a few steps forward, squinting between the shadows of the garden, searching for movement.

"You're getting soaked." Nick appeared in the doorway, sheltering himself from the torrent of rain that had become much harder.

The brightness of the lights in the designated smoking area dazzled her and she lifted her hand to shield her eyes from their glare.

Embarrassed, she was aware of how ridiculous she must look. "I only came out for air and then thought I saw something." Folding her arms across her chest, she realised how wet she had become. Behind her, the thunder continued to roll closer.

"I've missed you in there," he said. "You're quite a hit too. Edie's niece, the stunning blonde."

Rolling her eyes, Kate swatted the air. "Has anyone ever told you that you're a horrible tease?"

Grinning, he stepped forward to join her in the downpour and offered his hand. She took it. Deftly, he pulled her towards him. He was tipsy, the alcohol giving him a confident edge. She liked how attractive he made her feel. Even in the early days, she had never felt quite like that with Richard.

"And has anyone ever told you how beautiful you are when you smile?" he asked.

The question caught her off guard and she stammered to find words as she found herself locked in the intensity of his gaze. Rain beaded at the tip of his lashes. She felt the thrash of it on her hair, her cheeks and her chest. Droplets ran down her cleavage, cooling the heat that prickled her skin as she felt his hand in hers, watched his tongue lick away water from the fullness of his lips.

He pulled her closer so that their bodies collided. The firmness of his chest pressed against her. She felt his hand slip down the length of her spine to the small of her back, drawing her pelvis closer to him. Then he brought his fingers to her face, brushed away stray locks of her drenched hair and cupped the side of her cheek tenderly.

More than anything, she wanted to feel the touch of his lips, to know what it was to lose herself in him. The feeling was intense, a primal need deep inside her, and then they were locked together in an embrace. Their mouths hot and impatient, their hands running up and down one another's bodies, the urgency to explore electric on their fingertips.

For a few seconds everything around them became a blur; the thunder a distant echo, the music from the party faded to nothing, the laughter from inside belonging to another place entirely.

When they pulled slowly away from each other, Kate was hardly aware of the sound of her phone ringing. No sooner than it rang off, it started again. Irritated, she checked the screen. Chris.

Her heart thudded. Was it about Richard? She hesitated, staring at the screen mutely.

"Kate? What is it?" Nick squeezed her arm gently. She tilted her head towards him, the sensation of the kiss still tingling her lips.

"This could be important. I should probably take it."

They went back inside and offering to get them both another drink, Nick disappeared, leaving her alone.

The second call had rung off too and she would have to call him back. She manoeuvred herself over to the door of the utility, closing it for privacy.

Chris didn't pick up when she tried his number but her voicemail beeped, showing her that a message had been left. Shakily, she hit the call button.

The recording of his voice was tinny and distant, but the tone was urgent. It was a short message. "He's coming for you Kate. He knows where you are. He's not happy Kate. He knows everything." There was a lot of background noise distorting the words, as though he was in a car, and she wondered if he knew where she was too and was on his way to help.

Terrified, she pulled open the door and raced into the house. There was no way they could stay at Thornycroft if Richard knew where she was. The message that Chris had left echoed in her brain. What was Richard capable of? Up to this point, he had never hurt her, but after everything that had gone on, the way he had been so frenzied about Chris, accusing him, accusing her, behaving like a mad man, she wouldn't put anything past him.

Nick was carrying two more champagne flutes. "I think we're onto the Prosecco now, Francesca was all apologies that the good stuff has gone-"

"We need to stay at your house tonight," Kate interrupted. "You, me and Edie. We can't stay at Thornycroft."

"What?" Taken aback, he looked confused, the jovial smile wiped away. "What's going on?"

Kate was hurrying past him, not stopping to explain. "I'm just packing a few things. I'll meet you at your house in forty minutes." She stopped at the front door, resting her phone on the table whilst she kicked off her heels and scooped up the trainers that she had walked there in.

Nick's gaze shot towards the phone, its screen illuminated with the voicemail notification. "Kate, was it Richard calling you? What did he say?"

"Not Richard. Please just get Edie and take her back to yours. I'll explain everything when I get there. I won't be long. I'm literally just chucking some overnight stuff into a bag for us both and making sure I've got all of Aunt Edie's medication. I'd say we've got a good couple of hours grace. I'll call the police and let them know. Hopefully they can track him by the GPS on his car or phone."

She gave him no chance to ask anything more before sprinting out of the door, across the rain soaked driveway and into the road that wound down into the village.

CHAPTER 46

Present Day – Eyam

Watching the two of them cling to each other like it was the end of the world was enough to make him want to churn up the contents of his stomach. He had been watching them from afar all day, biding his time, working out his plan of attack.

In his wallet, behind the photograph of Kate, was a key. He had watched very carefully where the spare to Thornycroft was kept when she had left the house earlier that day with her latest conquest. It had been placed under the third plant pot to the right of the front door, just in case they were to return home at different times for any reason.

Locked in a deep and passionate kiss, it didn't look at all like either of them would be returning home at different times.

The kiss cut deep, a blade into his heart and Kate twisted it hard with every writhe of her body. Pain clawed at him as he noted the urgent way that she pressed herself against her new lover, the gentle almost inaudible groan that he had heard come from her.

Narrowing his eyes, he imagined pulling the blade from his heart, blood spilling from the wound that she had so callously made before he stemmed the flow with the plug of hatred that had begun to grow inside him.

He hated her, but he hated the man who he had seen her with more. Nick. That was his name; a name often given to the Devil. Old Nick. He spat on the floor, his saliva mingling with rainwater.

The glass of champagne that somebody had given him was still in his hand. Throwing his head back he drained it one go. He couldn't watch another second of their disgusting display. Dropping the glass to the ground beneath him, he smiled as he regarded the broken shards and how easy it would be to drive one of them in to Nick's neck and then hers.

The hatred inside of him swelled. Hatred was no stranger to him. He had felt so much hatred for his so called best friend, but never had he been driven to wanting to harm, to maim - to kill. He had always been cold and cool in the way he sought revenge, but Kate had really done a number on him. She really was a prime slut.

He spat again before crunching his heel over the broken glass and disappearing around the side of the house.

CHAPTER 47

Present Day – Eyam

K ate didn't stop once to catch her breath before reaching the gate of Thornycroft. Her heart felt as though it would burst from her chest with the effort that she had expended. There had been a time when she was much fitter, but with all the agony Richard had caused, she had stopped going to the gym as much, worried she would bump into him, or worse, bump into Chris and then into Richard.

Placing a hand on the gatepost, she doubled over, clutching her chest, taking the time to catch her breath before fumbling for the keys. They wouldn't need the spare one that they left out for emergencies. She would have to remember to remove it before leaving for Nick's. It was too dangerous leaving anything like that out with Richard possibly on his way to find her.

Pushing her wet hair from her face, she looked at the house, the brickwork illuminated spectacularly by another sheet of lightning. The wet ground beneath her feet vibrated as thunder crashed in overhead. She could only hope that the storm would pass swiftly.

Kate hurried down the path, desperate to get inside before the next clap of thunder. Finding the lock, she cried out as the garden around her flashed silvery blue and the next deafening crack shook her to the core.

Throwing the door open, she almost fell over the threshold, slamming it shut before blindly reaching for the light switch. Thornycroft was the last place she wanted to be alone in the dark.

Her mind whirring as she planned her every next move, she dashed into the kitchen, pulling open drawers to find candles and matches. There was no way she was going to leave herself exposed to being caught out by a power cut. Cutlery clashed together noisily as she scrabbled around. One partly burned red candle and a box of matches were off to one side, by the knives. It would have to do.

Kate stuffed everything that was needed into her shoulder bag and then grabbed the long nightdress and robe that had been neatly folded and left at the end of the bed in Edie's room.

Taking the stairs two at a time, she threw on the lights upstairs as she made her way to her room.

The suitcase was where she remembered leaving it, under the bed. She needed that case. There was something of the utmost importance in there, and if she was honest, aside from Edie's medication, the real reason she had returned to Thornycroft rather than going straight to the safety of Nick's cottage. The police weren't her only safety net.

Pulling the case out, she tipped back the lid and unzipped the inner most compartment. Silver glinted from inside and she reached in, the metal chillingly alien in her hand. If her father knew that she had taken the gun that she and her mother had disapproved of so much for so long, he would have a fit. The fact that she had taken three cartridges was even worse, but she didn't intend to use it unless she was put in the worst-case scenario.

Tucking the gun into the waistband of her jeans, there was no need to load it just yet. Just having it on her made her feel safer.

Her father had shown her how to load the gun once. It had caused a huge row between him and Kate's mother. At the time Kate hadn't been overly interested. Now she silently thanked him for doing so. She returned to the compartment of the suitcase, searching for the gun cartridges. Her hands flailed uselessly around the case's innards and she prised open the zipper further, looking inside. It was empty.

Cursing herself, she felt a frightened moan escape her. How could she have forgotten to pack them? She remembered getting them out of the desk in her father's study and she was sure that she remembered putting them in there, but her adrenalin had been working so hard at the time that the rest was a bit of a blur. The gun would have to do. It was enough of a deterrent and that was on the assumption that she would even need to point it at him.

She stood up just as there was a crackling noise and the lights flickered. From somewhere in the belly of the house, she thought she heard a woman hiss the words, "Not alone". The lights flickered again and one of the bulbs in the corridor sconces went out with a ping.

The house felt charged, its atmosphere threatening. She swallowed hard. "Not now, please not now." Reaching for the candle, she went to light it, willing the power to stay on for at least a little longer. Then she remembered seeing a reading torch in the room that she had made up for Nick. It wasn't much, but it was better than one measly flame. Hurrying through, she swore as the lights buzzed, persisting with their threat to blow.

With the torch in her hand, she felt marginally calmer. The rest of her stuff could wait until morning. She could borrow a t-shirt from Nick and buy a toothbrush from the shop. Finding herself at the foot of the stairs, she swore loudly once again. She had left her keys on the bed in her bedroom.

Rushing back, she didn't dare breathe as she willed herself to hurry. Sod breaking the law, she would be driving to Nick's. She was far too spooked to take another walk in the dark and the storm with Richard on the loose, as well as whatever it was that was haunting Thornycroft possibly following her. All she wanted was to get out and get to Nick's.

Reaching the bedroom, she gasped. It was unmistakable. A shadow in the corner. She caught it slipping away behind the curtain in an effort to remain hidden. Kate's eyes refused to leave the spot she had seen it move from. It wasn't Richard. In fact, she was pretty certain that it wasn't human.

The keys were where she had left them, on the bed. With the key to her car amongst them, they were her ticket out of there. Diving towards the bed, she yelped as the lights finally went out.

Kate froze. She was in the dark. Frantically she battled with the torch, searching for the switch that would give her some light, but when she pressed the button nothing happened. Whimpering, she pressed it again. Nothing. She dropped it on the floor, her eyes as wide as saucers as she willed them to get used to the pitch black, to at least make out the shape of the door, so that she could feel her way back down the corridor, down the stairs and to the safety of her car.

Something caught the side of her face, tousled her hair. The shifting of air was like cool breath on her skin. Then she heard it, the unmistakable sound of something dropping and rolling across the floor in the corridor.

Her body reacted, kicking into fight or flight and she retched as it tried to rid her of any excess that she carried, clear the smog of alcohol, enable her to focus.

Whatever had been dropped on the floorboards was rolling towards her room, the noise crisp and clear. It was the only sound in the house. The lights flicked back on and the air moved again, the curtains behind her billowing.

The rolling noise had slowed. She tiptoed out of the door and into the corridor, her gaze fixed on the wooden floorboards that had long lost their varnish.

The noise stopped abruptly.

Next to her foot, caught in the groove of the boards, was a gun cartridge, its pointed silver tip gleaming.

Shocked, she realised she was staring at one of the cartridges that she thought she had left behind in Surrey.

From the very top of the house there was a thud. A sudden draught of air hit her. Then she heard a voice.

CHAPTER 48

Present Day – Eyam

The cartridge lay in front of her on the floor, willing her to pick it up, to slot it into the barrel of the gun. She was vaguely aware of the slamming of a door from upstairs and she could feel the coolness of an unnatural wind against her cheek.

"I've never had you pegged as into guns Kate."

The voice took her by surprise, just as she was picking up the cartridge and slipping it into the pocket of her wet jeans. It was the welcome sound of the living against the backdrop of paranormal madness that had engulfed Thornycroft.

"Chris?" Kate gulped back the relief.

Chris was standing at the top of the staircase, the other cartridges in his outstretched palm.

"How did you know where to find me?" She felt herself wobble. In spite of her rebuffing him, Chris must have kept tabs on Richard, followed him, managed to get to her first. "Oh thank heavens you're here," she gushed, feeling some of the tension lift. "Have you seen him? Did you see Richard?"

Closing his hand around the two additional cartridges, Chris took a step forward and shook his head.

"I can't believe he's found me. He knew about Aunt Edie but I don't think I ever told him where she lives."

Chris had stopped, hurt on his face. "You should have told me where you'd gone Kate, let me come and help when I'd offered." He looked at her with regret and pity, his expression making her feel as though she was a foolish child. "It wouldn't take a genius to figure out you were here."

"But I didn't tell anyone where I was going."

He smiled and shrugged. "You've not been too good at covering your tracks."

She regarded the nod of his head, and his sympathetic smile. "Oh." Kate slumped against the wall and brought the heel of her hand to her forehead. "How could I have been so stupid? Was it the letting agency? Is that how you found me? Is that how he knows?" She couldn't remember telling them where she was going. Everything had been so hectic that she supposed she could have suffered a careless slip of the tongue.

"It doesn't matter, I'm here now and that's the main thing," he said. His tone was patronising, but he was reaching out for her, offering to draw her into his arms like he always had done when things had become turbulent with Richard. It had always been their way, his way.

Kate took a step back. This was how it had started last time around and she didn't want to give him the wrong signals. "Chris don't, if he's on his way and he finds us, there's no telling how he'll react. I mean, he's got to be mad to travel all this way to hunt me down when he's under a restraining order."

She was suddenly aware of the chill wind again and was surprised that Chris hadn't noticed. The atmosphere in the house was still electric, the storm outside heightening the tension. It was as though the house was waiting for something to happen. "We should call the police," she suggested, rifling through her bag for her phone.

Chris didn't respond. Instead, he stood calmly, watching her fruitlessly scrabble about. "Shit!" she exclaimed. "I must have left my phone at Francesca's place. We need to get back. Have you got your car?" She noticed the puddle of rainwater pooling at his feet.

"I'm afraid I left it in the main part of the village. It's just a rental, but I couldn't risk bringing it here."

"What?" Kate felt the atmosphere thickening. It felt as though the air was cloying at her. They needed to get out. "It doesn't matter. We can take mine. Come on."

"We're not leaving Kate." He positioned himself so that his body was a blockade between her and the staircase.

"But what about Richard? He knows."

"Richard? I'm surprised you even remember his name. You move on fast, don't you Kate? Richard, me, now Nick. How long will you toy with him for? How long before you discard him like a piece of rubbish?" Scorn dripped from his tongue and his face twisted into an expression of ugly hatred.

Kate stared at him, horrified by his icy tone, the malice in his expression.

"I warned Richard about you after your first date, but he was so intent, so very intent on getting one over on me, that he insisted on meeting you more."

Kate started backing away, edging deeper into the house. "What do you mean, you warned him?"

Chuckling derisively, Chris shook his head. "Oh Kate, you're so naïve and so fickle. You don't even remember that it was me who you met before Richard. You'd always smile at me at the gym, make small talk."

She remembered the greetings, casual, light-hearted, never anything more. "Yes we did meet first, but then you introduced me to Richard."

"No, Richard introduced himself to you. He knew I liked you but as he always has done, he had to win, to seduce you, to dangle you in front of my face. He even boasted about it, treated you like nothing more than a conquest to get back at me." He surveyed the expression on her face, "Oh don't give me that look Kate. That's your trouble. You've always thought so much of yourself, thought yourself too good for me, but the reality is that you were just a bet between friends. Richard fell for you, yes in the end he did, but you backed the wrong horse. If you'd even given me half a chance we wouldn't be where we are today would we?"

Kate felt sick as she digested the words that were coming from his mouth. The lights were flickering madly again and it felt as though the corridor was shrinking, the house swallowing them both up. "Richard was right about you all along. You're insane!" Panic was consuming her as she edged towards the stairs that would take her up to the third storey.

"And whose fault do you think that is Kate?"

Her mind racing, she gawped at him as it dawned on her how easily he had played her, played Richard and twisted everything. In a hideous way, his clever spin on everything was a stroke of genius. He had torn her and Richard's relationship apart. He had even managed to lead Richard to a restraining order. The reality hit her hard, a virtual punch to the solar plexus. To be that twisted, that cold and calculating, it would take a dangerous mind to do everything that Chris had achieved.

He was smiling at her, an arrogant confidence on his face. He had a plan for her. He had carefully thought out every next move and he had given her the gun cartridge, given her a chance to defend herself. Why? What sick thrill could he find in that, or did he want her to hurt him?

Fear was creeping up her limbs, a mixture of cold and hot, as she scanned her surroundings, desperately plotting her escape. There was nowhere else to turn. The stairs to the top of the house was all that she had left. Without hesitating any further, she fled up them, leaving behind the sound of his manic laughter.

When she reached the landing, another bang came from the end of the corridor. The door to the attic staircase had been thrown open. In the far recesses of her mind, she remembered locking it. She had tucked away the key. It seemed impossible that the door could have been opened. Chris surely couldn't have found the key? That didn't matter now though. It was her only means of escape.

A small orb of light lit the staircase that led to the space at the top. Something hissed at her to stop, to turn back. A sour smell that made her stomach muscles want to convulse was growing stronger. If it hadn't been for the sound of Chris behind her, she would have turned around, run all the way down the stairs to the bottom of the house, out the front door and into the mercy of the storm.

The orb winked at her, a shining beacon, showing her the way. She didn't stop to think where it had come from, or what it might be. Survival was the instinct that had kicked in, and that meant going upwards.

A sharp crack and all the lights went out. She heard Chris calling for her, his voice malignant and teasing. The door at the top of the staircase leading into the eaves had fallen open, inviting her to hide inside, offering her sanctuary. With a muted cry, she fell through it.

The space at the top of the house was dark and musty. Kate coughed, her lungs protesting against the dust that she had disturbed.

Downstairs, Chris was cursing, telling her that she couldn't escape, there was no way out, that it was just the two of them, like it should have always been.

The orb of light had disappeared, leaving her alone. She reached out, feeling for objects, for walls, mapping out what she remembered of the layout from when she had found the diary, box and Ouija Board.

Her knee nudged something, its edges prominent. Another dreadful clap of thunder shook the house and the room was illuminated. Pressing against her leg, the portrait of a once beautiful face glared at her.

Another flash of light and Kate stumbled backwards. The face in the portrait had changed. Firmly set pink lips were now twisted. Electric blue eyes were wide and bloodshot and the carefully styled black ringlets were bedraggled.

"Get out!" The voice took her by surprise. It hissed at her from one of the corners of the room, and she thought she heard something dragging across the floor. Kate turned, her eyes beginning to become accustomed to the lack of light.

Silhouettes began to take shape. She began to make out her surroundings: boxes, shelving and a door. Something jogged her memory. It was the door that led to the nursery. How did she know that? Had Rachel shown her? She didn't think so, not yet at least. The nursery had belonged to Lady Rosamund's child, the one who they said had been the last born…

With a strangled scream, Kate brought her hands to her head. She couldn't breathe. An iron fist was pounding at her brain. Images were forming. Her eyes squeezed shut as she attempted to block out the pain, but she needed to open them, to focus on the present. If she didn't keep her wits, Chris would find her. She needed to be alert, not rendered immobile, locked within the memories of somebody who had died hundreds of years before.

Forcing her eyes open, she looked around, focusing on what she could see of the room, ensuring that what she was seeing was of her time and not another.

Impossible shapes were beginning to form in front of her. Something tall and willowy was dead ahead, moving.

From the bottom of the house there was a loud bang. She jumped.

CHAPTER 49

25th August 1666 – Eyam

Rachel jumped at the loud bang. The noise pierced through her shock, stirring her back into action. The candle flames ebbed as a draught blew through her room.

There was a shout from downstairs. Benjamin. He was calling her name, practically screaming for her.

Folding the parchment, she slipped it beneath her bed.

In the main entrance hall, two voices were arguing. One belonged to Benjamin, the other to an older man who was standing on the entrance porch outside the house. He was gruff, angry, shouting threats.

Above them, Rachel heard a pained groan.

Despite the poor light, Rachel recognised the man as one of the night watchmen. He was holding his lamp high and there was a cloth pressed to his nose.

"Is it the pestilence?" Benjamin asked him, the question swathed in panic.

"Hard to say. She's been pummelled hard, covered in cuts and bruises, but she has a fever."

There was an impatient snort from a horse as a body was dumped on the doorstep.

Benjamin stepped back, afraid to go near it. "You can't just leave her here like this."

"You're lucky I brought her at all. She has defied the word of God, made a mockery of the sacrifice the rest of us have made."

"But look at her, what if she's with plague? What do we do?"

The man swung his lantern so that his pockmarked face was in full light as he regarded Benjamin, lips curled in something like disgust. "Do what us ordinary folk do, take care of her and pray. Let us just pray that it is only the cold and the shock of it all that has rendered her to this, lest she's taken the pestilence to the good folks of Tideswell too." He coughed as though to expel foul air from his chest. "From what she was able to tell me, she got off lightly. Talked her way past the watch until one of the villagers there recognised her as being from Eyam. She said that they were so terrified she had brought plague with her, they turned on her in a mad rage. They didn't stop. Would have pelted her to death to save themselves from her if she hadn't escaped. I still can't fathom how she did. Half dead she was when she stumbled in to my sights. 'Tis an almighty lump to her head there."

"She is a strong woman. That is how she escaped." Rachel emerged from the foot of the staircase and thrust the plague bag she still carried towards Benjamin. He stepped out of her way, allowing her to see what had been left on their doorstep. "I will take her from here," she commanded, sounding far older and wiser than her years.

The watchman gave her a nod of respect and stepped back, picking up his wooden watch-bill. He bid her a safe night and hurried back to his post.

Goody's breaths were laboured, her skin sticky and wet from sweat, blood and rain.

"Help me lift her Benjamin," Rachel ordered, gesturing for him to prop Goody on her shoulder.

Despite his fear, he helped her with Goody's weakened body, hoisting her up and taking her through to the blue parlour. "We need rags and water from the pot in the kitchen."

As Benjamin disappeared to gather what she had asked for, Rachel set about trying to determine how bad Goody's condition was. She pressed down her body, searching for signs of flinching and then tore at her kerchief, loosening it from her neck.

When Benjamin returned with the rags and water, Goody was attempting to speak, her thoughts and words a fevered jumble. "Forgive me child, I have been so wrong," she rasped and stopped to struggle for breath. "There is sickness within these walls. A sickness that I thought I could cure, but I can not." A low laugh gargled in her throat until she spluttered. "Did you know that they call me the 'Conjurer'? I could not conjure a cure this time though." Her eyes rolled back in her head as the fever took hold, sending senseless murmurings from her lips.

Rachel dismissed her words as delirium. She took the rags and squeezed them out, dabbing at the bruising and the wounds. As she worked, she hushed Goody from trying to speak, but all the while, the truth that she had found in Sir Edward's study was sticking in her throat, an uncomfortable wedge, choking her, making it difficult to focus.

Keeping his distance, Benjamin offered to fetch more rags, more water, any additional supplies, but Rachel could see that he was terrified that Goody had brought plague into the house. "Just fetch us something strong to drink," she said. "Find something that will hold off the pain."

Rachel dabbed some more at Goody's forehead before ensuring that she was as comfortable as she could be and promising to make up a poultice and bring it back.

When she returned from the stillroom, she was surprised to see Benjamin supporting Goody's neck, helping her drink.

Goody's eyes closed when Rachel applied the poultice to her wounds and her breathing calmed, but the fever was still raging.

Benjamin snuffed the fire that had been lit and suggested plunging her in a tub of cold water.

"The shock may kill her Benjamin," Rachel said. "We cannot."

They sat together, neither of them speaking, Rachel pressing the cool wet rags to Goody's forehead and Benjamin fetching more when needed. "Do you think it is plague?" he asked when Goody at last appeared to be sleeping.

Rachel shook her head. "There are no marks, she did not complain of any illness before she left. I am certain that this fever is from being so exposed to the rain and the shock of the injuries." She went to tend to the monstrous lump on the side of Goody's head.

Averting his gaze, Benjamin looked as horrified as she felt at the terrible injuries that Goody had sustained. The folk of Tideswell must have pummelled her hard to keep her away. It disgusted Rachel to think of how callous and cruel her fellow man could be, how low they could stoop.

"Rachel, I want to apologise for the way I have behaved." Benjamin's apology took her by surprise. She stopped what she was doing and faced him.

His head was bowed with shame and he couldn't meet her gaze. "I was scared and angry that you might have exposed yourself to harm. I could not stand it if-" He cut himself short, took a breath, air jarring in his throat as he swallowed his emotion. "I could not stand it if anything were to happen to you." He raised his head and looked at her in earnest. "I love you."

Those words again, filling the room with warmth, like beautiful golden threads weaving their way through the house, wrapping their way around her, pulling her towards him.

He reached out. Their fingers entwined, their bodies drawing closer to one another. "Whatever happens from hereon in, I am prepared to face it with you because I am in love with you. You have taken my heart Rachel Craven and I will do anything that you ask of me."

She wanted to tell him that she loved him too, wanted to tell him about Catherine, to ask him to take her in his arms, give her the comfort that she needed so that the empty chasm she had been left with could be filled. She said none of those things.

"I am not Rachel Craven."

He stared at her, bewilderment etched into his face.

She continued, trying to explain her real identity, the truth behind the huge lie that she had unwittingly lived. "My true name is Rachelle. Rachelle Maria Thornycroft." Even as she said it, she still couldn't quite believe it.

Benjamin dropped her from his hold. "I don't understand."

The truth of it all was still making her shake, causing her to feel unsteady. It didn't seem possible, but she had seen it written in ink, Edward Thornycroft's signature and the signature belonging to the man who she had grown up believing to be her father. "I found something today," she told him. "Wait here."

When she brought down the document that she had hidden in her chamber, she offered it to him.

With a look of trepidation, he took it.

For a while he was unable to speak. He read the agreement several times before responding, his complexion ashen. "But you work here. Lady Cecily, the way she treats you. The way my mother treated you. They treat you like a-"

"Servant." Rachel finished his sentence and nodded. "Because that's what I am. That's what I became when my father, my real father, signed me away into the care of a tenant farmer, one of his employees." Unable to keep standing, she sank into a chair. "Pa had always made it so clear how much he loved me. Now though, I cannot stop wondering if he had loved me at all."

"He loved you." Benjamin reassured her, his gaze bouncing between her and the document.

"He lied to me though. How could he have kept this from me?"

Benjamin shook his head as he stared at the words, at the signatures, still trying to digest the revelation in front of him. "I suppose he had to lie. How would you have reacted if you had known about this? What kind of life could he have given you if the money from the Thornycrofts had stopped and the farm had been taken away?" He looked up at her. "Rachel, after everything you told me about your Pa, it is obvious how much he loved you. You must hold on to that now."

Sniffing back the tears, she nodded. "I am still just struggling to believe it all, to accept that I'm a Thornycroft."

Benjamin's brow puckered as a thought struck him. "But the Thornycroft baby died. Mother said. A physician declared the death."

She shrugged. She had already had the time to piece together the possibilities from the fragments of truth that she had found. "He could have been paid off. Edward Thornycroft, my blood father, could have instructed him to say that the baby had died, just as he had paid off the Priest to cure my mother, and just as he paid off the man who brought me up, my Pa."

"God's teeth!" Goody had stirred from where she had been sleeping. Her head lifted as she looked over at them, her eyes moving up and down the length of Rachel. "God's teeth it is you. It is really you!" With a weak laugh of relief, her head fell back into the cushion that it was resting upon.

Rachel rushed towards her, wondering how much of the conversation she had heard, but Goody was looking at her with such reverence, as though she was a miracle. "Rosamund! Rosamund you are well, you are here. You are really here, with us." Her eyes were misty as she reached out for Rachel's hand. "Oh my dear heart, Rosamund." Her voice caught and she let out a sob.

"It is not Rosamund who stands with us Goody." Benjamin strode forward and tapped his walking stick on the floor next to Rachel's foot.

Rachel took Goody's clammy hand in her palm. "Goody, it is just me. Rachel."

Confusion furrowed lines in to Goody's face as she studied Rachel. "Ah Rachel," she said at last, a moment of lucidity returning to her expression. "Of course. Dear, sweet Rachel." She smiled fondly at her. "You look so much like her, like my Rosamund. My dear, beautiful Rosamund."

"Did you know about this?" Benjamin allowed no chance of a missed opportunity and waved the agreement in front of her face.

Goody looked confused. She refused to answer.

"Goody, you must tell us the truth now," he implored, keeping his tone soft, despite his growing impatience. "You need to tell us, for Rachel's sake. We are all stuck here until the pestilence takes us, so what harm can it do now?"

Goody squinted and he drew the parchment back, giving her opportunity to read the words. Her lips quivered, "I don't know."

"The baby." Benjamin's patience was beginning to wane. "Lady Rosamund's baby. She never died, did she? Edward gave her away. Why?" He leaned closer to her, forgetting his fear that the pestilence might be upon her. "You, their most trusted, closest servant, now their guest, you must know."

Goody shook her head, but the tears in her eyes and the expression that had come upon her gave her away. She knew the truth. She knew about the agreement, Rachel's true identity.

Rachel could see Benjamin's irritation, knew that his tolerance for Goody's silence would not last. She stepped in. "Goody, I know how you supported my mother. I have seen your letters in Sir Edward's study. I know that you stood by her during everything. I need to know what happened though. My life was taken away from me. I have lived a lie and I do not understand why. Only you can answer that for me."

Tears were spilling over Goody's cheeks. When she looked back towards Rachel, the mistiness had returned to her eyes. The fever began confusing her again, "Rosamund, I am so sorry I couldn't help you. I failed you."

Rachel took her hand and clutched it. "I am Rachel. I am Rosamund's daughter. Did she know that they took me away? Is that why she…" Rachel couldn't finish, didn't want to finish, to say the words that would confirm her mother had taken her own life.

Goody's milky gaze began clearing. "Rachelle." When she pronounced her name, it was with a much softer lilt, the way it had been given at birth. "Your mother loved you so very much. She loved both of you."

"Both?"

Turning her head, Goody was unable to keep looking her in the eye. "There were two. Two beautiful babes. Twins. Rachelle and Viola." She struggled to catch her breath and a fit of coughing gripped her. Rachel lifted her to be more upright.

Goody grimaced as Rachel's hand made contact with the bruises between her shoulder blades, but she continued the story. "We saved Rachelle." Sadness overcame her as she spoke. "'Twas too late for Viola."

Rachel's mind was racing. She'd had a sister? What was Goody suggesting had happened?

Goody turned to Benjamin and then back to Rachel, "We saved Rachelle. It was Rosamund's wish that the child was to be removed from Thornycroft Hall. She was so afraid that if the babe was to stay, she would suffer the same fate as all the rest."

Rachel recoiled, horrified by the possibilities surrounding the secret that Goody was still to fully impart. "Tell me how you saved me Goody? Tell me what happened to Viola?"

Goody looked at her sadly. "You have to believe me Rachelle, I didn't want to do it. I didn't agree to any of it at the time, but I know now 'twas for the best. Nobody outside of the family knew there had been two babies. Viola was born a short while after you. 'Twas me who delivered her." Goody turned to Benjamin, "Everyone who had witnessed Rachelle's birth had gone to announce the happy news to the rest of the house."

"Go on," Benjamin pressed gently.

"Viola was so much smaller, but so very beautiful and with a strong cry." As she spoke, Goody grimaced with the pain of the memory. "Rosamund warned me that baby was fated from the moment she was born, that the red mark upon her left shoulder made it so. I took no notice, thought it was superstitious nonsense, but then one day she was gone. It was just as she had portended. I'll never forget her face," she said, her bottom lip quivering with emotion. "Such a beautiful face, only 'twas blue when I looked into the crib on that dreadful morning. The other babe, Rachelle, she needed a good home, not the madness, the deceit and the lies of Thornycroft Hall. 'Twas what Rosamund wanted. She begged it of me. And she begged it of Edward." Her face darkened. "Not that he needed much persuasion with Cecily dripping her poison in his ear."

"What happened to Viola?" Rachel asked.

There was quiet as tears of remorse mingled with the sweat filming the skin on Goody's face. "There was nothing we could do to save her. She died. Rosamund was distraught, thought it was her fault, that she had let the demon get to her. 'Twas not her fault though. She did not allow anything to get to her babe." She shook her head sadly as she looked at Rachel. "I was with her the whole time. She nursed both of you herself. She loved you both so dearly. I saw everything." Her face twisted. "And then her madness returned." She began to cough, the effort of speaking taking its toll on her chest. When she regained her composure, she looked bitter, full of hatred. "Cecily had been with her, saying things to her, filling her head with all kinds of nonsense. That was what turned her, I am sure. Only this time, she was so much worse than before. She told Edward that Viola had died at her hand. 'Twas the tipping point for poor Rosamund."

Shutting her eyes again, Goody lay back, her energy sapping.

Rachel turned to Benjamin. "I had a sister."

He didn't respond. Everything that Goody had revealed was still registering with him.

Rachel looked at Goody, the regret and torment contorting her features as she lay there. "I still don't believe that my mother killed herself," she said. "She would never have done that if she had loved us both as much as you say."

Goody's eyes flickered open and she spoke again, her voice strained. "If what she had said about Viola's death had got out, even though there was no truth in it, she would have hung from the gibbet. Edward knew it. I knew it. We all did, especially Cecily. Rosamund was better off dead."

"So what happened?"

Goody's eyes had closed again. The effort of speaking, the emotion that she had felt, it had all been too much.

Rachel turned to Benjamin. "Benjamin, I need to know what happened to her."

He was pacing, his cane tapping endlessly against the floor. "I won't let them get away with doing this to you. I won't let them," he said. Then he looked out of the tall windows into the night. "I won't let either of them get away with any of it." He didn't pause to think, or to discuss anything further, and Rachel was too exhausted to stop him. She heard him gathering whatever he needed before the door slammed shut and the candles flickered.

A distant moan drifted through the house. The ghosts of the past had stirred again.

Goody's eyelids fluttered and she coughed again. "Rachelle," she said, her eyes bleary, but looking directly at her, fighting for clarity in everything she could see and say. "You are right, your mother did not end her own life. I need for you to know the truth now, but you must forgive me. Everything I have done, everything was at your mother's request. It was to protect you."

Rachel felt dread slither over her, coil around her torso and squeeze as she waited for Goody to continue.

"Your mother thought that a disciple of the Devil had penetrated her soul, that it wanted her to harm her children. She would not listen to reason. At night she would ask that I chain her. So I insisted on staying with her, keeping her company in that God forsaken room with those God forsaken chains." With effort she lifted her arm so that her sleeve folded in on itself, revealing the welted skin on her wrists.

At once, Rachel understood. Those marks were there as a result of Goody's own sacrifices. She had kept herself in chains at night to be with Rachel's mother, offer her companionship, equality and empathy. The marks must have scarred her. Old wounds, never completely healed.

Goody continued to speak, her chest wheezing with the effort. "I helped her put you to her breast when the madness took hold and she could not trust herself to hold you. I helped her until they took you away and then I helped her again. I was not cruel in anything I did. I did only as she asked of me. You must forgive me. You will see. You must see. You must-" Succumbing to another coughing fit, she spat blood into the rag that Rachel had given her.

"I am dying Rachelle. But you are so much like her. You must see. You must know the truth. I was wrong to come back because there is a sickness in this house. There always has been, but my work cannot remain undone. Take me upstairs so that you can finish what I have started. You are skilled in the stillroom. You must succeed where I have failed."

"You didn't fail Goody. You will get better. We can cleanse this house together."

Goody's smile was weak as she tried in vain to push herself upright. "You are a good girl Rachelle. Pure of heart, just like Rosamund. 'Tis too late for me now. I can feel death's icy hood upon me. When they pelted things at me, they hit me too hard, too much. Now please, take me upstairs. I am dying and I need to show you, to make you understand what must be done." Her breath caught again and she coughed up more blood.

Rachel tried to help her to a sitting position, to loosen the blood from her lungs, but Goody would not stop coughing and the blood would not stop coming.

"Forgive me lass." She looked at her with pleading eyes. "Forgive me for all that I have said and all that I have kept from you." The remorse she held on to looked like it was physically crushing her. She opened her mouth to speak again and the words juddered from her, almost indecipherable as they mingled with blood and mucus, but their meaning struck Rachel cold. "Lass, you must forgive me, for we are not alone."

Goody went to inhale. Something rattled in her throat. The thin trail of air that should have been expended back out of her mouth never came.

"Goody?" Rachel patted at Goody's cheeks, tried to get her to come around, but she did not move. "Goody, no, don't leave me here. Tell me what you need to say." Still there was no response. Rachel shouted her name, shook her. There was no point to it. Goody did not respond.

"Don't go!" she screamed. "Goody speak to me! Come back!" She pressed her palms on Goody's chest, sending a spasm of blood from her lips. Her eyes were open, their shade more of a blue than a brown. Behind them, the truth, only half told, was preparing to be buried.

Rachel cried out her name again, but her body was still, her eyes unblinking. Another person dead.

The sound of horse hooves could be heard thundering across the yard outside as Benjamin left the grounds of Thornycroft Hall. It was too late to call him back, to make him think twice and ask him to go up to Goody's quarters with her. He would be gone by the time she reached the nearest door.

To stop from shaking, Rachel wrapped her arms around her chest, wondering what she should do. Goody had been strong, her presence strangely comforting in the huge dark house. Now she was gone, leaving Rachel all alone.

Hysteria was building, a great monster unravelling. Rachel didn't know what to do with it. The enormity of everything that had happened was bringing her to the edge of her sanity. With Benjamin gone too, there was nobody left.

Goody's final words were still hanging in the air. "We are not alone," she had said.

Rachel's mother, Rosamund, had been haunted by a demon, and despite Goody denying its existence, with her dying breath she had suggested that something terrible was indeed with them.

As her mind teetered on the brink of sanity, Rachel recalled the rumour, the one that said Goody had bent to the will of the demon when Lady Rosamund had died. Now that Goody was dead, Rachel wondered, was it up there, waiting to prey on another living soul? Was that the sickness that Goody had referred to?

She wanted to run, but Goody had said that she needed to show her the truth, to show her what needed to be done to cleanse Thornycroft Hall of the dreadful sickness that was clinging to it.

Rachel still needed answers, to understand how her mother had died and by whose hand. There were so many answers that she needed, for her mother's sake and for the sake of her twin sister, who had been taken so early. No matter what might be lurking in the depths of the house, waiting for its next living victim, she had to find the courage and strength of mind to venture up there and find out what she could.

Fear wrapped its icy arms around her as she folded Goody's hands over her chest and swept her palm over her face to close her eyelids.

She picked up the legal document that she had found in Sir Edward's study, the first piece of the convoluted puzzle, and slipped into the shadows of the house, to take her first step up the stairs. Up she went, until she found herself outside the door that would lead her into the top quarters.

CHAPTER 50

Present Day – Eyam

"Edie, we need to go." Nick approached Edie, who was in the middle of a conversation with Lindsay. When she turned, there was stark horror on her face. "What is it?" he prompted, his panic growing.

"Lindsay says that a gentleman was looking for Kate last night."

Lindsay looked at them both tentatively, unsure whether or not she had said the wrong thing. "That's right, Richard. A very polite chap."

Nick swore and rubbed his palms across his face. "So he's here already, in the village?"

"You know too?" Edie looked at him with accusation, as though he had been keeping secrets from her. "She's told you about the stalking?"

He nodded. Lindsay was still confused. "I don't understand. Should I not have said anything? He seemed like a very pleasant chap."

Nobody had time to stop and explain. "Where is Kate?" Edie demanded.

"Kate's gone back to the house to get some things," Nick replied and reached into his pocket for his phone. "Shit, I'd better call her." He selected the number she had given him earlier that day and moved into the hall by the front door where it was quieter. The number connected and began to ring. There was a faint buzzing noise and he looked down at the table by the door. His name was flashing on the screen. In all of her haste, Kate had left it behind. "Damn it!" he shouted.

Lindsay had brought Edie into the hallway, preparing to leave. "Can you drive?" he asked her. She gestured to her soft drink and nodded.

That was one small mercy that was on their side at least. Nick charged into action. "Good. You'll need to take me down to Thornycroft. We need to go now." He turned to address Edie, "Call the police. Tell them they need to get straight to Thornycroft, that Kate's in danger. And for goodness sake, stay here. Don't follow us."

He didn't wait for Edie's protest, but pulled Lindsay by the arm out of the front door and into the driveway.

Thankfully she had been one of the last to arrive and her car had a clear route to the gates that had been left open. "I just hope we're not too late."

On the way down to Thornycroft, he filled her in on the situation with Richard, his knee bouncing up and down with nervous energy. "You'll need to help get me to the front door Lindsay because I don't fare well with seeing in the dark. I'll be alright when I get to the house and can put the lights on." As efficiently as possible, he explained about his deteriorating sight and when they had pulled up next to Kate's car, Lindsay was swift to help him. "Promise me you'll run straight back to the car once I'm inside and sit tight for the police?"

Lindsay murmured an almost inaudible 'yes', guilt colouring her voice. There was no time to feel bad for her, to reassure her that she had done nothing wrong. That could come later.

Thunder crashed around them, vibrating the posts either side of the garden gate. In spite of his impaired vision, the accompanying lightning bloomed white and stark in front of him. He imagined the house: a nightmare structure looming, silvery stone against a graphite night backdrop.

As the blinding white faded, his retinas began to recover. They approached the front door. It was unlocked. Kate must be inside already as the lights were on, although as Nick stepped over the threshold, they began to flicker. He groaned with dismay. If they went out, he would need to feel his way through the dark. Still, he supposed he would be at no lesser advantage than Richard if he had found his way there already.

He urged Lindsay to get back to the car before he disappeared inside.

Upstairs there were voices, Kate's and a stranger's - a male. So Richard had found her.

As he hurried along the hallway to the staircase, he was careful not to alert them to his presence. He had to be stealthy to avoid putting her in any more danger.

In his head he began working out how long it would take for the police to arrive. Fifteen minutes? Twenty tops? He wasn't sure, but he hoped that if things were going to get violent, he could hold Richard off until they arrived.

As he reached the foot of the stairs, the lights flickered one last time before they went out.

CHAPTER 51

Present Day – Eyam

K ate drifted in and out of consciousness, caught between the present and the past. This pull from Rachel, her ghost from the past, was more than just an inconvenience now. It was putting her in mortal danger. A shaft of light from the luminescent flashing sky outside lit the room and she looked around.

From what she could see, she recognised her surroundings as belonging to the present time. She sighed with relief.

Her mind quickened. She needed to find a hiding place. If Chris was to find his way up to the attic space, which she had no doubt that he would, she would need to take him by surprise, stall him so that she could run past him and make her escape.

She looked at the outline of the boxes that were perched on top of one another. If she could hide behind them, it would give her a vantage point. When he got up there, she could push them over, immobilise and disorientate him for a few seconds. It would buy her the time she needed.

More light flooded the room from the storm outside and she noticed the shape hovering at the edge. It was just an outline, but it was there, watching her. It wasn't Chris, but something else: the shape of a woman.

Behind the woman, Kate had seen panelling, subtle enough to just be part of a wainscot wall, except it wasn't really a wall.

She hadn't noticed it on the morning that she had found the diary and bogwood box, but a memory was firmly planted in her head, telling her exactly what it was. A door.

Fumbling through the darkness, Kate headed in the direction of the wall, carefully feeling her way.

"No!" A gust of wind pushed her back, the voice that breezed in with it ethereal yet powerful. Crying out, she slammed back against the exposed brickwork behind her, cobwebs tangling with her hair.

"I can hear you Kate. Not so stealthy are you?" Chris was nearing the door that would lead him up to this part of the house. The light from the storm must have helped show him where to go.

Panic filled her, giving her the strength she needed to propel forward and reach the handle. If she could open the door, he would think that she had gone down there to hide and if she was quick enough, quiet enough, she could shut him in and run like mad.

"No!" The airy voice resounded once again and this time, she felt icy fingertips squeeze her arm.

With a squeal she pulled her arm back. In front of her, the door burst open. There was an eerie glow in the space behind it, showing her a broken, crumbled staircase that led downwards. An ancient, musty puff of air billowed into the room.

She tried to move. Something was pressing her against the wall, paralysing her.

In the main part of the house, Chris continued his tirade of abuse. "Always hiding from me Kate, avoiding me. And after everything that I did for you when things broke down with Richard." His tone switched from angry to pleading, "Don't you remember that kiss we shared? You wanted that for a long time, I know you did. You felt the chemistry between us, didn't you?"

She wanted to shout, to tell him that he was wrong, remind him that she had pulled away, but she couldn't give away her position.

"I know you're up here Kate." He had moved to the stairwell that led into the attic space she was hiding in. "I can smell you. I know your scent. That's what love does Kate. You begin to recognise these small details. You'll do anything for someone, chase them across the country for their love in return, but then you're faced with a real kick in the teeth, a real punch to the heart. Did you think of me when you were kissing him Kate, or are you the kind of slut who has forgotten about what we had already?" There was danger in what he said, the words dripping with venom. "We were meant to be together Kate. All of this, I did it all for you and you've thrown it back in my face. There's a fine line between love and hate, you know. When I saw you tonight with him, I hated you. I truly hated you. So I made a decision."

Kate could sense he had reached the top of the stairs. Unless she managed to move, he was going to see her when the next flash of light appeared.

"I decided that if you're too foolish to return my love, then you're too foolish to get to love anyone. I'm ending it Kate. Tonight."

Everything inside of her went cold. In her chest, her heart was an icy hard rock. Chris meant to kill her. She fought with all her strength to move. Then, with a strained cry, she broke free.

Pulling the gun from her waistband, she clicked open the cylinder so that she could insert the cartridge that she had slipped into her pocket.

"There you are," he cooed as the noise gave her away. "You never were any good at hiding anything. Poor Richard is beside himself over what was going on between us. The police know that."

"You're bloody crazy Chris!" Unable to keep quiet, she responded vehemently. "If you lay a finger on me, the police will know it was you. Richard's got a restraining order."

Cruel laughter filled the space between them. "Richard's on his way here already. I made sure of it. He won't be long now. I called him in plenty of time, told him exactly what I intend to do and where you are. He thinks he's coming to rescue you. I've blocked his number so that he can't call me and leave any evidence to the contrary."

"You're not making any sense," Kate spat her retort into the darkness.

"Oh I'm making plenty of sense Kate. I have it all planned out. You'll die and Richard will get here when I've gone. He'll be crying over your dead body when they handcuff him. I've set it up perfectly you see. Everyone in the village should know by now that it was Richard who was staying at the guesthouse. Nobody has seen the car I was driving, not even that stupid woman who runs the place. Fortunately for me, she's far too busy fussing over making a good impression."

Kate could hear him moving, the sound of his voice creeping closer as he spoke. "It was Richard who was looking for you in the pub yesterday too. I imagine the lovely lady who helped me locate you will have spread the gossip already. It couldn't be neater Kate. And if I'm really lucky, lover boy Nick will come and look for you just before Richard arrives, so I can get rid of him too. I believe that they call it a crime of passion. Fitting for somebody like Richard, don't you think?" He sounded so pleased with himself.

There was a keen click as the gun cartridge slotted into place.

The next shaft of lightning revealed his position, standing in the doorway, looking straight towards her. He was holding something between his hands. A line of cord, pulled taut.

Kate pointed the gun at him, her hands shaking.

"Go on Kate. One bullet. Take your best shot. I dare you." He licked his lips, relishing the moment, toying with her.

Kate felt the familiar feel of urine slide down her leg. This had happened before, in this same room, in another time. She remembered how the taste of fear on her tongue had been just the same. It had been after Goody had died...

She shook her head. It wasn't her memory, but her brain was engaging her, asking her to look back at it. The memory continued its assault on her brain - Rachel's memory. She had been coming up the stairs and she had been scared, terrified.

Forcing herself to think only of the present, to fight the entity that was trying to hijack her mind, Kate strained to see where Chris was standing. She was painfully aware that she was fighting for her life. How many seconds were between him and her? Two? Maybe three? How many seconds before she would feel that cord he was holding around her neck, tightening, squeezing all the air out of her?

Chris was laughing again. "I knew you didn't have it in you to pull the trigger."

Slick with cold sweat, her finger slid over the trigger, threatening to squeeze it, but her hand was shaking dreadfully.

"You're weak," he sneered. "Still, that gun will come in handy." His footsteps were getting closer. "It's an added bonus that you thought to bring it. As you know, everyone will think it was Richard who was here tonight - jealous Richard with his restraining order. He might well decide to use it on your new boyfriend. I'm assuming that this Nick will be chivalrous enough to try and rescue you?"

His face was illuminated again, the whites of his eyes shining, the irises huge. He was the epitome of insane.

Kate squeezed the trigger.

CHAPTER 52

25th August 1666 – Eyam

Rachel's heart was pounding. The sound of gunfire confused her, throwing her off course. Its sharp crack gave rise to the wave of panic that was building inside her, threatening to erupt. She had no idea where it had come from but the noise reverberated through her head. Was this what it was like to start going mad? Is this how her mother had felt?

Tightly, she held the parchment containing the signatures that had signed away the truth of who she really was.

She had found the courage to climb to the top quarters and had found nothing but sadness and a sense of despair. Then she had seen the arc shape in the wall, the door to the truth perhaps? Only moments earlier, when she had opened it, the door had banged hard against the wall behind it. The noise had been like gunshot. That was all. She wasn't going mad.

Now she was balanced on the threshold, her head dizzy as she stared at the staircase that wound downwards. She took her first step, stepping into the thick stink of rot that was clinging to the air.

The room was a dim glow, lit only by the scantily spread candles from the sconces on the walls.

At the bottom of the staircase, to her right, she could see that the room stretched on and at the end, she could make out something red. Fabric billowed and throbbed like a ghoulish beating heart. A dress. Another. Then another. They must have all once belonged to the first Lady Thornycroft. The mad one. The dead one. Her mother.

Movement. Almost imperceptible in the darkness, but something had shifted. It was just a small movement, like the turning of a head.

Alert, Rachel's eyes were peeled as wide as possible, desperate to see, to spot any threat. There was not enough light to be sure of it, but amongst the dresses she could swear that there was a shape. As her vision adjusted, she felt with a sickening certainty that the shape was moving, only slightly, but it was moving all the same.

It started to grow, as if unravelling itself, until there was little room between the low-beamed ceiling and the top of its head.

With a cry of alarm, Rachel threw herself backwards, towards the base of the steps, preparing to scrabble her way upwards, but the door at the top had shut behind her. She was trapped.

There was an unearthly noise as the thing slowly closed the distance between them. There was nowhere left to run.

The thought sliced through her, that she had been right to fear what had skulked in the shadows for so long. Something from the wickedness of the past had remained, haunting Thornycroft Hall.

Before she could even find the first step to climb, the shape violently thrust itself forward and Rachel's shrill scream resounded through the desolate darkness of the house.

******

Pushing her hands out, she attempted to fight whatever it was that was flinging itself towards her. Her hands pulled through tangles of hair and fabric.

She screamed, drawing back her arms, putting the palms of her hands to the steps behind her in order to thrust herself upwards, leave behind whatever it was lurking in the darkness and shut it back in its chamber.

"Goody! Goody, please, where have you been?" The voice that cut through the room was weak, frightened, breathless. "The candles have almost gone out and I was afraid to come out. You told me to stay here in case she saw me. In case she saw my face."

Rachel stumbled and fell onto her bottom, the cold of the step penetrating through her skirts to her skin.

The shape in front of her stepped forwards. "I was going to secure myself into the chains. You know how it is at night, when I feel at my worst. I'm so afraid that without you here I'll succumb to the madness though. And oh Goody, this pain, this dreadful pain! Do you have the remedy now?"

Rachel stared in disbelief at the shadowy shape in front of her. "Mother?" The word was tiny but powerful, lighting up the darkness. The shadow moved closer so that the light from the wall sconces lit up a once beautiful face.

Feeling her body grow weak, Rachel's mind raced. What she could see was impossible. She considered the possibility that she was dreaming. "Mother?" she whispered. "Lady Rosamund?"

Lesions of red and brown scabs ravaged the woman's features. Eyes of the brightest blue stared back at her. Rachel remembered all the noises, all of the ghost stories, but this was no ghost. The woman in front of her was solid, living and breathing.

With trembling hands, the woman reached out. "Rachelle? Is it really you? My beautiful girl?" There was a gentle foreign lilt to her accent.

Overcome with emotion, Rachel was unable to answer. She stood up and took a step closer.

There was a strangled sob and the woman reached out to touch Rachel's face. The gesture was maternal, full of love, but the fingers were so cold.

Rachel recalled how she had once been wakened in the dead of night by the waxy feel of fingers against her face. Had it been this woman who had stolen into her room?

"My girl, my beautiful girl," the woman said through her sobs.

Rachel's heart was pounding fast. She had never known her mother. Her Pa had always told her that she had died after Rachel had been born. She supposed that in a way, he had thought he was telling her a part truth. Everyone thought that Lady Rosamund Thornycroft had died after her last child had passed. That was what Edward Thornycroft had allowed everyone to believe.

Trying to comprehend what she had uncovered, Rachel felt stunned into silence as she pieced together the truth. This woman was the person who had brought her into the world, who Goody had described as having nursed Rachel and Viola with unconditional love.

Her heart squeezing, she looked at the woman. She was a stranger and yet, she felt familiarity as she took in her features: her eyes, mouth and the long hair that was beginning to grey at the edges. In spite of the lesions and scabs, Rachel could still make out the beauty that matched what she had seen in the portraits hidden in the locked room. "Lady Rosamund," she whispered.

The woman nodded.

Rachel clasped a hand over her mouth, her legs threatening to collapse beneath her weight. "Mother," she cried and took a step towards her, wanting to feel her warmth, the love that she had missed out on for all of those years.

Rosamund's face crumpled and she pulled away, hid herself behind her hands. "Do not look at me child. The demon's ugliness is showing itself. Goody is doing all she can to fix it. She says it is a disease that is ruining me, not the demon. She is wrong. I know what this is." She turned away and lifted the hood of her cloak so that her face was shadowed. "I can feel it eating away at me. Soon it will devour me. It is my punishment for being so weak, for not fighting it, for allowing all of my precious children to be taken from me."

Moving towards her mother's thin body, Rachel put an arm around her shoulders.

The parchment had dropped to the ground and the signatures that had changed their lives were trodden on as Rachel carefully coaxed her up the stairs.

Rosamund tried to pull back, too scared to leave the confines of her chamber. "You must trust me," Rachel implored her. "Goody was right. 'Tis no demon that has caused this. 'Tis a disease. Have you seen a physician?"

Weakly, she shook her head. "Goody is as good as you can get. She has helped me fight this sickness these last months. She brought me here at the first signs of it, said that the majesty of the Peaks would fix it."

Rachel helped her slowly into Goody's chamber and then down the stairs into the main part of the house. "Goody has asked that I take over from where she left off."

Rosamund looked bewildered. "Where is Goody? Has she not returned from Tideswell?"

They had reached the main part of the house. The chill of night was seeping through the corridors and Rachel noticed how much Rosamund was shivering. "Goody

351

has returned. Let's get you in the warmth, get you some blankets," she suggested, unable to tell her what had become of Goody. Rachel was afraid the news might break her.

A wild look had come upon her and she stopped, refusing to go any further. "No, I must go back to my room, to the chains. Goody needs to secure me, lest the demon takes over and I lose control of my actions."

"There is no demon mother," Rachel reasoned, but Rosamund refused to listen as she attempted to return to the top quarters. In her weakened state, it was an impossible task. Rachel caught her as her body gave way beneath her weight.

"You need to trust me now," Rachel said, supporting her as best she could as she guided her down the stairs and into the kitchen where the fire was lit.

Rachel heated some wine, waiting for Rosamund's protests to die down. She knew she could not keep the news about Goody hidden for long.

After pouring the wine into two deep cups, Rachel took a seat next to her mother and held her hand as she began to explain. "Goody did return from Tideswell, but there was an accident." Taking a steadying breath, she studied Rosamund for her potential reaction, but she remained remarkably composed. "Mother, Goody was a strong woman, a good and brave woman, but she is gone now."

"Gone?"

Rachel nodded sombrely.

At first Rosamund said nothing. She took a sip of her wine, looked into the flames of the fire and then down at her hands. When she looked back up, her face was wet with tears. "I cannot believe that she is gone. Goody took care of me." Sadly, she turned her gaze to the flickering flames in the hearth. "She loved me, unconditionally. And I loved her. So much." Rosamund broke, began to cry again.

Rachel did not know how to comfort her. Goody had been everything to Rosamund. She had stood by her through thick and thin, given her love when everyone else had rejected her.

It was some time before Rosamund looked towards her again. The grief was still there, but there was something else too. Fear. "Rachelle, if Goody is gone, then I do not know what to do, how to keep us all safe. Goody helped me keep the demon at bay. If it was not for her, it would have ravaged us all by now."

Rosamund's vulnerable state was hard to watch. Rachel knew that she had to help her, guide her through her grief and give her the reassurance that Goody once had. "I am here now mother and I am strong. Goody wanted me to find you, to finish off what she had started to help cure your sickness, to take care of you."

Rosamund nodded mutely, her eyes hooded with grief as memories only known to her played back through her head. "I will miss her dreadfully," she whispered.

"I promise you that I will help you, just as Goody did, mother," Rachel reassured her. "I am good in the stillroom. I can find remedies, but we must bring a physician here." She stopped, realising the flaw in her plan. With the infestation of plague, there was no route in for a physician. She eyed Rosamund carefully, wondering if she even knew of the dreadful sickness that ravaged the once thriving and beautiful village.

Rosamund shook her head, insisting that she didn't want any outside help. "Nobody can see me. I have the spawn of the Devil inside of me." She turned away, shame upon her face. "Besides, Cecily told me that should any living soul find out about my existence, that she would tell everyone about what I did to my little Viola, that my punishment would be to hang at the gibbet for what happened to her, or worse." Her head fell forward and she collapsed into tears, the depth of her grief for Goody, and the years of despair that she had endured, shaking her to the core.

"You must listen to me mother." Rachel placed herself in front of Rosamund's quivering form, her voice firm. "Goody told me everything. You are not responsible for the death of Viola. She was smaller, weaker. Goody said that you did everything a mother should, how you nursed her, held her and loved her. 'Twas just her time."

Distraught, Rosamund wouldn't listen to sense. "No Rachelle, it was my milk. It poisoned her. Full of malice though she may be, Cecily was right the day that she whispered those words into my ear, told me I should be rid of myself before I infected you. This sickness inside of me fed your sister, fed you. She was too small, the weaker of you both. It killed her." She reached out and with a quivering finger stroked Rachel's face. "It is a miracle that you were spared, my darling Rachelle."

The ball of anger that had been building inside her exploded and Rachel beat the table with her fists. "No mother, 'tis no miracle. 'Tis the cruel way of life. Cecily preyed on your grief. She has as good as killed you, destroyed the life we could have had together." She stood up, her fury making her head spin. "I am going to find her and I am going to make her pay for this. 'Tis Cecily who will hang from the gibbet, not you. You will see mother. She has committed the most despicable of crimes. I will make sure that the truth will out."

"No Rachelle!" Even through her tears, Rosamund was indignant. "She has a son now, your half brother. If you take her away from that little boy, think what it will do to him. You will become no better than Cecily." Sinking back into her seat, she pulled at the hood of her cloak, ensuring that her face was still safely in its shadow. "I am getting older and I am sick. All that matters to me is that you are well and you are safe."

Rachel felt the injustice of the situation grinding her down. "But Cecily took me away from you. She wanted you dead so that she could take your place as Lady Thornycroft. She has stolen everything from you." Rachel could not understand her mother's indifference. Justice had to be served.

"It was not Cecily who decided that you should be sent away to another family. It was my decision, for your safety." She cupped a hand against Rachel's cheek. "I told Goody and I told your father that there was to be no more grief, no more destruction, that they must snuff my life from this earth, but they refused. They couldn't do it, wouldn't do it. So I told them to take you away. It was not enough to merely keep me in chains when dark thoughts peppered my mind. You needed to be moved to a safe place, where you would be loved and no harm would come to you."

Rachel groaned with frustration. Her mother was caught up in superstitions from times long gone. Things were changing. People were starting to be more reasoned in their judgement, not looking to blame all tragedy on curses, witchcraft and demons.

There was no convincing her, no consoling her. Still, Rachel persevered, "Babies die mother. Isn't that what the physician said when he examined Viola? There was no demon, is no demon."

She noted the ugly raised scars on Rosamund's arms and how they mirrored those that Goody had bore and she shuddered. Then she saw the deep cut, covered with what she assumed was a poultice, made by Goody's hand before she had taken her fateful journey out of the village. "Is that what this cut is from? Did you try to cut the demon from yourself?"

"No Rachelle, I did not." She retracted her arm from her grip. "Goody thought she might try to let some of my infected blood to get the disease out, give me some of hers in return. I allowed her to do it because she wouldn't hear otherwise." Her eyes pooled with tears again. "She was so determined to find a cure for me. She had been prepared to do anything, even put herself at risk." Ashamed, she looked away. "Made herself as weak as me for trying. It did not work. She got so angry, so frustrated, said she needed to find more ingredients for a new remedy to try."

Once again, Rachel was filled with respect for Goody Brown, who had so selflessly tried to help Rosamund. It made it all the more tragic that she had died trying to cure the woman who she had loved and taken care of for so long.

Rosamund stared into the flames of the fire, lost to her memories of Goody. "Before you were born, in my darkest hours here in this house, your father had the chains bolted to the walls to help contain me in my moments of madness." She looked up solemnly. "There were others before you. Countless others. My beautiful children, my babies, killed by this useless weak body, or ripped from my womb, their breath already cold."

"Mother, you can not believe that any of this is your fault, or the work of a demon? So many women lose their children." Rachel knew that her words were lost on Rosamund. The things that Cecily had whispered all those years ago, the poison that had been dripped into her ears had already done the damage. It had all stuck, had become embedded in her vulnerable mind.

Rosamund gave a bitter smile as she recounted her return to Thornycroft Hall. "Your father was not pleased to see us when we returned. He has always lived in fear that the crime he committed by marrying Cecily and sending me into exile will be uncovered. As for Cecily, she wanted us gone immediately of course. My very existence destroys any claim she has to being Edward's wife and the good fortunes such a title brings."

"But mother, they allowed you to live in chains, even in ill health."

"Goody hated seeing me in those chains so very much, but I insisted." Her eyes misted over and in spite of her deep sadness, she smiled at the memory of the woman who had done so much for her. "Rather than leaving me tethered to the wall like a wild animal, she would chain herself to me. Goody saved me from myself every day, but she couldn't save me from this." She winced as she traced a finger over the raised welts on her face. "This is my punishment. It is how I will meet my end."

Rachel tried to reassure her. "You are not being punished mother. Disease comes and it does so without warning." She thought of the Hancocks, of Catherine and of all her friends and neighbours who had lost their lives to plague. "Disease takes the innocent, the young and the old." She held Rosamund's gaze, deliberating over whether or not she should impart what had been happening in Eyam. "Do you know of what is happening to us, here in Eyam?"

Rosamund gave a sorrowful nod. So Goody had told her.

Rachel continued, "The plague has taken so many here. It has taken the best of us and the worst of us. There has been no method, no plan in how it has assaulted our village. And we stay. We stay here because God wants us to. He wants us to stop the spread of this wicked disease. But because we stay, there are so many of us, good God fearing people, who suffer every day. 'Tis not punishment though mother. 'Tis not the Devil's work and there is nobody to blame for any of it. I have lost my closest friends this past month, people who had the purest and strongest of hearts. Tragedy happens. You cannot blame yourself. I certainly do not blame you for anything that happened."

Rosamund did not respond. It was impossible to tell whether Rachel was getting through to her.

Ladling some more wine from the pot hanging over the fire, she gestured for Rosamund to have more, but her grasp had weakened and so Rachel helped her.

As she drank deeply, Rosamund calmed a little. "Can I see her?" she asked and Rachel knew that she wanted to see Goody.

Gently, Rachel took her hand, led her to the blue parlour where Goody's body lay, beaten and broken but at peace.

She watched as Rosamund knelt by Goody's lifeless form, cupped a hand in hers and looked on at her with such love. "My dear heart," she whispered before placing a kiss on her forehead. "May the Lord keep you safe in heaven."

Rosamund remained kneeling for a while before she took a seat in the chair opposite - Cecily's chair. When she spoke again, her voice was stronger, steadier. "She spoke of you. This past year, she told me all that she had seen of you." Her eyes were shining with pride. "When we returned and I found that you were here, I asked her to tell me everything that she learned about you. She told me what a beautiful and kind young woman you had become. She said I would be proud, that you have a strong heart, conviction and courage. And she spoke of how you are not afraid to stand up to the Belgrave boy." She chuckled as she recalled everything that Goody had told her.

"She said that you are a girl after my own heart, not afraid to show your opinions to a man, to influence him."

Rachel felt herself fill with pride as she noted the affection in her mother's words and the way that she looked upon her.

"I saw you once," Rosamund said. "It was just once, while you were sleeping. I wanted to see if what Goody had told me of you was true. Even in just that one snatched moment, I saw that it was."

"I remember," Rachel whispered.

"I am sorry I frightened you, but I had to see you." Rosamund's lips curved into a proud smile. "It soothes me to see you Rachelle. In here." She tapped the side of her head. "It dulls the pain, my beautiful daughter. You are growing into a fine woman."

Rachel reached for her hand and kissed it. "Thank you." She smiled at her and stood up. "I will fetch us something more to drink, to eat. You need to keep your strength up so that we can get you well."

As she opened the door to go out to the kitchen, she gasped. Benjamin was standing outside, his expression solemn.

She turned back to look at Rosamund, but she was lost in thought, in memories of Goody.

"You're back." Rachel was unable to disguise how much his presence had taken her by surprise.

"I could not leave you. I could not bring myself to break our oath." He stepped forward. "We have a duty to God, to our fellow men."

Rachel ushered him into the kitchen, her voice hushed as she told him about all that had unfolded, and he listened.

"We will look after her together," he promised. "I will help you. I will stand by the both of you and later, I will take Goody's body and bury her. We will hold a service for her."

Benjamin took her in his arms and held her whilst she cried for Goody, for her mother who had spent so many years torturing herself and for the great sacrifice that both she and Goody had made to try and protect her from harm.

She cried for Samuel too. He was a bastard child and with no rights to Thornycroft Hall if the truth of the situation was ever revealed. He was like her, an innocent, brought into a house of madness and lies.

It was in that moment that she realised that she could not tell anyone what she knew, at least not until Samuel was a fully grown man. One day though, she would need to clear her mother's name, exonerate her from the accusation that she had taken her own life and the life of her child.

Rachel held on tight to Benjamin, the two of them sitting up with her mother all night until the pearly streaks of first light, when Benjamin stayed good to his word and they buried Goody's body in the place where Viola had been buried almost two decades earlier.

They scattered poppies, herbs and interred a ring from Rosamund into the ground with her. They said prayers, cried for her and each threw a handful of soil over her body.

Benjamin and Rachel held Rosamund up, helping her pay her respects to the person who had loved her unconditionally and sacrificed her own life to try and save her.

"She was a good woman," Rosamund whispered through her tears. "She was a misunderstood woman."

"A strong woman," Rachel added and Rosamund held her hand tightly as they laid Goody Brown to rest.

CHAPTER 53

Present Day – Eyam

The sound of gunshot ricocheted through the house and Nick fell into the end of the balustrade at the top of the stairs. "Kate?" he shouted, forgetting about his quest for stealth, but his voice was lost amidst the thrashing of rain.

Feeling his way through the house, he steadied himself. He was on the top floor now. The gunshot had come from the eaves of the house, Edie's large attic space.

His ears were ringing, making it difficult to keep his balance. He tried to map out where he was, how far away he was from the door that would connect him to where Kate was.

"The police are on their way," he called out, hoping that both Kate and Richard would hear him. There was no disguising the tremor in his voice.

He pushed thoughts of Kate lying on the floor, bleeding to death, far from his mind.

Holding his breath, he listened for more noise. There was only silence.

Desperately, he tried to feel his way to where he needed to get to, but his arms flailed uselessly in front of him. His mind raced with panic, unable to count out how many doors he needed to feel his way past in order to find the one that he needed to enter.

A cry of frustration caught in his throat. He needed to keep his head if he was going to be of any help.

Then he felt the smooth coolness of what seemed to be an arm.

Recoiling, he held his breath.

Somebody was standing in front of him. Something brushed the back of his hand. Skin. Waxy. Cold. There was a smell. Death.

Gagging, he pulled away and his hand connected with another.

In his mind's eye he began to see. The layers of darkness in front of him began peeling away like the many layers of an onion. One after another they fell away until he was left looking into the house as it had once been. Bigger back then, but this part, the part that was still standing, remained unchanged in layout.

The corridor was lit dimly by candles and in front of him, a girl who it was impossible to append an age to, was leading him by the hand, showing him the way.

Just ahead of them, a door was open, the lip of a staircase behind it. He held the girl's hand tightly as effortlessly, they found their way through the door and to the stairs.

At the top, she turned and pressed an index finger to her lips. There was sadness etched into her pretty face. This was a face that had seen misery and tragedy too soon in life.

The girl pointed upwards, refusing to go any further but urging him to continue. Even without her hand holding his, he could still see everything with great clarity.

Then the edges of time blurred momentarily, allowing him to feel a pull cord in front of him. A light. Wasting no time he reached out and tugged it. Nothing happened. The power was still out.

Familiar with the experience of being engulfed in darkness, he focused his senses on the space around him. Footsteps were shuffling away from him. Somebody was breathing hard.

With trepidation, he took a step forward, and then another.

There was a neat pop and a whir as the power returned and the room was swathed in the bright light of the naked bulb that was swinging from the ceiling. He caught his breath, horror rendering him unable to move.

Kate was standing at one end, eyes as wide as a startled animal. One arm was outstretched. She was holding a gun.

Advancing towards her with great intent was a man with sandy coloured hair. A piece of yellow cord was held taut between his hands.

It was the shape behind Kate that had caused Nick to freeze in fright though.

Tall, thin, with hollow eyes in the skeletal face of what had once been a woman, it hovered. Hair grew in sporadic messy clumps from a dead scalp and clawed hands were reaching out, holding on to Kate as though to assist the man who was striding forwards, preparing to hoist the cord around her neck.

"You missed Kate," the man chimed in a strange sing-song voice. "Now it's my turn." He seemed oblivious of the creature that was busy pinning her to the spot, ensuring that she was unable to escape the fate that he intended for her. He took her roughly by a shoulder.

Nick found his voice, found his feet, lurched towards them, but an impossible gust of wind stopped him. A weight jarred into his stomach, sending him flying backwards. Sharp nails scratched at his neck and bony hands attempted to pin him to the floor. There was a voice that clanged through the air above him.

"It is my secret to tell, not hers," it hissed and Nick watched helplessly as Kate attempted to fight the man who was roughly taking control of her. He saw her swing the gun upwards, try to crack the barrel against his head and miss.

As Nick fought the hands that were unnaturally strong, he recognised the face above him. When he had painted, that face had been there, on the walls of Thornycroft Hall and in the memories that Rachel had revealed to him. Lady Cecily.

In life she had been a cruel, hard woman, but in death, the ugliness of her personality was magnified.

She glared at him with satisfaction as he fought her, knowing that if he didn't get up, Kate would die.

He kicked his legs and shouted, but she held him fast.

Then he saw the open arc in the wall. Beyond it, something was moving. A shape was gliding upwards, towards where Kate was struggling for her life.

Distracted, the man holding her turned his head just as the shape came into focus. Another woman. Her face was almost hidden by the thick navy cloak that she wore, but at an angle, Nick could see the angry, raw wounds and tumours that ravaged it.

She reached out, the movement jagged, her hand lashing out at Kate's assailant. It was enough for him to relinquish his hold and as Kate dropped to the floor, she gasped and gagged.

Nick felt the bony fingers weaken. He took his opportunity, diving towards Kate.

From behind him, there was an angry shriek. He ignored it, adamant that he would reach where Kate was lying, fighting for her life.

The man had pivoted to avoid the touch of the spectre in front of him. Nick recognised the wounds on her face as the merciless onslaught of skin cancer in its most advanced stages.

With a cry of terror, the man stepped away, his body backing into the black arc.

Everything seemed to play out in slow motion; the look of surprise on his face as he realised he was losing his footing, the way his hands clawed at thin air and the heave of his chest as he cried out, only at the last minute seeing Nick leap to grab his hand in an attempt to stop his fall. Their fingertips touched momentarily, but he was already descending into the chasm of black.

From the floor, Kate tried to shout out, her voice hampered by the pressure that had been applied by the cord.

There was a scream, bloodcurdling, brief. Then there was silence. It was Kate who broke it. "He's dead. There's nothing behind that door. The stairs have crumbled away. It was a steep drop." Shock made her tone deadpan. "Chris is dead," she said and then her body shook with both shock and relief.

Nick held her for a short time and only when she had calmed did he ask, "Chris?" He was confused.

Kate rubbed at her throat as she struggled to sit up. "That was Chris. It's a long story and I'm too sore to explain it all right now, but he was insane. He tried to kill me. If it hadn't been for..."

"I know." Nick scooped her in to his arms. "I saw her too." He felt her head rest against his chest as he looked into the gaping arc and at the hooded shape of the woman that was still hovering there.

The cancerous lesions and bumps on her face and neck had disappeared as the hood shimmied back. Thick ebony waves of hair cascaded over her shoulders and she smiled down at them, her electric blue eyes glinting. Another younger woman appeared by her side and their pale white fingers entwined.

Lady Rosamund and Rachel. Mother and daughter. He recognised them both. A glorious light engulfed them and there was a rushing noise, drowning out Lady Cecily's angry screams.

It took him a few seconds more before Nick came to his senses and realised that they needed to phone for help. "I'm calling an ambulance," he said, reaching for his mobile in the back pocket of his jeans, but Kate grabbed his hand, stopped him.

"Let them show us how it ends," she pleaded, but they had no choice. Like a great spectral curtain, the world around them was falling away again.

CHAPTER 54

November 1666 – Eyam

The buttery glow of summer melted into the amber skies of autumn. Rachel, Rosamund and Benjamin took each day at a time.

The anniversary of George Viccars' death, the first to die of the pestilence, came and went.

With Rachel's care, Rosamund grew a little stronger. Rachel convinced her to stay in a more comfortable chamber in the main part of the house. She gave her warm herb baths, tended to the ruptures on her skin with ointments and remedies and together with Benjamin, took her on gentle walks in the sweet apple scented air.

When autumn came in all its ripeness, the fruit on the trees in the orchards bowed heavily. There were not enough hands left to pick it and so apples browned, dropped to the ground, their sweet flesh turning soft and rotten as northerly winds began to blow a chill across the land.

The Reverend Mompesson visited three times, his shoulders heavy and his eyes aged, but his heart was still beating strong for the memory of Catherine and the hope that one day he would be reunited with their two beautiful children.

As she had asked, they kept Rosamund's presence a secret, but they refused to allow her to chain herself. Rachel slept in her chamber with her, nursed her, showed her kindness, love and compassion. The tortured look in her eyes lessened and the brightness returned, until late October, when she took to her bed.

Benjamin unlocked the room of hidden paintings and ensured that they were returned to their rightful place, where they could hang with pride, just as they should have done for all those years. When Rachel told her, she smiled, but she was too frail to get up and see.

One crisp morning, on a blue dawn in November, when the sun was slowly ascending over the crest of the highest peaks, Rosamund reached out for Rachel. She asked for her forgiveness.

Rachel told her that there had never been anything to forgive and kissed her head. She went to fetch her hairbrush, to run it through her mother's hair until it fell in gloriously soft waves, just as it had in the portraits of her youth.

"A new dawn mother," she said as she returned to the bedside, ready to help her to a more upright position.

Rosamund didn't respond. Her eyelids were closed, her face relaxed, and in spite of the painful swellings, scabs and blisters on her skin, she looked at peace. Her chest no longer rose and fell in raw, laborious bursts and her limbs no longer trembled.

Rosamund Thornycroft took her last breath on the same day that Abraham Morten, the last victim of Eyam's plague, took his.

They buried her next to Viola and Goody, at the edge of the apple orchard, when the sky was at its most beautiful, spreading a golden hue across the land.

CHAPTER 55

Early March 1667 - Eyam

After Yuletide, word was sent to the Thornycrofts, informing them that the plague was over. They refused to return until the spring, when the last of the snow had thawed and enough time had passed.

Rachel took the time to write another letter to the man who she now knew to be her blood father, Edward Thornycroft.

It was left in his study on the desk, next to the agreement that had changed everything. She had kept it short but let him know all that she had learned. She wrote that her mother's story would one day be told and Edward and Cecily's part in it revealed.

She gathered her things, noticing how silent Thornycroft Hall had become.

Benjamin was waiting for her, a modest carriage tethered to two horses. He instructed the coachman to wait whilst they tended to some final business at the house and he took her hand so that they walked together to Rosamund's grave.

They stood, their boots covered in the fine powder of what would be the last of the snow.

Snowdrops grew over the undulating earth. Soon they would make way for the golden crowns of daffodils and in the skies above, swallows would return from their winter haunt.

Rachel knelt, kissed the earth where beneath it her mother, sister and Goody lay. She promised that one day she would return, tell their story and do them all justice, that Cecily would pay for her malevolent part in it all and that her father would hang his head in shame.

Then she stood and looked out to the boundary stone, an icon that marked the sacrifice that so many in her village had made.

Two hundred and sixty of her friends and neighbours had lost their lives in the fourteen months that the plague had ravaged Eyam.

In that time Rachel had found grief, courage, love and truth. In Thornycroft Hall, she had uncovered a tragedy living in the shadow of another that had come to pass, its own victims dead and buried.

People would know of the hardship faced by the villagers of Eyam, of their courage, their loss and their selfless sacrifice, but they would not know anything of what her mother had lived through. It weighed heavily upon Rachel's heart, but she knew that all Rosamund would want was for Rachel to have a chance to live her life the way that she had been unable to: no chains, no walls imprisoning her, no deceit, pain or fear.

They had no firm plan mapped out ahead of them. Benjamin was well educated and had good connections across the country, but he was denouncing his title, his family. He could not find forgiveness in his heart for his mother and he did not want to return to any of the Belgrave residences. For many nights they had talked at length about starting a new life together, somewhere new, York.

Benjamin's fingers laced with her own and he placed a tender kiss on the top of her head. "What should we do now?" he asked, offering her the opportunity to choose to stay a little longer at her mother's graveside if she wished, or go.

She turned to him, tilting her head upwards so that she could see his whole face in the dazzling light of the morning sun. "We live Benjamin, my love. We live."

EPILOGUE

Kate hung the last of the baubles on the Christmas tree and stepped back to admire her work. The reds, oranges and gold were the perfect complement to the Stuart period décor they had used to offset the extravagant amount of space in Edie's living room. Nick had even commissioned an old contact of his to return the ceiling to its former glory. Smiling to herself, she folded her arms across her chest in satisfaction.

Since the court hearing things had felt much more settled. She glanced over at the cane in the corner of the room. With its proud looking wood-carved fox head, it was a wonderful antique ornament and a nod to the unsung hero that Goody Brown had been, her story, like the others, lost in the folds of time.

They had found the cane, along with many other items that had belonged to Goody and Lady Rosamund, in the hidden chamber, after Chris had been recovered.

Chris had been lucky, if you could call it luck. He had escaped death by the angle of his fall, but his body had been broken dreadfully with multiple fractures and snapped bones. When he had appeared in court, his injuries were still painfully obvious. He had sworn on the Holy Bible and confessed to everything.

Kate couldn't help but wonder whether his Solicitor had told him that he would get an easier break if he confessed on the grounds of mental health. There was a history - a clinical diagnosis for a mild personality disorder in his late teens. Mild enough to remain unchecked by the primary care system, the defence argued that it had got worse, that Chris needed clinical help.

The jury's decision had been unanimous. When he had been found guilty of the charges that had been made against him, he hadn't flinched, nor had he protested at the sentence. The court found that as he was an offender with a severe mental health disorder, he would be sectioned.

No charges had been brought against Kate for the illegal possession of a shotgun, or for firing it. Under the circumstances, she had been found to have only taken it to act as a deterrent, to have used it in self-defence and with no pre-calculated intention to cause physical harm. To be fair to Chris, he advised the jury that she had never directly pointed the gun at him. It was the one honourable thing that he had done.

He wore his shame well and Kate had almost felt sorry for him, but the memories of the cord tightening around her neck, the way he had not cared when her feet had kicked helplessly and the feeling of blood red panic that had flooded through her, were still so raw.

Within fifteen months everything was over legally. "I'll never understand how these things take so long. He's guilty as sin, they should just lock him up and throw away the key," Edie had complained several times whilst they had waited for the case to progress to the Crown Court.

When the conclusion was eventually drawn, Kate had felt flat, wrung out and deeply sad. Throughout it all, Nick had been her rock.

She had made the decision to stay living in Eyam with Edie and she had faced no protest.

Even Richard had agreed that a fresh start would be good for her. He had waved away any apologies for her part in the ordeal that he had been put through, insisting that none of it had been down to the fault of anyone other than Chris. It was a sad consequence that any romance they had once shared was long gone, but they remained friends, supporting one another through the emotional fallout of the events that led up to the arrest and the eventual sentence that Chris faced.

The festive scent of cinnamon and gingerbread wafted into the lounge, reminding her that Edie had been busy baking in the kitchen all morning. "Coffee?" Kate offered, joining her by the Aga.

Edie pulled a fresh batch of biscuits from the oven. "Perfect timing dear. How's the tree?"

"Very festive looking and ridiculously huge. We shouldn't have left it until Christmas Eve." Kate washed the smell of pine needles from her hands before switching on the kettle.

Transferring the biscuits to the rack, Edie inspected the holes that she had pierced through the dough in readiness for the ribbon. "It'll be fresher for longer and as for size, well in my opinion, the bigger the better. After all Kate dear, you know what they say, size matters." She gave her a cheeky wink.

"Aunt Edie!" Kate waggled a finger at her. "You need to clean up that sense of humour before mum and dad arrive. You know what a prude dad can be," she scolded, unable to prevent a chuckle as she reached for the mugs. "What time did they say they'd be here?"

"Around four, depending on traffic. That was the ETA when they last called." She accepted the steaming cup of coffee that Kate passed to her. "Should we do the taste test before the icing goes on the rest of them?" Edie pointed towards the cooling rack of gingerbread hearts.

"It would be rude not to."

The sound of the front door opening and closing gave them both a start and Edie slopped her coffee over the brim of the cup. "I don't think I'll ever get my nerves back," she said as Nick appeared from outside. He had been fixing some icicle lights to the house. Shortly after the court hearing, Kate and Edie had asked him to move in.

"Well Chris is gone now," Nick reminded them both. "He won't be coming out and there's very little he could do to pose any physical threat if he did," he reasoned, before disappearing again.

"Not Chris," Edie said, casting her gaze to the ceiling. There was no need for her to elaborate.

"Why? Have you heard anything in the house lately?" Kate felt the familiar palpitations in her chest whenever she thought about everything that they had experienced in Thornycroft.

Edie shook her head. "Not a peep, but it'll always be up here." She tapped the side of her head.

"I know." Kate stirred her coffee thoughtfully. "But the medium has been back twice, said the house is clear of any negative energy and that even Rachel and Rosamund have gone."

"I suppose they told their story," Edie said.

"Rachel always promised that she would, she just didn't get the chance to do so during her lifetime."

Continuing her research, Edie had decided to write about Rachel and Rosamund's story. They had found a record of Rachel, listed as Rachelle Maria Belgrave. She and Benjamin had married within six months of leaving Eyam.

Both of them had denounced their heritage as there was no reference to their lineage, but they had made their own wealth through Benjamin's work in political circles. It seemed that Benjamin held high favour and that he often visited the King's court, Rachel by his side. Their son, Anthony, had followed in Benjamin's footsteps and had climbed the political ladder well.

Rosa and Katherine, their two girls, had also survived well into adulthood, both strong women who clearly took after their mother.

The memories of Rachel's year of surviving plague, and of how she had unpicked the mystery that surrounded her mother, Lady Rosamund, were still as real in Kate's head as ever. At times, thoughts, feelings and echoes of the past would catch her off-guard, bringing a lump to her throat and tears to her eyes.

Kate looked across the table at Edie. "How's the book coming along anyway?"

"I'm writing what I can based on the facts that we've found, but I'll never be able to give any evidenced credibility to Rachel's full story." Edie dunked her biscuit, a morose expression on her face.

Kate squeezed her hand. "You'll get there and we'll keep helping all we can," she said. "She trusted us to put their story out there and regardless of how much we can prove by way of the written evidence, we have enough to share now. Have you got in touch with the ghost writer Francesca recommended?"

Edie nodded. "We're meeting after Christmas. It will be her project in the New Year and you never know, next Christmas we may have finally finished what we set out to achieve."

"Of course you will." Nick reappeared carrying a folder of neatly stacked papers. He had already helped them do so much to the place, but his enthusiasm for Thornycroft was nowhere near waning. "Now, before everyone arrives, I wanted to show you both something. Let's call it my moving in gift, if you like." He stooped to give Kate a kiss on the lips before taking a seat and opening the folder.

He spread the papers out on the table in front of them. "If you like it, we can submit to planning. I have it on good authority that it will sail through."

Flattening the paperwork with his palms, he began to explain the grand plans for converting the top quarters into a beautiful suite that would open out onto the resurrected area that had remained hidden for over three hundred and fifty years.

The arced door that Kate had thought had opened of its own accord was actually the result of the wall caving in following the force of the storm, or possibly even the ricocheting of the bullet sending the final but significant shockwave needed to at last reveal the secrets coveted away behind it.

Nick's thumbs caressed the neat lines that displayed his plans. "We can call it a reading room, anything you like. The important thing is that we open it out in memory of her."

"The rightful Lady Thornycroft," Kate put in and she gasped as she looked at the detailed drawing in front of her, admiring Nick's craft. "It's perfect," she breathed, emotion threatening to get the better of her.

"If they were still here, they would love it," Edie agreed and traced her finger over Nick's impressive work. "Thank you Nick." She looked up and winked at Kate. "He's a keeper."

Kate walked around to where Nick was sitting, his face filled with passion for his work as he talked them through the details. She draped her arms around his neck and kissed him on the cheek. "Did I ever tell you that you're amazing?"

He smiled back at her. The edges of a tiny box in his pocket pressed at his thigh. Kate had no idea about the box that contained a simple but stunning solitaire. He had been keeping it as a surprise for Christmas morning.

He pretended to mull the question over, "Hmmmm let me think…. I'd say once or twice, but not nearly enough." Playfully, he pulled her onto his knee and gave her a knowing smile as he recalled how the ring in his pocket had glinted in the winter sunlight. "But I'm hoping you'll be saying it again soon."

******

Upstairs, the house was still, except for the rooms in the attic, where the shutters to the newly exposed window rattled against the cool winds that were rushing in from the north.

Everything had been cleared earlier that year, to make way for the structural work. It looked empty, ready for its new lease of life.

All the relics that had been found were stored neatly away or had found pride of place within Thornycroft. Neither Kate nor Edie were ready to give them up or offer them to auction.

Old floorboards had already been lifted, ready to make way for the new flooring, but nobody had noticed the slip of parchment. Wrapped and protected in cloth, it had been placed there by a frightened, shaking hand hundreds of years earlier.

Here I am, back in Thornycroft Hall but no longer the Lady, no longer of any note.

Goody says that this is the place I need to be, within the majestic heart of the White Peaks. She says that this will cure me. Alas, I know otherwise. I can feel my body being devoured from the inside out.

Nobody but Goody can look at my face and not feel fear and yet, I long to see her, my darling girl, Rachelle.

Goody says that great torment has struck the village. Plague. Like me, they know what it is to suffer, but I am different to them. I deserve the suffering that I endure. Night and day, the guilt plays on me.

In the wee hours, when I am locked safely in the chains so that I will do no harm to anyone, as I believe I did to all those precious children before, I think that perhaps this accursed demon inside of me brought the pestilence here with it.

Goody says that these thoughts are nonsense, but I still feel so much grief and I have to pray so hard to keep up my strength of mind.

One night I saw her, I saw my dear darling girl.

Goody forgot to put me in the chains, although I did not insist, as I so often do.

When she was sleeping softly, I tiptoed through her chamber, down the stairs and into the heart of the house.

Oh how I remember it before, in all its grandeur, before I became infected by this eternally depressing presence that bore its way into my soul. I remember the parties, the chink of the finest crystal glasses that Edward spent a small fortune on. I remember how I could smile and the room would smile with me. I remember how they would always ask me to sing, how Edward would say that I had the voice of a songbird. Now Thornycroft Hall is like me, a sad shadow of its former self.

That night, as I descended the staircase and found myself in her chamber, my Rachelle's meagre chamber, my heart was beating so loudly that I thought it might wake the whole house.

Despite the pitiful room they had put her in, she looked so peaceful, so beautiful as she slept and I could not help myself. Just for one moment to treasure for always, I allowed my fingers to touch the velvety soft skin of her face. I wanted to touch her the way a mother should touch her beautiful, sweet girl. I wanted to feel what I have missed out on all these years. Of course, she awoke. I frightened her and I fled back to the top quarters.

Goody was furious and for once, she did not protest when I insisted that she return me to my chains.

Now, as I sit here and reflect on what I did all those months ago, I fear that had the demon inside of me got a hold, something dreadful could have happened to my darling girl.

Edward was so angry.

Before he left the house with his new family, he could no longer even look at me, even as he spoke and told me of their plans, remorse upon his lips.

I know that his refusal to look at my face was not down to his anger, nor is it for the same reason that I have known others to shy away from me. No, Edward can no longer look at me because he too grieves for what we once had, what I once was.

Once upon a time I had everything. I was a lady to be envied; dressed in the finest gowns, whose beauty, they said, could light up the dullest of rooms, and I had a husband who loved me unconditionally.

But all that changed and now I am here, scuttling about like a rodent in the hidden part of the house, the part where I lost it all.

I try to shut out the gaping hole of sadness that threatens to swallow me whole every time I think of what once was, what could have been.

They do not remember me for any of those things. Now I am thought of as a ghost, the spirit of a mad woman who took her own life.

I know that this is all born of my own making. It was I who demanded they take my only surviving child away from me. I demanded that they keep her from harm, but I did not ask for this. I did not ask to be given the shameful story that they concocted so that they could marry and make new heirs. I did not ask for this eternal misery.

Nobody remembers me for who I was. The memory of me will always be tarnished, for my story will never be known. And so I am writing these words because I know deep down inside that I am not a monster.

I am not the woman who took her own life because she could not abide the thought of living any longer. Like those who shackled themselves to this village, who died to prevent the spread of plague, I am someone who also knows what it is to make the ultimate sacrifice.

I am Rosamund. I am a shadow beyond.

AUTHOR'S NOTE

My short film, 'A Story of Eyam, the Plague Village', gives the fact behind the fiction and a visual walkthrough of the beautiful village of Eyam, featuring the important landmarks that tell its story. You can find it on my YouTube channel: Emma-Nicole Lewis.

It was during a short holiday in the Peak District that I found the beautiful village of Eyam. From the moment that we stepped out of the car, I was enchanted by its rich history and well-preserved beauty.

The village is a tourist trap, attractive to cyclists, ramblers and sightseers. At the end of August, Eyam celebrates the very old tradition of Wakes Week, beginning with the well blessing ceremony and culminating with a carnival at the end of the week.

I visited Eyam several times whilst creating 'A Shadow Beyond'. The more I read about the fourteen months of plague that the village endured, the more fascinated I became.

I began to question how people would have reacted to the Cordon Sanitaire, a quarantine that was imposed by their Rector, William Mompesson and the previous puritan Rector, Thomas Stanley.

My novel originally began exploring the idea of a family who rebelled against the quarantine, but as I researched, using the exceptional knowledge of the volunteers in the museum and church, as well as the rich supply of reading material in the public domain, I realised that this was not the angle that I wanted to take. I wanted to create a novel that was a mark of respect for the courage and selflessness of the villagers of Eyam and I hope that I have achieved that.

In those times, people feared God and for many families, they would not have had the means to leave their homes or their livelihoods. The people who lived in Eyam at the time of plague would have taken their duty to God very seriously, in spite of the sickening fear and impending doom that they must have felt. I tried to get this across when I was writing the novel, exploring Rachel's conflicting thoughts and throwing myself into what it must have been like to look out across the countryside towards the neighbouring villages in the knowledge that the people there were free of the onslaught of the pestilence.

My fascination with the Mompessons also grew as I researched, particularly Catherine Mompesson, the reverend's wife. I imagined that some villagers may have felt extremely bitter and cheated by the fact that prior to the quarantine, the